ALLAN MALLINSON

A professional soldier for thirty-five years, **Allan Mallinson** began writing while still serving. His first book was a history of four regiments of British light dragoons, one of which he commanded. His debut novel was the bestselling *A Close Run Thing*, the first in an acclaimed series chronicling the life of a fictitious cavalry officer following Waterloo (*The Tigress of Mysore* is the fourteenth in the series). His *The Making of the British Army* was shortlisted for a number of prizes, while *1914: Fight the Good Fight* won the British Army's 'Book of the Year' Award. Its sequel, *Too Important for the Generals*, is a provocative look at leadership during the Great War, while *Fight to the Finish* is a comprehensive history of the First World War, month by month. His major new work of military history, *The Shape of Battle*, tells the story of six defining battles – Hastings, Towton, Waterloo, D-Day, Imjin River and Operation Panther's Claw.

Allan Mallinson reviews for the *Spectator* and the *TLS*, and writes for *The Times*. He lives on Salisbury Plain.

Follow him on Twitter @allan_mallinson

By Allan Mallinson

AND FEATURING MATTHEW HERVEY
OF THE 6TH LIGHT DRAGOONS

A CLOSE RUN THING

1815: introducing Matthew Hervey, fighting for King and country at the Battle of Waterloo.

'I have never read a more enthralling account of a battle . . . This is the first in a series of Matthew Hervey adventures. The next can't come soon enough for me'
DAILY MAIL

THE NIZAM'S DAUGHTERS

1816: in India Matthew Hervey fights to prevent bloody civil war.

'Captain Hervey of the 6th Light Dragoons and ADC to the Duke of Wellington is back in the saddle . . . He is as fascinating on horseback as Jack Aubrey is on the quarterdeck'
THE TIMES

A REGIMENTAL AFFAIR

1817: Matthew Hervey faces renegades at home and in North America.

'A riveting tale of heroism, derring-do and enormous resource in the face of overwhelming adversity'
BIRMINGHAM POST

A CALL TO ARMS

1819: Matthew Hervey races to confront Burmese rebels massing in the jungle.

'Hervey continues to grow in stature as an engaging and credible character, while Mallinson himself continues to delight'
OBSERVER

THE SABRE'S EDGE

1824: in India Matthew Hervey lays siege to the fortress of Bhurtpore.

'Splendid . . . the tale is as historically stimulating as it is stirringly exciting'
SUNDAY TELEGRAPH

RUMOURS OF WAR

1826: while Matthew Hervey prepares for civil war in Portugal, he remembers the Retreat to Corunna twenty years previously.

'I enjoyed the adventure immensely . . . as compelling, vivid and plausible as any war novel I've ever read'
DAILY TELEGRAPH

AN ACT OF COURAGE

1826: a prisoner of the Spanish, Matthew Hervey relives the blood and carnage of the Siege of Badajoz.

'Concentrating on the battle of Talavera and the investment of Badajoz, both sparklingly described, [Mallinson] plays to his undoubted strengths'
OBSERVER

COMPANY OF SPEARS

1827: on the plains of South Africa, Matthew Hervey confronts the savage Zulu.

'A damn fine rip-roaring read'
LITERARY REVIEW

MAN OF WAR

1827: at home and at sea, crises loom.

'As tense, exciting, vivid and gory as we've come to expect from this master of military fiction'
SPECTATOR

WARRIOR

1828: in South Africa Matthew Hervey clashes with the warrior king of the Zulus.

'Hervey's thrilling battles against the vivid backdrop of the developing British Empire make for richly engaging old-fashioned storytelling'
DAILY MAIL

ON HIS MAJESTY'S SERVICE

1829: the stakes have never been higher as Matthew Hervey faces bloody war with the Turks in the Eastern Balkans.

'Mallinson . . . has done for the British Army what C.S. Forester and Patrick O'Brian did for the Royal Navy . . . splendid, irresistible stuff'
Allan Massie, SPECTATOR

WORDS OF COMMAND

1830: Matthew Hervey returns to take command of his regiment and becomes caught up in a bloody uprising abroad . . .

'One for the fans, who will not be disappointed by Mallinson's winning combination of scrupulous research and derring-do'
THE TIMES

THE PASSAGE TO INDIA

1831: blood on the streets of England, then revolt in India: Matthew Hervey and the 6th Light Dragoons must do their duty . . .

'Mallinson's series of early 19th-century military adventures are even better than Patrick O'Brian's naval equivalent . . . Faithful period detail. Rattling pace. Loveable characters'
A. N. Wilson, THE TABLET

NON-FICTION

LIGHT DRAGOONS
The Making of a Regiment

THE MAKING OF THE BRITISH ARMY
From the English Civil War to the war on terror

1914: FIGHT THE GOOD FIGHT
Britain, the Army and the Coming of the First World War

TOO IMPORTANT FOR THE GENERALS
How Britain Nearly Lost the First World War

FIGHT TO THE FINISH
The First World War – Month by Month

The TIGRESS OF MYSORE

ALLAN MALLINSON

BANTAM BOOKS

TRANSWORLD PUBLISHERS
Penguin Random House, One Embassy Gardens,
8 Viaduct Gardens, London SW11 7BW
www.penguin.co.uk

Transworld is part of the Penguin Random House group of companies
whose addresses can be found at global.penguinrandomhouse.com

First published in Great Britain in 2020 by Bantam Press
an imprint of Transworld Publishers
Bantam edition published 2021

A CIP catalogue record for this book is available from the British Library.

ISBN
9780857504401

Typeset in 11.25/15.75pt Sabon Next LT Pro
by Integra Software Services Pvt. Ltd, Pondicherry.

Printed and bound in Italy by Grafica Veneta S.p.A.

The authorized representative in the EEA is Penguin Random House Ireland,
Morrison Chambers, 32 Nassau Street, Dublin D02 YH68.

Penguin Random House is committed to a sustainable future for
our business, our readers and our planet. This book is made from
Forest Stewardship Council® certified paper.

Note on Orthography

At this time in India there was no standard spelling of words transcribed from Hindustani and Urdu. It was not until 1837 that the Honourable East India Company, which had recently been charged by Parliament with government and administration rather than exclusively with trade, replaced Persian with the local vernacular as the official language of government offices and of the lower courts.

Hindustani was the native language of northern India, historically the region known as Hindustan. The Mughals brought the Persian language with them to India, and Hindustani began to acquire Persian words. In parallel, the pure Persian of the Mughal court began to acquire words of Hindustani, becoming *zabān-i Urdū-yi mu'allá* – the 'Language of the Exalted Camp' – referring to the ruling classes and Mughal army.

Hindustani and Urdu were, and are, practically the same spoken language. However, the former was written in Devanagari script (as in modern Hindi), and Urdu was written in the Persian Nastaliq script (as in modern-day Pakistan and by the Urdu-speaking Moslems of India).

Transliteration in Hervey's time was, understandably, haphazard. Letters and diaries sometimes spell the same word differently on the same page. The vowels are the usual cause of variation. 'Hindustani', the modern preference, was variously spelled *Hindoostani, Hindoostanee, Hindustanee, Hindostani, Hindostanee*. Rendering the Indian vernacular in what might be called 'Times of India' style would have the merit of consistency, but would lose a certain sense of period. As in earlier books, I have therefore adopted the practice of the double-letter vowel, but not exclusively, for to do so would make some words look just too quaint.

CONTENTS

PART ONE: THE PRESIDENCY OF FORT ST GEORGE

PART TWO: THE NORTHERN CIRCARS

PART THREE: CHINTAL

Oh Allah the all-powerful! dispose the whole body of infidels! Scatter their tribe, cause their feet to stagger! Overthrow their councils, change their state, destroy their very root! Cause death to be near them, cut off from them the means of sustenance! Shorten their days! Be their bodies the constant object of their cares, deprive their eyes of sight, make black their faces in shame, destroy in them organs of speech! Slay them as was slain Shedaud who presumed to make a paradise for himself and was slain by command of Allah; drown them as Pharaoh was drowned, and visit them with the severity of the wrath. Oh Avenger! Oh Universal Father! I am downcast and overpowered, grant me Thy assistance.

Inscription at the palace of
Tipoo Sultan,
'The Tiger of Mysore',
Seringapatam, 1799

GOVERNMENT OF INDIA ACT, 1833

An Act for effecting an Arrangement with the East India Company, and for the better Government of His Majesty's Indian Territories, till the thirtieth day of April one thousand eight hundred and fifty-four . . .

SECTION 38:
PRESIDENCY OF FORT WILLIAM IN BENGAL TO BE DIVIDED INTO TWO PRESIDENCIES

The territories now subject to the government of the presidency of Fort William in Bengal shall be divided into two distinct presidencies, one of such presidencies in which shall be included Fort William aforesaid, to be styled the Presidency of Fort William in Bengal, and the other of such presidencies to be styled the Presidency of Agra; The court of directors to declare the limits from time to time of the several presidencies . . .

SECTION 39:
GOVERNMENT OF INDIA VESTED IN GOVERNOR GENERAL AND COUNSELLORS

The superintendence, direction, and control of the whole civil and military government of all the said territories and revenues in India shall be and is hereby vested in a governor general and counsellors, to be styled "The Governor General of India in Council" . . .

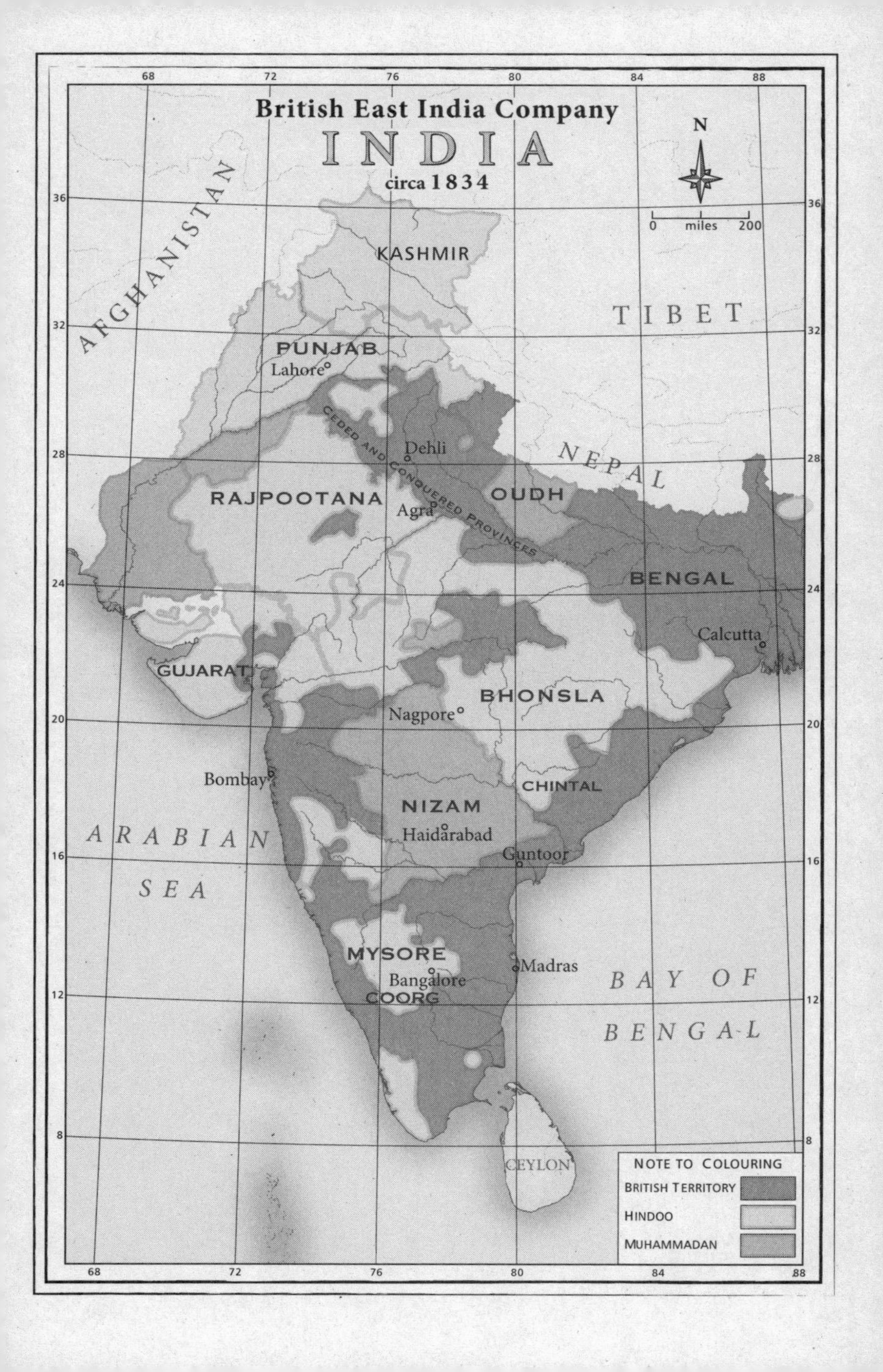
British East India Company
INDIA
circa 1834
N
0 miles 200
AFGHANISTAN
KASHMIR
TIBET
PUNJAB
Lahore
CEDED AND CONQUERED PROVINCES
Dehli
NEPAL
RAJPOOTANA
Agra
OUDH
BENGAL
Calcutta
GUJARAT
BHONSLA
Nagpore
Bombay
CHINTAL
NIZAM
Haidarabad
ARABIAN SEA
Guntoor
MYSORE
Madras
Bangalore
COORG
BAY OF BENGAL
CEYLON
NOTE TO COLOURING
BRITISH TERRITORY
HINDOO
MUHAMMADAN
68
72
76
80
84
88
36
32
28
24
20
16
12
8

PART ONE

THE PRESIDENCY OF FORT ST GEORGE

I

Thugs

Kothapore, Northern Circars, February 1834

Bunda Ali, late of Haidarabad and now of Madras, counted himself the most fortunate of men – *al-hamdu li-llāh.* For he was a *moonshee*, a teacher of languages. Yet no mere teacher to the writers of 'John Company', honoured though that position be, but moonshee to His Britannic Majesty's Sixth Regiment of Light Dragoons – 'most senior, most honoured of all regiments in entire presidency of the Fort Saint George', which he proclaimed proudly to each and all on first acquaintance. *Angreze* – Englishmen – of exalted rank paid him respects, he would tell them. There were, he said, many high-born officers in the regiment at Madras – sons of noblemen, sons of His Majesty's highest ministers of the Court, sons of great zamindars (landowners) and men of affairs. He esteemed especially their sirdar, Colonel Matthew Hervey-sahib, who attended to the Hindoostanee (so near to the Urdu) with exemplary purpose (even though it was not the native language of Madras), and who showed much aptitude for many other tongues, including that of the inferior Tamul people; also his wife, a very great lady, who had received also his own wife and spoken with her as if someone high-born also as she (though to tell truth the father of his wife was *bunnia*, a merchant of corn, and money-lender).

All this pleased Bunda Ali greatly, especially as with his position came a salary of eight hundred Arcot rupees a year (his servants received from him three rupees a month, and were most content).

And now, while the regiment was away in the west of the country on a mission of which he was not made privy (for he had no need of knowing), he was availing himself of the opportunity to travel to the place of his birth, with his wife and new-born daughter, to celebrate the wedding of his eldest to the man he had found for her some years before.

It was not the worst time of year to be making a journey. There was the better part of a month yet before the onset of the hot weather that would oblige them to travel by night. His little party had been on the road for three weeks – a well-made road at first, one of the dak roads that the Honourable East India Company made and maintained so that hircarrahs with their postbags, as well as troops and guns, might pass quickly between Fort St George and the garrison towns of the presidency. But once in the Northern Circars, they had left the dak road for the unmade track that headed north-west to Chintalpore, seat of the Rajah of Chintal, and then onwards to Haidarabad, for although the northerly route by Rajahmundree had the merit of being in Company territory, that by Chintalpore would save them many days.

In fact, to be precise, Chintalpore was the seat of the Ranee of Chintal: the rajah had died several years before, and, there being no male heir, the title had passed – though not without violent dispute – to his daughter.

Chintal in the time of the old rajah had been a proud and peaceable place, if troubled periodically by the Nizam of neighbouring Haidarabad. Hervey had himself observed one of these incursions – had taken up the sword, indeed, on the rajah's behalf – during his first sojourn in India fifteen years before. Since then, with the succession of Nasir-ud-dawlah,

Haidarabad had not troubled its smaller neighbour very much, having quite enough troubles of its own, yet not sufficient to tempt the Nizam to the distraction of a foreign war. Chintal had no permanent Resident of the Company, however, merely an agent, Fort William's interests being overseen from Nagpore, and since the death of the rajah there were many in the princely state who had come to wish there were, for where there was a Resident there was an interest, and where there was an interest there was the Company's Peace – now, in practice, the King's Peace, since the recent act of Parliament made the Company an instrument of colonial government rather than of trade.

Kothapore, but a league or so from the fork in the dak road that took the traveller from the Company's Peace to that of the Ranee, was a place of no great size, just an old fort with its outlying *bustees* (and mean dwellings they were at that, for in the hot season the land here was barren waste), but it served nevertheless as a *naka*, a customs post. Bunda Ali had no goods on which duty must be paid, but even so, he knew he must part with a good many rupees. The maidan was common ground; travellers could pitch their tents, fold their cattle, draw water from the wells and bathe in the stream, but the *pahra*, the watch, would want their dues. Not dues by right, but because they bore arms and stood between the traveller and his journey. And they might make trouble otherwise – tell him there was no fresh bread to be had or grain for his horses, or else search his belongings interminably, or tell him the maidan was needed for an official party. It was the way of the country – *baksheesh*.

And the pahra could expect Bunda Ali to be generous: he was a fine-looking Mussulman, bearded, turbaned – a *kazee* perhaps, a law officer. He rode a fine-looking Marwari, and behind him, on ponies of quality led by clean-shaven syces, came a girl of fourteen and a woman with a child in her arms. Behind them were five more servants and a bullock cart laden with the appurtenances of a man of position. Few men travelled with a retinue so large, yet without escort. (And among his baggage was concealed a thousand rupees' worth and more of jewels and coin – five years of savings – for his daughter's wedding and dowry).

The sun had almost set, and Bunda Ali wished only to make camp in a safe and pleasant spot. He was content to part with ten rupees for favour of a grove of banyan close by the stream, where his servants swiftly pitched the tents and began preparing the evening meal, and the grooms took the horses to water and to wash off the dust of the road. People from the bustees came to sell them bread, fruit and sweetmeats. Bunda Ali was content indeed – for this one night at least. Thereafter, his caution must be the greater. While he travelled the dak road he felt secure enough, for there was many another traveller and frequent bodies of troops, although near the forest edge he was always on his guard, for as well as wild beasts there were dacoits – robbers, armed and rapacious – who, though he felt sure he and his syces could see them off (they carried swords, and he a pistol too), would distress his wife and daughter. Beyond the Company's pale, however, he would have no such guarantee. The surest precaution would be to join another, larger party making for Haidarabad. Dacoits would fear to attack such large numbers of men, and it would be pleasant also to have travelling companions with whom he could relieve the tedium of this long journey. Agreeable also for his wife if there were female company. He was pleased therefore when soon after dark two men carrying lanterns came to his camp – one a policeman, he said, Ghufoor Khan, a Mussulman like himself, travelling to Haidarabad on official business; the other, Essuree, an officer of the magistrate's court at Etawah in Hindoostan, returning with depositions from Vellore in a case of criminal conversation. (They wore their badge of office with the habitual pride of the native official.)

'Huzoor,' they began; 'we have learned that you are travelling many days and must do so more. These roads are not as in the lands of *Company-bahadur.* Chintal people are not for trusting. We shall be honoured for you to join our party, which is more than fifty, all good and honest simple men. It will be our greatest pleasure to have travel with us an educated person.'

Bunda Ali was much relieved – *al-hamdu li-llāh* – and accepted at once. His servants brought sweetened coffee, and his two guests stayed an hour and more, hearing of the moonshee's good fortune in his appointment at Fort St George and in finding so suitable a bridegroom for his daughter.

Next morning, the two parties broke camp early and left Kothapore together. They intended making Sawangee, some twenty miles thence, before nightfall, where the old rajah had a hunting lodge – which perhaps the new Ranee kept also. It was near twice the distance that Bunda Ali would have travelled as a rule, but, said Ghufoor Khan, the road was good, not too rutted by bullock carts, and they would easily reach the little town by evening, with its pleasant camping ground and good wells. He would send on some of the men to keep the better part of it, and to have the *naan-baa'ii* (bakers of bread) make ready for them.

And the road proved as Ghufoor Khan said. It ran level and even, directly north-west, little deviating from its line except to skirt a hill, of which there were few. But it was a desolate country, the soil black and stony, unfit for the plough or even broadcast, and so villages were as few as the hills. The jungle through which they'd passed the day before had given way to forest edge, and there were but two rivers, both of them narrow and shallow enough to ford without hazard. Throughout, Bunda Ali rode between his 'hosts', finding them excellent company, just as they'd promised the evening before. Behind him his wife and daughter rode peacefully, speaking only to each other; and his newborn – another girl (a beautiful girl, but needful of another dowry in her turn) – scarcely cried at all. And now, as he beheld Sawangee ahead, with the sun still an hour above the horizon, he gave thanks yet again: '*Allhm rb alsmawat* . . . O Allah, You are the Lord of the seven heavens and all the things that are under these heavens and whatever is over these and of Satan who misled and all those misled by him and for the wind and all that it blows. Thus we seek the good of this town and the good of its people and seek refuge from its evil and the evil of its people, and from the evils of whatever is in it.'

Ghufoor Khan's *lughaees* – those who went ahead to prepare the ground – had done their work too, keeping another pleasing grove (of bamboo this time) not too distant from a stream. A dozen *bechne-walee*, sellers of all manner of good things, were gathered in expectation, and were not disappointed. Bunda Ali's servants pitched the tents as deftly as the evening before, watered and washed the horses, cut them grass, gave them a little corn, and then attached them to a running line before getting down to the business of pots and kettles. Soon afterwards, a small detachment of the Company's soldiers came in from the south, Native Infantry and two English officers, advance party for a magazine train (Chintal found it expedient to buy powder and fuze from the Company). They made camp but a hundred yards away, with just a clump of bamboo and the running line between them and the larger travelling party. Bunda Ali gave thanks once again, for surely Allah himself had sent these men for his protection, and thought he might present himself to the *Angreze*, and tell them he was moonshee to Colonel Matthew Hervey-sahib and His Majesty's Sixth Light Dragoons, who were also Princess Augusta's own (although of this latter he might not speak, for he himself did not quite understand how a regiment of the English king might also be that of a princess – and a foreign princess also). He might, indeed, offer them the hospitality of his own *shivir*.

But in the end, Bunda Ali would not present himself. Something stayed him, the uncomfortable thought that perhaps these *Angreze* might not be welcoming, for they might not be like Colonel Matthew Hervey-sahib and the officers of the dragoons. He had sometimes found that officers of the Honourable East India Company, having learned their languages for many years at their seminary in England, did not wish to treat with him in the same way. Oh, they were very good and fine gentlemen, but they were of very serious mind, and this perhaps made them a little unbending. That, at least, had been his experience at Madras.

Besides, as the hour approached eight (which he knew because not only was it darkling, but also, unlike any other of his acquaintance who was not *Angreze*, he carried a watch – a most handsome gold watch with a sentiment engraved on the inside of the cover, given him ten years ago by a general no less, in gratitude for his teaching), the khansamah brought him a washing bowl, and Bunda Ali turned instead to the *Maghrib*, the sunset prayer.

His wife and daughter had already retired. They shared the best of the tents, where they could eat in proper seclusion. He himself would take his *khana* later, in the great peace of the day when the cicadas and the crickets had at last hushed; and afterwards perhaps he would have one of his men play and sing a little, for he liked the sound of the sitar at evening. Meanwhile, the voices drifting from the soldiers' camp would please him.

After Bunda Ali had said his prayers and settled himself among cushions outside his tent, some of his new travelling companions joined him – Ghufoor Khan and three or four others who had paid him respects during the day, two of them with sitars. Their playing proved a little too unruly for his liking – his own people made sweeter music – but he would not object to it; not when they'd been so obliging as to let him accompany them on the road (indeed, he thought his bullock cart must have slowed them considerably). It certainly seemed to please Ghufoor Khan's party, for soon there were two dozen of them gathered by the tent, clapping in time with the increasingly erratic strumming. A dozen more strolled down towards the stream, where Bunda Ali's grooms would spend the night with the horses. And in the gathering darkness on the edge of the grove stood Essuree, the officer of the magistrate's court, watching, not pleased enough with the music perhaps to venture any closer.

In a quarter of an hour more it was black night, and Bunda Ali had become uneasy. These men could not be dacoits – surely? – for they'd had ample opportunity to rob him and be off . . . And yet they were crowding in a little too much for his comfort – and he could no longer see his own servants.

He felt for the sword, which he'd laid among the cushions at his feet – the sword his father had given him on reaching *baaligh*, the age of maturity.

But it wasn't there.

Two of the Khan's men had picked it up and were loudly admiring its workmanship – the jade on the pommel and the amber peen, the skin of the shark that bound the grip, the chasing on the blade . . .

Now alarmed, Bunda Ali stumbled to his feet and called for his servants. Someone shouted '*Tumbakoo lao*' ('Bring tobacco') – the signal.

At the stream it was all confusion: Essuree had loosed the horses.

Bunda Ali felt the scarf brush his forehead. He grasped at it and tried to turn as Bhawanee, the 'jemadar', the leader, yanked it tight round his throat, but a second gripped his arms from behind, while yet another kicked his legs from under him.

Bunda Ali was a big man; he fell heavily as the *roomal*, the scarf, gouged into his throat. The 'jemadar' crouched over him with one knee in the small of his back, gripping the two ends of the killing cloth, hands crossed. '*Accha*,' he hissed, jerking them apart with all the strength of the *lohaar* (blacksmith) that was his other trade.

Legs and arms flailed, then twitched feebly, and then fell still as Bunda Ali gave up the ghost.

The commotion brought the moonshee's wife to the flap of her tent, child in arms. She saw, cried out and turned, but the 'jemadar' was too quick. The same yellow scarf that had sent her husband to his maker was round her neck in a trice, and she too was sent to eternity – and the infant into the hands of the jemadar's second.

Another, Bazeed, lean and hungry looking, pushed past to finish the work. The promised bride was already on her feet, woken by her mother's cry. He seized her nightgown at the neck, rending the silk with such force that she fell back, exposed as never before to any man.

The back of the jemadar's hand struck Bazeed's cheek hard. 'No time!'

Bazeed staggered, then threw himself at the terrified girl as she tried to cover herself, fastened his hands on her throat and squeezed the life from her.

At the running-line Bunda Ali's syces, who seconds before had been squatting on their haunches, chewing betel nut and sharing thoughts of the day, looked up to see faces hitherto friendly but now homicidal. Two were dead before they could rise, but a third sprang free, making for the river, crying blue murder. Others of Essuree's who'd loosed the horses made greater racket, however. The plaintive cry of a single syce amid the stampede was not going to bring the soldiers running. Besides, he too was soon pulled down and the life squeezed out of him.

Murder, fast and efficient, and with a relish that was more than necessity – pure evil to any who could have observed. Eight men, a nursing mother and a girl who might still be thought a child had died like hens in a coop when the fox breaks in.

Then silently in the darkness, the jemadar's men searched the bodies. Those of the servants and syces returned just a few silver rupees, but Bunda Ali's yielded gold and the fine watch given him by the general at Fort St George, while his wife and daughter had about them jewelled bangles and rings. Their baggage of course would render much more.

Then the jemadar's men stripped the bodies. It would make it all the more difficult to recognize them if – Allah and all the gods of the Hindoos forbid – the bodies were ever found. The silks and satins would all bring coin at the bazaar, too; and even the coarsest dhoti was worth something as shoddy. Then they dragged them through the thicket to the long grass where that afternoon Ghufoor Khan's lughaees had dug two pits, practised as they were in judging precisely how deep and wide was wanted. They broke the joints of every one of them, and then out came the knives to slice through the sinews, all the better to pack the corpses into their secret tomb; and then as if this desecration weren't enough, they plunged the blades into the belly of each – even the wife and daughter – so that bloating would not displace the earth and reveal the murderous deeds.

Ghubbil Khan, the jemadar's second, who had plucked the child from its mother's arms as she lay choking, stood to one side with his mewling prize.

The jemadar gestured sharply.

'She is mine,' Ghubbil Khan protested; 'I shall raise her by my own hand, and she will marry my son!'

The jemadar cuffed him hard. 'She is not a peasant child. She will be recognized, and we discovered.'

So Ghubbil Khan tossed the child disconsolately into the pit, and the others shovelled in earth until the pitiful crying was no more. They trod the soil and then tamped it with the spade until there was no sign that the ground had ever been disturbed. Then they returned to the campfire to drink *bhang thandai*. In the small hours they took down the moonshee's tents, packed his belongings and stowed it all neatly on the bullock cart. An hour before dawn – before even the soldiers had risen – they left the bamboo grove with not a sign that Bunda Ali, his servants, his cherished wife, his fair bridal daughter or his nursling infant had ever been there.

II

Words of Command

Fort St George, Madras, Tuesday, 7 October 1834

'That's right, Miss Hervey: arm extended, locked at the elbow and wrist. Lower the piece onto the target, eye running the length of arm and barrel to the centre of the observable mass . . .'

Serjeant Acton could but instruct in the same language he would use with a recruit, if markedly less severe in tone. He supposed his commanding officer's daughter to have rather more education than the usual dragoon, even at the tender age of sixteen, and undoubtedly more sensibility. That said, a cavalry pistol was still a cavalry pistol . . . 'and firm but even pressure in the trigger . . .'

It kicked hard, and her hand would have shot upwards if he hadn't instantly closed his on hers.

He knew it would kick. The recoil could take the sturdiest dragoon by surprise first time, which was why his right hand had guided hers ever so gently into the aim, and his left had hovered ready to grasp her shoulder to steady her.

No man had ever held her so – except of course her father (but that was different) – and she thought she coloured a little with the intimacy. Perhaps it didn't show; perhaps, anyway, it was just the heat and the pistol's loud crack that made her redden – if redden she did. She certainly hoped she didn't; she'd no wish to discomfit Serjeant Acton, so fine a man said her father (said everyone): '*ein treue husar*'. And so he was, she'd decided – all that a serjeant of dragoons should look like (and be).

'A hit, Serjeant Acton?'

'A hit, Miss Hervey. High and to the right.'

'Oh.'

'It would have stopped the man,' said Acton encouragingly, if not altogether certain. 'Not that it'll ever be necessary, Miss, with a whole regiment of dragoons at your father's command.'

Georgiana smiled obligingly, for she knew he meant well; but it hadn't saved her mother. Although then, of course, her father had been a mere captain. Serjeant Armstrong – now the regimental serjeant-major – had been left for dead in his attempt to rescue her, but the Shawanese Indians had their method: they not so much left Henrietta for dead as to die, killing her horse and leaving her to the snow and ice. Georgiana had been in swaddling clothes still, with her wet-nurse, and her father had been with his dragoons and the Americans trying to intercept the migrating tribes; it had gone very ill with him indeed, his not being there when the Shawanese struck – Elizabeth, her aunt, had told her of his sending in his papers and the year and more trying to be a civilian – but it had been an age ago, now, and Kezia was his wife, and her stepmother; and she was come at last to live with them.

The straw round stood at just twelve paces, but Acton said that no dragoon under discipline would ever chance a shot at any greater range.

'Again, then, Miss.'

Acton gave her a percussion cap. Georgiana cocked the pistol, placed the cap on the nipple and eased the hammer down slowly again. He took a cartridge from his pouch, bit off the ball and gave the case to her. (She'd done it once; there was no need to blacken her lips any more than they were.)

Georgiana took it confidently – they'd practised 'dry' for half an hour before Acton would trust her with real cartridge – poured powder down the barrel, let him drop in the ball, pushed in the cartridge paper for wadding and tamped it firm with the swivel rod.

She fired, this time the ball striking a little nearer the mark. Three more followed – one closer in, two rather wider. She shook her head when they examined the round and chalked the holes.

'Those are nothing to be dismayed about, Miss Hervey,' said Acton. 'Accurate's not the same as being a marksman. Accurate's about getting them shots all close together. A marksman, though, *hits* his target when he's required to.'

Georgiana seemed reassured.

'Now, Miss Gildea, your turn if you please.'

Acton was being particularly correct in front of the daughter of his commanding officer, whose coverman he was, the most honoured position for any serjeant of the regiment. He'd first known Annie when she was a chambermaid at the Berkeley Arms at Hounslow, where Colonel Hervey had put up for several months before taking the lease on the former colonel's house at Heston, and Annie had gone to Heston too as housekeeper's assistant. She'd always been obliging to him – and to any other dragoon who'd come to the Berkeley: she'd come out with coffee and nice cuts on cold mornings, and then at Heston in the servants' hall if ever he'd had to wait. There'd been 'talk' in the canteen about her going to Heston, how as Mrs Hervey wasn't there – and why indeed *wasn't* the colonel's lady by his side? – and that Annie must be 'standing in for her'; but he didn't reckon it himself. Mind, she was a fine-looking girl. And then, after all, the colonel had asked her to come to India with them . . .

Well, it may have been the other way round. Annie had a brother who was a soldier, and he'd been posted to Bengal, and she'd thought she'd be able to see a bit more of him here, not really knowing how far distant Bengal was from Madras. In any case, Mrs Hervey had come to India too, so that was that. And Mrs Hervey must have thought highly of Annie, as when young Miss Allegra's governess said she wanted to go back home, Mrs Hervey promoted Annie in her place, which was why she had to be called 'Miss Gildea' now. And Annie was different now, too – not haughty or anything, just . . . well, quite the lady. (As he supposed she had to be, of course.) She spoke like a lady almost; and she dressed special. A lot of the NCOs were disappointed, naturally. They'd fancied their chances with Annie (he himself had), but it was different now she was 'Miss Gildea'; even some of the officers – not the Sixth's, of course, but some of the Foot regiments and the native ones – paid her attention after church parades and the like. To an NCO, he reckoned, she was probably now out of range.

However, Annie was not as naturally disposed to becoming a marksman as Serjeant Acton's other pupil, her additional charge, was. Colonel Hervey – or more precisely, Colonel Hervey and his wife (she wasn't exactly sure who'd spoken the words first) – had asked her to take on the care of Georgiana when they'd received word that she was at last bound for India, but not with a governess; with a chaperone only as far as Madras. And as both Colonel Hervey and his daughter were strongly of the mind that a lady abroad should be able to fire a pistol, she found herself here at the butts. Besides, since the affair of the snake she'd discovered in the stillroom, she had herself come to the conclusion that India was indeed a perilous place. (She hadn't heard Serjeant Stray say 'Colonel, that lass – Annie: as brave as a lion', but Mrs Hervey had given her a pearl necklace and said that nothing could truly express her thanks for saving her daughter; and the Colonel himself had left no doubt about his regard.)

Not that she would be elsewhere. She'd never thought meanly of herself for being in service; but to be a governess was the occupation of respectable people, and she cherished her new-found respectability.

Besides, although it was early days still, she found Georgiana most amenable. Indeed, she was certain that she herself learned more from her charge than the other way round. For what, in truth, could she, Annie Gildea, whose father had kept the tolbooth in Hounslow, impart to Miss Hervey, whose late mother had been 'Lady Henrietta', and whose paternal aunt, who'd raised her after her sad death, was lately married to a baron (and a German baron at that)?

Annie, too, had practised dry. She took up the pistol determinedly from the table and fixed on a percussion cap, Serjeant Acton handed her a cartridge and she bit off the end, trying not to grimace at the taste of the tallow as she took the ball between her teeth. She poured in the powder, spat in the ball and pushed in the wadding confidently enough, tamped it not too gingerly (she couldn't let Georgiana see a moment's hesitation – and she certainly wasn't going to give Acton the satisfaction), then extended her arm in the prescribed manner.

'I shall be well, Serjeant Acton,' she said equally determinedly as he moved to support her. (It seemed unnecessary that he should take hold as if they were dancing.)

'As you wish, Miss Gildea. In your own time, then; fire.'

The ball nicked the edge of the round, tell-tale bits of straw adding to Annie's dismay. But she'd been ready for the recoil at least, and her feet remained as they were.

'A little gentler with the trigger, Miss, and arm locked. That's all.'

'Another cartridge then, please, Serjeant Acton.'

He made to bite off the end.

'No, I must do it for myself.'

She bit off the cartridge with every impression of meaning business, and loaded deftly (she'd long observed how a woman's fingers were nimbler than a man's, and told herself there was no reason it shouldn't be so with powder and ball).

This time her arm was ramrod straight. She lowered the pistol and squeezed the trigger in one movement.

The ball was so close to the centre mark that even Acton couldn't suppress a smile. 'A fine shot, Miss. You need do no more.'

But Annie thought she must – at least as many as Georgiana had. Besides, she was not at all sure that her fine shot hadn't been a chance one.

Three more were enough to demonstrate Acton's pronouncement that accuracy was not the same as marksmanship – spread left and right of the centre mark – but both she and her charge could now leave the butts contented.

'Thank you, Serjeant Acton,' said Georgiana, smiling as winningly as ever her mother had, with the confidence of her station and the innocence of her years.

'An honour, Miss.'

'Thank you, too,' said Annie, though careful not to smile quite so much as she would have done before she became 'Miss Gildea'. She'd always found Acton the most decent of men – like Corporal Johnson and Serjeant Stray – and she wished to keep it that way. She'd been trusted beyond her station in being made a governess, and she'd no wish to let down Colonel Hervey – or indeed Mrs Hervey. What other secrets of her heart there were must bide their time, even if an eternity.

* * *

The regimental serjeant-major closed his order book. 'With your leave, then, Colonel.'

Hervey nodded. Not a bad orderly room today: no defaulters to speak of, and barely a dozen sick – and the new medals, for long service and good conduct, just arrived, a handsome idea of the King's, though why the infantry would have it after twenty-one years and the cavalry twenty-four puzzled them. Nevertheless, it was a fine pretext for a parade, and he'd get Somervile to present them – a dozen and more by the paymaster's reckoning.

'Thank you, sar'nt-major. And my compliments, again, to Mrs Armstrong. The durbar was a capital idea.'

Indeed, he'd often wondered if it might serve with the dragoons too, as well as the wives. He'd once seen a regimental durbar with Skinner's, and thought well of how the men conducted themselves. But, as Armstrong had been keen to point out, an English dragoon was not a Rajpoot silladar, who was likely as not a man of some standing in his village. And besides the evident perils in allowing a dragoon to speak directly to his commanding officer without the checks and balances of the chain of command, mightn't the practice actually weaken that chain? Three dozen wives, of course, was a different matter.

Armstrong looked gratified anyway. 'Colonel. I shall tell Mrs Armstrong the instant I am home.' (Hervey knew that that would not be before watch-setting, long after 'the patroness of the dames who follow the drum' had gone to her bed. For Armstrong was not a one to quit the lines till he was certain he'd find them in one piece the following morning.)

But there was no ignoring the darker cloud over the lines. Hervey picked up the single sheet of paper on his desk, and frowned. 'I fear there'll be no commutation for Askew. The sentence is subject to confirmation, of course, but I can see no grounds for clemency.'

Striking a superior officer, whether that officer be on or off duty, was punishable by death, and Private Askew had assailed Lieutenant Waterman in front of witnesses. It was a rare charge in the Sixth – the penalty and the NCOs saw to that – but . . .

'The Mutiny Act's the Mutiny Act, Colonel. We all live by it.' (Whatever the opinions on the justice of Askew's particular case, 'the interests of the service' took precedence. 'We are where we are' was not a bad maxim, however much they might wish they were somewhere else.)

And yet Hervey, perhaps because he was one remove from the serjeant-major when it came to discipline, remained uneasy, even while seeing no alternative. It was undoubtedly true that unbending justice kept discipline in an army that was still recruited by and large from the sweepings of society, but the cavalry prided themselves on a better class of recruit and a less draconian regime of discipline thereby. The Sixth, like several other regiments, did not flog, and therefore when some capital offence was committed the surprise was the greater. They'd not executed a man in some years, the last being for rape and murder rather than an offence peculiar to the Mutiny Act; and no one could look forward to the event with anything but distaste.

'I shall not permit it to be before the garrison, though. Askew's previous service was satisfactory; he's earned the privilege of meeting his maker with just his fellow dragoons as witness.'

Armstrong nodded. He'd already begun making plans for the parade; this was a welcome simplification. 'Colonel.'

'I still can't comprehend it, though. What could have possessed him?'

It had certainly not been drink, not that excess of it was any plea in mitigation. Provocation, yes – but there were daily provocations in the life of a dragoon, and far worse than being called the son of a whore. Hervey deplored the abuse – more appropriate for a roughrider chastising an idle recruit than an officer addressing a dragoon – and in a public place too. In a regiment of foot no officer would ever speak directly to a private man, but in the cavalry, with its fellowship of the stable, the rule was not so rigid. He'd not had a high regard for Lieutenant Waterman since his arriving from the Tenth, but once condone the striking of an officer, no matter what the provocation, and you made every dragoon his own judge and jury in the matter. And who knew what tongue-lashing an anxious dragoon might need when the guns began to play?

But they'd had this conversation before, and Armstrong had nothing further to say. 'With your leave, then, Colonel?'

Hervey nodded.

It was a slightly later hour for orderly room, the first day of the post-Monsoon routine. It could hardly be called the cool season, for although the thermometer no longer broached a hundred, it refused to fall very much below ninety during the day – at least in the first month. Nevertheless, Hervey was glad to have the day restored to something like usual, the hot weather stand-down from midday to four o'clock being rarely gainful.

The adjutant, who'd stood silent during the serjeant-major's report, beckoned to Sammy, the orderly room's bearer.

The little Tamul brought in a silver tray of coffee and two cups, the customary accompaniment to 'officers' memoranda' – the discussion of matters not requiring the presence of the serjeant-major. Lieutenant St Alban would one day command the attention of the House of Commons, and undoubtedly from the despatch box (and in the Whig, even Radical, interest): of that, Hervey was certain, for besides aught else, it was St Alban's own desire. But for the moment the adjutant's ambition was in abeyance, overtaken by the conviction that, as he put it, 'we do good here'. Besides, he found being adjutant the most agreeable work. Hervey had told him he'd be no use in the appointment unless he knew his commanding officer's opinion on everything and everybody, and had proceeded to give it him very decidedly. The confidence was beguiling.

Officers' memoranda had no fixed procedure. Unlike orderly room, however, St Alban usually tried to keep anything untoward till the end.

Hervey spoke first, though, this morning: 'This may amuse you,' he said, taking up a close-written sheet. 'From Lord George:

> *'I tell you that at the levee His Majesty, pursuant to a scheme of the Horse-Guards to raise an additional brigade of Hussars, said he was desirous of converting the regiment to that style, but that I begged a few days' consideration, at the end of which I informed His Majesty that I was grateful of the honour he implied in so doing (for I judged he thought it an elevation, and I thought it better to avoid discussion on the point) but that I believed the regiment would, for the time being*

at least, prefer to retain the distinction under which it served in the Peninsula and at Waterloo. You may treat with this intelligence as you see fit, but I surmise that it will not long be before it is out, especially as I understand the Eleventh are to be offered the "honour" instead.'

St Alban inclined his head.

'Quite,' said Hervey. 'I might add that it will be only prudent to share this singularly disappointing news with all ranks as soon as may be.'

Sammy waited for the first tasting of the coffee and sign of approval. Hervey's smile remained as he took a sip, unsweetened. '*Shukria*, Sammy. *Mikka nanri*.'

Sammy answered to Urdu and Hindoostanee, more or less – he'd been around cantonments long enough, and the two were all the same to him – and even to some English, but Hervey liked to use the odd word of Tamul as well, if only out of respect for the bearer's incomprehensible satisfaction in doing small things. Sammy owned nothing but what he stood up in, and lived each day without knowing – perhaps even without contemplating – where his bread would come from next. He swept the floors, ran errands for the clerks, made coffee *and* tea (and tolerably well), and smiled so continually as to make the blackest day a shade brighter. In exchange, the quartermaster gave him a few rupees from time to time to buy rice, and let him sleep in a little thatched lean-to by his stores. The dragoons called him all the names under the sun – and would then give him a few annas of their own, for a little old Tamul who smiled when he'd nothing but their company was comfort in a hard world. And one day, no doubt, they'd find him dead, with a smile on his face, and they'd give him a 'regimental' funeral, for as far as they were concerned Sammy was on the strength.

Hervey smiled the more as he contemplated the remarkable world of those who wore the King's coat. His Majesty spoke to Lord George Irvine, Colonel of the 6th Light Dragoons (Princess Augusta's Own); Lord George wrote thence to him, Matthew Paulinus Hervey, the

Sixth's commanding officer – Lieutenant-Colonel and Brevet Colonel, indeed; and in turn he conveyed His Majesty's pleasure to Lieutenant the Honourable Edward St Alban, while at the same time exchanging words with a man who probably didn't know even who was his own father or mother.

On the face of it, in Madras men like Sammy were as the sands of the sea. Were they all as he, though, in their simple virtue? On Sunday they'd sung of bringing them enlightenment:

From Greenland's icy mountains,
From India's coral strand,
Where Afric's sunny fountains
Roll down their golden sand,
From many an ancient river,
From many a palmy plain,
They call us to deliver
Their land from error's chain.

Good Bishop Heber had written it, a rousing hymn (and a fit memorial too to that tireless Christian). Hervey had known him a little in Calcutta when the regiment was there – and Kezia even better. But what chain fettered Sammy?

Yes, they did good work here, for it wasn't so much error's chain but *chains* – so many practices repugnant to civilized society. But for how *long* would they do good? Theirs, the Sixth's, was a temporary reinforcement, contrived in large measure by Sir Eyre Somervile, the pro-governor and Hervey's old friend, and the purpose for which they'd come here – the overthrow of the Rajah of Coorg, and the pacification of Mysore thereby – was accomplished. The court of directors of the Honourable East India Company would soon wish to see retrenchment.

'Is any more, Colonel-sahib?'

'No, thank you, Sammy.'

'I dismiss, Colonel-sahib?'

It had become a ritual. 'Dismiss, Sammy.'

When the door was closed, St Alban sat down. 'The sar'nt-major says he's the best scout in the garrison. There was adulterated flour brought in yesterday, and Sammy gave the quartermaster the word.'

'Did he indeed? How did he learn of it? I trust that Collins made much of him?'

St Alban nodded. 'These Hindoos and their damned "caste": it seems that when it comes to "untouchables" they never bother to guard their tongues.'

'And Sammy has a good ear, evidently.'

'Just so. And Collins has made much of him, yes.'

Hervey smiled. He could picture the scene – and when the quartermaster turned the tables on the corn merchants. Collins could make his one arm even more fearsome than two.

But there was work to be done, of a sort. 'Well now, Edward, what shall be the answer to the King's pleasure?'

'Oh, I can't suppose it will be of great moment to the serjeants and other ranks, Colonel. It scarcely affects their fortunes, I would think. I imagine it will provide diversion for the officers, though. I venture to say opinions will be equally divided. There'll be those who calculate it a financial advantage in the longer term – raise the price of their commission – and those who baulk at the cost of the uniform.'

'No doubt.'

St Alban opened his order book and smiled wryly. 'Well, it spares us the trouble of growing mustachios. There's an order from the Horse Guards commanding they be abolished.'

'The sky falls! What say the Horse Guards?'

St Alban read: '*The mustachios of the cavalry (excepting in the Life Guards, the Royal Horse Guards, and the Hussars), to be abolished, and the hair of the non-commissioned officers and soldiers throughout the regular forces, to be cut close at the sides and at the back of the head . . .*'

'As has been the regimental practice since time immemorial,' said Hervey, barely able to contain his amusement. 'I recall Lord George's dismay at the sight of the Hussar brigade in Spain: "More like Jews than British officers" . . . Is there anything else of moment from the commander-in-chief? Lord Hill must be sorely tried by our new sovereign, what with changing the uniforms of half the cavalry, and now hairdressing.'

St Alban raised an eyebrow, then shook his head. 'A month's worth of the *Gazette* came with the last Indiaman. I've made a beginning on them . . . I saw that General Greville had died of an aneurysm.'

Hervey sat up. 'Indeed?'

Sir Peregrine Greville had presided at the inquiry at Bristol. It had been an awkward business.

Hervey cleared his throat and assumed a sudden air of business. 'Then I had better write to his widow.'

St Alban said nothing. There were rumours, but there were always rumours about everything and everybody. Besides, they were the far side of the world.

A quarter of an hour passed on matters of regimental moment, yet which to an outsider would be of no moment at all – even if comprehensible. The one unmistakable detail was that a fresh cornet was to come – but, ominously, from the new military college at Sandhurst.

'Is he a gentleman, do you suppose?' asked Hervey. He'd every confidence in Lord George Irvine, but Lord George had been detained in the north of England a good deal, and had perforce to leave some matters to the regimental agents – and there'd been some shocking bad hats join these late years. They didn't last long, as a rule, but they left their mark nevertheless. The trouble was, the Horse Guards, for all their avowed intention to regulate purchase, had once again lost control of the practice, so that anyone willing to pay over-price was bound to be able to pick up a commission or promotion, since it was only natural that the officer selling-out should want to obtain the highest price. The old Duke of York, when commander-in-chief, had forbidden sales above regulation price, but the agents were not servants of the Crown, and while appearing to observe the order to the letter, were only too willing to negotiate the balance 'off the books'. Yet cadets at the military college were not notably flush with money, which did, of course, present other difficulties – though not so much in India, for there a man could live tolerably well on a smallish allowance.

'His letter of introduction is in your box, Colonel.'

Hervey nodded.

'Oh, and the Coromandel Cup,' St Alban continued: 'the committee has made the change to the rule. It will be run with couched spears.'

Hervey brightened. 'Capital. Jobbing's not a military practice, and the stand-off'll be a deal safer for the horse. I saw a boar all but sever a mare's leg once. Tusk clean through the ankle.'

'Though not so safe perhaps for the rival spears?'

Hervey smiled. He'd seen the long spear catch a rival's leg time enough – and worse; at least the shorter jobbing spear was wielded with less hazard. 'No, perhaps not; but the rival spears can shift for themselves.'

'Just so, Colonel.'

'Very well. And that, I suppose, is that?'

St Alban raised an eyebrow. 'I fear not quite. Channer has got himself into a fix: "Crim con" with Mrs Ellison, and Captain Ellison demands satisfaction.'

Hervey groaned. Criminal conversation – the common-law tort arising from adultery; but the injured party wishing to settle it with pistols rather than the court. Which was as well, perhaps, for Lieutenant Channer had no money to speak of. Yet an affair of honour rarely in his experience did honour to either party. He passed no judgement on Channer (how could he, indeed, given his former *amour* with Lady Katherine Greville?), but officers duelling, besides the question of homicide, was not edifying. 'Who, precisely, is Captain Ellison?'

'He is new, of the Engineers, the Survey to be precise.'

'And Mr Channer has wasted no time, evidently. You have forbidden him to give satisfaction, I take it?'

'He refuses anyway.'

Hervey's mouth fell open. '*Does* he, indeed.'

St Alban cleared his throat. 'He says . . . He says he gave satisfaction to Mrs Ellison and he fails to see why a man should be obliged to give more.'

Hervey angered. 'That is impudent as well as unbecoming. I trust it was not his reply to Ellison himself?'

'I fear it was, and in others' hearing.'

Hervey sighed. There was a rule, an understanding at least, that while a superior officer mayn't seduce the wife of a junior, the wife of a superior could bestow her favours as she wished. Both acts were abominable in the eyes of God, of course, but not in King's Regulations (the latter act being no abuse of rank). In all things, however, discretion was the better part, both during and afterwards.

'How do we know of all this?'

St Alban again raised an eyebrow. (As well ask a priest what his penitent had revealed as ask an adjutant how he came by his information.)

'Very well,' said Hervey; 'So not a matter to be settled quietly.'

'No. And in the meantime I've detailed Channer for duty at Bangalore. Waterman too.' (He disliked them both – Channer from Eton, where he'd thought him a blackguard.)

'Very well, I'll think on it.'

'And that is all, Colonel.'

'Then if you'll leave me in peace for an hour and Sammy will bring more coffee, I shall write the quarterly report to Lord George . . . You'll dine with our family party tomorrow, I hope? I intend shooting duck with Captain Fairbrother this evening.'

'With pleasure, Colonel.' St Alban rose and made to leave.

'By the bye. Where is the moonshee? Georgiana is keen to continue the instruction she had on the passage out.'

'I don't know, Colonel. I asked the same only yesterday of the quarter-master. He said the moonshee'd told him he'd be back before the monsoon.'

Hervey shook his head. 'These Hindoos.'

'Quite.'

Whatever their religion.

III

'Progress'

Next day

Morning exercise of a Wednesday was a regimental parade. All but the quarter guard, the picket officer, the sick and the prisoners turned out in cotton-drill stable jackets – 'drab' rather than the white preferred by many a regiment, for Hervey could see no reason to employ any more dhobi-wallahs than strictly necessary – to walk and trot for an hour and a half on the plain west of the lines. Three squadrons – five troops (the sixth still at Madkerry, former seat of the Rajah of Coorg), a little short of four hundred sabres – and the regimental supernumeraries parading in column of route, the sun not long up and the smoke of countless fires rising to make a meagre *hazree* with which to face the labour of the day. It was Hervey's favourite parade, assembled with all the formalities yet ridden at ease, the dragoons at liberty to chat with each other.

He rode at the very rear, as usual, better to observe – to admire – and with a party 'by invitation': the adjutant, naturally; the serjeant-major, without question; his covering serjeant, of course; and the major, though as a rule his second in command took the opportunity to ride freely and see the troop captains in the saddle. Major Garratt, a bachelor in the later part of the fifth decade of his life, had come to the Sixth on exchange from the Ninety-fifth (or the Rifle Brigade, as now they preferred). Hervey had been only too glad at last to have a man he could rely on in that post – shrewd, economical, efficient, not too active as to disconcert the captains, yet with a sure touch when tranquillity looked threatened; a bachelor content with a little soldiering, the pleasures of the table (including cards) – and sport. For to the sportsman, India was without peer: the tiger in the jungle, the great mahseer in the river, the wily snipe on the *jheels* (marshes), the strong-winged duck, the jinking pig . . . 'Everything that is necessary, and nothing that is not' was Major Garratt's motto, and of the Rifles, he said; and Hervey had told him it might equally be the Sixth's – what constituting 'necessary' being the opinion of the senior officer present, of course. And Garratt had laughed in a way that had reassured him. How, indeed, could it be otherwise when both had been at Waterloo – the only officers, now, saving Collins, at regimental duty. And when they'd marched into Coorg with Hervey at the head of the field force, Garratt had taken Hervey's place at the head of the regiment, exercised command admirably and then handed it back without the slightest resentment. Yes, he liked to give the impression of being the footiest of men around horses, but Hervey thought it a ploy, for he'd never seen him dismount involuntarily – and they'd taken some monstrous wide nullahs – dry watercourses – these past months in pursuit of pig – and Garratt's charger was not of a forgiving stamp. Indeed, it was the opinion of the Waterloo sweats in the serjeants' and the corporals' messes (few that they were, too) that the regiment had not been so godly and quietly governed since that day on the ridge of Mont St Jean, when Lord George Irvine had been the lieutenant-colonel, and Joseph Edmonds his major. And it pleased Hervey – these things always reached the ear of a commanding officer if the regimental staff and his body-men were of the right stuff – for he'd had his share of the opposite.

That said, he was of the opinion that tranquillity, before too long, was inimical to cavalry discipline (and quite possibly to that of the infantry as well); the dragoons would be pining soon enough for a little action.

'How was your sport last night, Colonel?' asked Garratt as they settled into a rising trot.

'Agreeable, most agreeable; though a modest bag perhaps – a couple of brace of sprigtail, a few egrets, a teal . . . oh, and a python. You should have come.'

'I should. The entertainment at the Bodyguard's mess was more than I expected.'

Hervey thought it best not to enquire. The Governor's Bodyguard had some fearsome customs. 'Fairbrother here got the teal, I should add – fast and high. There were no snipe, though, so you might have been disappointed.' (The major had soon established himself as the best shot of all the officers – and had even beaten Serjeant Acton at the regimental sports.)

'We did account for several thousand mosquitoes too,' added Fairbrother.

'Yes,' said Hervey, frowning. 'Corporal Johnson swore more than the army in Flanders.'

His attention, though, returned to Georgiana. It was not unusual for wives to accompany Wednesday exercise – Hervey's only stipulation being that they were not to ride with parasols – but Georgiana was the only female this morning save for Annie, who was riding with them for the first time.

Annie sat well, chatting easily with the riding-master, under whose instruction she'd been coaxed into the side-saddle. Georgiana, too, rode aside, chatting equally easily with the syce who was meant to be her pilot but who'd evidently concluded that his lead rein was redundant. Georgiana had protested that breeches were more suitable here, just as on the Plain in Wiltshire, but Hervey had no intention of presenting her legs for the contemplation of anyone, let alone the entire regiment. She'd been here but a fortnight, and he was still not accustomed to the change since last he'd seen her. It was a change he knew he ought to have expected, but he'd left her in England a child, and now in Madras she was . . . on the threshold of being a young woman. Youth notwithstanding, she'd be seen as 'a new-arrived angel', as the saying went. Indeed, for that very reason he'd not really approved of her coming to India, though it was delightful at last to have her company, for to all intents and purposes she'd been his sister's ward these past dozen years. But she couldn't stay here long; of that he was sure. She would need to find a husband – and a good match at that. She was not without connections after all: Henrietta, her mother, had been ward of the Marquess of Bath; Elizabeth, her aunt, was now a baroness (albeit the title German) – and he himself was not entirely without account. She should be presented at court, dances arranged, introductions made . . .

No, India was not the place for Georgiana Hervey.

And yet . . . 'The deuce, St Alban; she natters away like an old Company hand!'

'So I observe, Colonel. And that minds me: before parade I learned that the moonshee's chowkidar's become agitated by his absence. It seems he'd told him he'd return within four moons, and it's now gone six.'

Hervey shrugged. 'Well, it must have been a great tamasha, his daughter's wedding, but I do think he might have sent word . . . At any rate, Baboo-syce yonder renders service, though what his grammar is I can't imagine.'

'It cannot be worse than mine, I'm sure,' said St Alban, and not without some despair. 'I confess I feel the want of the moonshee's instruction.' (It was curious, Hervey observed, how a man so evidently well-schooled in Latin and Greek should find the Hindoostanee such a trial.) 'It seems the chowkidar fears something untoward has happened. He says the moonshee wouldn't have left so much business unattended.'

Hervey sighed. 'Anything's possible in this country, don't we know. I doubt we can do anything before we receive word, though. I expect he'll turn up in a day or so, full of stories, and a fuller purse than he left with. A good man, Bunda Ali, but . . .'

He lapsed into contemplation of Georgiana again, and St Alban decided to change rein.

'Were you in Jamaica long, Captain Fairbrother?'

It had been three years and more since Fairbrother had ridden with the regiment – in the Low Countries during the unhappy affair of the Belgian rising – and St Alban supposed that much of that time had been spent at sea.

'Six months or thereabout. Not long enough to be wholly reacquainted, but enough to see the change that Abolition will bring. It'll not be without its vexations.'

'How so, exactly, sir?'

St Alban, his family having no stock in sugar, was wont to see the Abolition Act, lately passed, as being a measure like Reform – a matter of liberal sensibility and nothing else. The owners were to receive handsome compensation after all.

'Simply put, Mr St Alban, the price of sugar may rise beyond what its consumers are willing to pay. The labour is extensive.' He said it with the detachment that was perhaps only acquired by the son of a slave who was himself – now, at least, with the death of his father, a planter – the owner of slaves. Or rather, now that the Act was passed, the *former* owner. He would be eternally grateful that he'd missed the late revolt, whose violence – of both slaves and the militia that suppressed the rising – sickened him.

St Alban nodded thoughtfully. 'That would indeed be a calamity, so many dispossessed suddenly and with no alternative means.'

Fairbrother smiled. 'You remain a man of humane but practical sensibility, Mr St Alban. India has not hardened your heart, evidently.'

Hervey's ears pricked, having contemplated the marriage stakes for long enough. 'Captain Fairbrother has a scheme to reduce the cost of production.'

'Indeed, Colonel?' St Alban was all attention. Schemes of improvement, anywhere, were always his delight.

'And one to appeal to your Whiggish notions of progress.'

'That I cannot promise,' said Fairbrother, knowing that some thought the Whig party's motive in Reform was merely to replace the divine right of kings with the divine right of Whigs. 'But I believe the future in all things to lie with steam. Have you seen an iron-rail road, Mr St Alban?'

'I have not, but I am certain of their capability.'

'On passage to England from Jamaica my ship put in at Kingstown, and I was able to see the railway just built to Dublin, all of six miles. Wholly remarkable. There's to be a railway-train from both ends each day, every half-hour from six in the morning until a half before midnight, some of them carrying mail bags for the English packets. I am urging my brother, and fellow planters, to consider such a scheme for the conveyance of sugar.'

'And is there coal for the engines in Jamaica?'

'There is not, but there's wood aplenty – the very name "Jamaica" means "wood and water" – and coal may be brought from England, I suppose. I came here by steamer from Suez, Mr St Alban, and there's no coal in Araby.'

'Nor wood, I think. Camel dung perhaps?'

Fairbrother glanced at him keenly (though he knew St Alban wasn't given to mock, certainly not a man his senior in everything but title). 'They port coal across the desert – that much I know. Is there coal here?'

St Alban hesitated. 'I'm shamed to say I don't know, Captain Fairbrother. Colonel, do you suppose there is coal here?'

Hervey's attention had once again wandered. 'What? Coal?'

'Is there coal in India, Colonel?'

'I should imagine so, yes. I think they dig it out in Bengal somewhere.'

St Alban was now thoroughly animated by the intelligence of the steam route through Arabia, not least because one day soon he would take passage home – though not without some regrets – and he saw no merit in spending more time at sea than was strictly necessary.

He pressed him: 'Was the Red Sea way greatly faster, sir?'

'The passage was ten weeks. It would have been nine had we not had to put in near Mecca for repairs. Yours was . . . what, twenty?'

'Twenty-four.'

'And I am very glad you hastened,' said Hervey, not wishing to hear again the details of Fairbrother's 'flight from Egypt'. His particular friend had been in Madras for three weeks, and his adventures in the footsteps of Moses (as it seemed) had delighted everyone he'd met – Somervile especially, whose plan it was to have a steamship ply between Fort St George and Suez. (The governor was especially pleased to have beaten Bombay to it, and more so to have persuaded Fort William to bear half the cost and engage a paddler of their own to take on packets and passengers to Calcutta.)

Hervey had scarcely been so glad as when Fairbrother had arrived that afternoon, soaked to the skin by the refreshing south-west monsoon, yet looking just like a hidalgo – a man of rank in the Peninsula. Hervey's own circumstances had been transformed since they'd seen each other last, when, as the saying went, he lived unaccompanied. For now Kezia was in residence. And not merely in residence, but in evident contentment. Would his good, dear friend, with whom he'd shared so much these past years, quickly tire of the new arrangements? He profoundly hoped not. But he'd do well to find him some proper occupation, for although Fairbrother was not one actively to seek work, he did – if not always recognizing it – grow weary of its absence after not very long. He still had his rank on the half-pay of the late Royal

Africans, which had proved handy in more than one adventure, but here in Madras it might not be so esteemed. Might he enjoy some commission from the Company?

They'd been riding for an hour when they reached the furthest point of the exercise, beyond the narrow isthmus between the Nungambakkam Tank and the Cooum River. Here they would debouch onto the plain of Chinglepoot, turning south to skirt the Long Tank and thence back to the lines. And here they'd have a bit of a canter, though that would depend on the dust – it could be the very devil, even at this time of year – and jump a ditch or two. But this morning Hervey would forgo the pleasure, judging it time to turn for the horse ferry across the Cooum and to make for the Fort. The general-officer-commanding had leave of absence, and as a brevet colonel Hervey stood in his place (until, he supposed, in an emergency one or other of the outlying major-generals was summoned). It was largely the work of administration, and principally of military justice, but three times a week the governor (or, strictly, in the interregnum, the pro-governor) held what he was amused to call his 'chambers'. Hervey enjoyed the occasion, for St Alban and the rest of the regimental staff were so efficient as to leave little to detain him at office and orderly room, and the major's eye was ever reassuring too.

He'd been in command now for three years; he could exercise that command with a longer rein.

'View Halloo!'

It echoed down the column like a regular order.

Hervey stood in the stirrups to see. 'A fine hog! A sanglier, I think . . . No, there goes another.'

A second boar burst from a tamarisk thicket thirty yards to the left of the leading troop. Off at once went C Troop's cornets, and then two from the following troop.

'May I go too, sir?'

Hervey smiled to himself – *Diana venatrix*. And Georgiana had the sensibility too not to call him 'Papa' in front of his officers, nor yet to presume the dragoons' prerogative of 'Colonel'.

'Very well,' he nodded, turning to St Alban. 'Make sure she—'

'Of course, Colonel.'

He was off before Hervey had needed to say.

He'd turned away as the 'hunt' began, with just Acton, Corporal Johnson and Fairbrother. Somervile had asked that he bring his friend, as he wanted to speak with him a little more about his passage out. He'd had word from Fort William that the governor-general had a mind to speed further the steam route via a system of fast posting across the desert from Suez to Cairo, where a paddler on the Nile already plied back and forth to Mahmoudia, and barges on the sweetwater canal thence to Alexandria. The Admiralty had for some years maintained a weekly packet service from Alexandria to London, and a relay across the desert would undoubtedly better expedite the whole enterprise of government as His Majesty's ministers envisaged by the new India Act. For Somervile, too, old India-hand that he was, embraced progress.

They reached Fort St George just before nine. 'Time, I think, for some of Ram Kumar's coffee and *'ki*,' said Hervey. 'The best in Madras.'

'I'd be pleased by even the moderately good, for my bearer made a very indifferent breakfast,' replied Fairbrother, handing his reins to one of the syces who'd doubled from the guardhouse.

'Then we must find you a better bearer. Or else you might reconsider the invitation to lodge with us.'

Fairbrother shook his head. 'You keep very early hours.'

'That is true,' replied Hervey, with a wry smile, 'but we keep late ones too. It's remarkable what India does for the constitution – inasmuch as fauna and infirmities permit.'

The syces led away the horses. They'd get a drink, a good rub down, some corn, and a few hours' rest, but Fairbrother's looked a shade tucked up.

'I shouldn't worry,' Hervey assured him. 'These mares can bear it. And these fellows could rub a dead horse to life.'

In the two years the regiment had been in Madras, Hervey had re-horsed half with 'New South Walers', as the riding-master called them. A dozen or so years before, the Madras cavalry board had turned down the remounts that the Bengal studs were sending them, and looked south instead. It was a prodigious journey from Australia, but only half that from England, where they might otherwise have found the improving blood (for there was only so much the Arab could do with the native breeds). His own charger, Minnie (her stable name; she was entered as Minenhle – in the language of the Zulu 'beautiful day'), was a three-quarter-bred, foaled at the Cape and brought to Madras as a two-year-old, turned away for eighteen months and then broken. She was rising ten now, and could outpace all but the full bloods. She'd strolled off with the syce as if the exercise had been nothing. Hervey reckoned that the regiment was at last, as they said of plants, 'acclimatized' – men and horses. Blooded, too, in the late affair at Coorg.

The question was, however, what use would there be made of them? What time would be left to make profit of their acclimatization and blooding now that the new Act turned the East India Company into administrators rather than merchant adventurers?

But there was no profit in excessive thought for the morrow, as Somervile was fond of saying; 'Sufficient unto the day is the evil thereof.' For the moment, he would enjoy the simple pleasures of this fierce and fickle land. He sipped his Arabica and crunched the *chikki* – how complementary were the tastes, bitter and sweet – and was gratified to see that Fairbrother appeared to think the same.

'*Eppotum nallatu,* Ram Kumar.'

'*Nanri, sahib.*'

Indeed, the coffee was so good he would ask for more; but suddenly from a window high on the other side of the courtyard came Somervile's habitual 'Salaam!'

Hervey smiled. 'The pro-governor does not stand on ceremony, as you see.'

This Fairbrother knew well from the Cape, when Somervile had nearly met his end – at least once – by excess of enthusiasm. But it had been some years, and he looked forward to more of his company again, elevated though it now was. Not least if he were truly an advocate of steam.

Steam, however, wasn't the governor's preoccupation this morning. All had changed with the arrival the evening before of a Company messenger from Fort William.

He welcomed them to the workaday rooms whence the presidency was governed, introduced his secretary to Fairbrother (a handsome way round, thought Hervey), poured them marsala and then sat down in the emphatic way he had when pleased with what he was about to impart.

'Well then, gentlemen: what do you know of thuggee?'

Hervey was well used to Somervile's interrogatory way of proceeding, though it was not his own. Nevertheless, he was in spirits enough to humour him. 'Do we speak of a proper or an abstract noun?'

'Abstract.'

'Frankly, I know neither proper nor abstract.'

'Captain Fairbrother, you look knowing, sir.'

'I met a Bengal collector on the packet out returning from home leave. He said his district was plagued by dacoits, of whom the worst belonged to a secret society which murdered any and all, whether necessary or not, and that these were known as *phansigars*, or sometimes *thugs*.'

Somervile beamed. 'Then my purpose is made so much easier. That, indeed, appears to be the essence of thuggee. And your collector will, by all accounts, find the situation in his district not in the least improved on his return.'

'He said he believed it would soon disturb Madras – the Northern Circars,' added Fairbrother.

'His reason?'

'That the authorities were quite unable to bring any of the thugs to justice for want of intelligence, so there was no impediment to their increase. Also that some of the nabobs must be party to it.'

'Hah! That is the material point,' said Somervile, turning to Hervey. 'The service believes this to be so.'

Hervey inclined his head, as if to say he was not surprised.

Somervile turned back to Fairbrother. 'I should explain, sir, by "service" I mean the Political Service. You are acquainted with its purpose?'

'I am not, Sir Eyre, but shall be happy to be so.'

'Most of the princely states – the greater ones at least – have a Resident, an ambassador of the Company, though his functions are considerably greater than merely embassy. It is a form of indirect rule, the object being the maintenance of peace, which was desirable in itself when the Company was principally engaged in trade but which now, since the new Act, is essential to the exercise of government. The service consists of officers drawn largely from the military, but also from the best of the Company's writers.'

'Admirable.'

'I confess a high regard for them . . . Well now, there's a political making his way here presently on instructions from Fort William. I should be much obliged, Captain Fairbrother, if you would lend an ear to our discussions.'

Fairbrother, having supposed their mutual interest lay in pistons and cylinders, was quite taken aback. 'I . . . should be delighted, Sir Eyre, though to what end my ear may be of use is quite beyond me.'

Hervey already had his suspicions.

IV

The Ways of Nature

That afternoon

'Why, Miss Gildea, whatever is the matter?'

Tears filled Annie's eyes and ran down her cheeks. She made to rise as Georgiana came in.

'No, please don't get up. Whatever can have caused you to cry so?'

Georgiana pulled up a chair and sat beside her. The nursery was quiet at this time. The infant Hervey slept, Allegra took her afternoon rest, and the work of the servants ceased for an hour or so. Annie herself used the time to read, or to write her diary or a letter home.

'Oh, Miss Hervey, it's my brother. He is dead.'

Georgiana took her hand. 'Annie, I'm so sorry— Oh, forgive me: *Miss Gildea*. Your brother here in India? How so?'

'Yes; I have no other.' Annie reached for the letter she'd not long laid aside on the little table next to her chair. 'I wrote to him three months ago – it went with the post from the Fort – and today there came this from his captain.' She handed it to her:

The Infantry Barracks,
Agra,
September 23rd 1834

Dear Madam,

I much regret to have to inform you of the death of your brother Private Thomas Gildea, who departed this life on July 6th after being seized by an illness. He was buried with military honours in the garrison cemetery, and his grave marked by a stone of regimental pattern. His personal effects were sent to his father in England together with a sum of money raised by sale of his necessaries and perishables among his comrades, as is the custom.

I may tell you that your brother was held in high regard by his officers. All in the company feel keenly his loss.

I am so very sorry to have to convey this news to you. If there be anything further that I may tell you for your comfort then I beg you only to inquire.

I am, madam, your obedient servant,
Robert Pattisson,
Captain, No. 3 Company,
13th (1st Somersetshire) Regiment (Light Infantry)

'It is indeed a sad letter, but a handsome one too,' said Georgiana, giving it her back.

'It is, Miss Hervey, but I wish I might know what was his illness. Perhaps his captain wishes to spare me distress, but I'm sure I'll keep thinking on what it may have been.'

'I pray you don't. His suffering, whatever suffering there was, is at an end. He is with God, and he would not wish you in anguish.'

Annie nodded, and dabbed at her eyes with a handkerchief. She folded the letter, put it aside and stood up in a determined way, brushing the creases from her skirt. 'I must make ready for Miss Allegra's walk.'

'Of course. I would come with you, but my lesson with the baboo . . .'

Annie smiled. 'I wish Bunda Ali were back. He is so fine a teacher. It is strange there is no word.'

Georgiana had heard the same, oft repeated – a fine teacher, and a good man. 'My father says that if he is not come by the end of the month he will have a notice sent to the Resident in Haidarabad to enquire his whereabouts. He believes it not unlikely that the Nizam – don't you think that title quaint? – has enticed him to join his court, his knowing so much about the military here, and being of the same religion as the Nizam.'

'To do us harm? Oh, I think not, Miss Hervey. Surely not. He gave me lessons too, though he need not have, for I am of no consequence.'

Georgiana clasped her hand again. 'Oh, dearest Miss Gildea, you are of the greatest consequence to me, and to my father – and to my stepmother too!'

Annie thought for a moment. 'Miss Hervey, please say nothing of this to your father, or to Mrs Hervey. I would not want to disturb them in any way.'

Georgiana was all surprise. 'Why, Miss Gildea, my father and stepmother alike would surely wish to know of your loss, to condole with you and offer what comfort they may. You are as family!'

Annie shook her head. 'No, Miss Hervey, if you please. I appreciate that sentiment, and no doubt you are right, but I have my reasons, and would wish, if at all, to tell them in my own time.'

Georgiana smiled warmly. 'Of course, of course. Forgive my presumption.'

'There is nothing to forgive, Miss Hervey. You are all kindness . . . And now there is work to be done.'

* * *

Hervey had returned to the lines just after stand-down at one o'clock. Second parade – which was always the preserve of the troop serjeant-majors – would follow in two hours, and then perhaps a little recreation. Afternoon was not as a rule a time for the commanding officer to be at office or even abroad, except in plain clothes, but as he didn't eat in the middle of the day save for a little fruit, he liked to keep 'open office' for an hour so that any of the regimental staff might have a word less formally.

The orderly room was otherwise a place of silence, even repose, the major asleep in his chair and no sign of St Alban or the chief clerk. Sammy, however, by some process that passed all understanding, stood ready with a tray of hot coffee as if he knew that the colonel-sahib would appear at this precise moment. There was, Hervey had long supposed, a means of communication among the native servants and vendors that they, the *gora log*, the white people, would never comprehend.

'*Nanri*, Sammy,' he said simply.

Sammy returned the smile broadly.

'But *two* cups? *Irantu kap*?'

'Yes, Colonel-sahib. Daktar wait.'

The surgeon appeared from the defaulters' room.

Hervey smiled still more widely. 'It is ever good to see you, Milne. But with tidings of joy, I trust?' He could say it with good cheer, for the morning 'states' said the regiment was in sound enough health.

'I wasn't able to attend your parade, Colonel, for I was called away. I thought I should report in person. Forgive my rather dusty attire.'

There was none whose company Hervey found more agreeably rewarding than Surgeon Milne's. In a regiment, it was said, one gentleman subordinate to another, the senior never mentioned it, and the junior never forgot it. The surgeon – a physician, indeed, formerly of some standing in Aberdeen – was Hervey's subordinate, but in his professional calling he was without rank (Hervey himself had joked that he was 'peerless'). This alone, in a society in which rank was of the essence, made his company welcome; otherwise it was forever a business of talking upwards or downwards. But it was more than just professional relief: Milne had saved Kezia from the 'puerperal melancholy', nursing her back to health after her collapse three years before.

'I'm just come from the Fort, and Sammy has brought us coffee. Sit you down.'

Milne took his coffee and sat in the gilded chair taken booty from the palace in Coorg, while Hervey settled into his green plush the other side of the writing table.

'Cholera in one of the villages beyond the Nungambakkam Tank. Francis, the senior medical officer, took me to see. Not a pretty sight. Nor smell indeed. But it's a native matter. It shouldn't enter the lines. We did what we could.'

Hervey grimaced. There were few things that could be of greater concern to a commander of men than cholera nearby, even if the other side of the Nungambakkam water. 'We'll not need sulphur pots then?'

Milne shook his head. 'But I've told Collins to make ready. It would be well to exercise south of the Nungambakkam meanwhile.'

Hervey nodded. 'Is that the worst of it?'

'Two deaths from snakebite in the native lines, and a third indirectly. One of them – one of the grass-cutters – this morning, in just three hours.'

Hervey shook his head. There was no escaping it in India, no matter where, or how exalted – as the encounter with Allegra in the stillroom had (almost) proved. But three hours . . . 'One of Corporal Johnson's "good" snakes, evidently.'

'Colonel?'

'He'd heard it somewhere: "the good ones kill quickly, the bad ones take days." Who were the other two?'

'A most intriguing case, a woman and child found dead this morning on their charpoy by the husband, a chowkidar returned from watch. We couldn't at first fathom why she'd died, nor the child, till we found two puncture wounds to the ankle, so small as to want a glass to see them. She must have been bitten while she slept; probably didn't even realize, then passed the poison in her milk sometime in the early hours. The child hadn't been dead long.'

Hervey shook his head again. A mother poisoning her own child – of all the ways that Nature inflicted death in this country . . . 'I confess I shudder each time I think of Allegra's brush with the cobra.' Had Annie not been so bold – and Serjeant Stray not so swift with the sabre – Allegra would now be laid in native earth (like her father, though he at least had succumbed in battle).

Milne nodded. 'Indeed.'

But Hervey was intrigued, still. 'Might you have saved the child had you found her alive, do you think?'

Milne inclined his head, as if to say the question was unanswerable. 'Poison ingested directly? Deadlier than a bite, I should suppose.'

'It seems to me strange that there's no native medicine – none at least that I've heard tell of – after so many hundreds of years. My mare was bitten when first I was in India, and Johnson got hold of a Brahman who gave her some potion of mungo root, and she recovered. But I suspect now it was nothing of the kind – not a snakebite. Though there were distinct marks on her muzzle. Hornets, perhaps. Was it ever a subject of your medical society meetings?'

'There were more pressing cases. I never heard tell of a snake in England kill anything but a dog.'

'Quite.'

'Mungo root, you say?'

'Yes. I recall it has a botanical name suggestive of a cure, though I can't remember what.'

'*Ophiorrhiza* – snakeroot. The *samperas* – the snake-catchers – say the mongoose eats it and acquires immunity thereby. I'm not disposed to dismissing these things merely because they come from such an authority, but in this case I confess I'm sceptical. There was an interesting work published fifty years ago or thereabout, by an Italian monk, on the venom of the common viper. It can't compare in potency with those here, of course, but I'm interested to know why. He was able to precipitate its constituents by alcohol, and observed that it produced not only coagulation of the blood, but puzzlingly, fluidity as well.'

'Was that not observable in those who'd been bitten?'

'Of course, but it's only possible by careful examination of the blood. By microscope, I mean, and it seems he had none.'

Hervey would freely admit that he himself had no science to speak of. 'What conclusions did he reach?'

'Nothing of substance, except that vipers are immune to the venom.'

'But how might they not be, since it comes from within?'

'It comes from within, yes, but from poison sacs quite discrete from the circulatory system. But the good monk discerned also that the venom remained toxic in the prey.'

Hervey nodded. In truth, he'd had enough of snakes. If Milne wished to bring his faculties to bear on the matter, all well and good – some dragoon might be glad of it one day – but it didn't conduce to conviviality.

'But, this apart, the regiment is in good health, I believe I can say – have just said, indeed, in my letter to the colonel.'

'Oh, quite so. I think we've come through the sickly season well, inasmuch as any season here's more sickly than another. But the monsoon seems to bring with it particular ills . . . And the damned snakes washed out of their holes. Dearly should I like to know what was the Almighty's purpose in them.'

Hervey sighed resignedly. Sometimes Milne could be persistent. '*And I will put enmity between thee and the woman, and between thy seed and her seed; it shall bruise thy head, and thou shalt bruise his heel*. Doctor, you will not let the work of the Devil tempt you too much?'

Milne shook his head. 'No, no; the serpent merely intrigues me as a physician, which means also that I am drawn to their part in natural history. I can't fathom, say, why the venom of the cobra is so much greater than that of the viper, since its purpose – the killing of prey, we must suppose – is no different.'

Hervey would concede that the philosophical aspect of it was stimulating, and nodded as much. 'Well, I'm glad this place affords you opportunity for study, since there's evidently so little work in the infirmary to occupy you fully.'

Milne was not always quick to diagnose irony, however. 'The business of prevention is as compelling as that of cure, Colonel. There's a most active chirurgical society here, corresponding with Calcutta, and no shortage of subjects for inquiry. Nor, I may add, corpses for dissection.'

Hervey wished he'd steered the talk to something more wholesome, though he had to accept that his purpose in being at office at this hour was to allow his staff the opportunity to speak. 'Is that of importance, bodies for dissection?'

'To my mind, Colonel, it is of the first importance. You may take notes for twenty years – and believe me, I have – and all will likely be to you a confusion of symptoms and incoherent phenomena. Open a few bodies and this obscurity will disappear.'

'Tell me how so, exactly.'

'By comparison of the change in – principally – the organs. Come to one of our dissections and observe for yourself.'

Hervey frowned. There was all the difference in the world between wielding a blade in battle and cutting cold in a dissecting theatre. 'I may think on it.'

Sammy came with more coffee.

'But by the bye, Colonel, I must tell you of two particular matters. Serjeant Cottam, I fear, must soon be for discharge. Pronounced cataracts.'

Hervey nodded. Cottam was a steady man (Worsley thought highly of him, as long as book work wasn't too demanding), but he had no family; it would be a long and dismal passage home. 'We might find him something here – lighter duties, on the civil side, say – though perhaps you'll object that the climate isn't favourable.'

'He likes the climate, Colonel, and the climate likes him. Alas, the very intensity of the light exacerbates things.'

'Have you spoken of it to him, and to Worsley?'

'I told Cottam yesterday that I'd defer his medical board for one month, but that I couldn't risk it beyond. I haven't had opportunity to speak with Worsley.'

'And Cottam was . . . content?'

Milne sighed.

'I can imagine. Speak with Worsley as soon as you're able.'

'I will. Also . . . How do you find Mrs Hervey . . . now that the monsoon's at an end?'

Hervey smiled. 'Exactly as at the beginning of the monsoon. In splendid health. Have you a concern?'

'None whatever. You reassure me. I merely wondered if she found the weather enervating, as some have.'

'Quite the opposite, I believe.'

'Then I shall speak no more of it.'

Hervey's brow furrowed. 'You were called to Dorothea Worsley's this morning, I understand. *She* is well, I trust?'

'She is very well. Her time nears – two months, I'd say; these things are difficult to be exact about – but the season has fatigued her.'

Hervey wondered if there was something more; but he put it from his mind. Milne, he found, was invariably frank – as frank as may be – and if he were anxious for Kezia's condition he'd given him ample opportunity to say so . . .

Instead they saw out the coffee with general chat about the healthiness and otherwise of the garrison, though he began to regret indulging Milne in so vivid a description of the plague of boils visited on the Madras Artillery.

*

Hervey didn't stay long at office. St Alban had returned soon after Milne left, saying there was no business to detain him. Hervey had been doubly content, for Sammy had told him that a tiger had come close to one of the villages near the Long Tank the night before. The ryots had chased it away, but were sure it would return as their goats had not long yeaned, and although they kept dogs and a watch, they feared they'd be unable to drive it off for good now that it had scent of the fold. There was nothing that he, Hervey, could likely do, but it would be a fine thing to get sight of the beast, if only at a distance. Georgiana, he was sure, would wish to; and St Alban was all eagerness, for leaving India – whenever that would be – without seeing a tiger would be too much to admit at a drawing room. He was certain that Fairbrother would say the same.

Kezia wasn't tempted, however, when he proposed the idea on returning to Arcot House; she had to pay a call on Dorothea Worsley. Besides, she reminded him, she'd seen tiger in Bengal, 'where they are of no little size'. (She'd thought it would be in vain to suggest he took care, for himself or Georgiana.) She was, though, pleased that Major Garratt would accompany them. Knowing that he'd not yet seen a tiger, but that it was his avowed intent to have a skin on the wall by the year's end, Hervey had woken him playfully – '*Dekh, dekh, samne – baagh!*' – and Garratt had sprung up, all anticipation. And when Hervey had explained, he'd been all activity. His plans for a grand *baagh shikar* in the Nilgiris were well advanced, and of tiger hunting he'd read everything he could lay his hands on, but a glimpse of the noble creature hereabout, this very evening, could only serve his object.

'One thing I would say, though,' warned Hervey, thinking it right not to let eagerness entirely overtake caution; 'a thing that was told me when first I was here: you may take your chance with a leopard in thick country – as once I did at the Cape, and not by choice – but you have none with a tiger. The leopard when startled isn't so intent on killing as on escaping, whereas tiger – man-eater or no – is so prodigiously strong, it makes no odds why he attacks, for he'll crush you instantly.'

But Garratt, composure returned after his rude waking, needed no cautioning. A man whose soldiering had hitherto been on his feet rather than in the saddle was all too alert to the threat of ambush. 'And from all I've read, too, wise words, Colonel,' he said tactfully.

They set off just after four. There were two hours to sunset, about the best time of day, said the major, tigers disliking the heat of the fore- and afternoon as much as did he. Their smaller prey was anyway nocturnal, but the tiger also favoured dusk, he supposed, so that it could carry off or devour its kill under cover of darkness.

Between them they carried a good weight of shot, though the major's pair of capping rifles seemed to Hervey to be somewhat undue. Service pistols and carbines would be more than enough, though admittedly a volley of lead would not make for the prettiest of trophies. Georgiana wanted a pistol too, but Hervey said he thought it better to wait till she'd had more practice. Annie was relieved, for then she would have felt obliged to carry one as well, and she was not yet confident that pistols behaved exactly as bidden. Besides, in the company of men it was scarcely necessary. Not, at least, in the company of Colonel Hervey.

They trotted fast for most of the way. The village lay at the lower end of the Long Tank, south of the Audeaur River, five miles or so distant, and Hervey's design was to find a place a few hundred yards short of the objective – the merest mound would do – from which to observe the approaches. Had there been time he would have skirted the village on its northern side so as not to lay any scent across the path of the tiger – it came, said Sammy's informants, from the Vandalur Hills to the south – and then to observe with the sun behind them. Instead they might have to shade their eyes.

Finding any elevation proved difficult, however, especially as the lemon grass stood high. They'd closed to a furlong of the village before they could see anything of it – so close indeed that the evening breeze, slight that it was, brought them its scent, more than usually rank. They would have to stay in the saddle to have any chance of spotting a crouching tiger, but the horses had had only light exercise earlier and could bear the weight. In any case, dismounting, even in company, was perhaps not the most prudent thing when the shadows lengthened.

They waited silently but for the odd equine grunt and sniffle – sounds natural enough not to dismay a tiger. Annie felt the need of a shawl as the sun neared the horizon, but she'd not brought one, and nor had Georgiana. She hoped she'd not have to bear it long, for what with the sun in her eyes and the lemon grass she could see next to nothing, and felt sure that when the tiger appeared it would be so fleeting that she'd not be rewarded with so much as a glimpse to write home about. But she was where she ought to be – where Georgiana was – and where, in truth, she'd have wished to be. For she'd never seen Georgiana's father in the field – or any soldier; a mystery she supposed would intrigue any woman.

She watched keenly. Hervey stood a little in advance of the rest of them, peering periodically through his telescope – one day she hoped she too might be able to look through one – just as she imagined he had when the French were in the field, or any number of the savage people he'd fought with, the King's enemies. (She'd observed the land from the deck of their packet out with a telescope, but it wasn't the same.) Just behind him, watching as fixedly too – not into the distance but close about – was Serjeant Acton. She knew that as covering man it was not his to observe what was far away, rather what threatened at hand. Then behind him (and just to the front of her and Georgiana) stood Corporal Johnson, observing not quite so intently, but alert enough and his horse as quiet as a mouse; and to the left of him, facing south to their south-east, were Captain Fairbrother and Lieutenant St Alban. Only Major Garratt, standing rifle in hand several lengths of horse to their rear, did she have to turn to see – not that the major noticed, for he looked the most intent of all.

She began to marvel at being here. She, Annie Gildea, who'd been a chambermaid at the Berkeley Arms in Hounslow, sat side-saddle like a lady with these finest of gentlemen (and Serjeant Acton and Corporal Johnson, gentlemen too in their way), and in this distant, strange land. She wondered what purpose the Almighty could have for her, for her fortune in being here was hardly of her own making? She wondered if her own heart would count for anything in His purpose, or whether it would simply be taken up in the great stream of events as everything else? Would she, in truth, ever be more than mere Annie Gildea, late of the Berkeley Arms? Perhaps, like her brother, this place would one day see her passing – suddenly, by some malign hand, the Grim Reaper or one of his many attendants. She shuddered. Perhaps she ought never to have quit the sphere in which she was brought up.

But no (she almost shook her head); she had looks, airs – she knew she had, because some had told her so (Georgiana for one) – and she fancied, though how could she truly know, that although she had no formal learning she had intelligence. These past two years she'd read a great deal, and learned already much useful native language, both Hindoostanee and Tamul. *No*; she might not be a lady, but she might soon pass for one and then she—

A squeal, a shriek – the horse plunging then bucking, the tiger still fast on its quarters.

Georgiana fell hard, the horse tumbling after her, pinning her leg.

Annie's reared and threw her.

St Alban leapt to Georgiana's side.

Hervey levelled his pistol, but—

Crack!

Garratt's rifle fired first, taking the beast in the shoulder. It fell thrashing with bloodied claws, then grunted and lay still.

Hervey put a ball between its eyes to make sure, and slid from the saddle as calmly as he could to head for Georgiana.

'Stand fast! There's another!' shouted Garratt, on his feet and making into the lemon grass.

Fairbrother went after him.

Annie had scrambled to Georgiana's side almost as fast as St Alban. Only Acton and Johnson stayed mounted, the one to cover his colonel, the other to gather loose reins.

St Alban managed to get the stricken mare to her feet. Hervey and Annie got Georgiana to hers. There were no bones broken – none apparent at least – and though winded she was composed enough to brush the dust from her skirt.

The mare stood stock still, her quarters badly torn. He'd seen worse in the Peninsula, but Hervey contemplated putting a bullet in her brain nevertheless . . . 'Annie, get back into the saddle. Georgiana, you'll ride with me. Corp'l Johnson, take her in hand,' he said briskly, giving him the mare's reins.

But Annie couldn't settle her mount to get a foot in the stirrup. Hervey grabbed her by the waist and lifted her roughly, but then recollected himself enough for a smile of sorts – reassurance.

Acton remained restless until Hervey was back in the saddle, only then letting his sabre drop into the shoulder, at ease, as if sighing with relief.

Garratt and Fairbrother reappeared. 'Gone away,' said the major.

Hervey nodded. It wasn't the time to enquire – nor to congratulate or thank. 'We'd better have the villagers retrieve your trophy.'

V

The Penalty of Death

Next morning

Burra hazree: the governor breakfasted heartily only occasionally these days, mindful of his constitution. *Chota hazree*, 'little breakfast' – a dish of tea and a sweet biscuit or the like – was all his physician recommended as a rule. This morning however he had business to transact, and it was as well to do it with the aid of the table. They began with furmity made with almond milk, which Somervile confessed to liking immoderately, and then the khitmagars brought a silver tureen the size of a bucket.

'I imagine you'll have had *kichree* since your landing here, Captain Fairbrother, though in the hot weather it's not eaten so very much. I venture to say, though, that you'll not have eaten so good as this. Every establishment in Madras has its own receipt, but here my cook excels. Such a way with fish and the smoke box; and the rice – not a grain that sticks to another; and a spiced sauce he makes at midnight when no one is abroad to observe. *Servez-vous, servez-vous!*'

Fairbrother helped himself liberally. He'd returned late after the evening's exertions, lain down and fallen into a deep sleep, waking only with the dawn and his bearer bringing tea. He'd eaten nothing since the middle of the day before, and the kichree – all saffron yellow rice, pink fish and golden-yolk eggs – was a picture.

Hot bread in silver bowls, piping hot coffee from silver pots, and then chilled porter from bottles wrapped in white linen – the khitmagars were practised at their art, bowing as one to be dismissed. Somervile could hardly wait for his guest to pass the spoons to him.

'And so, tell me, Captain Fairbrother – I'm excessively intrigued: your good friend and mine was for once at a disadvantage in battle? What do you suppose would have happened had it not been for the presence of the good major – *La Longue Carabine*?'

Fairbrother sighed. 'Mr St Alban would likely as not be dead, Colonel Hervey and his coverman much hurt, but the tiger killed nevertheless.'

'Quite probably so.'

The truth was, as well they knew, Hervey had several times before been at a disadvantage (how might it be otherwise in a lifetime of making war?) but always there'd been a man to cover him.

Fairbrother smiled. '*La Longue Carabine* indeed; Major Garratt was already called "Hawkeye".'

Somervile tapped the table approvingly. 'I'm very glad you're come, Fairbrother.'

'To breakfast?'

'To India. Our friend is in fine spirits – and he has a major at last worth the name; but – and I've known him these twenty years, almost – he is never better than with you at hand.'

'I am glad to be here. But how long is not for me to say. Hervey thinks the Company will dispense with his services – and the rest of the reinforcement – very soon.'

'My days are spent trying to persuade Fort William otherwise, though until late I'd thought Hervey'd be recalled on promotion. Now that

Melbourne's prime minister, however, I fear the call *won't* come – not, at least, for some time. That pleases me as governor, of course, but not as a friend.'

It was only the day before that Fairbrother had learned that Earl Grey was no longer prime minister, and he'd thought the news favourable to his friend.

'How so? I understood that Lord Melbourne commended his action in Bristol, that the city would have fallen to the mob had not he taken command.'

'That is true, on both counts, but Lord M is so very contrary – a Tory masquerading as a Whig no less. No sooner was the danger to the King's Peace gone but he began loathing the means of quietening that danger. Hervey ought by rights to be general now. The French do these things much better.'

Fairbrother smiled. 'And yet we beat the French always.'

'I grant you that, yes, but perhaps if we arranged things better we might do so more expeditiously, more economically? Be what may, we are most fortunate here to have his services. His subduing of Coorg – its rajah – was most brilliantly done, and at very little cost.'

'I've heard the same from everyone, although he himself is still much affected by the death of his brigade major. He's lost some good young men of late, and feels it keenly. And the business last evening . . . St Alban would for certain have succumbed without Garratt's shot. War is one thing, Sir Eyre, but . . .'

'Quite.'

'And he troubles too over the court martial – of the dragoon, the one who struck an officer – the penalty of death withal.'

'Ah yes, I know of it. I am apprised of all capital sentences in the presidency, for the simple fact that they're ultimately mine to remit. But he hasn't spoken to me of it. Why does it trouble him?'

'I don't know the particulars, but the man is not of fundamentally bad character, it would seem.'

Somervile, already helping himself to more kichree, though his plate was not yet empty, sighed and raised his eyebrows. 'Cruel necessity.'

Fairbrother sighed too, resignedly. 'No doubt.'

'Or is the colonel become sentimental in his seniority? Perhaps if the regiment were to flog, the odd execution wouldn't seem so harsh.'

Fairbrother smiled. 'You deliberately try me, Sir Eyre.'

The Sixth had held flogging in abeyance for many years, even during the late wars with France. No one doubted its efficacy in maintaining good order and military discipline – not least the Duke of Wellington himself – but in a regiment of cavalry, its recruits brought with care and the whole under good regulation, its application ought rarely if ever to be strictly necessary. That had indeed been the tradition of the Sixth for as long as any had served, save for one unhappy instance when they'd a martinet for a colonel – a man from another regiment who'd bought command and exercised it as he would a stallion that he couldn't master save with sharpened rowels and wire bit. Besides, he too, Fairbrother, had a deep contempt for flogging. It couldn't be otherwise, he'd say, if anyone had seen the backs of recalcitrant slaves (especially knowing that he himself might have been on the receiving end of the lash if his father had left him the wrong side of the blanket).

'I shall await our friend's application for remission, though I must say that any plea in mitigation would have to pass muster with his fellow commanding officers here to be successful. I couldn't risk an outbreak of violent insubordination – in King's regiments or Company's alike. It's tricky enough since Bentinck decided – quite without consulting – to abolish flogging in the black regiments.'

'The governor-general? He has?'

'Very decidedly. And now every sepoy thinks he must be superior to a man wearing the King's coat. No good will come of it. Not, at least, in the Bengal army, "the martial races" as Fort William's wont to call them – deuced hotheads for the most part. The Madrasee's made of sounder stuff. But it won't be easy. The Nairs especially can be refractory.'

Fairbrother nodded. He hadn't heard of the Nairs – or indeed of many other tribes – but was content to let the question go. In truth, he'd admit, he was only too content that he himself was not called on to make decisions requiring great exercise of the mind. He was a man of some means – even more so now since the death of his father – and was content to wander through life taking his pleasure in whatever amused him. That he could, when roused, fight with unmatched skill, had first recommended him to Hervey – that and his ability to see things not as others, a particular instinct for the native man's way of thinking, which must stem, so he (and Hervey) supposed, from his own quarterings. At the Cape he'd often known what the Xhosa and the Zulu were thinking, and in consequence what to do, even though the veld was a far cry from the forests of the Ashantee whence his mother's people had been taken. The people of India were another matter again, however; another matter entirely. He might share their coffee complexion (those from the northern parts, at least – coffee and cream – not the Tamuls and those hereabout), but how and what they thought he didn't suppose he'd any notion of.

'But you've not invited me here, Sir Eyre, to discuss our friend. Nor indeed matters of steam, I fancy.'

Somervile smiled. 'My engineer says you had a most useful exchange yesterday, and that you expressed surprise that we've a railway here; or, I should say, shall soon have – and with a fair wind for the Indiaman bringing the engines, a steam train to run upon it.'

Fairbrother admitted his surprise. He'd not supposed there'd be the need, or indeed the expertise until he'd learned of the Madras Engineers. 'I look forward to seeing the line of survey as soon as may be.'

For it was twice the length of that in Ireland, all of thirteen miles, though for a less picturesque purpose – to bring ironstone from the quarries in the Red Hills for the roads in the city.

Somervile shook his head, quizzically. 'But I am yet undecided whether to call it "rail-way" or "rail-road". What say they at home? I read both in the papers.'

Fairbrother had no especial opinion on the matter. 'I believe that "rail-road" is preferred in America.'

'Mm. I shall reflect on it further.'

Fairbrother was now quite baffled. Could this really be the reason he was being so royally entertained? He understood that the governor of the presidency in which the first of these great works was to be undertaken must decide when the name was in dispute, but it hardly seemed a matter for prolonged study.

But then Somervile turned grave. 'You are, however, correct in assuming that matters of steam locomotion were not my purpose in asking you this morning. I have a commission I would offer you, which would be of greatest service to His Majesty and to the people of the presidency – and, it must be said, to me also.'

Fairbrother put down his spoon and fork.

'It is this business of "thuggee". Bentinck is of the opinion that it is become a very present danger, and that under the new . . . "arrangements" – I mean the Act changing the Company's preeminent function in India – its suppression is of the first importance. Now, I have very capable politicals here at Fort St George, but they are not so practised as you in what I have in mind. It seems to me that I ought not to be in ignorance of so great a threat to the peace as the governor-general suggests. Not that I question his judgement in this – I know Bentinck to be a man of highest principle; he's been unstinting in the suppression of suttee these past five years.'

'Suttee?'

'Ah, I'd supposed . . . widow-burning.'

Fairbrother nodded. 'Now I recollect.'

'But Bentinck's in a hurry, for he leaves Fort William next year, and it may yet be that his judgement in this is . . . precipitate. When this political from Fort William comes, I would have you listen to him – as you've agreed – but then to go yourself into the Northern Circars and explore on my behalf. The Duke had his exploring officers in Spain did he not?

I would have you do as they did: bring me intelligence by whatever means you judge best. You'd have a free hand . . . and well provided for by the Secret Fund. Would you think on it, and give me your answer as soon as may be? Before the political arrives, so that we may speak further.'

Fairbrother put down his spoon and fork again, and nodded slowly, as if turning it all over in his mind. 'Sir Eyre, I have no need of time to think. I will take up the commission, and eagerly, but on one condition, that our mutual friend has no objection. I am not obligated to him in the strict sense, but my coming here is at his invitation.'

Somervile bowed. 'A very proper sentiment.'

He rang a silver bell, and khitmagars came to replenish the cups and glasses.

'And now, Captain Fairbrother, we shall speak only of sporting matters.'

* * *

Kezia's piano greeted Hervey on return, as so often it did. He'd stayed at office throughout the day, then ridden home at a gentle trot. It was a little before five, and there were still the usual outdoor servants to attend his arrival. The *malee*, an old sepoy of the 40th Native, stood at attention with flower pot in one hand and trowel in the other; a syce, who'd been apprenticed as a boy to the Artillery, led away the Marwari that Hervey liked to keep for sport and which served him day to day, while the chowkidar, a turbaned Maharatta (of undisclosed background), saluted with his stick.

Inside, Corporal Johnson took his hat, but Hervey dismissed him silently so that he could listen to Kezia's playing without her knowing he was there. Perhaps his ear was better attuned to fine music these days, for once where her playing had been . . . (frankly) disquieting, now it pleased him. It might be, of course, that she played different music; he joked that besides 'God Save the King' he could recognize only two tunes – one of them the regiment's march, and the other not. But he thought he recognized this piece, for he'd heard her practising before – Beethoven, which as a rule he didn't find pleasing. This, however, pleased him very much. And – though heaven knew, he was no judge in these things – it sounded no easy piece to play.

He stood unobserved until she was finished.

'Matthew.' She sounded as content as ever he'd heard.

'You *have* played that before, or am I mistaken?'

'I have,' she said, rising to kiss him. 'I have tried to, that is.'

'Beethoven?'

'Yes. I thought you might think it apt, for it's supposed to suggest a horse galloping. I think it must be so, for it's in three-eight time, the rhythm of a gallop.'

'The rhythm of a canter, certainly,' he agreed, though he'd no very clear idea of what was three-eight time.

'I'll ring for tea. Georgiana's riding with Annie, and Allegra.'

He looked mildly anxious.

'And Serjeant Stray,' she added.

'Then no great harm can come to any of them,' he said, with a sigh.

Kezia raised her eyebrows and smiled. 'It was by all accounts a venturesome affair last evening.'

They'd got back late, what with the retrieval of the tiger and a good deal else, and he'd left early that morning. 'Georgiana was a little knocked about by the fall, a little bruised no doubt, but evidently it's not dampened her zeal. Nor Annie's, for she was thrown too. Did Georgiana say more?'

'She said that Annie came at once to her side.'

'She did indeed. The girl's unconscionably brave.'

'Georgiana said there was a second tiger, but unseen . . . that Major Garratt somehow divined its presence.'

Hervey smiled. 'He has a remarkable eye. He says it's the Rifles' way.'

A khitmagar came with a jug of lime water, and then another with a tray for Kezia to mix and make their tea.

'I wish I'd been there to see it . . . Although perhaps on that I am not so sure.'

Hervey wasn't surprised. Kezia was full of spirit, but Annie's account – and Georgiana's the more so (with, no doubt, corroborative detail from Corporal Johnson) – would have been vivid, and, as she'd implied, she was herself by no means unacquainted with the hazards.

'It is well that you weren't. Besides, if you're so inclined, Garratt is gone for the second beast. We might ride out to see the sport.'

'I am all admiration for Major Garratt, but I shall forgo the pleasure, for it might otherwise be thought reckless.'

He smiled. 'There might be talk, yes.'

She laughed.

'By the bye, do you know what is an ophicleide,' he asked, drinking a glass of lime water in one go.

She shook her head. 'Yet another sort of snake?'

'Oh, yes; I hadn't made the connection – serpent. It's an instrument of some sort is all I know – a band instrument. Garratt said to me this morning he intended procuring one. I confess I didn't want to disappoint him by appearing not to know. You recall I asked him to make good the band as soon as may be. He does sterling work already.'

'We shall all be happier for a little more music,' said Kezia decidedly.

It was one of the minor calamities of the passage to India that but a dozen musicians had come with the regiment, and that most of their instruments lay on the bed of the sea in the Madras roads, practically the only loss in the transfer of men, women and chattels from trooping ship to shore.

'He really is quite extraordinary. He's conceived the most fantastical scheme of reprieve for Askew.'

Kezia looked at him keenly. She knew every detail of Private Askew's transgression. Although it was rare for Hervey to speak of the discipline of the regiment – it was merely part and parcel of everyday life – a capital offence was a different matter.

'He came to see me this morning. He says that once a tiger has scent of easy prey it will return, so he intended lying in wait for it this evening, but to quieten the villagers he'd set a bait some distance out. Then he said he proposed Askew act as the bait—'

'*What?*'

'I know; we've denounced more than one rajah for baiting with village boys. I said it was fantastical, but Garratt proposed to skin a goat and for Askew to wear it.'

Kezia was all astonishment. 'Like Jacob? Why cannot the goat simply be tethered instead?'

'Because to be reprieved will require an exceptional act of valour, and the tiger will be wary of human scent. I should add that Askew will have his carbine.'

'I am relieved to hear it! And he has agreed to this?'

'He has – and without *promise* of reprieve. I considered that if I were to ask Somervile first he'd forbid it, not least on grounds of connivance. But in truth, what choice does Askew have? One way or another he might at least die a hero.'

Kezia sighed, still shaking her head in disbelief. '*And Jacob went out from Beersheba and went toward Haran . . .*'

Hervey smiled. 'That is the intention, or rather to New South Wales, where he can do hard labour for some Australian Laban and then make his fortune and marry.'

She shook her head. 'You have a good heart, Matthew Hervey.'

'I trust so. But not a soft one. My concern is first for the good order of the regiment, not for Askew.'

But he'd no need to tell her that. She'd long understood, from the time of her first marriage, that 'the interests of the service' – of the regiment indeed – were above all earthly things. Except that she also knew that Askew, being of the regiment, was a part of that interest.

Then her eyes twinkled. 'If they return alive from the venture, and with the goat meat, I shall have the *langree* spice it to taste like venison.'

He laughed – not least in delight at her blitheness. The dark days were truly gone (even if the memory of them lingered obstinately). If the monsoon had done nothing to decrease her spirits, then plainly little else would. And he'd not heard her sport with scripture before. India, it seemed, banished care as well as sorrow.

'Matthew . . .'

'Yes?'

But Serjeant Stray appeared. 'Begging your pardon, Colonel, ma'am, but Lady Somervile is come.'

VI

La Longue Carabine

Later

The major took with him a syce who had better English than he himself had Hindoostanee – the man might be useful when it came to parleying with the villagers (unless they were all Tamul, in which case they'd have to rely on gesture) – but just one dragoon as escort, the provost corporal. His own coverman was detailed for guard duty that evening and he'd no wish to disrupt the serjeant-major's carefully laid roster. For his part, Armstrong had been obliging in detailing a provost man largely because Askew remained in close arrest, and it wouldn't do for him to be in the direct charge of an officer. Corporal Simpson was a sturdy man, and if anything untoward were to happen – Askew proving himself unworthy in some way – he could be relied on to do the right thing. Not that he, Armstrong, expected anything particularly; it was just that men did the strangest things when death stared them in the face, whether by tiger or a squad of carbines.

Garratt didn't speak on the ride out. He didn't know Askew from Adam, and the man was, after all, under sentence for striking an officer.

Had he been longer with the regiment he might have probed him a little, but he was still strange to many of its ways.

When they reached the village the syce found the headman and told him they'd come to kill the tiger that would surely return to feast off their fold – again and again – and they wished to slaughter a goat as bait. This he was able to explain easily enough, but the headman said they were poor people and could not give up one of the fold without silver.

'If the sahib here does not kill the tiger, you will lose many goats rather than just the one,' argued the syce.

'*Accha*,' said the headman, 'but that would be by the will of Shiva, whereas I am lord of the single goat's fate.'

The syce told the major of the headman's hesitation.

Garratt studied him for a moment or two, brow furrowed, eyes narrowed. He was more than used to sharpers, malingerers and chancers, but here was either folly of a high order or else equal cunning; or yet, perhaps, a wholly genuine display of religious scruple. How was he to know?

Whichever way, he wasn't inclined to spend time investigating. 'How much does he want?'

'Sahib, I say you offer one rupee.'

'Very well.' He sighed; he'd probably end up paying double – two Arcot rupees for a goat with no more meat on it than . . .

Two minutes' bargaining followed – in truth a minute doubled by the need for translation.

Eventually honour was satisfied. 'He say "thank you", sahib.'

Garratt shook his head. He was better off than he'd expected to be, and yet he still wasn't sure of the bargain. He supposed he'd never understand the ways of this country. He gave the man a silver rupee, nodding sternly.

'But as we are here in the service of his village, *we* shall choose the goat.' (He had every intention of making a meal of mutton when it was all done.)

The syce told the headman, who protested loudly; but he'd taken the silver, so there was little he could do. Garratt felt that honour was now even, and chose a yearling.

They then retraced the steps of the evening before – doubling back eastwards to begin with so as not to lay any trail between the village and the likely line of approach – until coming on the place of the previous night's execution, of which there was now neither sight nor scent. Standing in the saddle atop the little mound, Garratt searched the country first with the naked eye – by which any movement was best detected – and then with his telescope to examine shadow and shape in the sea of lemon grass. He could see the further track which the villagers used plainly enough, and the one where he'd gone with Fairbrother – not so much a track as a trail, the lemon grass parted rather than trampled or cleared – and, fifty yards or so beyond and towards the village, a lone tree that he reckoned would serve as the baiting place. Here the grass became low scrub; a tiger wouldn't be able to crouch unseen before springing. Private Askew would have a fair chance – a closing shot, yes, but more time therefore, and no aiming off.

Over they rode.

Garratt got down to spy the approaches. The tree was too spiny to climb into, but the trunk was cover enough to lean against, to steady the aim, and the grass was so poor that naught but a mouse would be able to get within twenty yards without being seen. It would do very well. He turned on his heel and slapped his thigh as if overcoming a great dispute. But Corporal Simpson had a knife out.

'The deuce! Leave the blasted goat be. It can't possibly stink more dead than alive. Tie it to the tree, Simpson.'

'Sir.'

It would also have the merit of being fresher meat on return to barracks, but that was a lesser consideration. Garratt told the syce to put away his knife too: 'Unlike Abraham, I'll spare the goat also.'

'*Accha*, sahib.' He hadn't the faintest idea what the major meant by 'Abraham', but he'd no objection to leaving the goatskin where it was for the moment.

'That were a ram, though, weren't it, sir? This 'un's a she-goat.'

'Admirable knowledge of scripture, Corporal. I shall commend you as a reader to the chaplain.'

Simpson could only hope the major was in jest – he'd said it with some asperity – and set about tethering the bait.

'When you're done,' he continued, indicating a clump of bamboo fifty yards towards the village, 'take Askew's horse with you yonder, and field at Long-stop.'

Cricket – another of the major's passions. Simpson wondered if Askew was to be batsman or wicket-keeper, but it wasn't the time to try the major's humour. Besides, though Askew was a prisoner, a man under sentence, he saw no reason to add to the dragoon's disquiet. 'Sir.'

'And Private Askew . . .' added Garratt, beckoning the syce to remount, and gathering up his reins.

'Sir?'

'Screw your courage to the sticking-place, and we'll not fail.'

'Sir.'

The Bible, cricket, and now Shakespeare – *officers*. Corporal Simpson sighed to himself. He'd certainly have plenty for the wet canteen's hearing later that night – if he ever saw it again.

Garratt now withdrew to his vidette post, as he put it, except that for several minutes he was undecided whether or not he could remain mounted. A shot from the saddle was always perilous, but at least he'd be able to see his quarry. From the ground it was uncertain, and his aim would be unsupported anyway, though he might risk resting on the saddle if his horse was quiet. If he lay down he'd see no further than the end of his rifle.

In the end he decided to stay astride. Without line of sight, all effort would be to no avail; he was the best of shots, so the risk at least was as small as may be. The syce sat down nearby with his reins over his shoulder and began cleaning his old Company blunderbuss. It had killed many a meal and many a man, though never a tiger. What would be the point? Its shot made so great a mess that no sahib would ever buy the skin.

Garratt reckoned they had an hour at most. He'd no intention of being here after dark, for there'd be no moon worth the name to see them out, and they'd need half an hour of what light remained after the sun set to find the road home (which would anyway be tricky enough to follow if the cloud continued to roll in). And if the tiger chose to hunt at night, then so be it; but he reckoned that if it were indeed a juvenile, it wouldn't yet be inclined to, for what animal powerful enough to hunt by day would do so instead by night?

His mare was obliging. In fact she seemed only too glad of the respite. There were no troublesome flies either. He let out the reins a good length, catching them in the crook of his right arm so that he could aim quickly without losing them, while she lowered her head to doze.

From time to time he glanced at the sticking-place. Askew looked commendably upright and steady, with his back to the tree rather than shrinking behind it. Evidently he intended facing the tiger squarely, and if he succumbed it would be a noble death, a better thing for someone to write home of – he himself perhaps – to whoever was his kin, instead of . . . what exactly? Did the Sixth write also when a man had been hanged, or shot? He'd never thought of it until now. What had they done in the Rifles? They'd certainly shot a few in his day – in Spain at least . . .

He marvelled again at how quickly the sun fell at this hour. He'd not take out his watch, though, for his mare was sound asleep – as good as; he wouldn't risk a pull on the reins. But an hour must have passed – three-quarters, certainly, for the sun couldn't have fallen *so* fast . . . He supposed he'd better end the vigil soon, for once it was below the horizon here the night was on them before they knew it. Besides, his leg was . . .

His mare started. He almost lost the rein. He made to turn—

The blunderbuss deafened him.

But it missed the target.

The tiger sprang.

Garratt ducked right while bringing up his rifle.

Crack! A desperate shot – instinct, not aim.

The years repaid, though: the brute fell dead as the mare suddenly squealed and bucked, tumbling him from the saddle – but he rolled in one movement to his feet, making to reload even as he did so.

'Sahib! Sahib!'

'*Raghav*, what the devil . . .'

'Sahib, I very sorry, sahib. Tiger came from long grass like Kali sudden from Durga's brow, all terrible look, sahib. But Raghav not afraid, sahib. He shoot tiger.'

'Shoot *at* tiger, Raghav! *At* it! How the deuce did you miss with that artillery?'

He'd no more idea who Kali and Durga were than the syce probably did Abraham, but whatever Raghav was prattling about, to his mind a thunderous great weapon like that was worth it only once in a campaign – and this would have been the once.

'Yes, sahib. I thank very much, sahib. Raghav he not afraid of tiger.'

Garratt swore and picked up his reins, his mare stock-still as Lot's wife. He made much of her. Even a cavalry charger shouldn't have to suffer a blunderbuss going off next her – and a tiger springing.

She whinnied after a while, and Garratt got back into the saddle. 'Now,' he said, taking his telescope from its holster; 'how is our tethered goat – *goats* indeed.'

The light was fast fading, but there was Askew at his post still, and perfectly upright.

'Good man; good man!'

His orders had been that no one was to move – tiger or no – until he himself gave the word. He didn't for one minute think there'd be yet another beast, but he'd known of more than one piquet that had shot a sentry of its own who'd moved to ease himself or the like.

All looked clear.

'Come on, Raghav, let's away.'

'Sahib, what of tiger? He many rupee.'

'Damn it, man; how in heaven's name d'you propose we skin it? He's jackal meat, unless the village bring him in.'

He'd try to get them to, of course. The tiger was no great size, and he'd certainly prize the *pair* of skins – tigress and progeny. But he'd no intention of trying to find it in the dark with them, not with a long hack to barracks afterwards, his stomach empty and his throat dry – even if he *could* get the village to search. He'd just have to trust to promising more silver.

They trotted smartly to the tree. Askew saluted. Corporal Simpson cantered up looking anxious, having thought he'd get there to untie him before Garratt saw.

'Damned useless goat,' was all that Garratt said, though, ignoring the rope. He'd not remark on Askew binding himself to the tree, like Odysseus to the mast to resist the sirens. If that's what it took, then all the greater his courage . . .

'Would you cut me free, Corporal Simpson, please?' asked the prisoner calmly.

Simpson's sabre did quick work. Garratt, new-come still in so much, could but admire the deftness with which dragoons handled the *arme blanche* – though a little more practice with the carbine wouldn't go amiss . . .

But now that he looked – that knot, a reef, surely? And the other side of the trunk. How on earth could Askew have tied it?

VII

Major Sleeman

The governor's council chamber, a week later

The introductions were a little stiff. Hervey was not in the best of spirits, for an attack of the remittent fever had kept him in his bed for the whole of the two days before. And although Milne had dosed him so powerfully with an *antipyretica*, as he called it, that he'd been on his feet again that morning, his head was by no means entirely free of the pounding that accompanied the sweats. (Or perhaps it was, as the saying went, the heavy fire of medicinal artillery?) Besides, he was conscious of his position as a commanding officer of cavalry, as well as a brevet colonel – not to mention acting commander-in-chief in the absence of Sir Robert O'Callaghan. This visitor was important – superintendent of the *Thagi Daftar* (department) of Jubbulpore, no less – but he wished first to be sure that his importance was of consequence.

'Major Sleeman, Colonel, at your service.'

Hervey bowed.

'And this is Captain Fairbrother,' added Somervile, 'who is to act as my particular exploring officer.'

There were others in the room, a dozen or so military and writers, of whom Hervey took no notice except to nod. The superintendent was three or four years his senior (as he'd learned from the Army List), an inch or so taller, a little stocky, with a round and open face – a shade care-worn perhaps – and reddish-gold hair beginning to recede. Not, perhaps, a picture of entire good health, but a rather more striking figure than he'd expected, for it was held that long service in India generally diminished men in stature.

Hervey refused the offer of Madeira and took lime water instead, and a seat at the table. 'How long was your journey from Jubbulpore, Major?'

'The better part of two months, Colonel, but I took the opportunity to call on the residents at Nagpore and Haidarabad, and the agent also at Chintalpore.'

Hervey nodded. 'And how did you find Chintal?'

'Not, I fear, a place of contentment. There continues dispute with the Nizam, and forever skirmishing – banditry – with Nagpore. The state is not without enterprise, though. Some very fine rubies have been found these late years, and exploration goes apace, in the course of which coal, too, has been found. There are steam engines that pump water from the excavations, and haul out the earth – a very advanced thing – and plans for a steamer on the Godavari. Do you know Chintal, Colonel?'

'In the late rajah's time, yes. I'm surprised there's no full-blown embassy still, especially in light of what you say. Does the agent have like status to resident?'

Somervile, looking slightly anxious, raised a hand. 'This I think we may speak of later, respecting other matters, if you will.' Then, turning again to Sleeman, 'I would that you tell Colonel Hervey what you told me earlier of the extent now of your remit.'

'Of course, Sir Eyre . . . Colonel Hervey, sir, five years ago Fort William charged me with directing a campaign against what has generally become known as thuggee. The word *thug* means, simply, "deceiver", although here in the south of India, where the cult is not so general, they are sometimes known as phansigars – Hindoostanee also, from the Persian, meaning those who use a noose.' . . .

Sleeman explained that during his time as a political officer in the Central Provinces, which lay along the boundary in Bengal with the presidency of Madras, he'd come to make a study of this particular and murderous cult of Kali, the Hindoos' goddess of destruction. 'The thug associations which we are now engaged in suppressing have been taught by those whom they revere as the expounders of the will of their deity that the murders they perpetrate are pleasing to her, provided they are perpetrated under certain restrictions, attended by certain observances, and preceded and followed by certain rites and sacrifices, and offerings. The deity who, according to their belief, guides and protects them is ever manifesting her will by signs; and as long as they understand and observe these signs they all consider themselves as acting in conformity to her will; and consequently, fulfilling her wishes and designs.'

He looked at Hervey for leave to proceed, and Hervey nodded. (He couldn't see what business it was of his, but it would at least make for an interesting page or two in his next letter home.)

'On all occasions they believe these signs to be available if sought after in a pure spirit of faith, and with the prescribed observances; and as long as they are satisfied that they are truly interpreted and faithfully obeyed they never feel any dread of punishment either in this world or the next.'

'They are all Hindoo?'

'By no means; it appears that the creed is held by Hindoo and Mussulman alike – of which latter there are many. However, I've sometimes observed that when death is at hand, in the case that they fear they've not been strict in their observances, they're apt to believe that a deathbed repentance will appease a justly offended God, and secure their pardon.'

Hervey nodded again. It seemed to him not dissimilar to the beliefs of many a Catholic brigand.

The discourse continued, until Hervey held up a hand to ask what the ryots, the simple peasant people of the villages among whom the thugs must live, made of them.

Sleeman shook his head and sighed. 'This is perhaps one of our greatest hindrances. In some cases the village communities and the local authorities in the native states have a notion that the thugs are under some supernatural influence, and dread the consequences of being made in any way instrumental to their punishment. Such people oppose their arrest and conviction as they would oppose the killing of a snake or a wolf.'

'Wolf?' He knew of the superstition regarding snakes right enough.

'In many parts a village will lament the killing of a wolf within their boundary as a great calamity, even though it would have taken a child every week. They consider the wolf an instrument in the hand of God, and dread the consequence of any violence to it. Indeed, in some parts the thugs are accustomed to leave the bodies of their victims unburied, having no fear of inquiry or pursuit from the local governments. Though I have to say that in the main they conceal them very thoroughly.'

Hervey frowned. 'It puzzles me that they should murder as well as rob if there's no likelihood of arrest, but I suppose you will say that the two are as one to them . . . But why is their trade so lucrative?'

'Oh, that is the aspect of the problem over which I can have the least influence. If I may, Colonel?'

'Proceed.'

'The practice all over India of sending remittances in precious metals and jewels – whenever the rate of exchange makes it in the smallest degree profitable to do so – by men on foot and in disguise, without any guard or arms to defend themselves, at once provides opportunity. Likewise, I regret to say, the necessity of drawing recruits for our armies from distant provinces, and of granting a certain portion leave to revisit their homes every year during the hot season, when they set out every morning before daylight in order to avoid the heat of the sun during the day.'

Hervey's eyes narrowed. 'They murder sepoys, you say?'

Sleeman nodded. 'We know it because, fearful of being found with any piece of uniform, which they certainly cannot sell, they bury their victims without stripping the body, which otherwise they always do.'

'Damnable.'

'And, of course, the mode of travelling on foot or on small ponies, being almost universal among those who have occasion to make long journeys whatever their rank or condition, makes the thug's work easier. As well, the unreserved manner in which travellers of the same caste mix and communicate, and the facility with which men can feign different castes.'

Hervey, though repelled by the murder of any man in a red coat (and troubled yet by headache), was becoming impatient. 'It appears to me to be a hopeless case.'

Somervile said that at first he'd thought the same, but was now inclined to take a less passive view – not least because thuggee was no longer confined to the native states, and the honour of the Company, and thereby the Crown, was at stake. 'I think we might compare it with the state of England in past centuries – when highwaymen and footpads, brigands of all sorts, were not uncommon. The King's Peace was won only by degrees.'

Hervey nodded. 'I am not an antiquarian, but I accept the premise: a start has to be made. But with so much traffic, I cannot see how.'

Sleeman raised his hand. 'If I may, Colonel: I believe that here, we are so to speak in England before the canals and the turnpikes. The pace of transport – of every aspect of daily life indeed – where all is carried on foot or bullock carts, provides opportunity, and likewise the assassin has little chance of being overtaken and intercepted in his operations.'

Hervey saw where this was leading, but bid him continue anyway, not least out of regard for his old friend.

'Thuggee, Colonel, is a spider's web of family connections, and I am convinced that this very fact will be its undoing. The strength of a web lies in its unity. Careful gathering of intelligence – in which I've been engaged now for a considerable time – will take apart that unity strand by strand.'

'I understand that. Continue.'

Sleeman looked gratified at last. Five years ago, he explained, he began systematically to record every known instance of thuggee crime. This depended on the evidence of 'approvers' – turncoats: 'The first point I make always to ascertain from the approver the time, place and mode of the murders as near as possible – the place whence the murdered persons came and whither they were going – and the property they had with them. On these points the approvers are always well informed. I then send to local officers of my acquaintance and have the bodies dug up before the people of the neighbouring villages, whose depositions on oath are taken down by the local authorities of the district on a form of my devising for the evidences. If the bodies are not found, the people of these villages may have seen them at the time, before their murder, and their depositions to this point will answer the purpose.'

Hervey was puzzled. 'But from all you said previously I'd have imagined there to be reluctance on their part to furnish such information? They don't fear reprisals?'

'That is the encouraging part of it. If the village is of good character – and much depends on the headman – and the inquiry is well conducted, as fatalists they will cooperate. If not of good character, they will fear intrusion into the village and thereby the uncovering of all sorts of misdemeanour, but even this can be used to advantage – the threat of turning every stone. The gangs – who are not from the parts where they do their marauding – make a point of not molesting any from those parts. Nor as a general rule do they prey on European travellers, which would bring down the severest wrath of the authorities, but once they move on, there is opportunity for a diligent policeman.'

He explained that over the past five years he'd accumulated several thousand names of active thugs, and also their genealogies. Most of those he'd interrogated personally confessed to being born stranglers, and the older ones to have initiated their children into what they saw as their rightful inheritance. 'They don't hesitate in the slightest to tell you, or blush to confess the number of murders they've committed. They show no moral disquiet in what they've done – nor indeed any fear of what awaits them on the gallows. They take it as part and parcel of life. It's very strange to the English mind, Colonel Hervey, but not at all to theirs.'

Hervey nodded again.

Sleeman unfolded one of his genealogies.

Hervey was astonished by its detail.

Then he unrolled a large map hanging on the wall, on which were marked the different gangs' areas of activity, and explained how he used it to predict their future movement.

Hervey got up to study it closer.

It even reached some distance into the presidency.

'Truly, I am all astonishment. This is a most particular collation of intelligence.'

'The governor-general has been generous with his encouragement and subventions, without which, I fear, we would not make progress.'

Somervile seconded the opinion. 'Major Sleeman has also discovered that some of these gangs work with the connivance of certain zamindars, and perhaps even princely rulers. There has of late been increase in the waylaying of treasury parties despatched by sahoukars – bankers, that is – who as a rule follow set routes and are expected to arrive at their destination by certain dates. We are speaking of considerable sums, Colonel Hervey, such as would be attractive to a nabob.'

'They travel with an armed escort, I imagine?'

Sleeman nodded. 'They do, but some of the gangs are thirty and more, and, as their name suggests, they do their work first by deception – only then the roomal, the strangling cloth.'

He spoke for an hour in all, explaining how with the genealogies, the maps and the approvers he would soon be in a position to take the offensive against thuggee rather than, as up to now, gathering intelligence and biding his time, content simply to put before the magistrates the open and shut cases. When the time was right, and soon, he would concert a campaign to capture the gangs and at the same time arrest all who were named in his charts as connected with them. 'That way I trust that the material evidence gained from the gangs, together with the increase in approvers once our success becomes widely known, will be enough to send most of them to prison, or even to the hangman. But for this I'll need the assistance of considerable military force to supplement my nujeebs.'

'Nujeebs?'

'They are a kind of mounted militia. They've come on admirably this past year.'

Somervile looked at his old friend.

Hervey frowned. 'It is not a job for a soldier, Sir Eyre.'

'I understand perfectly; but only a soldier can do it.'

Hervey inclined his head, his least signal of acceptance.

Nor could he deny that it would be good sport. And the regiment was in need of some diversion other than practice for war.

'What do you propose for the nabobs by whose let the gangs do their work, Major?' he asked drily.

'Within the Company's own territory or that of its vassals, the governor-general has given me leave to do as seems fit. Where the thuggee is supported from any princely state, the matter is to be decided by Fort William.'

'As is only proper,' said Somervile, in a slight agitation. 'Colonel Hervey, this is something for consideration.'

Hervey nodded again.

Somervile rose. 'I believe I will now withdraw to allow the politicals – and Captain Fairbrother – to discuss what further detail there may be with Major Sleeman. Colonel Hervey, let you and I confer privately.'

Once in his 'chambers', Somervile became grave. 'What do you make of Sleeman?'

Hervey frowned. 'How may I judge? He's been here a good many years – since I was a cornet in Spain no less. I certainly can't judge his method, but evidently he's hanged or put away a good many of these devils, so it must have merit . . . And, if you were to press me, I'd say he were a man to have by one in a tiger hunt.'

Somervile smiled just perceptibly. 'I had judged so too, though, frankly, my instructions from Bentinck give me no choice in the matter. Besides, the reports from the Northern Circars have become disturbing. In September alone several lakh of rupees were spirited away in Guntoor, my old district, you'll recall – and the carriers too, doubtless strangled. If the sahoukars can't shift around coin, then the whole system of land rent becomes impossible, and with it the tax. The collector at Guntoor says there are arrears now of six months.'

'Then something must indeed be done, but I remain of the opinion that it's not a job for soldiers. Our best course would be to raise more police – these nujeebs – and with that we may certainly help.'

'I've no objection to such a scheme. Nujeebs under proper regulation should suffice, once things have been quietened. I've no wish to engage regular troops on such a business, though until more nujeebs are raised I fear that someone in the King's coat must make safe the roads – the dak roads most certainly.'

Hervey nodded. 'If you command it, I shall arrange it.'

Somervile's brow furrowed again. 'Madeira?'

'Is it a one- or a two-bottle question you're about to pose?'

'I can't say yet.' He poured liberal measures of his best Blandy's. 'Have you heard of the principle – the doctrine – of lapse?'

Hervey shook his head. 'The fall of man from innocence? The sin of Eve?'

Somervile indulged him with a smile. 'The court of directors have lately decided that the consent of the government of India to adoptions in the case of rulers of princely states dying without male issue is to be treated as an indulgence, and the exception, not the rule, and is not to be granted but as a special mark of favour and approbation.'

Hervey raised an eyebrow. 'The heirless state thus lapsing to the Company?'

'Just so. But further, that if a state be not governed with real authority, and for the good of the governed, it too may be deemed to have lapsed.'

Hervey was puzzled. 'That, surely, was the principle on which the Rajah of Coorg was deposed, was it not? How's this doctrine novel therefore?'

'In part it was the principle, but as you'll recall, the intervention was at the invitation of one who had the greater claim. This new doctrine puts the interest of the governed above that of the prince, and the judgement in the matter is that of the governor-general.'

'It seems a rather fine distinction to make, in light of practice to date.'

'Perhaps, but an important one nevertheless.'

Hervey was unconvinced. But then, he was not a political.

Somervile frowned again. 'Chintal . . .'

'Ye-es?'

'Bentinck deems that it is in lapse.'

Hervey sat upright. 'I see. And am I to suppose that somehow we are to deliver it from evil – secure its redemption?'

Somervile nodded slowly, as if gathering his thoughts. 'There are other concerns. Preposterous as it may seem, the Ranee has designs on Mysore. Apparently some panjandrum in Chintal's persuaded her that she has a claim on Tipoo Sultan's inheritance – I'm not aware how, precisely; doubtless some obscure bloodline – and he's begun a scheme of agitation, possibly with the help of this web of thuggee. Bentinck says it's not unheard of for minor rulers – like Chintal – to garb themselves in the glories of greater men, but that usually it's little more than an irritation. But Mysore's a tricky place yet, and on that he's right.'

Hervey frowned. 'This isn't the Ranee I quite recollect, for all her faults.'

'That's as may be, but with evil counsellors anything's possible. Bentinck says she's been deluded into believing she's heir to Tipoo's tiger mantle.'

Hervey smiled doubtfully. 'The Tigress of Mysore?'

Somervile tilted his head. 'You may well be right, but Bentinck intends proclaiming the lapse, and supposes the Ranee will resist, and therefore will direct the Army of Madras to expedite the proclamation.'

'"Expedite the proclamation"?'

'His very words. Moreover, because of Coorg he asks that, unless I have compelling objection, you personally take command of the field force.'

'And you have no compelling objection?'

'I have none. But more to the point, do you?'

Hervey looked at him disbelievingly. 'For I am a man under authority, having soldiers under me: and I say to this man, Go, and he goeth; and to another, Come, and he cometh.'

Somervile finished his glass and poured another. 'Verily I say unto you, I have not found so great faith, no, not in . . . India.'

Hervey bowed.

'But as a man of rank – with a brevet indeed, as well as acting in command here – you are not obliged by blind obedience. You have some discretion in these matters.'

Hervey was now intrigued. 'What cause for discretion, as you put it, might there be? If the governor-general in his wisdom deems Chintal to be a threat to the King's Peace, then who am I to gainsay it?'

Somervile nodded.

Hervey smiled. 'And I could hardly admit that there's anyone more capable than I of commanding the field force.'

Somervile looked grave once more. 'I had in mind distaff matters.'

'Ah.'

'Forgive me, Hervey, but I ought perhaps to have congratulated you on the news.'

Hervey smiled again, conceding. 'And I perhaps should have thought to tell you, except that these things are always more seemly done by the ladies, are they not?'

'Hah! Quite so; Emma told me only last evening, though she'd known for a week. Yes, they're judicious in choosing their time.'

Hervey didn't say that Kezia too had told him only the day before. 'But it can make no difference.'

'Ordinarily, no, but in light of Kezia's former . . . *distraction*, how wise was it, I wondered, to follow the precept of "duty" so narrowly?'

Hervey raised both eyebrows. 'Dorothea Worsley's time is near. Can you suppose Worsley would take leave?'

Somervile bowed, content. 'Then we'd better begin on a plan without delay. I'll call a council tomorrow. Another glass of Madeira?'

Hervey nodded.

And then he thought it the moment to press his advantage. 'Might I ask, by the bye, if you are near to a decision yet on my dragoon?'

'Hah!' The governor banged the table so hard his glass fell over. 'What a business indeed! I never heard its like. The fellow binds himself to a tree when there's tiger about? Splendid! Splendid!'

'The honour is all Garratt's, the humiliation all mine. I wasn't aware of the subterfuge until it was abroad that Askew had done so, by which time . . .'

'Come, come! I'm excessively obliged to you for your candour in the report. This corporal of yours, he ties the dragoon to the tree for the man's own good, without – he admits – his express consent, and out of duty also lest the man's courage fail him and he attempts to make his escape? A really very remarkable initiative, Hervey. What resourceful NCOs you have!'

'Unfortunately, perhaps, as I explained, Garratt detected the dodge. He got to the tree before the corporal could untie him, but it wasn't until later that Armstrong had the truth from him.'

'Yet the dragoon was a volunteer; that is to his credit. No one need know any other.'

'But as I explained, there's no knowing if Askew intended to use the opportunity to escape. Except that he's of previously good character.'

'God preserve us from corporals with good ideas?'

Hervey frowned again. 'I can't regret having men who are willing to think and act – even if at times they do so to unfortunate effect. Some need driving, most need encouraging, few need restraining.'

Somervile smiled. 'I believe I've heard you say so before, but it's no less compelling for repetition.' He refilled his glass and took an ostentatiously modest sip. 'You know the most grieving clause in the new India Act? That neither Bombay nor I can make laws without the consent of Calcutta. It's of no moment to the case of your dragoon – the death penalty's an altogether different matter – but I would have abolished flogging as soon as Bentinck abolished it in the native army. Indeed, I would have done so before, had I had the unequivocal support of the commander-in-chief.'

Hervey looked at him sombrely. 'I've never heard you speak thus . . . Oh, forgive me; I don't mean to suggest you never *thought* thus.'

Somervile put down his glass. 'Some years ago, Hervey, before you first came to India, when I was in Guntoor, I had occasion to speak on the subject with a man raised from the ranks into a regiment of cavalry – King's cavalry – and which I never forgot. He told me that from his observation of its effect on others, he could most solemnly affirm that flogging was, and always will be, the best, the quickest, and most certain method yet devised to eradicate from the bosom of a British soldier his most loyal and laudable feelings.'

Hervey was about to speak, but Somervile's expression became even more earnest.

'He told me that during the whole of his service, which included a period of upwards of thirty years, he never knew but one solitary instance in which a man recovered his self-respect and general reputation after having been tortured and degraded by the punishment of flogging – and this isolated case was of a private soldier, who had, on previous occasions, received altogether some thousands of lashes. Since his first flogging his name had been constantly in the guard reports, and he'd scarcely ever done a day's duty. His offence on the most recent occasion was being drunk on guard, and his sentence was three hundred lashes. His regiment was paraded for the purpose of seeing punishment inflicted and the court-martial findings were read, but even before it was finished, said the officer, the man began to undress with apparent – indeed sullen – apathy. He knew the heinousness of his offence and was well aware of its certain consequences. When he was stripped and tied, however, his naked back presented so frightful a spectacle that his commanding officer, kind-hearted as evidently he was, turned his head from the sight and stood absorbed in thought, as though reluctant to look on it again. When the adjutant informed him that all was ready, the colonel seemed to start, and then walked slowly up to the prisoner and stared even more closely at his lacerated back – on which there were, apparently, the most visible large lumps of thick and callous flesh, and weals distressing to behold. The colonel contemplated the wounds for some moments, unknown to the delinquent, and, when at length the man turned round (more from surprise that the flogging didn't commence than from any other motive), his colonel addressed him along these lines: "Clarke," or whatever was his name, "you are now tied up to receive the just reward of your total disregard and defiance of all order and discipline. Your back presents an awful spectacle to your surrounding comrades, and, for my own part, I would willingly withdraw it from their sight, but I fear that your heart is as hard as your back, and that I have no alternative but to see that justice administered which the service requires. What possible benefit can you expect to derive from this continual disobedience of orders, and disregard of the regulations of the service?"'

Hervey frowned. He'd seen a similar parade at the Canterbury depot before first going to Spain.

'And do you know what happened next? The poor fellow seemed touched, and wept bitterly. For a time he could say nothing; but then, "I wish to God I was dead and out of your way, sir; I am an hopeless fellow, and I pray this flogging may be my last, and put me beyond the reach of that cursed and vile liquor which has been my ruin." Well, the colonel and the whole regiment were now much affected, and many of the soldiers turned their heads. Seeing this, the colonel called the attention of the offender to the commiseration of his comrades, and the man did indeed seem much distressed. The colonel then said that he couldn't bear to see his brother soldiers so much affected without removing the cause, and that his sentence, therefore, for their sakes, he'd remit, and, instead of the chastisement awarded him, would the man pledge, in the presence of his comrades, that he'd behave well in future? If so he would not only pardon him, but promise, when his conduct merited it, to promote him to the rank of corporal.'

Somervile leaned back in his chair. 'A long story, but an instructive one. What next do you suppose happened?'

'I imagine the man swore on his sainted mother's grave that he'd mend his ways, and in six months was again arraigned for drunkenness.'

Somervile looked pained. He perfectly understood that his friend wasn't a Sunday-school teacher, but he'd expected something a little nobler.

'The astonished man called on his comrades to bear witness to his words, and in a most solemn manner protested his firm resolution to amend. A short time after, he was indeed promoted, and proved one of the best non-commissioned officers in the service.'

Hervey sighed. 'The problem is that the case might also be said to prove the efficacy of flogging. Do so remorselessly enough and eventually the man will be made. While those that *aren't* made don't have the character in the first place.'

Somervile was no Sunday-schooler either, as Hervey well knew. He shook his head ruefully. 'Quite. I did say that my informant said it was but one solitary instance.'

Hervey nodded equally ruefully. 'Where, therefore, does this leave my dragoon?'

Somervile chortled. 'Damn the business. I signed his commutation last night.'

* * *

'Adjitan-sahib, colonel-sahib he come now!' Sammy had already decanted coffee into the silver pot. From his lookout on the verandah he could see for half a mile, and no scout had sharper eyes.

St Alban was mildly surprised; he'd supposed that Hervey would spend the rest of the day at the Fort. 'Well, Mr Kynaston, you had better sit yourself in the ante-room, and I'll return to matters later.'

'Sir.'

St Alban reckoned he just had time to change his shirt. '*Qu'hai!*'

His bearer came in an instant. '*Saaph shart*, Amit, *shukria – jaldi*.'

''Es, sahib – *turant*!'

And immediately it was brought. Amit helped him out of his morning shirt and into the clean linen.

St Alban thanked him. He'd persevere with this strange language of the Hindoos. He'd not be beaten by it, even if he did intend going home in a year or so. It was his duty; and besides, he hated a show of incapability. Perhaps, like others, he ought to engage a 'sleeping dictionary', but women could be a deuced distraction; *native* women especially. Besides, he wasn't sure he'd be able to look Miss Hervey in the eye.

If only the moonshee were back.

At the guardhouse the picket turned out and presented arms. Hervey checked the reins with the merest flex of the finger, bringing Minnie to a walk – no one rode past the guardhouse at the trot, even when there was but a single sentry – touched the peak of his forage cap with the top of his whip, then made across the empty parade ground for regimental headquarters. St Alban stood waiting on the verandah.

'Good afternoon, Colonel.'

'I trust you'll think so,' said Hervey, giving Minnie a pat and handing her to an orderly.

St Alban knew the pat meant there was work afoot.

'Is the major at office?'

'He's not. He and the quartermaster have gone to the Black Town.'

Hervey looked puzzled. 'Why so?'

St Alban looked equally puzzled. It was true that there was no detail of a regiment that was beyond an adjutant's purview, but there were limits to a man's capacity. 'I'm afraid I don't know, Colonel. Is there anything amiss?'

'No . . . I . . . I had wished to tell the major of his success in his scheme. The governor has commuted Askew's sentence to transportation for life. You may make the arrangements forthwith.'

'I shall, Colonel, and very glad of it.' The arrangements, given the interminable ways of the law, would now mean an appeal against the commuted sentence by Askew himself. It would be months before his passage, even if there were a ship working south. 'I'll go with the sar'nt-major at once and inform him . . . No, that won't do. I'll send word to him.'

'No, Edward, I think your first instinct was the better. Bad news directly from the top, yes, and good news down the chain of command, but there are exceptions: a life and death business is no small thing.'

As they passed the defaulters' room Hervey caught a glimpse of home service uniform.

'That was Cornet Kynaston, I presume,' he said sympathetically, taking off his cap as they came into his office.

'Yes, Colonel. Arrived this morning and just presented himself. His letter's on your desk. I've sent for the senior cornet.'

'Well, we must hope he arrives before Kynaston expires, and gets him into tropicals. Have you had chance to speak?'

'I have. A fine fellow. Oh, and he brought out a draft of fifteen.'

'I would see him now, then, before he wilts any further. Give me chance to read his letter . . . Has the sar'nt-major braced the new draft yet?'

'The orderly serjeant's gone for them.'

'Splendid. Then I look forward to seeing them. Tomorrow at riding school. What a treat's in store for them.'

'For Kynaston too, Colonel.' (Every new cornet fancied himself a rider, until his first encounter with the RM.) 'I'll bring him and then go and tell Askew of his new lease of life.'

'And then I'll tell you what we're about these next six months.'

Sammy came meanwhile with coffee, while Hervey read.

St Alban returned a few minutes later with the Sixth's newest joined officer. 'Cornet Kynaston, Colonel.'

Hervey rose and held out his hand. 'You are very welcome, Mr Kynaston. Remove your shako and be seated.'

The punkah had begun to swing, but it produced only a disturbance of heated air rather than anything cooling.

'Thank you, Colonel.'

'Sammy, coffee for Mr Kynaston please.'

It was probably the last thing that Kynaston wanted, Sammy thought, replying to Hervey's Tamul with an additional '*Nimbu pani*, Colonel-sahib?'

Hervey nodded, and saw that Kynaston evidently understood too – a promising start.

'How was your passage out?'

'A little faster than expected, Colonel, and without incident, though I regret to inform you that one of the draft in my charge died not long after leaving the Cape – of an aneurysm.'

Hervey nodded. Another letter to be written by someone, St Alban probably, and without the consoling words of one who knew him, or that he'd died bravely in action against the King's enemies, or that he was held in high esteem by all ranks – and so on and so forth. But this was India, and even getting here was not without its perils.

'I am sorry to hear of it. He was given a Christian burial, I trust.'

'He was, Colonel. There was no chaplain, but the captain spoke the words.'

'Then please give to the adjutant before the day is out what details you have so that he may write to his people.'

'Of course, Colonel. I presumed to write, myself, already, and sent it by way of an Indiaman we passed off Mozambic.'

Hervey hid his surprise, saying simply 'Good man', and then, 'The draft – a likely cohort, are they?'

'I believe so, Colonel. There were no defaulters to speak of. The serjeant, from the Thirteenth, with a draft for his own regiment, had them under good regulation.'

'Capital. Thank you for your letter, by the bye. Tell me, was it India or the regiment that claimed your interest?'

Kynaston smiled readily. 'Both, Colonel. I had the great good fortune to be recommended to General Irvine, and I have a relative in Calcutta.'

Sammy came back with the lime water. Kynaston thanked him for his in confident Tamul.

Hervey was not minded so much to enquire about the recommendation to the colonel of the regiment – it was as it was – but he asked out of civility and mild curiosity what was his connection with Calcutta: a fellow officer, preferably; or a writer, perhaps (not entirely to be sneered at); but he hoped not a box wallah.

'He is governor-general, Colonel.'

Hervey managed to keep his countenance, just. He didn't relish a spy in the camp, for good or ill. Not that it was fair to call Kynaston a spy, but a cornet on terms with the governor-general was a confounding prospect.

He was, however, a fine-looking subaltern: tall, fair, with a good leg for a boot, and an openness of expression, without hint of guile – exactly the cut of officer he, Hervey, prized. Evidently, too, from his Tamul, he was a man of application – as already it seemed by submitting himself to the unnecessary and no doubt toilsome regime of the military college.

'Tell me, what of Sandhurst? I am not well acquainted with its method.'

'There is much drill and equitation, Colonel, and the military sciences – administration, topography and fortifications especially – and field sketching.'

'Admirable,' said Hervey, though warily. He knew perfectly well of the several academies that purported to prepare a cadet for service, of which that now at Sandhurst was carried on at public expense, but he was of the opinion still that a gentleman born, brought up to horse and hound, God-fearing and of good appearance and constitution, was best brought to his regiment quickly, so he could learn its particular ways and the regulation of men. It was not so for officers of the Ordnance – the artillery and engineers – for they had practical matters to be expert in before they joined, but a cavalryman . . .

'Well . . . I am glad you're come. There's work to be done.'

Kynaston rose to take his leave.

He was sensible of cadence, at least, thought Hervey, whatever the military college had drilled into him – and which the regiment might have to drill out. Indeed, he was already inclined to like him, whatever his status as 'spy'. He certainly didn't have the stamp of a Channer or a Waterman.

St Alban returned a little afterwards. 'Well, Colonel, Askew is apprised of his fortune, and pretty humbly. How did you find Kynaston?'

'Did you know his uncle is Bentinck?'

St Alban started. 'No, I did not, else I would have told you at once.'

'To his credit, he didn't volunteer it, nor yet try to conceal it. Which troop is he for?'

'You'd said Oliphant's.'

'Had I? I think better it is B.'

'Very well.' St Alban supposed he knew why. There wasn't a place to fill in B Troop, but if there was to be communication with the governor-general, better that it be informed under Worsley's command. He knew that, to Hervey's mind, there was no surer troop captain than Worsley – not even Vanneck, who was sure enough. Worsley had first commended himself by his address and courage in the affair of the gunpowder mills at Waltham Abbey – long before he, St Alban, had joined (but it was still spoken of) – and he'd seen himself how Dorothea Worsley had been the staunchest of supports at Hounslow. And, of course, they'd both come to India . . .

'And tell me when he's first at riding school.'

Just as he'd thought. St Alban nodded, with a smile.

'Now, send for the sar'nt-major, and I'll tell you what we're about.'

VIII

Salvete et Vale

Riding school, two days later

'Att-e-en-shun!'

Fifteen recruits – they'd not be given the distinction 'dragoons' until they'd passed out of riding school and skill-at-arms – came to attention sharply, testament at least to the daily routine the serjeant of the Thirteenth had maintained aboard ship.

Roughrider-Corporal Walcot saluted as if his life depended on it, which with Armstrong standing by Hervey's side he almost certainly thought it did – a life worth living, at any rate.

'Recruit-ride all present and correct, Colonel.'

It was their second morning. They'd been in uniform for the best part of a year, but only now had they come under the prodigious regulation of a regiment. Hervey insisted on seeing recruits in their first raw days, before they'd been made so 'regimental' as to lose the frankness that might reveal just a little of the man. Not that he'd be able to remember them exactly, but that didn't matter. He'd pen a few words about each in his order book. He might never have need or reason to read them again, but the Sixth were a small corps. Singletons mattered, for good or ill. It was different in the Guards or the Line. His late and much-lamented Coldstream friend D'Arcey Jessope used to say that he could never recognize his company unless the serjeants were posted. Except that Hervey always suspected it a conceit – and, indeed, in Jessope's baggage after Waterloo his friends found a pocket book wrapped in oilskin containing the particulars of every man in his erstwhile command.

'Name!' Armstrong barked, but not unkindly.

'Steele, sir!'

'Steele, *Colonel*!'

Armstrong turned and glowered at Walcot.

'Why, Corporal, have you not instructed these men in how the commanding officer of His Majesty's Sixth Light Dragoons is addressed? Or is there some new regulation of which I am unaware and to which you only have been made privy?'

It happened not infrequently even with the dragoons. In the tautness of the moment a man could forget that if the commanding officer was on parade, any question, remark or order, no matter by whom it was asked, made or given, was answered as if direct to the commanding officer. And in the Sixth, it was the duty – and privilege – of all ranks to address the commanding officer as 'Colonel' rather than 'sir'; even a recruit who was not yet accorded the distinction of being called a dragoon. (It didn't require 'the brains of an archbishop' to grasp these particularities, as Armstrong was fond of remarking, but it did require alertness – although on a man's second day it didn't merit too excessive a verbal flogging.)

Corporal Walcot knew there could be no answer to the serjeant-major other than to repeat the instruction he'd already given them half a dozen times that morning (and which Armstrong knew of perfectly well, though he'd never say).

When he'd finished, Armstrong tried again. 'Name!'

'Steele, Colonel.'

'Well, Private Steele,' began Hervey at last; 'you are very welcome in the regiment. Where did you enlist?'

'Stow, Colonel.'

The orderly corporal accompanying them made a note.

'Gloucestershire,' said Hervey, both to be certain and to put the man a little at ease.

'Colonel.'

'And your occupation before?'

'Shepherd, sir – sorry, *Colonel*.'

'Retained or hireling?'

'Hireling, Colonel.'

'How were you brought, by recruiting party?'

'Yes, Colonel, at the hiring fair.'

'The good shepherd giveth his life for the sheep. But he that is an hireling seeth the wolf coming, and leaveth the sheep, and fleeth: and the wolf catcheth them, and scattereth the sheep. The hireling fleeth, because he is an hireling, and careth not for the sheep?'

The orderly corporal wrote simply 'Colonel says some Scripture.'

'No, Colonel, I'd never've fled. But there was no more sheep, Colonel.'

Hervey nodded. The country parts had been much depressed since the war with France – the natural check to the unnatural growth in demand. But it was an ill wind that brought no good, and this ill wind brought good countrymen into the army. 'I had heard it. And I don't doubt you'd have stood by your charges . . . You know those words, do you?'

'Oh yes, Colonel, but the parson, he said they weren't to be taken as meaning an *English* shepherd would.'

Hervey smiled to himself. Shepherd Steele would do. He asked of his family and sundry things, then nodded and moved to the next man.

'Name!' rasped Armstrong.

'Beale, Colonel.'

'Well, Private Beale, where were you listed?'

'Hungerford, Colonel, but originally I am from—'

'As you *were*, Beale!' roared Armstrong. 'The colonel asked where you enlisted. If he wishes to know the particulars of your childhood, or indeed of your paternity – if, that is, you are yourself aware of the latter – he will ask!'

'Colonel! I just thought—'

Corporal Walcot winced. Armstrong thrust the head of his whip under Beale's nose.

'You don't think, Private! You does as you're told. You speak when you're spoke to, an' you keep it short!'

'Colonel.'

Hervey was intrigued by the 'originally from', for here seemingly was a more articulate recruit than usual, and perhaps with some sort of story. But he could hardly enquire now, what with Armstrong telling the man he'd no interest in his particulars, which thwarted somewhat his purpose in addressing them direct. That, however, was discipline.

'Your previous employ?'

'Apprentice bookbinder, Colonel.'

Corporal Walcot winced again. Armstrong's eyes narrowed.

Hervey nodded, and sensing 'trouble', moved to the next.

'Name!' Armstrong's bark somehow managed to convey a note of warning.

'Stratton, Colonel.'

'Listed where?'

'Braintree, Colonel.'

'And where is that?'

'Near Colchester, Colonel.'

'In which direction?'

'West, Colonel. That is, to the west of Colchester, Colonel.'

Hervey liked that reply. Not only did Stratton know the points of the compass, he had the presence of mind to realize his answer might have been ambiguous, and therefore clarified it. He'd be a corporal in eighteen months no doubt.

'And before enlisting?'

'Silk-thrower, Colonel.'

'Handloom, was it?'

'No, Colonel: was in a factory, power-loom, Colonel.'

'And you found that . . . insufficient?'

Stratton reddened. 'Most of the others there were women and girls, Colonel.'

Hervey nodded. There was no further explanation needed. He moved to the next.

'Name!'

'Prettyman, Colonel.'

And so it continued – Prettyman, a postboy from Kent; Newing, a farmhand, also from Kent; Shaw, an engineman from Somerset, the first engineman they'd ever had (Hervey asked why he'd joined the cavalry and not the Sappers, and Shaw said that he'd grown wary of 'exploding things' and would rather take his chances face to face); then there was Lange, the son of a corporal in the old King's German Legion; Needham, a tall, good-looking youth from Warwickshire who'd been in service with the Earl of Denbigh; and Harben, who'd come by way of the Canterbury petty sessions – the option of enlistment or a month at the treadmill (for common assault). And six more, all different and yet all somehow the same – men who'd not sought out the recruiting serjeant, but whose fortunes or otherwise had propelled them his way. He, Hervey, could never abide the Duke of Wellington's 'scum of the earth' remark (though he didn't doubt there were some who answered that description), not least because the Duke had meant it fondly, that the army took men whom the world rejected – and see what the army made of them. He supposed there must be an unsuspecting hero or two among these now. Why should there not be, indeed?

'You have all of that, do you, Corporal Spence?'

'Yes, Colonel. I'll make a fair copy for you at once.'

Hervey returned his salute and let him cut away to the orderly room. (He'd pay one of the clerks to write in a fine hand for him; it would be a good investment.)

'I suppose a likely enough lot, Mr Kewley. Nothing out of the ordinary run of things,' he said as they left the draft to Walcot's tender words of advice.

The riding-master said they'd had a bit of schooling at the depot, but that Canterbury wasn't much of a place for equitation, and that, anyway, six months at sea was a sure way of forgetting everything. 'Two are promising, though. That Lange's been around horses for sure; and Needham's got capability. Four months, I reckon. The usual, Colonel.'

Hervey wished it were less, but there it was. At least they'd had plenty of sabre and carbine on the passage out. 'Mr Armstrong?'

'That Beale'll get knocked about a bit till he's learned what's what, Colonel, but 'e didn't flinch when I shoved the whip at 'im. Good sign, that.'

'Promising, certainly.'

'And what of Cornet Kynaston, Mr Kewley?'

Hervey had watched that morning as the RM put him through his paces.

'I've rarely seen the like, Colonel. Specially not after six months at sea. It is very pleasing to see a young officer ride so. I couldn't fault 'im.'

Hervey smiled. 'No doubt you tried.'

'Round and round the jumping lane sans saddle and bridle till I got dizzy watching. You saw it, Colonel. Horse was blown afore young Kynaston broke sweat. Not once did 'e even look like 'e'd lose 'is balance.'

Hervey had indeed observed it. Evidently the military college taught *something*, though a seat like Kynaston's was a gift of God. (He was already inclined to overlook the unfortunate connection with Fort William.)

'Very well. Carry on, RM.'

* * *

'Mr Channer, sir,' announced the senior subaltern, looking testy (whether because of distaste for the task or for what he supposed was Channer's offence – the dalliance with the survey wife and refusal to fight her husband – was impossible to tell).

St Alban looked severe. 'Thank you, Mr Hastie. Have him come in, please. Then dismiss, if you will.'

Channer was not in arrest; there was no need of Hastie as escort. But St Alban intended leaving Channer in no doubt. It was rare that the senior lieutenant was required to attend at adjutant's orderly room, and that alone would serve his purpose. Hastie himself was scarcely delighted by the duty, for he had six years' seniority in the rank over St Alban, but the appointment of adjutant carried with it in effect the seniority of the commanding officer himself, and so there could ultimately be no resentment. But any temporary vexation would only serve St Alban's purpose; whether Hastie blamed him or the unfortunate Channer was by the bye.

The door opened again, and Lieutenant Channer entered in undress, the day uniform when not on picket. He saluted, and prudently remained at attention until St Alban bid him stand at ease – which St Alban did not.

'Mr Channer, a most disturbing letter has been sent to the commanding officer by an attorney in London acting on behalf of the parish of Chelsea claiming that you are in breach of a bastardy bond. That you have, indeed, been in breach of the said bond for three years, since its signing in fact. Can there be any substance in this allegation?'

'With respect, Mr St Alban, I regard the matter as being entirely my affair, and think it impertinent in the extreme of this attorney to write to the colonel. He ought, if there be any complaint, to address it directly to me.'

'He writes that he has, on no fewer than six occasions, and without reply, and that on learning of your departure here felt he had no alternative. Is there nothing to these allegations, then?'

'I really must protest, St Alban: this is not a matter for gentlemen to concern themselves with.'

St Alban angered. He would have damned his eyes had he not thought it demeaned his appointment.

'*Mr* Channer, let me be rightly understood. The matter is to my mind of the essence. The lady is of a respectable family, but it would scarcely matter less if she weren't. There is a child to whose paternity you have admitted – sworn indeed – and for whose maintenance you therefore in all decency must make provision. Need I say more? The colonel does not know of this – *yet*. The letter was addressed to him impersonally and I therefore opened it. *Were* he to know its contents, I cannot vouch for the consequences. His temper is uncertain at this time. But I am of the opinion that he would refer the matter to a court martial on a charge of behaving in a scandalous, infamous manner, such as is unbecoming the character of an officer and a gentleman.'

'I—'

'You would be ruined whatever the verdict, which I cannot see could be other than "guilty", in which case you would very likely be cashiered.'

'I—'

'You will therefore, this instant – at once, indeed – resign your commission. There is pen and paper in the antechamber. And having handed me your resignation you will quit the lines this very day for lodgings in the Fort and take passage home by the first sailing. Before leaving the lines, however, you will attend on the paymaster and sign an authority for recovery of the full amount owed to this unfortunate woman. He expects you.'

Channer was stunned, so complete and categorical were the terms. Then his aspect turned to insolence. 'I see you have very well fixed me. A very willing little colonel's fag.'

St Alban simply held his gaze.

Channer cleared his throat. 'Very well. I bid you good day.'

'Dismiss.'

Channer saluted, in a manner just compliant with regulation, and strode out.

When the door closed, St Alban leaned back in his chair and sighed with relief. He hadn't been at all sure that Channer would leave without a fight (and even now he couldn't be certain he'd not resile, cursing him for a prig and heaven knew what else), and nor had he been certain that he read the mind of the commanding officer rightly, who was perhaps more bound by strict procedure, but . . . For now, however, it looked as if there was just Waterman; and then they'd be shot of blackguards. There'd be just the usual run of idlers, scamps and dunces that were found in any regiment – with, thank God, one or two capable of greater things – though all of them, no doubt, brave enough when the call came.

IX

Council of War

Two days later

'Gen'l'men!'

The serjeant-major's usual bark was more moderated for regimental conferences, but imperative enough, and singular – just the 'G' and the second 'N' distinct, with those in between rolling into one in the rising minor third of the Tyne.

Hervey entered at nine o'clock precisely with Garratt, St Alban and Major Sleeman. He took off his cap, and smiled. 'Be at ease, gentlemen. Be seated.'

The council of war – orders – was assembled in an open-sided marquee on the maidan beyond the horse lines. Hervey didn't as a rule hold conferences seated. A seated conference somehow invited more discussion than was strictly necessary. Besides, men who spent a good part of the day in the saddle ought to favour standing upright to hear their colonel. This morning, however, he wanted his troop captains to have opportunity to take in the purpose and design of the coming months, so that as events unfolded – and doubtless unravelled the well-laid plans – they might better judge for themselves how to regain the scent, so to speak.

A dozen comfortable cane chairs were arranged in two ranks, with several more as flankers. Outside, a serjeant's picket patrolled resolutely, ready to intercept the curious – if such were likely.

In the front rank sat the five troop leaders, numbered from the right, A to E (the sixth, F, Hardy's, would remain on detached duty in Coorg for a good few months more). Vanneck – the Honourable Myles Vanneck – perhaps the most experienced, sat with his order book resting on a foreleg crossed confidently over the other. Hervey hadn't expected him to come out to India, for he'd money enough to arrange a transfer and stay in England, and he was unmarried (India could offer him little prospect in that regard, even if plenty of consolation). To his left sat B Troop's leader, Christopher Worsley, hardly less experienced, and even more agreeable. Hervey hadn't expected him to come either, for he had a wife used to finer society than she'd find in Madras (but then, so had he such a wife . . .). Then Lord Thomas Malet, C's captain, who'd been his adjutant when he'd assumed command – the best of men. His coming here too had been something of a surprise, although he was not yet of an age when dutiful thoughts of matrimony intruded. And to his left was Hayes, lately come on exchange from the Royals, wanting a troop – a quiet man, but whom the Chestnuts (although D now, like the other troops, were a mixed bag of remounts) seemed pleased with, their efficiency much improved of late. Then E, Oliphant's – Leslie Oliphant of Bachilton – another extract, exchanged from the Ninetieth, who but for some long-disputed entail would have been Clan chief and inheritor of ample acres in Perthshire, but who instead had to eke out a modest annuity in service overseas. Hervey had yet to get the measure of him; he seemed quick of temper but not so quick of thought – though it might have been mere native prudence, for the Ninetieth were after all light infantry, meant to cut about. F Troop's lieutenant, returned from Coorg with the monthly states, stood in for the captain.

In the rank behind sat Lieutenant & Quartermaster Collins and the rest of the regimental staff – Gaskoin, the veterinarian, unpolished but skilled; the surgeon, Milne; the paymaster, Cowper, grey-haired, untroublesome; the riding-master, Kewley, come to the regiment in Hounslow full of the gospel of St John's Wood, delighting in his new commission after twenty years in the ranks of the 7th Hussars; the chaplain, Coote, a Welshman, a widower of some years come from a battalion leaving Madras for home, a literate rather than a graduate, which occasioned some disdain in the mess at first, but who had endeared himself by his work on the comforts committee.

And at the rear – his post on parade, whether mounted or on foot – and this morning 'resting' on the silver-topped Malacca cane brought out on special occasions instead of the day-to-day whip, stood the serjeant-major. For twenty-five years he'd braced-up dragoons for Hervey to address (in section, then troop, then squadron, and now regiment), and for twenty-five years Hervey had taken his counsel – for better, for worse, for richer, for poorer, in sickness and in health. (The old sweats said 'until death do them part'.)

A map of the country some eight feet square, from Fort St George to beyond Haidarabad in the north, and to Coorg in the west, hung at the front of the marquee. It had aroused much interest as they assembled – what clues as to their work, and where exactly. 'Quite a reredos, eh, Coote?' the paymaster had said. Malet had heard, and smiled. More a backdrop, he'd reckoned, for this was theatre.

'Well, gentlemen,' began Hervey, with a distinct note of relish; 'there's much country to hunt this morning, which no doubt is evident from the map. The regiment has two distinct but associated charges. Together, it may be a business of some heat, and perhaps some months. First, we are to pinch out the brigand tribe in the Northern Circars known as "thugs"; and then we are to stand ready to take prisoner the Ranee of Chintal in order that the government in Calcutta may annex that princely state – for the reason that will be made clear.'

No one spoke, but there was a collective stirring, a keen anticipation. There was very likely no one who'd known where Chintal was before seeing the map – not with any precision at least – or anything about it. Nor, until now, that its ruler was female. Still, they'd lately deposed the Rajah of Coorg; so unseating a woman should hardly be troublesome, an affair of only moderate heat at best. Hounding out these 'thugs' sounded far greater sport.

'First, I have asked Major Sleeman, the general superintendent of operations against the bandits, who will by now be known to most if not all, to give his intelligence of thuggee, and its irruption in the Circars.'

Hervey took his seat and Major Sleeman rose to address them.

'Gentlemen, many of you will be acquainted with stories of banditry, but I ask for your forbearance, for in order to convey the extremes of thuggee, I feel I must relate an actual account of their depravity – a deposition by an approver, a man turned King's Evidence as it were; a deposition taken by me personally, and touching on the particular gangs which I believe are now active in the Northern Circars.'

The assembly sat back to listen. It was always pleasing to hear an account of crime and punishment at first hand.

'The first relates to the murder of a party of silk merchants and their families . . .'

Sleeman spared them no detail. The fate of Bunda Ali and his party, had he known of it, could not have served his purpose better (except that the murder of a man in the regiment's employ was an affront to honour as well as to all else). Then having revolted them thoroughly, he concluded with a depravity for which no officer, no dragoon indeed, could wish other than the speedy justice of the noose. 'Having thought they'd killed every man and woman, and stripped and disposed of the bodies in the usual way, the thugs sat down to their hookahs and *bhang thandai*; but their attention was soon arrested by the figure of one Ghufoor Khan, their chief, dragging along a girl, who resisted to the utmost of her power, but who was evidently nearly exhausted: "Ha!" cried he, "Meer Chopra, is that you? Here have I been working like a true Pindaree, and have brought off something worth having; look at her, man! Is she not a Peri? a Hoori? The fool, her mother, must needs oppose me when I got into her tent, but I silenced her with a thrust of my sword, and lo! – here is her fair daughter, a worthy mate for a prince. Speak, my pretty one, art not thou honoured at the prospect of the embraces of Ghufoor Khan?"

'Meer Chopra, my approver in this vile crime, says he could have killed him, for the girl was their sentence of death were she to denounce them. He appealed to Khan to follow their rule – to kill the girl – but the Khan laughed in his face and dragged her off. Meer Chopra says that she would fain have fled, and attempted to do so, but the Khan pursued and caught her, for her tender feet were cut by the rough ground. Ghufoor Khan told him in the morning, with a hellish laugh, that she'd tried to possess herself of his dagger to plunge into her own heart. "I spared her the trouble," said the Khan.'

The disapproval was marked in the extreme. The faces of the front rank showed it, and the exclamations of those in the rear rank put words to it.

Sleeman was pleased. It wasn't often he was able to address King's officers, especially ones who were about to assist him in his work. 'But not, I fear, before he'd defiled her in ways that no Christian ought to hear.'

'Monstrous,' said Worsley; 'bestial.'

Sleeman closed his order book and said nothing more for the moment, allowing the outrage among his audience to do his work.

He'd calculated well: a tale or two of highway robbery, even accompanied by violence – by murder indeed – might be shrugged off in this land, especially the murder of money merchants and the like who took their chance, without precaution; but the murder of women and girls – even of low estate – and especially their defilement, must for any

Englishman demand justice. Demand revenge, indeed; and above all for officers of His Majesty's cavalry . . .

'Gentlemen,' he said, finally, 'this Ghufoor Khan, who masquerades as a nujeeb, a militiaman, is abroad again, even on the road from Guntoor to Chintal. But to date he has eluded all our endeavours, for these depositions were made two years ago. With your help, however, I am confident that we shall apprehend him, and with his arrest, such will be the dismay, the fear, among the other bands – for the Khan is looked to as their leader – that there will come a check in their activities, so that there will then be an increase in approvers, and we might then take the chiefs and jemadars of all the bands one by one.'

At this, there was much appreciation, with calls to 'take 'em to the gibbet'. But Sleeman had one more card to play. 'Gentlemen, I am conscious that this is not a job for cavalry, for I am myself a cavalryman, albeit a native one, but I am persuaded – as is, more importantly, your colonel – that *only* cavalry can do it.'

And thus, said Hervey to himself, Sleeman elegantly enlisted every man assembled, whatever his first thoughts. For here addressing them was not a zealot, but a measured officer of infinite native experience. He himself had first thought the suppression of thuggee to be an impossibility (as well bid the incoming tide to stop, Canute-like), and yet he'd been persuaded these past few days that it might be reduced to a status that could not long stand, and that time and the ordinary sanction of law would see it dwindle to nothing, an occasional and minor irritant.

And not just that it might be reduced, but that it must.

Besides, there was the hideous possibility that Bunda Ali, the moonshee, might himself have been taken by thugs. And if so, then his wife and – God forbid it – his daughters also . . .

It was now his moment. He rose and stood square to address the 'council'.

'This, gentlemen, is not a job for soldiers; indeed it is not. But only soldiers can do it. And only cavalry, for celerity and ranging long will be of the essence, as well as the prowess of each dragoon in scouting. Now, the adjutant will issue the scheme of deployment and the march-tables, but my design for operations against the thugs can be simply put . . .'

X

The Distaff Side

Arcot House, that evening

'Captain Worsley, Colonel.' Serjeant Stray said it with a note of doubt. He was quite used to officers calling without notice at this time, but . . .

'Indeed? Show him in.'

Hervey was sitting in an armchair by the open doors of the verandah in the west-facing room he used as a study. He put down the *Madras Mail* and rose as Worsley entered.

'Colonel, I intrude.'

'On nothing but the *Mail*'s comings and goings, I assure you. Whiskey?'

'Thank you.'

Hervey poured two glasses, added soda and nodded to the second armchair. 'Dorothea's well, I trust?'

'*Very* well. Thank you.'

Worsley took a sip, seeming to search for words. On the lawn outside, a coucal alternately pecked and called, its hooping distracting him further.

'Griff's pheasant, Somervile says they're called,' said Hervey, seeing his hesitation; 'on account of some new-comes thinking them game then finding it rank to eat. Allegra puts out food for them – and the others.'

It seemed to do the trick. 'Colonel, I'm excessively obliged to you for arranging things so that I might stay until Dorothea's given birth, but – with respect – I believe it improper.'

The march table the adjutant had issued at the end of the conference placed Worsley in command of rear details until F Troop returned, his lieutenant taking the troop to Guntoor instead.

Hervey sighed. 'Not improper. Unnecessary, perhaps, but in the circumstances . . .'

'Colonel, my troop takes the field; I must be at their head.'

'We're not facing the French, Christopher!'

Worsley shook his head. 'If there's a scrape . . .'

'You scruple commendably, I can't deny. But Hardy's troop'll be back in no time. All Edgeworth's got to do is get them to Guntoor. They'll not begin operations at once.'

'All the same, Colonel . . .'

'What says Dorothea?'

'We've not spoken of it. I know she'd be of the same opinion.'

Hervey took a large sip of his whiskey. It was quite some thing that a man should know his wife's opinion so decidedly. He thought for a good minute or so. 'The firstborn, and all that. And here, not at home . . .'

'But even so, Colonel.'

Hervey sighed, then smiled. 'Very well, if you're certain of it. I'll have Garratt do duty instead. It's a small matter. And is that all?'

'It is all, Colonel, yes.'

He made to leave.

'Kezia will be at hand, of course.'

'Yes; it will be a great comfort for Dorothea, and for me to know.'

It had been the other way round in London, at the concert, when Kezia had had her 'seizure', as Milne called it, the culmination of what he diagnosed as 'chronic puerperal melancholy'; and what the less clinically practised called derangement. (Without Dorothea Worsley there, he was sure they'd have been in a greater lather – without Dorothea *and* Milne, that is.) He supposed that giving birth in India was not greatly different from in England, but Kezia having now done so – and a fine, healthy infant he was – he imagined she must be some support.

He saw Worsley off with a word or two about Chintal, how it was quite impossible to say how these things would go, but that he hoped he might bring it off without a shot. 'I was there fifteen years ago. Queer place. If it comes to a fight, though, I'll certainly need your troop.'

They shook hands. It was unusual, but it passed for many more words. They'd spoken of matters that men as a rule didn't speak of; a handshake said it was all done – *hukum hai*, 'the matter is closed', the way the silladar regiments ended things at durbar.

Hervey returned to his *Mail*.

Ten minutes later, Serjeant Stray reappeared.

'Beggin' yer pardon, Colonel . . . Dr Milne.'

He ushered in the surgeon – and much less stiffly. Milne was a regular visitor, and always gave his report after seeing Kezia if Hervey was at home.

'Good evening, Colonel.'

Hervey poured him whiskey. 'Nothing amiss, I trust?'

'No, not in the least. I've just paid a call on Dorothea Worsley, and before that, Serjeant Twentyman's wife – she carries her fourth, and well.'

'Kezia's not yet returned from Government House.'

'No, I'd not thought to see her today. No need. I thought not to trouble you at office, though.'

Hervey looked at him quizzically. 'Proceed.'

'I thought to say that if you wished it, I could arrange for the surgeon of the Fifty-seventh to do duty, and I his.'

Hervey nodded appreciatively. It was delicately done. He knew Milne's mind exactly. Milne, his senior in age by some ten years, was already much respected in the Sixth. Few regiments could boast a physician as their surgeon, and fewer still, if any, *Medicinae Doctor Aberdonensis*. But, he knew – else Milne would never have suggested it – the Fifty-seventh's man must be every bit as capable, and perhaps even more so with the knife, for Milne always protested that he disliked cutting, let alone cutting deep (although he'd saved Collins's life in the Belgian skirmish by amputating). Nor did Milne lack stomach for the fight, as the late business in Coorg had shown.

Hervey knew both what he wanted to say and what he must, but took a moment or two nevertheless to wrestle with himself.

'My dear doctor, I am ever in your debt, but on this occasion there can be no question of where duty lies.'

Milne nodded, with a look of resignation. It was as he'd expected, if not as he'd hoped – not *perhaps* as he'd hoped, for while as a man he would have admired his commanding officer's devotion to his wife, as a man under authority he might surely have thought the decision unfitting.

'Very well, Colonel. I shall look forward to the change of air.'

Hervey always found Milne's gentle Buchan reassuring. 'You'll not have dined. Will you sup with us? Kezia can't be very long returning.'

'That is most generous, as ever, Colonel, but there are two men sick in the hospital that I would see before staff parade. Nothing serious in the acute sense, but . . .'

Hervey smiled, though to himself. *Milne*: if there was a single dragoon bedded down he wouldn't pass the evening without attending.

'Of course, but nothing to trouble the chaplain with.'

Milne raised an eyebrow. 'No, there'll be no call for burials, but if only the chaplain had been able to close the door ere the horse bolted, so to speak . . . but I'm afraid it's now a case – *two* cases – for mercurous chloride.'

'Ah.' Many a dragoon consulted a 'sleeping dictionary' too, but in their case the vocabulary was all too limited.

'I've spoken to the sar'nt-major. The particular house will be made known.'

'And these two: the prognosis?'

'They'll be back at duty in a day or two. They could do duty now, indeed, but they'll be bilious with the mercury. Then it will recur at some distant time, as it always does.'

Hervey sighed. Milne had addressed every troop on the subject of what he called 'public hygiene', admonishing them that if they couldn't control their carnal desires, like wild beasts, they should at least satisfy them 'in armour'. When it came to the pleasures of the bazaar, however, in the management of men – some, at least – a surgeon (or a chaplain) might as well speak to the hand.

'How many is that now?'

'Forty-seven, Colonel.'

Hervey sighed again. The better part of a troop; it was unconscionable. His only consolation, perverse as it seemed, was that it was worse in the foot regiments.

Then he inclined his head in irony. 'Strange, is it not, that many a dragoon will now live longer for chasing thugs and making war in Chintal, for I doubt there'll be opportunity for such comforts in many a month.'

* * *

'Well, lass, that's about it an' all. Six months, the colonel reckons, mebbe more.' Armstrong said it matter-of-fact, but to reassure; it was best to square up to these things.

The punkah swung silently, and Mrs Armstrong poured him more tea and spread dripping on another slice of bread – his staple no matter what the heat. Six months at least – and only a week ago they'd been talking of next summer in the hills. Mrs Armstrong was not a one to fling her arms around her man's neck, but five children and two dozen dragoons' wives and *their* children were going to be a handful.

There'd once been *eight* children – three by her late husband, Serjeant Ellis, and Armstrong's by Caithlin, his late wife, but the Reaper had not been kind. The older ones minded the younger, as was the custom, though now at least a little army of servants was also at hand. Edie Armstrong was no Caithlin, who'd had book learning and had run the regimental school, but there was no better seamstress in Madras, and she could manage both men and women. She'd never known material comforts such as those now, and was all too aware they might vanish in an instant.

And she cared fiercely for her husband, too; for, she reckoned, he cared not enough about himself. 'I'll want you back, Geordie Armstrong. Don't you be going for the hero.'

Armstrong laughed. 'Chance'd be a fine thing for me now, bonnie lass. Serjeant-major? I'm nowt but a clerk.'

She frowned. She knew he was no such. She'd heard how he'd charged at Coorg with the colonel – which they'd no right doing, except there was no choice, so they said – and how he'd sabred two. And it'd be the same again this time no doubt, and although there was no one handier in a fight than he (Serjeant Ellis used to say so, and every NCO), the time would come when a lucky shot or an unguarded cut would . . .

But there was no point trying to talk him out of being at Colonel Hervey's side. She might as well try to teach their old pug new tricks.

But she might just get him to think beyond, a little. 'I don't want to say it, Geordie, for you're every inch a man and more, but even I can't sew as nimbly as once I could.'

Now Armstrong frowned. It was true; he'd been mightily long in the saddle, already a corporal when Hervey had joined. He'd own to forty-five years on this earth – but no more. And no one could prove otherwise. His attestation papers had long been lost – an old dodge – though the paymaster kept careful note of his reckonable service. (He'd be able to take his pension at any time.) These days, however, no one bothered about a few grey hairs, any more than they did about a man trying to enlist before he shaved. As long as he looked the part and was useful.

'I'll be right. Depend on it.'

'They say Colonel Hervey won't be long before he's going. They say he'll be a general and away before a year's out.'

That was different, and he knew it. They hadn't spoken of it before, though. Not that he hadn't wondered what his own position might then be. Who knew who'd then take command? Even if it were someone from the regiment it wouldn't mean they'd want him as serjeant-major for long. And what then? Collins was set for life in the quartermaster's chair, and besides, it wasn't a job for him. Yes, he could do it, he reckoned – he *supposed* he could, with a decent quartermaster-serjeant – but he knew he'd not be a patch on Collins. RM? He wouldn't mind, not if it were that or nothing; but 'babby-minding', as he called it, wasn't his idea of soldiery. Besides, Kewley wasn't going to give up any time soon. What *could* he do? Now that the Sixth had gentlemen for adjutant, whereas before they'd been commissioned from the ranks, there was no prospect of anything. No, he supposed he'd a couple more years at most, and then it would be the end. He'd tried it once, and been heartily glad when Hervey had brought him back to the colours – *and* made him serjeant-major, which he'd never for one moment thought he'd be.

Anyway – Lord in heaven – who could he hand over to?

'When it comes to it, Geordie, do we *have* to go home though? Can't we stay here? You know how far a rupee goes. We can have a place ten times bigger than in England. We could even buy our own. They say there's a new law, and you can buy here now. We could run a guest house – for officers and the like.'

It was more than he'd have liked to contemplate at this time, what with a regiment to get to Guntoor all of three hundred miles away, but he must say something by way of reply. In truth, though, it wasn't Edie Armstrong's intention to have a decision from him there and then – merely to plant the thought in his mind, for him to contemplate during quiet moments in the coming months, of which there must surely be some?

'Aye, well, it's an idea, bonnie lass.'

And that was all he needed to say, and all she needed to hear.

* * *

Not long after Milne left, Georgiana and Annie returned from their afternoon promenade with Allegra. Annie and her younger charge, with the ayah and her assistants, went straight to the nursery; Georgiana joined her father while her bath was being drawn.

'Papa, Serjeant Acton says the regiment is to go north for several months. May I go too?'

She took him by surprise. It wasn't unusual for memsahibs – or a regiment's women – to accompany their men on expeditions, and there'd certainly be some of the dragoons' wives on this one, but . . .

'Why would you wish to?' (Even as he said it he realized how absurd a question it was.) 'I mean . . . would it not be better that you stayed here, in the circumstances?'

The 'circumstances' were Kezia's confinement (when, in the strict sense, her confinement began). But again, even as he spoke he realized how much he took – continued to take – for granted. He'd presumed on his sister for many years after Georgiana's semi-orphaning, and now he presumed on Georgiana herself.

'If you wish me to stay here, and my step-mama too, I shall, of course, Papa.'

'Your step-mama wouldn't, I think, object to your going, for she wouldn't wish to stand in the way of your being with me after hazarding the passage here, but she might have a concern, I think, for . . . your company; for I believe Annie would have to stay.'

'If Annie must stay, I should be perfectly content if Anjali or Sarah were to come.'

Hervey put down his glass. He'd never thought to prepare himself for this – the child he'd always left behind, seen only occasionally and supposed would somehow remain a child, now making her own way, and most assuredly. What, indeed, could he say? 'Very well, we'll ask your step-mama's opinion on her return. And in truth . . . I shall be pleased if she approves.'

They dined quietly that evening, just Kezia, Georgiana, Annie and himself. St Alban was dining with the Bodyguard, the major was garrison field officer of the week and therefore dined at the Fort, and Fairbrother was with the Somerviles. The conversation was diverting enough, thanks in large part to Georgiana, who'd learned of yet another of St Alban's seemingly incomparable qualities and wished to share her enthusiasm, but it had hardly been taxing. Annie had seemed pensive, however. Not that, as a rule, she spoke without first being spoken to, though with assurance enough when she did (and sense). Hervey wondered if they asked too much of her of late – the oversight of three children (well, Georgiana, and Allegra who was not yet eight, and Master Hervey who did not yet speak), although there were Anjali and Sarah, admirable ayahs, and innumerable maids of all work. Perhaps she pined a little for home?

There was a triumph with the pudding, though. For a year and more Kezia had been considering the attempt, but getting chestnuts brought from the hills beyond Patna had defeated her several times, and only now was there ice enough to be had to continue with the experiment.

The cook had been bewildered at first, and only Kezia's persistence – herself in an apron, no doubt shaming the poor man – had brought off the success.

'I have wanted to do this since first I saw it, but . . .'

And the sentence had been left unfinished, for there was no need to recollect the difficulties there'd been since that time – the time of her seizure – and their coming to India. It was a pudding, she explained, that Monsieur Carême, Count Nesselrode's chef, had devised. And now that she was confident that it could be brought to table, it would be brought as often as the season would allow (and, Hervey trusted, the accounts). For no matter how imperfect the soup, how mean the relevé or unpalatable the entrée, such a pudding would not be forgot, and the homeward diners therefore content.

When they were alone, outside, Kezia poured coffee for them both, nodding to the khitmagar to dismiss. It was so much cooler of an evening now, almost time for a shawl. Torches ringed the lawn, and lanterns hung from the tamarinds fringing the further parts of the garden. Citronella burners kept away all but the most determined mosquitoes, and the lanterns distracted the rest of the flying tribes. Georgiana and Annie had withdrawn as soon as they'd all risen from the table. It was, as she liked to say, their time of day.

'Is all well with Annie?'

Kezia frowned. 'I had thought to ask you the same. Nothing untoward has occurred here, I'm sure. I wondered if the tiger hunt had troubled her.'

'I think I may ask Georgiana.'

'I think that would be wise. Brandy-water?'

He shook his head.

'You are not ill, are you, Matthew?'

He smiled. 'I confess I'm a little tired. I think brandy would not conduce to sleeping – or rather, to waking with a good head. Did Milne have anything to say this morning? He told me he'd paid a call.'

'He thought it best if I took to a carriage for exercise, rather than the saddle.'

'And you will?'

'Yes, though I so very much enjoy riding with Allegra – and with Georgiana; and Annie.'

He was pleased she enjoyed her exercise so, but relieved that she'd moderate it. He was about to say 'The time will pass quickly enough' – the time until her birthing – but suddenly thought better of it, for how could he know how time passed for a woman with child?

Instead he pondered a moment or two. 'By the bye, the strangest thing: Somervile told me that the commissary had got word that money has been changing hands – bribes – over the forage contracts. I said I thought it so preposterous as to consider it a slander, and that the commissary should produce his evidence, sworn as necessary.'

'That is indeed very ill. I am sorry for you. But surely no discredit attaches to you personally?'

He shook his head. 'It can amount to nothing, or else I'm no judge of horseflesh at all. Garratt, Collins and the quartermaster-serjeant are the only men engaged in the business of forage contracts. It's unconscionable.'

'I should think so myself, even though I know them but little.'

He nodded, and pondered a few moments more. 'Somervile was, though, eager to tell me that my dragoon is reprieved. So God bless the major and the tigers of Madras.'

'That is indeed happy news.'

He related the details – Australia, appeal, delay; she listened patiently.

Then it was silence again but for the cicadas. Kezia turned to gaze at the distant lanterns . . .

'You will return to me, won't you, Matthew?'

She said it not anxiously but insistently, yet with a note of affection that made him catch his breath.

'But of course! I said to Worsley that it's hardly the French we face – and we beat *them*.'

But she knew her husband. She'd known his reputation long before they'd married. Her late husband, then his commanding officer, used to say there was no handier officer in a fight; and she'd heard how he'd charged at Coorg, with Armstrong alongside (naturally), which they'd no right doing, except that (it was said) there was no choice; and how he'd sabred one and then been first through the sally port of a stockade. And doubtless it would be the same again this time. She'd never been happier, she supposed, than now – no, not even as Lady Lankester – and she was all too conscious of the miserable journey to that happiness. Yes, it was all in the past, but how could she know if contentment – the foundation of contentment – might vanish in an instant? A random shot, an unseen blade . . .

But there was no dissuading him from the cannon's mouth. As well bid the incoming tide recede. Could she bear the blow, however, not least for Allegra and now Georgiana – even for Master Hervey, all unknowing still? The material comforts, here, were of no concern; at home in Hertfordshire she'd be as well attended. But she cared for her husband – not least, she believed, because he cared not enough about himself. How else was it that a man who'd saved the government's skin by his action at Bristol remained a colonel still?

'Let me ask you plainly, dearest: is Lord Bentinck quite to be trusted? I don't know the particulars, of course, but it seems very convenient for the Company that Chintal be deemed to be in lapse. From what you've told me of the place, it wasn't in the least worth Fort William's regrets. But now there are *rubies* – and coal indeed! It is really most convenient. Even if Bentinck does act entirely honourably in this, he's to leave India next year – you know that – and his successor will be a Whig, and decidedly against these encroachments. Shall you not be . . . tarnished?'

'I am a man under authority; I am not responsible for the orders given me.'

She sighed, and put a hand on his. 'Oh, Matthew; of course you're not responsible. But I don't trust these Whigs. They make all sorts of mischief and absolve themselves because it serves a higher principle, they say. And Somervile will be of no help because he too will have gone.'

Kezia was beginning to sound like Henrietta: anxious for his reputation, ambitious for his advancement, mistrustful of any who might do him down – and he loved her even more for it.

But he smiled, intending to reassure her that she need have no fear in that regard. 'You'll recall that Bentinck's a Whig himself. We might reasonably suppose continuity therefore.'

Kezia said nothing. She'd said enough. She knew her husband to be a reflective man. It was sufficient now to plant the question in his mind, for him to contemplate during quiet moments in the coming months, of which there must surely be some?

And there was the reassurance that Georgiana would be with him, a present reminder (and, of course, Annie must go with her). There was also the chance that St Alban would notice and reciprocate her admiration.

PART TWO

THE NORTHERN CIRCARS

XI

Ghufoor Khan

The road to Chintalpore, eight weeks later

Fairbrother was not to be discouraged. In the course of November he'd tramped the road from Guntoor to Sthambadree, and beyond to the border with Chintal, then back again via Bezwada to the east, three times – seven hundred miles in all, perhaps, trailing his coat in the red earth, hazarding the ferries on the Krishna and a dozen other rivers of this vast plain in the hope of tempting thuggee. Not just any band, however: Sleeman's intelligence was, if not precise, very definite. The man they sought was known to all as Arjan Brar, 'the last of the Pindarees', the freebooting horsemen of the Maratha wars, though Brar himself was reputed to be of a noble Jat family. But Sleeman said he'd welcome any encounter with thugs – of course – for there was always the possibility that one of the captives would turn approver, with information that would lead them to their prize. This was how he'd come to know of Arjan Brar in the first place, for four years ago he'd captured the infamous 'Feringhee' and turned him approver. It was, he said, like taking the plan of a maze: where before, all he'd seen as he tried to find the route to the middle were high hedges, with Feringhee's collaboration he now knew his way about blindfold. But there was, he said, another maze – perhaps even two – connected in some way with the first, and for this, Feringhee had told him, he needed Arjan Brar. For Brar was key to the secrets of thuggee in Mysore.

At least the heat now was bearable, even at midday. Indeed, in another few weeks they'd need a blanket at night. But the country was without feature or charm – except the rivers – so that he spent as much time gazing at the sky as the ground. Such an abundance of avians there was too – gaudier than at the Cape or in Jamaica, or for that matter any other place he'd been. Bigger, too – the kites and crows, even; and the bustard. These were his consolations in the weeks of tramping the dusty roads. The collector at Guntoor, Somervile's old post, had given him an excellent *rahbar* (guide), who knew also what the birds were, if not always their English names. It passed the hours pleasantly, and Fairbrother was ever curious. As long as none of the travellers they encountered heard them speaking English, there was no danger in it. They were in all other respects convincing enough, just ten of them, dressed respectably but not showily, walking by the bullock cart or riding ponies – exactly as the sahoukars did. Fairbrother called his party the live-bait troop.

Yet so far there'd not been a single bite. No other party of travellers had seemed in the least wanting to combine with them. None had even fallen in with them for a mile or two, though there were comings and goings enough. Each night, it was true, they'd put up at some resthouse, or even a corner of a village maidan – where a thug wouldn't risk prying and where they could mount a good watch – but, he trusted, not so as to give away their game.

He'd certainly chosen his party with especial care. He was strange to the country and would not risk what he might at the Cape. He had with him as covermen two dragoons whom Armstrong had particularly recommended: good, active corporals whose complexion was sallow enough to escape interest, especially with a prodigious growth of beard. Sleeman had also sent him one of his best approvers, who could recognize fifty thugs known to be active in the Circars in the past five years. A 'half-cast baboo', one of Somervile's best writers, was his interpreter. He it was who'd speak for 'my master' to any they encountered, a not-unusual practice, Sleeman said, despite the tendency for rank to count less on the road. His syce was industrious, a Tamul whom the RM had proposed (and Sammy had seconded), and the other servants had proved reliable, too, especially the langree. Half the reason, he was sure, was that money was no object, as Somervile had assured him. (The Secret Fund was, it seemed, almost infinite.)

Most industrious of all was his 'bearer' – Private Askew, whom St Alban had assigned to him in open arrest. With no ship bound for Australia in many months, Armstrong had said he was damned if he'd let a man idle away his time – even on constant fatigues – while others sweated in the field, and St Alban had agreed. Besides, there was just the possibility that Askew might further redeem himself, and the transportation be commuted therefore. 'The performance of a duty of honour or of trust, after the knowledge of an offence committed by a soldier, ought to convey a pardon for the offence', the Duke of Wellington had written, which, though he now held no official position, was good enough for any officer.

The sun stood a hand's span above the horizon; it was time to make camp, although Fairbrother had hoped to reach Mattapallee that evening, five miles distant. Knowing the road as they did, however, it would be enough to find a place to bed down. In the next village there was more than one good billet, and he decided to send the baboo ahead with Corporal Smale to make arrangements. If there were any need to exchange words between now and reaching the village he'd rely on the approver or the rahbar. He didn't entirely trust the approver – how could he? – but one false move and he'd put a bullet in him without hesitation, which he'd had the baboo tell him in no uncertain terms before they'd set a single foot on the road. And if for any reason he wasn't able to keep his word, then Corporal Smale – or else Corporal Spence (another of the roughriders) – was to carry out the sentence. The approver – Banji Lal – had shown no terror at the threat, and Fairbrother had concluded that either he was a man of honour, if of a peculiar kind, or else wholly possessed of the Hindoo's fatalism. Whatever it was, Banji Lal had so far been an exemplary support.

The baboo found them comfortable quarters in what until lately had been a police post but was now in the care of an enterprising old *sipahi*. They were in the Nizam's territory, although there was no customs house until Mattapallee and the ferry on the Krishna, for the road from the border led only there. It made no difference to Fairbrother's method, except that if they came to call on the police for help they would have to do so as travellers, and thereby take their luck, rather than within the presidency as agents of the government and therefore able to command assistance.

Not that he expected to have need. Indeed, he intended to rest himself and his party well here, for after crossing the Krishna they'd have to be doubly vigilant. It was a stretch of road that had apparently seen many murders, and if Sleeman and his predictive system was right, there must surely be one if not two thug bands active now between there and the crossing into Chintal.

And restful this place would certainly be for the night. Fairbrother even had his own room, with a door he could bar and a window likewise.

They'd not been long there, however, the sun not yet quite set, when they had a visitor – visitors. There were always visitors, as this evening, but always intent on selling them something. This particular one, older than most and carrying just a basket of dried coconut, told the baboo when the other sellers were out of earshot that he wished to speak to the huzoor.

The baboo scolded him, telling him he'd get no more money for his coconut than offered, but the man spoke softly and said he wished to tell the huzoor something to his advantage: 'I am a poor but honest farmer. I was one time a *sipahi* in the army of the *Angreze*.'

The baboo went to tell Fairbrother, finding him in the courtyard with Spence and Smale drinking boiled milk.

Two former sipahees – first their landlord and now this fruit-seller. Fairbrother was intrigued. This was good fortune, truly. Or did they all say they'd served when they thought they were in the presence of Company men?

'Bring him here, baboo-sahib, but not a word of English, mind.' He nodded to the corporals, who came and sat close.

The baboo brought the sometime sepoy to the presence. 'Tell the huzoor what it is you have to say, *sipahi*.'

The man made *namaskar*. 'Sahibs, you are sahoukars, I think, with much gold and rubies. I have seen you pass by three times since the last moon. Today I overhear bad men speak of robbing you. Sahibs, I am poor farmer, with much debt. I wish only to help. I wish that bad men be punished and honest men like you and me live in contentment.'

Fairbrother listened keenly. He understood just a few words, but his intention was to suggest the opposite. When the man finally stopped – he spoke for some time – the baboo looked at 'the huzoor' for a sign. Fairbrother nodded slowly, giving the impression he was weighing the words, then rose and went to a corner of the courtyard with the baboo.

'He says a party claiming to be pilgrims intends joining with you tomorrow at the ferry, and accompanying you on the road to Chintal, and when it is night falling upon you to take the gold and jewels, and that there will by then be thirty of them, so that they will overwhelm you before you can defend yourselves. They will send lughaees ahead to dig a great pit into which they will cast the bodies, near a place they have used many times before for murder.'

'Ripe intelligence, baboo-sahib. You trust him?'

'I believe I do, Captain-sahib. How could his telling us help the thugs in any way? He says he knows where is their camp tonight, but says it would be unwise to move against them, for there will be little moon and the place is set about with bamboo.'

Fairbrother cursed. His instinct was to do just that – turn the tables on them before even the tables were laid, so to speak. That was certainly what his good friend – Hervey – would have done. But he didn't underestimate the hazards, nor overestimate his advantage; to start with, this little *purana sipahi* might be cunning, tempting him to try by urging him not to.

'Do we suppose that Banji Lal would recognize these men? We can't presume to. We'll need this old soldier to point them out at the ferry, shall we not, for each time we've crossed there've been many hundreds waiting. I'd want to take their leaders as soon as possible. Did he offer to identify them to us? Did he name his price?'

'He asked for fifty sicca rupees, sahib.'

It was a monstrous sum: and *sicca* rupees – gold. It was more than he could possibly be in debt for, unless his standing was much greater than appeared.

Yet it was reasonable enough as a measure of a *seth*'s – a rich man's – or a sahoukar's life and the treasure they must be carrying. Besides, Fairbrother admired the man's pluck, for one way or another it was his forfeit life that was the stake.

'Very well. Tell him I'll pay twenty at once, and the rest when he's marked the ringleaders at Mattapallee. Have him come back when the sun's up.'

Next morning the old *sipahi* rose with the larks, the *chandools*. They were in good voice, too, so that even in the village Fairbrother heard them. They sounded as they did at the Cape, and in Jamaica, and he wondered how it was that birds sang the same in places so far from each other, yet here a man might go a dozen miles and hear so many languages, each strange to the other. Would it even matter if anyone heard them speaking English; for would they recognize it as English? But their business was discipline, especially now that, at last, the mahseer seemed to be rising to the bait.

Breaking camp was by now a practised affair. They were up, breakfasted and on the move in an hour. They saw no one on the road but the odd bhisti carrying water to the fields for the ryots who'd been up since dawn to till the red earth in their unhurried way. It reminded him of the plantations at home, although here there was no overseer with them.

They reached Mattapallee in an hour and a half. It was not a large place by presidency standards, but because of the ferry there were many more people than its size suggested. On both sides of the river there was a crowd waiting to cross: a hundred, perhaps more, mainly men, and their impedimenta – bullock carts, packhorses and the like – and importuned by every sort of vendor. The Krishna here was three hundred yards wide, at least, but sluggish enough to permit a raft to be roped across by hand. How many could safely be taken aboard was a question Fairbrother had pondered the first time he came here, and was a question still. It looked haphazard in the extreme.

There was no order to the crowd – no system, no queue. He'd seen before how those with the means might be first rather than last. The baboo said there were men who earned a living by never themselves crossing but crowding the landing and taking baksheesh to make way for those willing to pay. But Fairbrother was in no hurry to cross. Rather, he was keen to see the men who would waylay him. So they bought fruit, found a little shade, and settled down to wait.

They were not long at rest when the old *sipahi* suddenly became agitated. 'There, in yellow dhoti kurta: he is man who I hear say will rob sahoukars.'

The baboo whispered it in Fairbrother's ear.

Fairbrother tried to take the measure of him, a man of his own height and build, perhaps even of his age, with the appearance of rank and respectability. He could certainly pass for a pilgrim, although the half-dozen or so with him were less refined looking.

What to do – wait for him to make his approach? What if his design, though, was to wait until they'd crossed, away from the police and customs men?

Suddenly, Banji Lal himself became animated. 'Huzoor, that man, the one in yellow kurta, I know him. He is Ghufoor Khan. He is thug of great reputation. If he see me, all is lost.'

Fairbrother had always supposed this might happen, Banji Lal recognized and the game then up. His plan had been to have one of the corporals bundle him away until the threat was past or they'd made their move and taken the thug. Here, though, it would split their little party if he himself was then to cross the river (and he hadn't the men to risk that). But he could hardly cast Banji Lal adrift. The approver was one of Sleeman's best, and besides, he still couldn't entirely trust him.

But he must act fast, both to preserve their disguise and to take their man. It wasn't Arjan Brar, Sleeman's prize, but Banji Lal made him sound almost as good as.

'Tell him to get into the bullock cart and pretend a fever, baboo-sahib.'

He got hold of the corporals – Askew too – and pointed out Ghufoor Khan. 'Pistols primed. We're going to make our crossing, and if we're followed we'll move at once to take him. If luck goes with us, it may be the end of our work.'

The ferry was mid-stream. They hadn't long to get through the press of people, therefore, but Fairbrother reckoned it might work to their advantage, for the hubbub would surely draw in the Khan. He paid off the old *sipahi*, then told the baboo to ease their way through the crowd with handsome quantities of coin, if necessary telling people of the fevered passenger in the bullock cart. (He reckoned, too, that Ghufoor Khan might think it a ruse to protect the gold and rubies they were carrying.)

Corporal Spence led the way, roughly pushing aside vendors, travellers and placeholders alike, for as soon as the baboo produced the coin, the press became greater. It worked though: by the time the ferry touched the bank they were at the ramshackle pier, with no one in front of them. Close behind, however, and Fairbrother smiled to himself in satisfaction, was Ghufoor Khan.

But now he would have to separate him from the rest of his thugs. Thirty would be altogether too many to manage, even with a pistol at their leader's head.

'Tell the ferryman that only our party is to cross – tell him of the fever – and offer him gold enough that he doesn't think twice about it.'

'*Accha,* sahib.'

The ferry was heavy-laden. It would take many minutes for its cargo to shuffle off, and in that time the baboo ought to be able to complete the transaction. Fairbrother tried to see without looking how many were in Ghufoor Khan's immediate party. He seemed to be talking to two, but in the press behind him there could be any number.

He'd have to be bold. When the Khan importuned the ferryman to let him on, he'd tell him he wanted no more than three, for the sake of his fevered brother.

As soon as the raft was lashed to the pier, baboo-sahib pushed aboard to harangue the ferryman. He asked how much he'd taken for the crossing from the other side. The man was reluctant to say – who knew whether he was indeed a traveller, or a tax inspector? – so the baboo tried the more costly tack: 'The huzoor will double the sum!'

The ferryman thought for a moment, then came up with a patently inflated figure. There was no time to bargain, however; and besides, reckoned baboo-sahib, the man would be so surprised that he'd be even more eager (no small thing when the crowd were told they'd have to wait another hour and more).

'Very well, twenty sicca rupees!'

The ferryman, astonished, sprang to his work, laying about with his *lathee* several men already trying to board.

Fairbrother saw the look of dismay on Ghufoor Khan's face. He was sure he wouldn't simply give up. It amused him, indeed, to think with what ingenuity he must now be concocting a ruse by which to inveigle himself and his followers onto the ferry.

The bullocks were a little more intractable than usual, which at first held up the boarding, but in a quarter of an hour it was done. Then, just as Fairbrother and the baboo were about to follow, the Khan made his move.

'Huzoor, I am a pilgrim bound for the great and holy shrine at Sthambadree. I will pray at the shrine for your companion who has the fever. Let us accompany him now, my three fellow pilgrims and I' (he indicated each of them) 'so that we may pray for him as we cross the holy river of Krishna.'

Fairbrother nodded without waiting for the baboo to translate. It was plain enough that just four would come aboard – better odds, indeed, than he'd expected.

Once the bullocks were quietened and the lathees had done their work – more than one traveller had swum to the side to try to get aboard – the ferryman cast off and his men began hauling on the ropes. Fairbrother took himself to the front, deliberately apart. This, too, seemed to suit Ghufoor Khan, who spent the half-hour of the crossing in chanting and earnest hand clasping.

At the other side, all went well, the hubbub among the waiting crowd masking the instructions Fairbrother gave the corporals. He didn't intend waiting long before his move – a mile or so, out of earshot of the ferry.

The bullocks were obliging, and the party set off at a good pace, Ghufoor Khan and his men attaching themselves, just as Fairbrother had anticipated, and continuing their chanting. Again, it amused him to think what the Khan had planned: the lughaees would already be this side of the river, digging a pit at the appointed place; the *bhuttotes*, the stranglers, would be across next, in an hour or so, and would move quickly to make up time, joining their master before evening, or wherever it was they'd arranged. Doubtless the Khan was confident that he himself and his three henchmen could do the deed if it were necessary, for to him this sahoukar and his servants – and their sick companion – must hardly look fearsome.

The sun was now high, the heat growing – the time for refreshment and rest. It would be no strange thing to find some shade and boil up a little coffee, and rice. Ghufoor Khan would be only too pleased at the delay; the rest of his men would be with him sooner.

Three-quarters of a mile on, Fairbrother found a good spot. The road was clear in both directions, not a soul even in the fields, such as they were, and no village for another mile and more. A sal grove offered shade – and cover for what he intended.

The syce led the bullock cart to the edge, just as the baboo instructed. Ghufoor Khan and his men kept so close to it that they didn't see the corporals and Private Askew slip into the grove. When the baboo said, 'The huzoor invites you to take refreshment with him', they were at once delighted.

A bearer spread a mat and Fairbrother bid them sit – exactly as the thugs would with their victims. He couldn't resist a smile of satisfaction, but again to himself.

The instant they were settled, Fairbrother still courteously on his feet, out from the sleeve of his kurta came the service pistol, and out from the sal sprang Askew and the corporals.

Surprise was complete. Fairbrother lost no time: while Askew and the corporals pulled the three others aside and the bearers bound their hands and feet, he slipped a yellow scarf round the Khan's neck.

'You are Ghufoor Khan. You are wanted for murder. Tell me why I should not strangle you here and now, as you have strangled others!'

The baboo translated excitedly.

'No, no, huzoor! I am humble merchant and pilgrim!'

Again baboo-sahib translated, but there was hardly need.

'Banji Lal!' shouted Fairbrother.

Out from the bullock cart jumped the approver, though none too boldly.

'Do you recognize this man, Banji Lal?'

'*Accha*, sahib. He is Ghufoor Khan.'

The Khan's eyes – murderous – left no doubt.

Fairbrother yanked the scarf and dug the pistol into his neck.

'You will tell me where is Arjan Brar.'

'I not know who is Arjan Brar.'

'Speak to him, Banji Lal. Tell him we know all, and will hang him and his accomplices here and now if he doesn't oblige.'

Banji Lal spoke animatedly, reinforcing his words with gestures that left no doubt as to the fate of Ghufoor Khan and his party if they didn't cooperate, though he said it more with anxiety than menace, for he couldn't quite believe this considerable man of thuggee could have exposed himself so, and feared that at any moment the rest of his men would appear and put them all to the sword.

The same thought hadn't escaped Fairbrother. But he might use it to his advantage yet. The Khan still vehemently denied that he was who he was, and all knowledge of Arjan Brar. For what had he to fear if he could play for time?

'Corporal Spence!'

'Sir!'

Fairbrother whispered his orders. Spence nodded grimly.

'Very well, Ghufoor Khan, which of these three men of yours is the most honoured, and which the most lowly?'

Ghufoor Khan looked puzzled, but if the game won him time, he'd play it willingly enough.

'Akash Roy, of the blue turban, is my oldest friend; Bhargava, of the beard, is my servant.'

'Very well. Bhargava shall die at once unless you tell me where is Arjan Brar. And then the next in importance, and then Akash Roy, and then you yourself, Ghufoor Khan. For if you will not tell, you are of no use to me – a burden, indeed, as your men try to catch us and we flee for the safety of the police post at Sthambadree.'

The Khan was alarmed. He hadn't expected such a threat.

But could it be real? Would these agents of the British Company – or whatever they were – hang them like dogs at the side of the road?

'I know not this Arjan Brar!'

'Very well. Proceed, Corporal Spence!'

Spence beckoned to Askew to unbind the feet of the least of the accomplices and drag him to the bamboo thicket beside the grove.

Once out of sight he gave him the nod. 'Good and clean, Davey lad.'

Askew swung his fist so fast the man was flat on his back before he could even flinch.

'Stone cold. Nicely done, Davey. Get ready.'

Spence fired into the ground, then stepped out of the thicket for all to see, the pistol smoking obligingly, while Askew dragged the unconscious Bhargava into view for a second or so, as if moving him to make way for the next.

'So, Ghufoor Khan, you think I am not a man of my word? Where is Arjan Brar?'

'Tell him, Ghufoor Khan, tell him!' shouted the next to die.

'Yes, tell him, Ghufoor Khan,' echoed Akash Roy, the next-but-one. 'Why should we die for that rich fellow who takes more than his fair share?'

Ghufoor Khan shook his head.

Fairbrother feared he was thwarted.

But then the next-to-die gained heart. 'I will tell you, huzoor, if you spare me!'

'I too, huzoor,' said Akash Roy.

Fairbrother brightened. 'Take them aside, separately, baboo-sahib, and make note of what they say. If they differ . . .'

'*Accha*, sahib!'

It was done, and quickly. And the name of the place was the same.

Fairbrother smiled. 'So, Ghufoor Khan, these men have told me where is Arjan Brar, and I shall spare their lives. Yours, though, is forfeit. Corporal Spence!'

Spence hauled him to his feet.

'And further, Ghufoor Khan, you are a Mussulman, but you will not enter the kingdom of heaven. Rather, I myself shall smear you in the blood of Bhargava, your Hindoo accomplice, and shall shed on you my own, an infidel too, so that you will be doubly defiled!'

The Khan was now much alarmed. He looked anxiously about him, then fell to his knees and beat his breast. 'It is better that Arjan Brar, an infidel also, is taken than I dishonour Allah by dying defiled. I will tell you his hiding place, ḥuzoor.'

The baboo explained, and Fairbrother nodded. 'Tell him that if the name of the place is not that which is given by the other two, I will have all my men defile his body, in every way, and then shoot him with my own hands.'

Ghufoor Khan bowed meekly, trembling, and gave the baboo the name of the place.

It was that which the others had given.

XII

And All His Pretty Ones

Two days later

Fairbrother cursed. If only he'd come himself instead of wasting time reporting to Sleeman, but those were Sleeman's express orders: as soon as a likely approver was taken, he was to be brought at once for interrogation. The information he'd volunteer in the early days of capture would be far greater than if he were left to mull over his condition. That, at least, was Sleeman's experience. Yet what information could be more valuable than taking Arjan Brar, who might then himself turn approver? Usually Fairbrother had no great liking for the rules; he was, he liked to say, one of Nature's irregulars, but respect for his old friend – Hervey – had this time bound him to Sleeman's instructions.

He was doubly annoyed with himself because when they'd handed over Ghufoor Khan and told him the whereabouts of Arjan Brar, Sleeman decided to stay and interrogate the Khan and instead send one of his inspectors to arrest Brar. Fairbrother therefore found himself acting under orders of a native officer – and a policeman at that – which severely tested his pride, though not perhaps as much as that of his two corporals. Except that the inspector's zeal was not to be faulted.

The following night found the party – the inspector, a dozen of Sleeman's sepoys, and Fairbrother's men – lying up in a grove of coral trees half a mile outside a village of no note astride a track on which even a bullock cart would have struggled to make progress. Fairbrother had argued for closing at once, but the inspector was certain they'd find the house empty – at least of Arjan Brar, who, having probably heard of the taking of Ghufoor Khan, would be lying up at a distance from the village during the day. It made sense, and Fairbrother conceded that they'd have only the one opportunity to close on the house, but in the pitch darkness how would they know when he returned? They wouldn't, said the inspector, so they'd have to lie up most of the night as well, descending on the house only in the early hours.

And a shivery night they had of it too after the ground had given up the heat of the day, such as there was. Nor could they risk a fire to cook with. There was a bit of a moon, such as the unseasonal cloud would allow, but at least it was dry. Likely the whole month would be, which was one of the reasons he knew Hervey wanted to make progress with Chintal, and he sympathized with his chafing at the delays. This thug-hunting was goodish sport, he supposed, but it wasn't soldiering . . .

'Captain-sahib, now is time to go.'

Fairbrother sat up. He'd not slept. Not much, certainly. 'Very well, Inspector-sahib. Your men in place at the rear?'

They'd agreed that the best course was to have half a dozen sepoys creep around the edge of the village to the back of the single-storey walled house in case there was a watch at the front. There'd be little chance of catching Brar if he bolted now, not with two hours to daylight.

'No, Captain-sahib. I changed the mind. Men are good, but most unready still.'

Fairbrother swore to himself. It was too late to do so to his face; and besides, it didn't do to undermine the inspector's authority, however 'unready' his men were. But if only he'd told him earlier he could have sent Spence and Smale . . . 'Then the quicker we move, the better.'

'Accha.'

They could at least do that – move quickly – 'unready' though the sepoys supposedly were. They were up and stood-to-horse in minutes. Silently too. In no more than ten they were mounted and away, but in a walk to keep down the noise.

At least, too, the house would be unmistakable said their intelligence – new-painted white. Fairbrother began to feel confident again.

The cloud thinned obligingly as they came to the edge of the village – a trifling place, a dozen or so dwellings, twenty at most. There were no lights of any kind, and no watchman they could see.

There was just room to ride two abreast into the maidan, Fairbrother and the inspector leading. The whitened house stood the other side, clear as day, just as promised. Fairbrother took his pistol in hand. He hoped not to use it – he wanted to see this Arjan Brar die by the drop – but if it came to a fight he wanted it to be he who dispensed justice. Ghufoor Khan had left him in no doubt as to Brar's depravity.

The inspector's best naik and three sepoys rode to the rear of the house while the rest dismounted. Horse-holders took the loosed reins, and the remaining six and Fairbrother's four made ready to storm the last refuge of the secrets of thuggee.

There were two high, shuttered windows and the solid, studded door of the better sort of village dwelling. It was still too dark, even with the cloud gone, to make out detail, and the inspector told the havildar to light the lanterns. It took a minute or two, but the result was immediately impressive, the white walls helpfully reflecting the light. Confident, now, that if Arjan Brar made a dash for it he'd be seen at once and caught, the inspector advanced on the door, flanked by two naiks with drawn swords and Fairbrother with his pistol.

Doors and windows in the sturdier dwellings were invariably barred at night, or even secured with a lock. The inspector banged with his fist.

No sound came from within.

He banged again and shouted for all the village to hear: he was an inspector of police and whosoever was inside must open the door at once.

Still nothing.

'Havildar, fire your musket at the window.'

'*Ji*, sahib!'

The noise was twice that by day. The ball struck dead centre; splinters flew; one of the shutters swung open.

The inspector told him to reload and fire again.

As the havildar came to the aim, however, they heard the bar being drawn.

'Wait!' The inspector held up the lantern, and his sword.

The door opened just enough to show a face, and another, that of a child.

The inspector spoke firmly but politely: was this the house of Arjan Brar?

The woman said it was, but that he wasn't there. Another child's face appeared.

Where was he, asked the inspector.

The woman said she didn't know.

Fairbrother caught the Hindoostanee and became impatient.

But the inspector wouldn't be hurried; he had the house in a noose as tight as the thug's roomal. 'You are his wife, and these his children?'

'*Ji*, sahib.'

He asked if there were any others in the house.

She said there was a third child, an infant – a boy.

He asked if the boy were Arjan Brar's son.

'*Ji*, sahib.'

Only then did the inspector say he was obliged to search.

The woman made no objection.

The sepoys returned their swords and lit more lanterns.

The inspector began his search.

It was soon evident, however, that the woman had spoken the truth – at least that Arjan Brar wasn't in the house. Whether or not she was his wife, and the children his, was another matter; as was his whereabouts.

The inspector now ordered his havildar to make a search of everything that was in the house: 'Light all the lamps, and examine every last item.'

Fairbrother went outside again and told his men to make what breakfast they could: he expected they'd be here till daylight at least.

The inspector came out half an hour later, his face both anxious looking and exasperated. 'Captain Fairbrother-sahib, he is gone, this instant I believe.'

'This instant? How in heaven's name—'

'Sahib, there is door in floor of house, under bed of infant. There is hole in earth under wall, just one, two yard.'

Fairbrother quickened. 'You mean he may have escaped us?'

'Sahib, there is sandal in hole, and other door is open yet.'

Fairbrother angered. 'But your men – didn't they see him?'

'They see nothing, sahib. It is black as the pitch, and door is hidden by wall.'

'Wall? What wall? Oh, in heaven's name . . . Too late now. We've just got to find him.'

'Yes, sahib, but how?'

Fairbrother thought for a moment. This was the inspector's business after all; surely they were used to hue and cry?

'See, he can't run far, not even with *two* sandals. It'll be light enough in an hour to search every house in the village. And if he *has* run, then he can't be more than a mile away now. We must make a cordon at once: four parties, two or three in each, to ride out a mile at the four hands of the clock – you understand, inspector-sahib?'

'Accha.'

'Then let my men take the lead, and give me four sepoys, and after you've searched all the houses you can begin searching within the cordon. There's not a lot of cover as I saw. You'll be able to search well from the saddle.'

'Accha, sahib; it is good plan.'

But he sounded dispirited.

Fairbrother softened. 'Inspector-sahib, we have his wife and children, and we can catch *him*.'

XIII

The Deceiver

Sthambadree, twelve days later

'Not a job for cavalry, but only cavalry can do it.' Hervey sighed, and none too contentedly. His regiment was strung out along the roads of the Northern Circars like the old Bow Street redbreasts. To see all of his five troop leaders in less than a week was no small achievement. The devil of it was that when they deployed in this way – not even as squadrons – they didn't in truth need his command. Sleeman had devised a very promising scheme to overwhelm the thug circle south of the Godavari, and it was now just a business of awaiting results.

There was no doubt that the dragoons were enjoying the sport. He could see for himself, and Sleeman said the same. But pleasant as Sthambadree was, and comfortable his quarters – a fine *haveli* whose widowed chatelaine was only too glad of their company – he chafed at wasting his time here. He might as well have stayed in Madras and tried his hand in the Coromandel Cup. With Granite, his Marwari-Arab, he'd had a good chance of winning. Except that he could hardly prize chasing pig over even more dangerous quarry.

Perhaps there'd be opportunity next year. *And* a good many years after that. He smiled ruefully. The Indians always said they never saw a British grey-hair: the officer-sahibs either died or were posted home, the Company men took their fortunes and returned to England for a life of leisure. Yet *he* seemed destined to prove them wrong.

Not that prolonging command wouldn't be the greatest satisfaction – he'd thought of little else but command for twenty years – but command prolonged was ultimately command exhausted. He didn't feel exhausted – he *wasn't* exhausted – and was sure that others didn't think so; but five years, as soon it would be, and with little prospect of action . . . Action, at least, as he knew it . . .

Except this business of Chintal, perhaps. Yet somehow he couldn't think it would come to a fight. When last he'd seen their army it was scarcely more than a rabble militia. A show of red-coated force would have scattered them like chaff before the wind. Nor was Chintal like Coorg: there were no mountains to speak of, no hanging forests, no rushing rivers. Above all, their 'rajah' was a woman.

And yet, as Garratt himself had said (and many another), in cleverness and fortitude – in sheer gameness – the female of the species *Felis tigris* was greatly superior. Garratt respected the tigress because she raised her cubs and fended off predators, and would die in the act if need be. A tigress was like a fighting cock, which gives battle though knowing it will be killed.

Well, he, Hervey, had seen tooth and claw enough in the Princess Suneyla when first he'd been in Chintal, and perhaps would do so again when it came to his mission of observation (in truth a reconnaissance for war). The Ranee was mercurial, said Sleeman, as well as venal – Hervey certainly knew of the quicksilver – and quite possibly on the lookout for a pretext to make war with Fort William, if only a war of words and martial bluster. And yet, Hervey would confess, he was himself animated by the prospect of seeing her again. Yes, Suneyla had schemed against her father, paying the price with banishment to the forest of the Gonds; but that apart, he'd admired her as a woman of spirit (and, he must admit, of some beauty), as well being intrigued by her . . . difference, as formed wholly in so alien – exotic – a place as this. Indeed, for a week or so they'd enjoyed some intimacy; it had been vocal only, but in the forest, when they'd gone to see the hamadryads, it had verged on something more. Later he'd trembled at the thought, for he was then affianced to Henrietta. He put it down to the heat, the humidity, the strangeness of the surroundings. No, there was not impropriety in his desire to see her again; just . . .

Meanwhile the honour of the regiment rested on his 'Bow Street patrols' – and, he'd be first to admit, on the address of his particular friend. For Fairbrother's gambit would surely prove the ace in Sleeman's game, and he was determined that his friend should have recognition. Indeed, he'd already resolved with Sleeman that they'd jointly write the citation, directly to Bentinck. It was a pity, to say the least, that Fairbrother having discovered the whereabouts of Arjan Brar, Sleeman's men let him slip. But then, although Sleeman had seen service, he seemed at heart a political. Hervey didn't suppose he'd had opportunity to acquire that *coup d'oeil* which was the mark of the true cavalryman.

And yet he couldn't condemn him, for he'd seen how calmly he'd received the information that Brar had evaded his policemen. A lesser man would have railed against the incompetence of the inspector and his sepoys, but instead he'd congratulated them for taking captive the wife and children, and thereby made a half-capable officer an entirely loyal one. Besides, with all his pretty ones in custody, Arjan Brar wouldn't lie low indefinitely, he said – and this time there'd be no escaping. (And, no doubt, he secretly chided himself for sending an inspector rather than going in person.)

In truth, too, Hervey recognized the predicament Sleeman had faced. Arjan Brar's house was in Chintal, if only a league or so. Sending his native police into a princely state was risky enough; going himself might have set back his entire scheme. Fort William had enacted the 'hovering laws' to prevent malefactors from taking advantage to carry on their trade – a right of 'hot pursuit', as the Americans called it, and the native rulers had shown no objection, but it was in their nature, said Sleeman, not to take issue with a proclamation in principle, hoping instead to circumvent it as the need arose.

Besides, he, Hervey, had another concern. Their newest approver, Ghufoor Khan himself, had told Sleeman all in a contract to secure his life no matter what crimes were subsequently uncovered; he'd sung, as Sleeman put it, like a cock linnet. That meant, likely as not, that they'd soon be sharing the road with a vile murderer – and hardly a repentant one at that. It would stick in his craw. Was it right to grant a man such as this Ghufoor Khan his life when the full extent of his crimes was not yet known? He recognized that his own world was, as the saying went, black and white (which was why the business of Major Garratt gave him so much unease), while Sleeman's was of types and shadows. How Sleeman managed being Solomon in this place he couldn't conceive. They'd spoken of it, of course, the 'greatest and continuing dilemma', and Sleeman had said simply that he slept at nights only in the knowledge that such things as condonation, repugnant that it was, might – should – in time mean the obliteration of this savage guild, and the saving of thousands of other men's lives. For to Hervey, with his Mutiny Act and King's Regulations, condign punishment (inflicted wisely) was the surer, the proven way. And Sleeman had replied that in the early days he couldn't be sure, for he too had been hard-schooled in military discipline, and his uncertainty had troubled him very greatly. Now that he believed that intelligence of the entire guild of thugs was within his grasp, however, he didn't hesitate so much, though even so there were occasions when the discovery of past crimes brought him close to revoking his pardon. That, of course, would have been the end of his system of approvers, he said; for who would betray the guild only to be hanged later, doubly damned?

Meanwhile, Hervey could console himself that he had Arjan Brar's people (his wife – one of them at least – and children) hostage, fast within the sturdy walls of the old fort of Sthambadree atop a great hill – massive, impregnable for five centuries – and under close watch of Serjeant-Major Armstrong. Nothing was impossible, but with Armstrong, the improbable was not worth a moment of his consideration. So until Sleeman returned and they could discuss their next moves, and although he would have relished any diversion, there was office to which at last he could attend.

Or rather, there were letters, for with the regiment dispersed there was really very little of routine to detain him. Indeed, that morning he'd dismissed St Alban before ten to accompany Georgiana on her daily exercise. The hircarrah had brought a full bag from Fort St George, including several letters from England. These – with a single exception – he looked forward to reading, but first there were the official papers, one in particular that caused him the keenest disquiet. Indeed, he'd been turning it over in his mind since first breaking the seal the night before, yet could find no answer, for he'd never dealt with its like. Yet the statement, from the chief book-keeping officer of the Commissariat, was categorical:

> *I am now in possession of a sworn statement by an Indian of the highest reputation that the sum of 800 Arcot Rs was paid by him to the person of Major Garratt, in inducement to tender for supplies to His Majesty's Sixth Light Dragoons at Fort St George, this Thirteenth Ultimo . . .*

He couldn't believe it. Or was it simply that he didn't want to? There was some consolation at least in reading that there was no impropriety on the part of Collins; but *Garratt*? How could a man who'd proved so faithful and active in so short a time be just as corrupt as the run of native merchants? After all his years of being under authority and having soldiers under him, was he really no judge of men at all?

But it was not a time for excessive pride. How now was he to proceed? 'Always strive to do the right thing, because it is the right thing to do.' Oh, the voice of his father, and of many a master at Shrewsbury! But what struggles of moment were theirs compared with matters of the regiment? Besides, doing the right thing was the easier part; it required only courage. How did one first discern the right thing? What indeed *was* 'right' in the profession of arms, an occupation encompassed about with a great many rules and regulations, but with rather more questions than the rules and regulations provided answers for? Was the right thing the most prudent course? Prudential judgement was the true practice of command, Lord George Irvine had been wont to say, not the blind practice of the King's Regulations and the Mutiny Act. And that, he trusted, had ever been his own conviction, albeit conscious of the human tendency towards convenience. Was it for mere convenience – the regiment's, but more particularly his own – that he now sought some way of avoiding the due process of military law?

He trusted not. He cared nothing – well, nothing very much – for what the chiselling, fraudulent merchants of Madras would think. (They would likely never hear of it anyway, for what villain would complain to another of his own corruption going unrewarded?) But the confidence in the regiment of both officers and the rank and file – the confidence that their seniors were men not only of courage but of honour – was everything. Yes, he might use this case as an exception to prove the rule – 'be ye ever so high, there is nothing higher than the law' – but what might be its dispiriting effect? He simply had no precedent to consult – or even another whom he could trust, save, perhaps, Fairbrother.

No, the decision would be his. That was the price of command.

It helped, however, that he was still in acting command of the army. It gave him some latitude – some time at least. For with the papers from

Fort St George had come a most opportune solution. But to gain that time he would have to move apace. Under the provisions of the new India Act, control of the island of Saint Helena would pass from the Company to the Crown. There was to be a three-year period of transition – the new governor, a major-general, would take up his post in a year's time – and Madras was instructed to send forthwith a lieutenant-colonel to act meanwhile as garrison commander. The appointment was thus in his, Hervey's, gift. He had the right to promote to acting rank, with the associated pay and privileges. He would appoint Garratt. Thus exiled, albeit not as permanently as had been St Helena's most notorious resident, the whole business might conveniently be forgotten. (It could certainly not be pursued except at great cost, not least in time.) And promotion would contradict any hint of taint.

It would serve, he concluded, for the greatest happiness for the greatest number.

He took up his pen and began to write the posting order.

Georgiana, meanwhile, had never enjoyed herself more. In so short a time – not even a year – she'd seen so much of the world, whereas in the whole of the fifteen years before, she'd seen but a page in the great volume. A delightful page – Wiltshire was very bliss, and London, what little she'd been able to observe, was full of wonders – but *India* . . . And now she was riding in the company of the finest of men: Lieutenant & Adjutant Edward St Alban was the handsomest, cleverest and most upright subaltern officer in the whole of the army!

'Miss Gildea, do you suppose we might ask Mr St Alban if we may cross the Krishna today?'

Annie, ever cautious – she had, after all, the care of Colonel Hervey's firstborn – wondered what there might be on the other side to justify risking any more perilous encounters with ferries than absolutely necessary. The military ones she'd been confident enough of, but the native ones were to her altogether too lackadaisical. But Georgiana was so full of zeal to see the country – she told her what the chatelaine at the haveli had said about the temple carvings in one of the villages – and the weather was as perfect as could be . . .

'Shall I ask him, Miss Hervey?'

Georgiana blushed a little. She'd thought to ask him herself, but perhaps it was more proper for her governess to.

He was anyway within earshot almost. He'd only trotted up fifty yards or so to have a word with the syce acting as guide – though what he could be saying when all he had was the stock words of command, she couldn't imagine. She did think it funny that some of the officers seemed not to be able to make any headway with the language, and not for want of trying – though St Alban himself was undoubtedly so conscientious an adjutant that he could have little time for study. And it certainly didn't help that the moonshee of whom everyone spoke had so inconsiderately abandoned his post. But that, they all said, was Indians. As Corporal Johnson had explained: 'Tha sees, Miss 'Ervey, these 'Indoos don't think like us. They reckon as they do things cos God makes 'em. Well, not t'real God – t'one they 'as. Except they 'as so many as it gets confusin' for 'em because one god says one thing an' another says another.'

It may not have been expressed with much erudition, but she'd found it a good deal more enlightening than much of what she'd read. She was glad her father let him ride out with them this morning. She'd known him for as long as she'd known anyone who wasn't family – indeed, in many ways he *was* family – and he always had a cheerful word. Well, perhaps not to everyone's mind, but she herself thought it cheerful, even if to others it sounded crabby. It was nice, too, for Serjeant Acton to have someone to talk to. She'd have been as happy to talk away with him as with St Alban – well, not quite (she blushed, again, to admit it) – but Annie didn't approve. Or rather, she reckoned, Annie didn't approve of Serjeant Acton talking to *her*. For it was plain as a pikestaff that Serjeant Acton – who was without question the finest of men and soldiers too, all that a serjeant of dragoons should look like and be – admired Annie. And Georgiana would have jumped with joy had Annie said 'yes' to a proposal . . . except that, as Corporal Johnson said, 'Officers' wives have puddings and pies; a serjeant's wife has skilly' (to the tune the trumpeter played for the mess call), and she didn't suppose that Annie liked the prospect of skilly any more than would she, especially now Annie was 'Miss Gildea' – although in character, she felt sure that Annie was now as she had always been, and that she would no more have sold herself for a bowl of skilly when there was none other to be had, as now when she dined at their own table. No, Annie deserved puddings and pies.

'Mr St Alban, Miss Hervey asks if we may take a ferry at the river today.'

St Alban had dropped back alongside them. 'Indeed? Why, Miss Hervey, do you wish to take a ferry?'

'To get to the other side, sir.'

Johnson, riding behind, snorted. He liked it when young officers – even ones like St Alban – got a smart answer.

St Alban smiled. Nor was it merely an indulgent smile for the child of his commanding officer. 'And what, Miss Hervey, is so particular to see on the other side?'

'Begum Mansoor says there are temple carvings in one of the villages that are very old.'

St Alban wasn't sure about temple carvings – there were some, he knew, that were not for the contemplation of ladies – but he supposed he could send Acton on ahead to have a look. 'Of course, Miss Hervey. We'll enquire at the next village where is the nearest horse ferry.'

Annie steeled herself to ordeal by ferry once more. She'd have to dismount, which meant that she'd have to remount, and Serjeant Acton would try to assist her, and she'd probably have no alternative but to let him . . .

But she did like being in the saddle now. The RM had even complimented her on her seat, which everyone said was no little thing, for he was a stickler for position (nor one to flatter), although how he was expert in riding aside as well as astride she didn't know.

And riding in weather such as this, fresher at last, the sun not so fierce that she had to carry a parasol (just a broad-brim bonnet served) was even more delightful. She hoped they'd get a gallop later, for this soft red earth was fine going for her mare. Granite, on the other hand, went well on any going; Georgiana had even managed to give St Alban a run for his money on the wet sand of the Saugor river a few days ago.

So they went at a trot for the next village, and found it practically empty but for dogs and an old man selling sweet lime. St Alban bought up most of the limes, while the syce asked about the ferry.

There was one a couple of *cos* straight ahead – four, perhaps five miles, said the man.

St Alban nodded. 'That's within reach. How many horses will it take?'

The syce frowned. 'Sahib?'

He tried again, in Hindoostanee.

'Sahib, it is for horses,' replied the syce, puzzled. (Had he not said that already?)

'No, what I mean . . . Curse it; Miss Hervey, can you help? I wish only to know how many horses the ferry can take at a single crossing, for if it can't take us all . . .'

'*Accha*,' she said assuredly, then rattled off the question with such clarity that the syce had no need to elaborate.

The sweet-lime-seller replied to her direct.

'It is a large ferry,' she told St Alban. 'We shall all be able to cross together.'

'Thank you, Miss Hervey; I'm obliged.'

The lime-seller glanced left and right, then spoke to her again, in a low voice.

Georgiana lowered hers too as she posed his question to St Alban. 'He asks if you are an officer of the British king.'

St Alban smiled at him civilly. 'You may tell him "yes", of course.'

She did, and the lime-seller nodded and then lowered his voice to a whisper.

The syce looked anxious, unable to catch much.

Georgiana looked confident, asked the man a question or two in clarification, and at length turned again to St Alban. 'He says he is very glad to see you, for there is no *kotwal* – policeman – here any more, and there is no one who will protect honest men. He says that a short time ago, this very morning, a large band of dacoits passed though – twenty, perhaps thirty men, not from these parts – carrying much baggage. All the people of the village ran into the fields at their approach, but he could not because he is old and infirm. They would have plundered the village, he says, but they seemed in a hurry to be on. He believes they are phansigars.'

So complete was the report that St Alban had no question to ask of their informer, only of himself: what might they do about it?

'Thank him for his information, Miss Hervey. Tell him he's an honest as well as a brave man.'

She did, and the lime-seller smiled. He replied that, being old and crippled and possessing nothing but a few lime trees, he had nothing to fear.

'Then if he is right and we apprehend these bandits,' said St Alban, 'he shall have some reward – but don't tell him that. Ask where are the nearest *kotwals*.'

She asked, and the lime-seller shook his head. He thought there were no policemen nearer than Sthambadree.

St Alban frowned – Sthambadree, a ten-mile point. And likely as not there'd be no *mounted* police there either. Except there'd be Armstrong's men, and Worsley's nujeebs waiting for tomorrow's sweep towards Kothapore. An hour to get there; then an hour back, and then beyond to the river, however far that would be.

No, they'd never be able to intercept them, not before the ferry, and once the other side . . .

Better therefore to gallop for the river and order the ferryman to stay the other side until . . .

But that wouldn't work, for they'd have to gallop past the thugs, who'd soon tumble to what was happening (they weren't fools; that's why they remained at large), and then they'd scatter, or lie low in some hideaway. No, he'd have to think of something else . . .

'Serjeant Acton, gallop for Sthambadree and tell Colonel Hervey what's t'do. Ask for every spare man to hasten here at once – here to this village and wait concealed till I return with the thugs.'

'But sir, with respect, how are you to bring them back when they're so many and there'll be just you and Johnson?'

'And the ladies, Serjeant; I'll have need of Miss Hervey to speak for me – if, that is, they're agreeable.'

Georgiana's eyes brightened. Annie's, less bright, were nevertheless resolute (the price, perhaps, of 'puddings and pies').

Acton looked horrified. '*Sir*, with *respect*—'

'I know: yours is to cover the commanding officer and anyone he appoints you to, but these are the exigencies of the service. And the ladies have their pistols, and facility with them – thanks to you.'

Acton now looked only slightly less horrified, but he was reconciled to the facts of life. 'Sir!'

'Go to it, then.'

Hervey's covering serjeant looked once more at Georgiana, as if for assurance, then saluted and reined about. 'Here, Johnno,' he said, sternly, handing him his own two pistols; 'you'll know what to do.'

Then he dug in his spurs.

Hervey broke the seal and began to read. A letter from Lord John Howard at the Horse Guards was always welcome, but now perhaps especially, for there must surely be something of especial intelligence, there being so many comings and goings in the *London Gazette*. As a rule, everything was at least six months out of date, though – even despatches by the steam route were four months gone as a minimum – but as events anyway took their time to have material effect, a considered commentary instead of a mere report was much to be preferred.

Howard, lieutenant-colonel of Grenadiers, had in successive ranks and with very few interruptions served twenty years and more at the Horse Guards (it seemed that every commander-in-chief, including the Duke of Wellington, had thought him indispensable), and was a staunch friend and supporter. Somehow he'd managed to get the letter into the official bag, and thus overland; so its date was not *too* antique . . .

It began with the whys and wherefores of various comings and goings in uniform, adding explanation to the announcements in the *Gazette*, and then (Hervey supposed) the gossip of White's club, or whatever drawing room his old friend had been gracing, relating to Lord Melbourne:

> *After my lord Grey resigned in July, His Majesty, obliged to appoint another of the Whigs in his place, as the Tories were not strong enough to support a government, sent for my lord Melbourne. Lord M however was not at first inclined to go, for he thought he would not enjoy the extra work that accompanied the office! Tom Young – his secretary you'll recall – told me Lord M said to him 'I think it's a damned bore. I am in many minds as to what to do' and that he, Young, told him 'Why, damn it all, such a position was never held by any Greek or Roman, and if it only lasts three months, it will be worth while to have been Prime Minister of England' & that Lord M replied 'By God, that's true. I'll go!'*

Hervey smiled. He'd take pleasure in showing that to St Alban. It would do no harm to tilt a little at his certainty of Whig high-mindedness. But as he read on – there were four close-written sheets – he found nothing touching directly on himself. Yet if Melbourne were now prime minister, surely it couldn't be long before Lord Hill thought it meet to approach him on the matter? After Bristol, his lordship had told him he'd put his name before Lord Goderich, the secretary at war, as a mere formality before submitting it to the King, and that Goderich had said that in the present circumstances he felt he couldn't countenance it – and that he, Hill, knew that Goderich had canvassed Melbourne's opinion and several others', perhaps even Grey's. Goderich had apparently said that once the sea was calmer he'd have no objection whatsoever. He, Hervey, had then asked Lord Hill how long he thought that might be, and Hill had said after the passage of the Reform bill. Well, the bill had been enacted these good two years, and still there was nothing. Would the 'sea' ever be calm enough? For there was but one consolation on relinquishing command – the gradation list.

So what now stayed Lord Hill's hand?

He sighed and took up Kat's letter, which had come by the Cape. He'd stared at the seal long enough; now he would screw up his courage to break it.

The trouble was, he'd not written to condole with her on the loss of her husband. The last time he'd seen her was at Bristol, when Sir Peregrine Greville had presided at the court of inquiry. She'd been dismissive, to say the least. Not that he'd no right to be dismissed, but it had been Kat herself who'd invited him to their supper party. It had been an altogether disagreeable evening, for not only had she behaved strangely, so had Sir Peregrine. It had been as if each, in their own way and for their own reason, wished to warn him off. And there could have been no reason but the birth of a son – as *The Times* had it, 'The twelfth of March at Rocksavage, County Roscommon, to Lady Katherine Greville, a son and heir.' It had struck him at the time as being a curious wording: the heir was surely to Sir Peregrine? The child had no title to inherit from him, for his was *KCB* not *Bart*, so perhaps succession in the Irish peerage followed a different rule? Perhaps the child really was the heir, through Kat, to some Athleague remainder? But why did he concern himself? Only because of the nagging doubt that Kat reserved, as it were, the paternity – and that that was the cause of Sir Peregrine's *froideur* that evening. And yet for several days afterwards he'd studied the announcements in *The Times* and found the wording entirely usual. What, therefore, was her design now in writing?

The first two pages gave him no clue. They merely told him of not so much her widowing but Sir Peregrine's passing, as if he'd been a distant cousin of theirs both. There were expressions of sorrow, but they lacked the quality of being heartfelt. Perhaps it was that she'd steeled herself to writing, as she must have done to many another. Sir Peregrine had not been a bad husband, only an absentee one, and considerably older than her. Or rather, in truth, it had been Kat who was the absentee, for she'd chosen not to accompany her husband to Alderney, where he was military governor, a post he'd held for nearly ten years before another sinecure was found for him in Ireland, which suited her more in her sudden and unexpected pregnancy. And so here was she now, a widow with child, about his age, undoubtedly left well provided for, and, he supposed, with looks and figure undiminished in the three years since he saw her last – and quite probably enhanced. What indeed was her design in writing?

The third page revealed it in part, perhaps. She'd returned to London, already disdaining widow's weeds, 'for Greville would not have wished it' –

I hear talk that you will not be long in India, that Lord Hill has need of you and that you will be major-general in Ireland or in some such place. I dined with the Duke quite lately and he was of the opinion that your promotion was much overdue, but says that he has no influence in the matter these days because the Whigs are so much in the ascendancy and he is so heartily disliked by them and said I should petition Earl Grey, but that it would almost certainly be to no avail for he is so unbending a man, and that matters would be so much better arranged were Lord Melbourne to be in his place, for Lord M is a sensible man in these tempestuous times. I do of course know Lord M, he came to dine at Rocksavage on occasions when he was Chief

Secretary but have not seen him in many months, he is so oppressed by the troubles in the country and I suppose you will have read there was a great tumult over his transporting some labouring men to Australia who had taken some secret oaths or some such and they are being called martyrs in the newspapers and even Parliament, but I shall endeavour to call upon him as soon as I am out of mourning, or even before if occasion presents itself, for I do so believe, as the Duke, that there is none more deserving of promotion after your exertions at Bristol, which Greville himself wrote to Lord M of in approbation or so I believe.

Hervey cursed. He wished she wouldn't meddle and intrigue so. It was no way for an army to arrange promotions. She'd meddled, even, with admiralcy, though in truth he couldn't regret it. She'd told him of her efforts on behalf of his great, good friend Commodore Peto, who against all the odds – confounding even the surgeons by the extent of his recovery from the terrible wounds of Navarino – was now a port admiral. But had this really been her doing? The secret, black, and midnight process by which their lordships advanced a post-captain to flag rank might well admit of petitioning, for as Peto himself had said more than once, he'd known many an officer with red, white or blue at the mizzen whom he'd not trust to take a single ship to sea. Who knew what heads could be turned by a good ankle?

And yet, if it helped his cause now, did it matter in the end? When it came to the time that he must, if with all reluctance, hand over the reins of the Sixth, could he bear to bide his time in that military purgatory between command and generalcy? Would it not be better to write in reply that he appreciated any effort on his behalf – doing so of course in a way that did not in the least suggest there remained any *tendresse* on his part – or indeed obligation – except the wholly proper feeling of friendship towards one whom he'd known before his marriage?

He suddenly, more so than since leaving Fort St George, wished that Kezia were beside him.

*

St Alban wouldn't risk a fight, even one in which he knew that his and Corporal Johnson's pistols and sabres would prevail. Not when he'd Georgiana and Annie in his care. This was not 'the exigencies of the service'. Besides, the whole idea of being here was to apprehend these villain thugs, to turn some of them into approvers, and then to hang the rest – publicly, *pour décourager* – or else transport them. And there was nothing like a gallop to stimulate the mind. By the time their quarry had come in sight he'd decided against detaining the ferry and instead to attempt a ruse.

'Miss Hervey, do you know what is the word for "opium"?'

She didn't, but the syce understood (if only the syce could string a few words of English together, or understand a few more, so that he, the adjutant of the 6th Light Dragoons, didn't have to rely on a girl of fifteen or sixteen . . .).

'*Ahiphen*, sahib.'

'*Mehrbanee,* syce-bahadur.' He turned to Georgiana, and looked resolute. 'Miss Hervey, we are from the Opium Prevention.'

Georgiana couldn't yet guess his game, but she began rehearsing the words in her mind.

They had but a minute before they overhauled the thugs.

'Salaam!' cried St Alban, pulling up sharp and raising his hand.

He wished he were in red, but blue would have to do. His cap and white face would probably be enough – that and the pistol holsters.

'Salaam, huzoor!' The party shuffled to a halt and made gestures of deference, the leader salaaming with particular cordiality.

'I am an inspector of the Opium Prevention. You have contraband opium in your possession, and sowars from Sthambadree have been ordered to take you back there.'

He nodded to Georgiana. She turned to the leader and spoke quickly and fluently, with the same note of authority. The look on the leader's face – innocence, puzzlement – told St Alban she translated well. He had to make an effort not to show his admiration.

'But huzoor, we are pilgrims! See, here is our baggage. Search it – see for yourself!'

'That's as may be, but you'll have to come back to the village you passed through last, to the customs post there, or you'll be in trouble for evasion. If you have no contraband then you'll be given a ticket of clearance to go on without further hindrance.'

It was Georgiana's turn for hiding admiration. These thugs, these phansigars, these deceivers – *they* would know they had no contraband; not, at least, the type the 'Prevention' were looking for, so they'd get a pass from the authorities that would see them safely through the whole of the Circars. It was *so* clever of him! And it was *they* who were called 'the deceivers'!

She repeated exactly what he'd said, looking as grave as she might.

The leader looked delighted (and again she had to suppress a smile). What was a delay of a few hours, of a night perhaps, to gain such a pass? He'd walk back gladly.

'*Accha,* memsahib! *Accha,* huzoor!'

'You left her? You left her with just the adjutant and Johnson? What in hell's name were you thinking of, man?'

Armstrong's voice carried across the courtyard to the guardroom. Serjeant McCarthy came running.

'Sor, is everything all right, sor?'

'No it bloody well isn't! Get every man you can on 'is 'orse. Who's guard commander?'

'Corporal Verity, sor!'

'Jesus!'

'He'll be fine, sor. What do you want for him?'

'To make damned sure them prisoners stay put!'

'Right, sor; I'll tell 'im just that. And where's it we'd be going with the others, sor?'

'Never mind yet. Just get 'em 'ere!'

'Sor!' Out scurried McCarthy like a bookie's runner. When the serjeant-major's temper was up, it was best to cut about even more than usual.

Armstrong could scarce believe it – an entire regiment, *his* regiment, and all they'd be able to muster were a few 'odds and sods'. And they'd have to leave these prize prisoners in the care of Fanny Verity and a handful of sick, lame and lazy, for Christ's sake! It was bad enough having Pat McCarthy as provost.

'Shall I find the colonel and tell him, sir?' asked Acton.

'No, Serjeant, there's no bloody time,' growled Armstrong as he buckled on his swordbelt and grabbed his carbine. 'An' I'm not letting you out of my sight till you've led us back to yon colonel's daughter – *who you should never've left in the first place!*'

Acton bit his lip. There was no answering back a serjeant-major in any circumstances, not least when he'd just left the commanding officer's daughter to a fate that couldn't bear contemplating. Besides, every dragoon knew that Armstrong had nearly died trying to save her mother from the savages in Canada. The worst thing that could ever happen was to make the same mistake with another bunch of heathens. And if a few NCOs got a chewing up in the process, what of it?

A good ten minutes passed before McCarthy returned with a corporal and eight men, but mounted ready enough.

Armstrong muttered to himself. McCarthy, who'd first been an infantryman, and as Irish as when he'd left the Bog of Allen or wherever it was (certainly when it suited him), was still the footiest serjeant on a horse – and from time to time, the footiest corporal – but his cheeriness whatever the circumstances was worth a dozen sabres.

'Pat, there's a bloody band o' bastards th'adjutant's tricked into going with 'im to a village a dozen miles off, an' the colonel's daughter with 'em an' all. Let's be about it!'

Armstrong wasn't a man for throwing over the punctilios of drill lightly, but if by now a handful of dragoons couldn't follow in good order, then he might as well hang up his spurs this moment. Out they went through the gate arch without a word, and into a trot at the foot of the ramp. He'd have to pace it; it wasn't hot compared with Fort St George, but twelve miles was a long point. He'd warm them up for ten minutes, then they'd be clear of this place and on the road south, and then he'd take it at a steady canter for a couple of miles, see how they were faring – and then they'd bloody well gallop for it.

St Alban and the others rode behind the 'pilgrims' and their carts – three of them, each pulled by a bullock – for the party knew where they were going, and he wanted to see they all got there. There was no cover beside the road, but it wasn't impossible that one of them might just manage to conceal himself in a furrow of red earth. And he wanted to keep the pace up, too. (Let them dawdle and it might be dark before they got to the village – and with fewer than they'd started with.) Even so, after an hour they were strung out like women come from a fair.

One of them had straggled so far behind that the horses were almost on top of him. The syce trotted up and gave him a push and a sharp word. The man clasped his hands together and began jabbering, but quietly.

'Memsahib,' called the syce.

St Alban nodded, and Georgiana rode forward.

'*Kya baat hai*, syce-sahib?'

The syce told her what he'd said.

She looked uneasy suddenly. St Alban saw and came up alongside her.

'What is it?'

'This man says he's a thug, that all in the band are thugs, not one a pilgrim. And there is one of them of very high rank, who's not one of their band but who hides within.'

'His name?'

Georgiana asked the man himself rather than through the syce. He in turn apologized but said he didn't know, only that they addressed him as 'Guru'.

'Why does he tell us this?' asked St Alban.

Georgiana put it to him.

The man looked directly at St Alban as he answered. 'Huzoor . . .'

Georgiana listened, asked another question, then thought for a moment. 'He says if you will promise him protection and pardon, he will show where are all the *beles* . . . the places where they bury their victims hereabouts. And he will tell the names of every thug here, and of their village, for he no longer has confidence in the jemadar, the leader.'

St Alban frowned. 'Tell him, please, that I cannot give him that assurance, but that I will speak on his behalf to the *wakeel*.'

Georgiana told the man firmly, yet with just enough of a note of sympathy to reassure him.

'*Accha*, memsahib, *accha*.'

It was two hours more before they reached the village. The bullock carts had creaked along at the pace of a lame horse, and St Alban had begun to think he might have to detach them, except that that would probably give the game away, for if the pilgrims were to be searched for contraband, how could the inspector-sahib let the better part of their baggage go? They'd guess that it was they themselves he wanted at the village, not contraband, and then all hell would be stirred.

But what to do now? How was he to detain them till help came from Sthambadree? All he could think of was making them turn out their baggage for inspection, and telling them the customs men would soon be here – delaying, equivocating, humbugging. But how long would they fall for it? What if there was no relief till nightfall? What if there was no relief at all? That wasn't possible. Acton of all men wouldn't fail. But wouldn't it be better to take prisoner now the leader, and this 'Guru'? The others would scatter, no doubt, but did it matter if he had these two? But what if there were concealed weapons and they tried to stop them taking the 'Guru'? They could, he supposed, barricade themselves in a house to wait for relief, but – in truth – two dozen armed thugs might prevail against them even then.

No, all he could do was keep Georgiana and Annie at a safe distance so they could make away fast if the tables turned. It was all a gamble; of course it was. Yet Hervey himself always said 'First reckon, then risk', and this he had. But he'd risked a great deal more than he ought, had he not?

The village had seemed empty enough when they'd first passed through. Now it looked deserted, with no sign even of the sweet-lime-seller. (Doubtless there were lookouts at even the meanest of places, and a returning dust-cloud spelled trouble.) Whether the villagers would have been help or hindrance was a moot point, but a deserted place might easily unnerve the thugs.

He made his decision. As soon as they got to the little maidan where they'd stopped and bought the sweet limes, he'd order them to lay out their baggage and unload the carts, while he and the others stayed mounted. At the first hint of trouble he and Johnson would loose off their pistols, charge and set about them with the sabre. It would be furious, bloody slaughter and they'd take down a dozen maybe. The rest would flee. That was the rule in India: when confronted by a superior host, charge without hesitation. But for the moment, it was shepherd work, and the flock was biddable.

As they reached the maidan, though, the 'sheep' suddenly became restless.

'Johnson!' he barked.

But before the pistols were out, the wolf was on the fold. Or rather, the wolves – Armstrong and his men – and circling it.

'Mr St Alban, sir!'

'Sar'nt-Major!'

Sabres sealed the exits. The maidan was now a pen; there was no escape.

'Mr St Alban, sir, a *word* if you please . . .'

XIV

Prudential Judgement

Sthambadree, a week later

'Arjan Brar taken by ruse – the nicest work you'd imagine. And all accomplished without my knowing a thing; indeed, while I took my ease here with a month's worth of the *Gazette*.' Hervey smiled at the thought of it.

Somervile sipped his coffee with a look of satisfaction. His arrival, though causing something of a stir – the Governor's Bodyguard was no less splendid a sight for being ten days on the road – had come as little surprise, for Hervey's old friend could never quite resist seeing things for himself. It was a weakness, if weakness it was, that had nearly cost him his life at the Cape. Besides, when they'd first met, Somervile had been at Guntoor. The Northern Circars he regarded still as his. It was entirely proper, he said, that he should make a personal visit, as he did to many of the districts. A single visit saved a hundred letters.

'So you've commended St Alban or reprimanded him?'

Hervey smiled again. 'My informants told me that Armstrong left no words unsaid in the latter regard. And Georgiana certainly didn't in the former.'

'I am glad to hear it. *Audaces fortuna juvat*. I look forward to hearing what Sleeman has to say.'

'He's wholly delighted. Brar is, *was*, the pivot of the system throughout the Circars – through Chintal and beyond to the headwaters of the Godavari indeed. I have to say that Sleeman judged it perfectly: he said that Brar'd be forced to try to spring his wife and all, and that's what he'd been about when they passed through the village – a reconnaissance of the fort. Really, it was quite astonishing, though, how he'd been able to go about the place without discovery. Sleeman says he doesn't know if it was by disguise or the fear of people to expose him. But that's by the bye now, since he's joined his club of approvers, and with a will.'

'And no doubt it will encourage others.'

'Really, Somervile, it's quite extraordinary to me how some of these fellows go to their deaths so readily – putting the nooses round their own necks on the gallows even – and yet others will turn coat and denounce men who'd hitherto been bosom associates.'

'I have observed that every man wishes to go to heaven, but in truth that few wish to die in order to do so.'

Hervey nodded grimly. 'Fairbrother, I might add, was first to gain the advantage. It was his address that led ultimately to Brar's capture. I've mentioned his services in a despatch to Bentinck – through Sleeman, who has his ear. I trust you'll not object.'

'Not in the least.'

'And the troops themselves have taken many thugs and common dacoits, some from information that Sleeman got, but a good many others by opportunity. The captains have done sterling work.'

'I didn't doubt they would. But this additional intelligence of Chintal, it is thoroughly opportune.'

'In what sense exactly?'

'Her Highness's complicity in all this. Don't misunderstand, me, Hervey. The charge of "Lapse" is irrefutable – her scheming in Mysore alone's sufficient, and the provocations with Haidarabad – but scheming with thugs is simple, base law-breaking. And, I have it on good authority, she puts to the sword any who disoblige her – and summarily. In the past months, several of her household have been impaled alive, barbarously mutilated, on account of their not wholeheartedly throwing in with her schemes. It seems as if she's determined to be the tigress in Chintal no less than she would be of Mysore.'

There was no gainsaying it. Hervey had not been in India so long as to believe, like the cynic, that intrigue was the natural condition of life; but then, nor was tranquillity. And the female of the species must surely be on especial guard, in a way quite different from the male. The tigress, it was said, had first to protect her cubs from the tiger.

'The problem is, Hervey, the seclusion in which the Hindoostanee woman's obliged to live isn't favourable to the development of the female character, nor does it tend to soften and improve the heart.'

Hervey raised his eyebrows, conceding. 'You, of course, know the country far better than do I.'

But, the Ranee – wayward, yes; cunning, certainly; but corrupt, cruel . . . evil?

And yet one of her bands of thugs, said the approvers, had been Ghufoor Khan's, and, as Fairbrother had discovered – with his own hands, digging out the grave (if the pit of putrefying corpses might be dignified thus) – it was Khan who'd murdered the moonshee and his family. (The child's remains had sealed the testimony.) Their blood was upon her.

If, that is, the approvers spoke – or really knew – the truth.

'I have to say that Sleeman and I are in dispute. The thug who murdered my moonshee may be a most valuable informer, but it can't expiate his sin. I'd have him hanged before the entire brigade. Indeed, I can't but think of it as a question of honour.'

'Ah,' said Somervile, with the air of a world-weary philosopher: 'we are here in the realm of judgement, are we not? Judgement as opposed to merely judging. "Prudence is right reason in action", you'll recall.'

'Aquinas? I wonder what he'd have made of India. The Gospel appears to make little headway here.'

'Aquinas was merely echoing Aristotle: *Prudentia auriga virtutum*.'

Hervey frowned. Somervile was first, foremost, a scholar. But he'd always liked that image – Prudence, the charioteer of the virtues, the one that guided the others – though chariot-racing was a ferocious sport, was it not? 'Frankly, I'm of a mind that Courage is above all things, since without it there's no guarantee of the others.'

'And I myself could not gainsay it.'

'The fact is, this Ghufoor Khan, who's murdered heaven knows how many, is to profit from his evil, whereas I am obliged to punish each and every offence against the Mutiny Act. How is discipline to be served when the regiment learns that the man who butchered Bunda Ali – who was practically on the strength – and his wife and bairns, shall walk free?'

'Ah,' replied Somervile, with the air of a man who knew he was about to preach a doctrine he didn't entirely believe: 'their reward shall be in the next world, whereas this Ghufoor Khan faces sterner judgement.'

Hervey frowned again.

'Besides, it is cruel necessity.'

'On that, perhaps, we may agree. But I shall continue to press Sleeman nevertheless to find a means of satisfying regimental honour on this account.'

Somervile smiled wryly. 'I wish you well. Now, supposing that your work in suppression of this thuggee is coming to an end, may we talk about Chintal? I have a mind to go there myself.'

Hervey groaned. 'With respect, I can't see how that would serve.'

'It would serve to assure me on certain matters.'

'On what matters?'

'Hervey, it may surprise you, but I do myself have misgivings about the new India Act. I see in it the seeds of alienation. I don't doubt – indeed, I know – there was corruption in the old system, the Company chiefly engaged in trading, but traders are by the nature of things dealers with people, the native people. Now that we're to be just governors and tax collectors and magistrates, there'll be a tendency to draw apart, and if we do so we'll lose the approval of the country, on which the whole accidental enterprise rests. This new place in Hertfordshire – Haileybury: they'll come here with high Platonic ideals as a class apart, minded to keep their virtue by distance from the "producers".'

Hervey inclined his head in a gesture of sympathy.

Somervile looked wistful suddenly. 'I suppose not the juniors, for once the smell of canvas and smoky fires gets in their nostrils, and a horse got between the knees on a dewy morning, or a walk home in the darkness and rich scent of a regular native village . . . Well, then they'll understand it's impossible to think of the Hindoo in deprecatory terms. I have, perhaps, only a few months here still, but I intend to have the smell of canvas and dew and native village in my nostrils once more, else I can't be sure of my own judgement in what we're to be about.'

'I understand, perfectly. But if you're to go, how shall I be able to make my own reconnaissance?'

'I don't propose to interfere with that.'

'My preoccupation will be your safety!'

'Hervey, what do you suppose the Bodyguard is about?'

'They would fight to the last man, I'm sure – like the Swiss Guard for the Pope. But I as the senior officer would not be at liberty to cede responsibility to them. You must see that.'

Somervile scowled. 'Yes, of course I see that. I merely supposed you'd find a way.'

'No,' said Hervey, shaking his head determinedly; 'I can't. It would be different if we were *invading*. Besides, what are these things on which you seek assurance? Why can't I answer for them? Why can't the agent?'

'The agent's dead.'

'Indeed? I'd not heard of it. How so?'

'That, I don't know either. The news isn't abroad yet. It may not even have reached Fort William. It came to the collector at Guntoor yesterday, the exchange point for Calcutta. Seems he succumbed to a fever.'

'And you suspect foul play?'

'I don't discount it.'

'Mm. But it's not, I submit, a matter requiring your personal attention.'

'I can't deny it.'

'I must say, unhappy as is the agent's death, it gives me more ostensible cause for visiting. And – how can I put this? – you didn't find me wanting in political matters in Coorg.'

'On the contrary.'

'Then I fail to see how Chintal is in any way different. Except, perhaps, the close attention of Fort William.'

Somervile narrowed his eyes. 'You think me fearful of Bentinck?'

'Forgive me. I know you to fear no one. But I know you to have a nose for trouble, if I may put it crudely.'

Somervile took some time to reply. 'There is, I concede, no compelling reason for my coming with you to Chintalpore. And also that to do so would place too great a burden on you, and to the detriment of your mission.'

'Then may we discuss my exploration on that presumption?'

Somervile smiled at last. 'We may.'

Hervey sighed with much relief. 'I'd value your opinion. I've had no opportunity to consider things further than when we last spoke in Madras.'

'Indeed, indeed,' said Somervile brightly, suddenly his old self and reaching for his case of papers. 'I ought to have said: here's the composition of the field force. It is, I'm assured – indeed, I've proved that it is so myself – substantially as you requested. Bengal's sending two battalions, as it's best we keep some strength at Bangalore, in light of the uncertainty in Mysore – and, until time satisfies that it is otherwise, Coorg too.'

'Thank you,' said Hervey, taking the papers. 'It was my best assessment, given the intelligence at hand. There may of course be need of modification – augmentation – after I've seen the country for myself.'

'Of course, though there mayn't be much time. My presence here, however, ought to serve in that regard.'

Hervey smiled. 'Assuredly.'

Somervile let him look over the papers for a minute or two.

'By the bye, you'll dine with me this evening?'

Hervey was amused that he phrased it as a question. But he supposed his old friend knew his days as governor were not long now. 'Delighted, as ever.'

Somervile slapped his thigh. 'Splendid! Do you have any sherbet?'

* * *

'Good morning, Annie. Where is Georgiana?'

Hervey had left the governor to his secretary and the correspondence that now came and went daily by hircarrah. There was an hour or so before Sleeman was due with his 'bill' for the next few days – the final few days, he trusted – and he thought they might take a stroll in the Mogul gardens.

'She has a headache, Colonel, and is resting. She said she wanted to be well for dinner this evening.'

'Oh; is she afflicted by headaches often? I hadn't . . .'

'No, not as a rule.'

'Has anything in particular occasioned it?'

He was anxious, as Annie saw perfectly well, though she wasn't sure how to reassure him in the matter. 'It is nothing to be disturbed about, Colonel Hervey. It happens . . . periodically.'

'Oh, well, if it's nothing more – not a sudden fever or some such, for they strike in this place with no notice – I'll take no account of it.'

Only then did it occur to him what Annie might be saying. It wasn't a matter that had crossed his mind before. There'd never been occasion. He tried not to look awkward. Annie herself had lowered her eyes.

'Ah, yes, something that will please you much: your brother's regiment, the Somersets – they may be coming here in a month or so . . . Yes, indeed they will be coming.'

Annie looked suddenly pained.

'I'm sure there'll be opportunity to see him.'

Tears came.

'Why, Annie, whatever's the matter?'

She told him, dabbing at her face with a handkerchief.

Hervey stood awkwardly. 'I am so very sorry. But why did you not say before?'

'Oh, sir, there wasn't cause to trouble you in it, or Mrs Hervey. Miss Hervey knows because she saw me crying one day, but I begged she would say nothing.'

His instinct was to comfort her, in the way he would Georgiana if she were distressed, but instead kept his distance.

'Please, sit down, Annie. I really am very sorry indeed, for I know you were a small family, and close. It is a perilous thing, soldiery, and the worst of it, often as not, isn't the enemy but the country and its peculiar sickness. India's a fierce and fickle place, as you've seen for yourself, and I shouldn't in the least try to persuade you otherwise if you wished to return home now.'

Annie dabbed at her eyes again, and thanked him. But she knew there wasn't the least need for him to persuade her. Her people's days were probably not long – they'd said so themselves when she'd asked them if she might go to India – and they'd said she must make her own life, and make of it the best that she could. She couldn't tell him this, of course – it wouldn't seem right, as if she were . . . well, some sort of fortune-hunter – but she could make *some* of her own feelings known at least, and plainly. (*And* if she could stop being tearful and behaving like a housemaid, and bear herself like someone respectable.)

'No, Colonel, I would not wish to return on that account.'

'Well, I am glad to hear it, of course, for neither I nor Mrs Hervey – and certainly not Georgiana – would wish to see you go. And I do commend you for your consideration in keeping the sad news to yourself, but please recollect that you are as family to us. Neither I nor Mrs Hervey would wish you to withhold something so distressing again.'

'Thank you.'

It was the first time, she'd later recollect, that she'd ever answered as a woman rather than as servant – no 'sir' or 'colonel'. What was become of her?

'Well now,' he added briskly; 'I would not have you unhappy. You'll be joining us at dinner this evening? I think Sir Eyre means to put on quite a show.'

She nodded, and managed a smile. 'I shall.'

'Capital . . . Then, what say you to a walk if Georgiana isn't able to? In the Mogul gardens. I'm greatly in need of a little exercise after so many letters this morning. You might tell me a little more of what you've observed of this place, and the business of the thugs.'

She said she would.

Half an hour later, under Serjeant Acton's ever-watchful eye, they began their stroll in the cool greenness of what had once been the private precincts of a considerable palace long dismantled.

'I can't pretend to knowing a great deal about Mogul gardens – and these here are far inferior to those at Dehli and . . .' (he was going to say 'Agra', but thought better of it, since that was now the place of her brother's grave) '. . . and Fatehpur Sikri.'

'Fatehpur Sikri is near Agra, is it not?'

He smiled to himself at his unnecessary delicacy. 'Yes. The fort and palace there are quite extraordinarily fine – red sandstone.'

'And the Taj Mahal. I have read a little about it.'

'Ah, yes, the Taj Mahal.'

'You have been there, Colonel?'

'Yes, when last the regiment was here, in Calcutta.'

'And seen the Taj Mahal?'

'Yes.'

'I had very much hoped to go and see my brother, and while there to see the Taj Mahal. *Is* it the most beautiful building in the world?'

'Well, I am at a disadvantage in that I have not seen all those that would claim to be more beautiful, but I would say that there is something to its situation – by a great river, the Jumna – and the brilliance of the marble stone, and the symmetry, and its dimensions and proportions, which are very great. It is certainly without comparison with anything I've seen, or indeed seen images of. And it's come upon from Agra – where too, incidentally, is a fine sandstone fort, which your brother would have known well; it's come upon via some miles of desert, and so it stands most impressively on the eye.'

Annie smiled. 'I wonder what my brother made of it. He may not even have seen it, of course, for he was never a one for churches and such like. He was a very active boy. But I know who were the Moguls, and that they liked to make gardens that were enclosed, but to keep out the world, rather than to keep what was within. And that they liked water for fountains and pools to reflect the sky, and that it was to remind them of the mountain streams where they came from.'

'You have indeed been reading, Annie. I understand it is exactly so.'

The fountains at Sthambadree, though, were of no great height – hardly that of a man, where those at Dehli and Agra were twelve feet and more; and the hedges and flora ran wild, though the trees gave shade, and doubtless fruit in due season. And the walls, though tumbled down, still somehow kept out the world. Besides a couple of gardeners who were not greatly exerting themselves, the place was theirs.

'Why is my brother's regiment to come here, Colonel? Will they no longer be in Agra?'

'They will return there.'

'Oh, I am sorry to ask. It's not my place.'

'You are at liberty to ask what you please, Annie, though I'm afraid that I'm not always at liberty to answer as I please.'

'Of course. It's just that I heard we might be returning to Madras soon, now that the regiment has caught these men, and I wondered if his, my brother's, regiment were to replace us – the regiment, I mean.'

Hervey warmed to her 'us'. It never went better than when a regiment's camp-followers thought themselves on the strength.

'The answer to that, Annie, is "no", on both counts. Before the regiment returns to Madras I have to visit with the ruler of Chintal, a Ranee, a princess, and then afterwards there might be need of them here a little longer. But in all probability I shall send Georgiana back if there's need for us to stay, for I don't think it would be especially agreeable to remain here then, my being away and all. Besides, I think Mrs Hervey will be nearing her time.'

Annie found this disappointing. She hadn't really supposed she'd ever be able to see Agra and the Taj Mahal, certainly not now her brother was dead, but she was finding these country parts very agreeable, not least because so was Georgiana. She'd never before enjoyed such freedom, the freedom that the horse granted – to jump a stream, to gallop, to see so much from a position of security . . .

'Of course, Colonel, though for myself I would gladly stay and see more.'

She knew that half her duty lay at Madras with Allegra, and that loyalty demanded she be with Allegra's mother for her time (which she didn't in the least resent), but there was Georgiana, whose care she'd been given . . .

'Colonel Hervey, I hope you won't think it impertinent of me, but I know that Miss Hervey, given the chance, would stay longer.'

Hervey stopped. 'You're sure?'

'I am. She knows you're to go to Chintal – oh, perhaps I ought not to have said – but I am sure she wishes to go with you. She knows the ruler is a princess, and that you saved her father's life.'

He wondered how she knew he was to go; but that was no matter. There was always camp gossip. Nor could he remember what he'd said about his time there; it couldn't have been much, for Georgiana always complained that he'd never speak of soldiery, unless a parade or some such. Doubtless, though, Corporal Johnson had woven a rich pattern of tales . . .

'Well, I'm not altogether sure it would be entirely safe. It's not the Crown's territory,' he said, taking up his stride again.

Annie wouldn't argue with him on that point; for how could she (though Georgiana had shown herself cool enough when it came to dacoits and pistols)? But her expression was obviously more than mere disappointment.

'I've already told Sir Eyre Somervile that it would be most imprudent for him to come, so I can hardly now say "yes" to Georgiana.'

This, however, seemed to permit her some latitude. 'I would say, on Miss Hervey's behalf, Colonel, that women perhaps see country and people different from men, and that this might be of assistance.'

He almost missed his step.

XV

Diplomacy

Later

'The surgeon to see you, Colonel.' St Alban laid a sheaf of papers on Hervey's desk.

It was four o'clock, and the heat of the day, nothing compared with Madras when they'd left, was comfortable without the punkah – a good time for office, however tedious, especially after so diverting a walk.

'Excellent! I trust he brings no ill news, though,' said Hervey.

It had been a week and more since he'd seen him (Milne had insisted on visiting each troop, strung out as they were around the Circars), and there were matters of business to discuss, as well as the pleasure of his company.

'I fancy that no surgeon brings wholly welcome news, Colonel.'

Hervey looked at him quizzically. 'You are a little sombre, today.'

St Alban looked awkward. 'Colonel, I have to tell you that Lieutenant Waterman has died.'

'Oh.'

The death of an officer wearing the same device on his shako – the death of *any* rank, indeed – was ever a reason for gravity. That he'd not much liked Waterman, and disliked even more the business of Askew, for which he'd held him in part responsible, was by the bye.

'Of what cause?'

'I believe that that's what the surgeon wishes to speak about.'

'Was it in Bangalore?'

'No, he'd returned to Madras. I detailed him for the rear party.'

Hervey raised an eyebrow, perplexed: first Channer sending in his papers, suddenly and without explanation (though no loss – indeed, in truth, he was glad of it); but Waterman dead? This was the solution that no one could have wished for.

'Nothing untoward?'

'Colonel, I sense that that's something on which the surgeon wishes to speak directly with you. I didn't press him. He knows where I stand, and I trust his judgement.'

'Handsomely put. Very well, show him in. And then, perhaps too, you'd better withdraw.'

St Alban bowed.

Milne came in saluting and taking off his cap in one motion.

'My dear doctor!'

He took the chair as Hervey indicated. 'A relief from the saddle, Colonel. My poor mare's carried me well this past week, but more miles than I'd foreseen.'

'Some refreshment?'

'St Alban said he'd send in tea.'

'Very well, what's to report?'

'On the whole, as regards the troops, very little. B had a man die of a convulsion, one of the new draft and—'

'Which of the new draft?'

Milne took out his notebook. 'Newing.'

Hervey shook his head. One new recruit was much as another, but Newing, the farmhand from Kent, who'd shown promise at riding school . . .

He'd only reluctantly agreed to letting them join a troop instead of the rear details (all bar two, whom the RM was certain weren't yet fit to pass out) on condition they were under the strict eye of a serjeant.

'How do you account for the convulsion?'

Milne said he couldn't, that it was almost certainly a latent condition.

'So not the fault of any neglect.'

'No, I judge not.'

'Proceed.'

'There are one or two sunstrokes, but nothing likely to prove fatal. No, I should say that the exercise is to the greater health of all.'

'And what of Waterman?'

Milne sighed. 'Now *there's* a strange case. Gibb, the Fifty-seventh's surgeon, who's doing duty, wrote me that he'd been called to his bed, Waterman having been discovered lifeless by a servant in the middle of the morning, and found no obvious sign of the cause of death, but a great odour of alcohol – brandy, he thought. He therefore had the body brought to his hospital and carried out an extensive post-mortem examination. Waterman's stomach didn't contain the excessive alcohol he'd expected, and he began to think it possible that there'd been some sort of violent reaction and Waterman had spilled the contents of his flask. An examination of his nightclothes suggested this was in fact so. He then made an examination of the exterior of the body – I have to say that I would have done so before any incision, but that's by the bye; we each have our methods – and he found two wounds on the left ankle.'

'A snakebite, you mean?'

'A krait, he believes.'

'How might he know that?'

'The bite's usually deeper than the cobra's.'

'So he died of a snakebite. Yet another, if this time more exalted than your chowkidar's wife. Though I must say I don't think I've heard of an officer being bitten in his own room, though one or two close shaves . . . I presume we may suppose he *was* bitten in his room, not elsewhere?'

'Booted, I doubt the snake could have made such an impression on his ankle, so we may presume he was indeed bitten in his room. Unbooted, perhaps, if he were in his cups, he mightn't have felt the bite, and changed into night attire and gone to bed. Or perhaps he lay with his ankle exposed. It's deuced odd, be what may.'

'A cobra came into the stillroom at Arcot House.'

'But there was no glass or flask or bottle to be found in his room. So either his nightclothes were soaked in brandy outside his room, or else the container was removed.'

A khitmagar, one of the begum's, brought them tea.

'You're saying there's something irregular in his death?'

Milne looked quizzical. 'Gibb has entered the cause of death in the register as probable snakebite, and burial has taken place. Beyond that, his profession doesn't require more of him, but as an officer he's unquiet and has reported his suspicions to the provost marshal.'

'Then there we'll have to leave matters. What a thoroughly wretched business. I'll write to his people at once, even if no more than to say he is dead and the cause is uncertain.'

Milne nodded. 'I should think that best, yes.'

'Very well, you'll join us for dinner? Sir Eyre is host.'

'Very gladly, Colonel,' he said, rising. 'If you'll excuse me, meanwhile, I should like to visit the prisoners before I take my bath.'

Hervey opened the door for him, and when he'd taken leave he called in St Alban.

'Milne has told me the deucedest thing . . .'

St Alban listened warily; then when it was finished he shook his head. 'I should have warned him to be on his guard. Sammy told me he'd heard all manner of threats, though he couldn't – wouldn't, perhaps – say who uttered them. I merely dismissed it as the stuff of the wet canteen.'

'It's conjecture only, Edward. At this stage the evidence is but circumstantial.'

'Indeed, Colonel, but if true it bodes very ill.'

'I don't need reminding of that. I don't think I ever heard of an officer being dealt retributively in so calculating a manner.'

'I should hope not.'

Hervey sighed. 'I'd better write at once. Who are his people, do you know? Sussex, I think.'

St Alban shook his head. 'I'll have the chief clerk look. Oh, and the major has arrived, and with letters for you,' he added, handing him a small bundle.

They dined in some state that evening, and a tent as sumptuous as any nabob's. The governor's baggage train had come up from Guntoor and his quarters made under canvas in the fastness of the great fort. It was here at Sthambadree that Hervey had planned to assemble the field force, and Somervile was determined to see it. He fancied (as soldier manqué *par excellence*) that he was never happier than when pointing a pistol or wielding a sabre in the company of those whose profession it was, and he was certain that it would be his last chance of military adventure. (He'd leave the reconnaissance to Hervey, but he'd not concede if and when it came to a campaign.) What would then follow after his governorship came to an end was as yet uncertain. The best he could hope for was a not too disagreeable colony somewhere, though how he'd receive such a preferment with a government of Whigs he couldn't imagine. The trouble was, he was a little too senior for a plum in Leadenhall Street, and a little too junior for one of the more sought-after posts. He'd lately been sounded for Van Dieman's Land, not long detached from New South Wales, but, as he'd said to Emma, his wife, if he had to be a prison governor he'd rather it were Dartmoor.

They were twelve at dinner, all in uniform save Somervile himself and his secretary, who both wore plain white kurtas, and Georgiana and Annie, who both wore silk. Fairbrother, released from his disguise as a *seth*, shaved, scrubbed and his hair cut and dressed, was immaculate in rifle green; the commanding officer of the Bodyguard and Somervile's aide-de-camp were equally immaculate in red; Sleeman wore the frogged kurta of the Political Service; while Hervey, Milne, St Alban and Major Garratt were in their best blue, their red put away until it could no longer be avoided.

Hervey was surprised by how pleased he was to see the major, for all the trouble he'd given him lately (the anticipation of trouble, at least). Garratt was as affable as ever. To all, he could only appear the ideal of the man of candour, the man altogether confident in his ability as a soldier, who took delight in simple pleasures – the hill and the stream, the table, and cards – content in his comfortable-enough circumstances, even though in age senior to his superior. There was really nothing more that he, Hervey, could reasonably have desired in his second in command.

And yet this wretched . . . misfeasance (there was no denying the word). And the worst of it was that if it were so, there was no knowing what else the major indulged himself in. But he'd decided on this already, had he not, in seeking to arrange the appointment at St Helena? He'd judged that the corn dealer's inducement (if it was no more than that) was a peccadillo rather than a crime; for a crime could not be overlooked. And it must surely be so, for Garratt couldn't possibly be the man he saw before them now – brave, resourceful, sociable – if at heart he was corrupt?

Then why had he not just told the commissary to bring charges, and let the major refute them and a court martial decide?

The answer was, in truth, that in his heart he feared the accusation was true, and that it might amount to a crime, and he simply couldn't bring himself to let such a friend as Garratt be brought down, and on account of a merchant who was himself corrupt enough to have bribed in the first place. He told himself it was prudential judgement; but he feared that St Helena was a stratagem of evasion.

The die was cast, however, and for the time being he had back with him a man he could trust to command the regiment in his absence, first during his exploration in Chintal, and then when he took command of the field force. For he'd done so, admirably, in Coorg. Ought he not to have told him, though, about St Helena? Yes, in the ordinary course of things, but . . .

'And so tomorrow you'll hang another half a dozen, Major?'

Sleeman was somewhat taken aback by Somervile's bluntness, if only because there were ladies present and the khitmagars were still serving.

'I shall indeed, Sir Eyre, the very worst of a Sabar band from Odisha – a thoroughly criminal tribe – brought five days ago on account of an approver. And thanks to your Captain Vanneck's troop, Colonel Hervey.'

Hervey, sitting opposite and to Somervile's right, nodded appreciatively. 'But not the worst of Ghufoor Khan's band yet, Major Sleeman?'

'Their time will come, Colonel, I assure you,' he replied firmly.

'But not the *very* worst, I fancy: Khan himself.'

'With respect, Colonel, we have discussed this already, and at some length. I must choose the greater good.'

Somervile, warming to the discussion, decided to press him. 'So, Sleeman, you play God.'

'I fear, Sir Eyre, that from time to time we must do so.'

The governor tapped the table. 'I heartily concur. That indeed is our burden. I myself would declare the entire thuggee caste – for a caste apart is what it is – outlaw, and then there'd be an end to the elegant points of what our American cousins are wont to call "due process of law". No honest Hindoo I've met in all my years – and they're mostly honest, in their own way at least – would ever object to such methods.'

Hervey had no argument with that, or indeed with Sleeman's doctrine. He wished only for retribution for the murder of Bunda Ali and his family, the more so since hearing Fairbrother's account of finding their remains.

He glanced towards the end of the table to see how Georgiana was faring – if she was listening indeed – and saw both she and Annie were quite oblivious to the talk, and instead engaged in diverting conversation, Georgiana with St Alban, and Annie with the aide-de-camp. Except that whereas St Alban managed wholly to engage Georgiana's attention, Annie's eyes were still able from time to time to take in the rest of the table.

He smiled to himself; she really was a most diligent governess.

'So this Ghufoor Khan, Hervey, will have to fall prey to a hungry tiger, or to one of his own band, except that Sleeman here will've hanged 'em all,' concluded Somervile, taking up a spoon to his soup.

'I've no hesitation in saying "Amen" to that, however profane,' replied Hervey.

Somervile nodded. 'By the bye, I gave my travelling chef licence to surpass himself this evening, for I fancy you've been on meagre fare these past weeks.'

Hervey smiled again, but this time not to himself. Somervile's delight in the pleasures of the table would surpass that of the hungriest cornet.

'*Potage à la Julienne*, gentlemen. Not St Sulpice's best soup, but lobsters are not too many to be had, if at all, this side of the Krishna.'

He smiled again. When first they'd met, not long after the French wars, Somervile had called himself a Hindoo, and damned the eyes of those setting themselves apart from the country – those who on every occasion insisted on 'the roast beef of old England' instead of curry and rice. John Bull himself would have eaten curry and rice were he to have come to India, said Somervile. Yet here he was, now, 'Frenchified'.

Somervile had his reasons, though, as he'd already explained. If it came to the removal of the Ranee of Chintal, as it must, the manner of her exile would be of the first importance. There was already disquiet in London over the annexation of Coorg, and if that were so, the tendency would be to even greater revulsion in the case of a helpless female. He would therefore receive the Ranee not as a captive, but as an honoured guest. He intended somehow crafting a tale of deliverance from evil, of rescue indeed. She would doubtless receive a considerable pension (Fort William had yet to inform him of the terms). An Elba or St Helena did not await her. Rather did Monsieur St Sulpice's cuisine.

Whatever the case, he was determined that he himself would not be made a scapegoat. Nor, indeed, would he have his old friend made one either.

So in that great cause of diplomacy, Somervile's guests proceeded through a menu of sardines brought from Marseilles by means that could scarcely be imagined, broiled partridge and quail shot on the plain west of the Ghats three days before, 'Madras venison' – wether mutton (or more probably goat) fuddled and rubbed with allspice and claret – and then blancmanges and sweetmeats; and all with the finest burgundy and sweet white wine. The Bodyguard's little band played airs throughout, and the conversation was plentiful.

When the cigars had been smoked and the brandy imbibed for digestion, and thanks to the host offered and leave taken of him, Hervey got into the gharry hired for the evening with Georgiana and Annie to drive the half-mile or so to the haveli. There was a moon, and the walk would have been easy as well as pleasant, but he wouldn't risk it. Sthambadree was a peaceable place, with a good native police inspector, but beyond the pale of a garrison town it was never wise to be too certain. The Sixth had stirred up a good deal of trouble these past weeks, and Serjeant Acton had been adamant – riding even now close behind with carbine and pistols primed.

Georgiana was smiling yet. (Was it her first dinner in state?)

'How did you find Mr St Alban this evening, Georgiana? You appeared to be in quite animated conversation.'

'Oh, Papa, he is so learned in everything. He has such decided views on all manner of things: the new Act – the India Act, I mean – and the government at home, and so much more. And he has just read, for the second time, Mr Gibbon's *Decline and Fall of the Roman Empire*!'

She continued for several minutes, keen to retell what was St Alban's opinion on this and that and everything.

Annie sat silent, but content-looking, as if pleased for her charge.

At length, courtesy alone required that Hervey say something to her. 'You found the dinner and the company agreeable, Miss Gildea?'

Annie smiled, almost as if to laugh. 'Oh, it was delightful, Colonel.'

'Really? How so? The aide-de-camp appeared to me to be a little earnest.'

'Oh, Colonel, do you know that in the Third Madras Light Cavalry, the lieutenant-colonel is not called the commanding officer but the commandant; and that the officer's sword has one half of one inch less curvature than the sowar's; and the peak of the officer's shako is made of sealskin whereas that of the sowar is made of goatskin; and a lieutenant's sleeve braid has four ounces more silver bullion thread than a cornet's; and—'

Hervey began to laugh; and then Georgiana – and Annie.

PART THREE

CHINTAL

XVI

A Nine-Gun State

Ten days later

They'd passed through the customs post at Kothapore two days earlier without hindrance. The papers had been sent to Chintalpore a month ago, and in any case there was little that a few customs officers could do to bar the way to a half-troop of cavalry. But since then they'd hardly seen a smiling face, even a child's. Sullen, wary, or else resigned (whatever it was), the face of the Chintalee ryot was not that of his cousin in the Circars.

Whether they themselves – his dragoons – were the reason, Hervey couldn't tell. No doubt the unexpected appearance of soldiers from the Company – or elsewhere for that matter – didn't bode well for a ryot. If he were, say, in some manner connected with thuggee, it might mean his livelihood was about to be taken away; and if he were an honest man he could scarcely expect to profit from war, for both sides would trample his crops without remorse and take his livestock, such as it was, and probably his womenfolk too.

But it was hardly his, Hervey's, business. Fort William had decided that Chintal must be annexed, and he therefore must make a plan of campaign; and as the Duke of Marlborough said, no war could ever be conducted without good and early intelligence.

'I'm intrigued to see what the palace has become, how the Ranee's spent her rubies. It was a rather delightful affair, as I recall, a jumble of styles, Hindoo and Mogul, all domes and pyramids jostling along side by side – rather like the people. Much marble and alabaster, too, with a vein of red I hadn't seen before, nor since. Most attractive. But that was the late rajah's time. I fancy the Ranee has her own tastes; and, rather more to the point, the means to indulge them.'

Annie didn't think she'd ever seen a ruby, but thought to keep that to herself. Besides, it was the least of her concerns. If this Ranee, who was clearly a woman of intrigue, were to receive them, she'd be at pains to flatter, and probably therefore to pay Georgiana great attention, which would mean she'd probably keep her – Annie – at a distance. Yet Georgiana was her charge. How could she exercise it if this Ranee thought she was just a servant? A princess was surely going to know she'd risen from nowhere; women had instincts about these things, Hindoo women especially, for 'caste' seemed to be everything in this country, or so they said. And, in truth, Colonel Hervey had spoken of her with evident admiration – 'she has much intelligence, and her English is quite excellent' – and he'd thought her, then, perhaps eighteen or nineteen; so now, she reckoned, this admirable princess would be grown to the full attraction of womanhood. It made her uneasy, for no matter how much she herself observed and imitated, and read, she knew it could never be the same . . .

She was pleased, at least, that Mr St Alban had assigned two pack-horses to her, so that she could bring some silks. She'd no jewellery though, just the pearl necklace given her after the business of the cobra (even now she shuddered each time she put it on, minded of that terrifying encounter with Eternity), and she supposed the Ranee would be spangled with all manner of precious stones.

In truth, at that moment she'd have been glad to return to Madras and take up embroidery.

Except that Georgiana was thoroughly enjoying the adventure, and she herself wanted very much to see a real palace. Besides, Colonel Hervey had asked them to be his eyes and ears when he couldn't see and hear for himself.

No; she'd not just be Dorcas again.

They reached Chintalpore towards the middle of the afternoon, exactly as he'd planned: it was cool, and there were four hours of daylight left. Worsley's lieutenant, with half a dozen dragoons and the Guntoor baboo as translator, had ridden ahead to make the arrangements, and found quarters laid out for them by the Ranee's bodyguard in the old zenana (the women's quarters) on the edge of the city, a place of security with its high-walled gardens running down to a canal which took water from the Godavari to the palace half a mile to the west.

They'd had a good view of the palace as they approached, and all agreed it was a sight to behold. Hervey told them how it had been built two centuries before to celebrate the birth of the rajah's great-grandfather, whose own father had visited the water gardens of Italy and had wished for fountains of his own. But the Moguls, although they'd always prized the play of water, hadn't been able to achieve the height of the fountains of Rome, and so he'd brought home with him a Venetian engineer.

The palace sat prettily on a shallow hill. There were several higher ones, but the engineer had chosen the site to produce the most spectacular cascades. It was imposing, therefore, rather than dominating, and when he, Hervey, had first taken up his sabre, the rajah had rued the compromise, for it was overlooked by three hills within cannon range. Since then, however, the palace had been much fortified, with bastions, a curtain wall and a vast moat.

He, himself, was not to be quartered in the old zenana, however, but as the guest of the Ranee, at the palace. He could hardly decline the hospitality, though he'd considerable qualms about accepting it while at the same time taking advantage to calculate how best to deprive her of her inheritance: *The hand that mingled in the meal / At midnight drew the felon steel, / And gave the host's kind breast to feel / Meed for his hospitality!*

True, he'd done the same in Coorg. But at least in Coorg it had been a clear-cut affair: the rajah was an oath-breaker, a usurper, a tyrant, a murderer. He was yet to understand how the Princess Suneyla he'd known had become 'Queen of Thugs'. Was there a single shred of evidence that an English court would accept; only the word of 'approvers' – thieves and murderers turned King's Evidence to save their own skin? And whence, indeed, came this intelligence of her claim on Mysore? The more he thought of it, the more his unease.

Except that in this land, nothing was beyond belief. Suneyla had once told him of Ravana, the great King of Lanka, who on finding the mountain of Kailasa barring the way of his chariot, asked the mighty peak to step aside for him; and when the mighty peak, as the abode of Shiva, refused, he climbed from his chariot and of his own strength lifted the mountain clear. And when he, Hervey, replied that it was a fine *mythos*, she'd protested that it was truth.

So he must trust in the lord at Fort William, and do his duty. And as soon as he'd satisfied himself that Worsley and his half-troop were quartered safely and comfortably, therefore, he'd set off for the palace with the largest party he dared – Georgiana and Annie with their two ayahs, Serjeant Acton and Corporal Johnson, Fairbrother and St Alban, with the baboo, two orderly dragoons and half a dozen bearers and syces.

As that first time, when he'd worn the aiglets of an aide-de-camp and the two Bath stars of a captain, they were met by the rissaldar of the Ranee's bodyguard at the foot of the *droog*, the great earth ramp that led – over the drawbridge – to the inner bailey. Here they dismounted to be borne ceremoniously by palanquin to the turreted gates commanding the ascent, where, as also on that first occasion, they observed the customary propitiatory offering to Pollear, the protecting deity of pilgrims and travellers. One of the bearers silently unwound his turban, gave one end to the other bearer, and then they stood either side to bar entrance. Hervey placed some silver into their palms before passing over the lowered cloth and through the portals into the courtyard.

He'd no more idea now than when he'd first been carried up, why it was the custom, and imagined that neither had the rissaldar or the bearers. Things were done in India because they'd always been done, and anything that involved silver passing from one hand to another was doubly cherished.

The rissaldar spoke no English – by choice or otherwise he couldn't tell – but the baboo was at hand. The Ranee had been visiting with the Raj Kumaree of Nagpore, he explained, and would be returning tomorrow. Meanwhile the household was at the service of her guests, adding that he and the other officers of the rissalah, the bodyguard's cavalry troop, would be hunting pig soon after sunrise and that Hervey and his guests were most welcome to join them. Hervey thanked the rissaldar in as much Hindoostanee as he could fluently muster – he knew it was a besetting fault of his, to be averse to making mistakes – and said he'd be delighted to. The khansamah and a small army of servants showed them their quarters, arranged baths and told them of their evening's fare and entertainment.

They were being treated royally, of that there was no doubt. Hervey wondered if it were by command of the Ranee herself or by her dewan. Perhaps it didn't much matter; an embassy from the Company would hardly be treated with discourtesy, no matter how ill-disposed the host.

Had he met this Ashok Acharya, the first minister, that time before? Then, it had been Kunal Verma who'd been dewan, and who'd met his end by an unknown hand (an end that few could not have welcomed, so thoroughly corrupt was he). Somervile had said he was surprised that the politicals, both his own and those at Fort William, knew so little of Acharya, and voiced his disdain for the late agent, who ought to have been reporting every detail.

In any event, their quarters were light and cool – high, airy rooms with fretted windows opening on to the water gardens. He couldn't recall which had been his the first time, but Johnson said he thought they were the same – just with more gilding (doubtless the bounty of the rubies).

'And them,' he added, pointing to two lattice gratings high in the walls.

Hervey looked.

'Eh, *bien vu!*'

'Colonel?'

Walls had ears – the 'ears of Dionysius' – just as before. He made a sign of appreciation. Johnson understood.

Then it was time to bathe; and afterwards to dine, which they did in a room furnished in the European style (and, again, with 'ears'); just the five of them – Hervey, Fairbrother, St Alban and 'the ladies', although Acton insisted on being present, upright in a corner resting on his sword throughout (though he did concede to hospitality by not drawing it from its scabbard). Later he would keep guard in the corridors with the two dragoons, catching a little sleep when he could. A coverman's capability was judged in one way only, the safety of his principal. Success would bring promotion, failure oblivion. It was a powerful spur to vigilance.

XVII

The First Spear

Next day

'*Chota hazree*, Colonel.'

Johnson had taken to announcing his customary 'dish o' tea' like the bearer who brought it at Arcot House (though without the 'sahib' that ended every one of Sutty's statements) and who'd kept with them these past months no matter what the heat and dust. (His name was Sutantu – the Lord Shiva – but Johnson thought 'Sutty' was more regimental.)

'And Sutty's made some 'oney cake.'

It wasn't yet light, and none too warm, and in truth Hervey would have preferred to lie a little longer, but tea was always enough to fortify him. At least his razor could stay in its place, for he'd shaved before dinner.

'Who roused you?'

''Ave been awake for 'ours.'

He didn't ask why. It wasn't the time to hear the litany of instincts, misgivings and suspicions that invariably came with the first night in a new billet.

He looked at his watch. 'Ragjiv's making ready?'

''E is, Colonel. Been up for ages. Gave Minnie 'er corn an hour ago.'

Hervey counted himself doubly blessed with his bearer – he didn't like 'dressing-boy', as they called them in Madras – and with Ragjiv, his syce. Johnson had trained them well, though he said they hadn't needed any training, just acquainting with regimental ways – which was tantamount to meaning his, Johnson's, ways.

But as he sipped his tea, the perennially unwelcome thought came to him: how much longer would he – could he reasonably – be able to count Corporal Johnson his man? Twenty-five years it had been, as good as. Perhaps it had been that morning on the ridge at Mont St Jean that sealed the bond, when with the rain still beating down the then Private Johnson had brought him a canteen of tea – hot, *piping* hot, and he, Hervey, a cornet, when not even his captain's groom had managed more than brandy. *Were you too at Waterloo? / 'Tis no matter what you do, if you were at Waterloo . . .*

But the hour before dawn wasn't the time for philosophy, or for addressing the future. *Sufficient unto the day* . . . There was pig to be hunted – and, no doubt, the reason for the invitation to be revealed. For nothing here could be taken as merely incidental.

Sutty came a few minutes later with a bowl of hot water, and a new-boiled egg, and then in an hour, as the sun rose, he joined Fairbrother and Serjeant Acton in the courtyard – just the three of them, for he'd thought better of asking Georgiana, wanting no distraction. For then too St Alban would have had to come and play the escort, and there was work for him elsewhere. Nor would he take the baboo, for he reckoned his Hindoostanee ought to be up to chasing pig.

Minnie looked as fresh as the day they'd left Madras. He'd thought he might instead ride Granite – he'd schooled the gelding for the chase, after all – but Georgiana had taken to him, and he to her. Now, though, he was having second thoughts. Minnie had a big stride and plenty of speed, but Granite was perfection, a clean-bred little horse, quick to turn and light to the rein, and fast over a quarter of a mile, with a bold eye and courage beyond praise . . . There again, they weren't competing for the Coromandel Cup. Whatever was the rissaldar's game this morning, he was sure that Minnie wouldn't be outrun by native cavalry.

They were in the saddle when the rissaldar's party arrived, so the introductions were brief, no handshakes. Acton, in his red, with carbine and sabre, looked them over with his usual suspicion. Three officers (the rissaldar and two jemadars) with three orderlies, none with long guns, but holsters on the saddles and the orderlies with swordbelts – quite a fight if it came to it, two spears against three, and he against the sowars. He reckoned he'd take two with the sabre before they knew what was happening, and the third would then bolt, likely as not. Their pistols probably weren't capped either, so he'd have the advantage if it came to that too. He'd just have to trust that the colonel and Captain Fairbrother could hold off the three officers with their spears, or else their Derringers, till he could bear down on them in turn . . .

The rissaldar explained that they'd be drawing the country to the west. There were nullahs there, and some of them difficult to see till on top of them, but plenty of *jhow*, the tamarisk, the bushy manna tree – common cover for pig. At this time of year there were numerous sounders, as well as singleton boars, he said. They usually took three or even four in an hour.

Fairbrother had yet to wield a spear. They hadn't hunted pig at the Cape. 'Just recollect that a horse can go where a pig goes, and let him have a long rein,' said Hervey as they broke into a trot, clear at last of the rings of earthworks, all of which had been thrown up since his first coming here. (What troops there were to man these fortifications no doubt he'd find out.)

'Chintal's not famed for its country,' he added as they debouched onto the grassy plain. It was on the whole rather flat, much of it jungled; and there was nothing very much ancient about Chintalpore which, in decay, would give it the consequence and grace of other princely seats. It was nothing to Coorg, with its hills and noble forest, its fast-flowing streams and sudden vistas. But trappy jungle had its fascination, he supposed, not just for sport but for its mystery. Who knew what it concealed, of past or present?

Fairbrother heard him without remark. It was an unconscionable hour to be abroad, even for sport, and to hear that the country sounded no more appealing than Goree (of late memory) didn't conduce to conversation.

There were no beaters that Hervey could see, so he imagined they'd simply be riding-up, springing the game themselves. He'd no objection to that. Perhaps he might learn something of value, if there was any conversation with his hosts, though so far the rissaldar seemed disinclined.

But they did seem to be making very determinedly for a particular patch of jhow. He supposed they must hunt the ground regularly.

Sure enough, as they got close to fifty yards a huge boar – a single pig, a 'sanglier' – broke cover.

But not as if they'd bolted him. And as he spurred after it he saw it was let slip from a frank. (They'd long given up the practice in Madras, too many beaters gored in the process of taking a pig captive and then carting it elsewhere.)

No matter; the boar ran hard.

Hervey raced straight ahead – the first rule – then on to the line. For not to ride exactly the line that the pig ran would lose ground, and often as not bring a spear to grief – a lesson he'd learned the hard way. There was no seeing the country; the horse did that – a good horse anyway. Let the pig be the pilot, to tell the horse where to put in a fifth leg, and where to shorten its stride. There was never so much trouble riding hard on a boar's line; the trouble came with trying to ride a parallel one – or a general stern chase.

Fairbrother was to his left some lengths back, but the rissaldar was coming up hard on the offside – too close for comfort if the boar jinked, and with it Minnie, as she certainly would on a long rein. The fellow risked a foul, indeed, except this wasn't the Coromandel Cup; there was no umpire – no rules.

Hervey gave a touch with the shaft of the spear, and Minnie lengthened. The boar ran straight and fast for half a mile, just the one nullah giving it a bit of a scramble, which Minnie took without check, gaining a little more ground. Fairbrother was with him still (Acton too), but the rissaldar and cohort were beginning to crowd him, more intent on riding him off it seemed than getting to the pig first. He'd have cursed them had they been his, but there was nothing for it now but to give Minnie her head and trust to her blood.

Another fast half-mile, the boar still not tiring but the rissaldar several times close to colliding, forcing Hervey to keep drifting off line and swear like the army in Flanders. Two more nullahs, one so wide it needed three full strides, the boar losing ground again, but still not enough for him to close, and Minnie starting to blow. Then three narrow ones in a row, unseen. She jumped big each time, but one of the jemadars didn't, and fell hard. Fairbrother stayed clear on his nearside, but Acton had closed on the rissaldar. (If the colonel fell it would be the rissaldar's fault, in which case . . .)

Still the boar ran straight. He'd surely need cover soon to catch his wind? There was jhow to left and right.

But he wouldn't yield. On and on, without slowing – not as much as the field at least. Two more nullahs checked them (needing a stride and a half) and nearly tumbled Fairbrother, yet somehow increased the boar's velocity. Never had Hervey seen pig run like this, even in Bengal. If they'd been at Fort St George he'd have pulled up and touched his peak to him. But it wasn't Fort St George, and – no doubt of it – the rissaldar was harrying him . . .

Yet another nullah, half hidden by tiger grass and camel thorn: Minnie stumbled, recovered and then jumped big.

But the boar disappeared.

Hervey pulled up and stood in the stirrups. He'd not let it get away, no matter how long it took. But all around was thick cover . . .

He began casting about looking for 'pug' (spoor), but the thorn was close set and the horses had roiled the open.

Nothing – not a clue.

They'd have to beat him out. But from so much thorn – *how*? What would—

'Christ!'

It burst from cover not twenty yards off – massive, fast and straight for him.

He just got the point down in time to spur Minnie to meet it square. The impact nearly pitched him from the saddle, and he struggled hard to hold it off, though the point had gone deep.

Minnie, nostrils flaring but answering loyally to the leg, kept her ground until at last the boar, exhausted, gave way, toppling like a sniped stag.

Hervey jumped down. 'Carbine, Sar'nt Acton!'

He'd no intention of just letting it bleed to death; and a Derringer wouldn't do.

Acton unshipped the carbine – it was ready primed – and handed it him. 'A good size, Colonel. And a fighter.' (He'd leave his observations about the native officers till later.)

'Indeed.'

A shot, a grunt, and then it was over. Hervey handed back the carbine and touched his cap to the trophy.

The rissaldar, come from the other side of the jhow, jumped down beside him.

'The colonel is a great *shikaree*,' he said in English, and with a smile that was almost warm.

Hervey simply nodded, and coolly. He'd no desire to be complimented by a junior, especially one who'd nearly unseated him. But the admonitions could wait – and the fathoming of what on earth he'd been about.

'The village chief will come with his men to take the boar,' said the rissaldar, pointing to the smoke rising in the distance. 'Please come away now, Colonel, for there is someone who wishes to meet with you.'

Fairbrother heard, and gave Hervey a quizzical look, as if uneasy.

'Who, Rissaldar?'

'I am bound not to say, Colonel-sahib. Please come.'

Hervey managed to suppress his irritation, just. 'We'd better accept, I think,' he said to Fairbrother, mindful that he didn't know just how much English the rissaldar understood.

'Very well.'

The rissaldar looked relieved. '*Mehrbanee*, Colonel-sahib.'

It was the second time he'd added 'sahib' to 'colonel' – a definite sign of subordination, of submission even. Hervey couldn't fathom his game.

Tired though they were, the rissaldar put his horse into a canter and turned north towards the forest a quarter of a mile away. Only now did Hervey appreciate they'd come so close, for he was sure the boar had run in the straightest of lines – though perhaps it was the forest which bent south?

Then he saw: spectators, mounted, two dozen and more, by the forest edge.

A little further and he realized who it must be.

The rissaldar slowed to a trot as one of the party – an officer in the uniform of the bodyguard – advanced to meet them.

Fifty yards short, they halted.

'Colonel Hervey, I am Rissaldar-major Natu,' said the officer, in the clearest English. 'I am sirdar of the household. The Ranee wishes you to be presented.'

Hervey angered. He'd been sported with. For what purpose? He kept it close, however. It wouldn't do to show.

He nodded, and followed keeping Minnie collected, weary though she was.

He looked the Ranee straight in the eye as they neared. She sat composed, astride, splendid in blue silks, and flanked by sowars and an assortment of courtiers – men, all; not another of her sex in sight.

Had she played him as a cat's paw, if at a distance?

But he'd not given her cause for triumph, at least; if that had been her intention. Neither pig nor nullah – nor rissaldar either – had unseated him. If she, the would-be 'Tigress of Mysore', had intended humbling the Company's representative – the British Crown's, indeed – she'd not succeeded.

In fact, she'd surely set back her cause by challenging the supremacy of the Company in front of the court – albeit in sport (though wasn't sport the image of war?). Indeed, was it not perilous to have done so before not just her courtiers but her bodyguard – her praetorians, who like all praetorians might unseat *her*?

He was defiantly triumphant.

Minnie was blown, however, her neck and flanks drenched, her breathing heavy. His every instinct was to dismount, run-up the stirrups, loosen the girth and lead her in hand. But he couldn't present himself on foot to any man or woman who remained in the saddle. Minnie would have to bear it a little longer. She'd have every attention as soon as may be.

He pressed forward, but the Ranee herself suddenly dismounted – and as elegantly as it was unexpected.

He cursed beneath his breath. She'd outplayed him, forcing him now to dismount, Acton taking the reins before himself springing from the saddle, along with Fairbrother.

'Your Highness, may I present Colonel Hervey,' said the sirdar.

It had been eighteen years. How long she'd spent in the forest of the Gonds – in just what circumstances, comfort and liberty – he'd no notion; but the years had been kind. Excessively kind, perhaps. She was the same slender figure of their first encounter; her face, lighter than the Madrasi women whose complexion he'd so much admired in those days (and did yet), was unlined; her hair, jet black, was just as he remembered, and her eyes larger still. Though unadorned by any jewel save a gold pendant on her forehead, she remained, by any estimate, a beauty of high degree.

'Her Highness Princess Suneyla Rao Sundur.'

If the sirdar knew of their tryst in the forest all those years ago, when the sampera – the snake-catcher – had hissed to bid them be silent as they crept to the nest of the hamadryad, and Suneyla had taken his hand and squeezed it in a gesture of reassurance, and he'd not loosed it, so that then, moving a little ahead, she was leading rather than walking with him in that place of primal instincts . . . If the sirdar knew, he concealed it perfectly.

No, the sirdar could have no idea. He himself had thought almost nothing of it until now. *Now*, when ceremony made memory suddenly vivid by contrast.

What *was* this game she was playing? Why had she prepared this . . . contest, this spectacle, like the *munera* of Ancient Rome?

'Your Highness,' he said simply, saluting.

She had once called him *Matthew* – for a moment or two, in the forest – and now all was formality.

But she smiled as she held out her hand – a confident, regal smile (meant no doubt for those who watched). Even so, it disarmed him in part, for a smile – however devious – was hard not to reflect. And to be other than gracious was anyway to risk the resentment of her followers, and therefore his purpose in Chintal. He took her hand and bowed.

'Colonel Hervey, it is good to see you again. Or is it "General"?'

The enquiry might be innocent enough, but it might also suggest remarkable intelligence (of his coming command of the field force). 'Colonel, Your Highness.'

'I observed the chase keenly, Colonel. I hope you enjoyed it. It was close run.'

He wasn't sure if she meant with the boar or the rissaldar, but he wouldn't give her the satisfaction. 'A noble beast, Highness.'

'Your horse is fatigued, let me find you another.'

'Thank you, ma'am, but she'll recover soon enough. She has bottom, as we say.'

The Ranee smiled again. 'I had thought your daughter might accompany you this morning.'

'I hope I may have the honour of presenting her later, Your Highness. Meanwhile, may I present my good friend Captain Fairbrother of His Majesty's Cape Mounted Rifles.'

He beckoned his good friend forward, and they went through the formalities again. Suneyla was all politeness.

She asked how long they intended staying. 'I understand there will be matters requiring attention with the sad death of Mr Weller.'

'There will, Your Highness, but not, I think, detaining us much more than a week,' said Hervey.

'Then I look forward to the pleasure of your company in that time, and of your daughter, and of course Captain Fairbrother. You will dine with us this evening, I trust.'

'Thank you, ma'am.'

'Oh, and while you are in Chintal, I hope you will take opportunity to visit with Colonel Bell – you recall? He came to assist my late father. He is old now, and rather – as you say' (she smiled as she turned the phrase) '*infirm*, but I believe he would wish a visit by a fellow-countryman.'

Hervey had met Colonel Bell but once. Evidently he'd taken residence, though this was the first he'd heard of it. Yet what interest could

Suneyla have in such a man, who was plainly no longer of use to her – not, at least, the use for which he'd first come to Chintalpore, command of troops?

Curious, too, that she singled him out for mention now, rather than later.

He would speak with Fairbrother.

XVIII

The Tamasha

Later

Hundreds upon hundreds of candles: they filled the marbled dining hall with the warmest light and most pleasing of perfume. The guests, a good many in addition to Hervey's party, sat on cushions at a table laid with a gold cloth and jewelled dishes of pomegranates and jujubes. Hervey sat on the Ranee's right, the place of honour, just as on the first occasion he'd sat in the place of honour next to her father the rajah. To his right was the sirdar, all affability; on the Ranee's left, the brooding presence of the dewan, Ashok Acharya, first minister and keeper of the treasury. Musicians in the gallery played lively ragas, and a steady procession of khitmagars brought yet more delights for the table: oranges, peeled and dusted with ginger, finger-lengths of sugar cane, figs and mangoes. This was the Indian way, he'd told Georgiana beforehand. Whereas in England a feast could not begin with sweet things, sweetness being earned by progression through much sourness – as in life itself – in India it was different, for those at the banquet table had earned their title to indulgence in this incarnation through preparation in earlier ones. Or so Suneyla's father had explained. (Only later did he learn that it was a doctrine in which the rajah did not believe.)

Georgiana sat between the rissaldar and St Alban. The rissaldar had good, at times excellent, English. He was perhaps five or six years St Alban's senior, with – as Hervey observed, and rather to his surprise after the morning's chase – a ready smile and pleasing manners. He was from Rajpootana, he told her, his father a zamindar who'd engaged a former writer from Fort William as his tutor.

Annie, too, seemed to be finding things agreeable. Every time Hervey looked to see how she and Georgiana were, he saw her talking easily – to her left with a jemadar of the bodyguard, and to her right with the wife of another, whose father was a man of business in Bombay but who'd lived for some time at the Cape, and who spoke English almost naturally.

He'd observed how the Ranee had received her, though, which vexed him – suddenly 'regal', as if minded she must display her superiority, show no deference simply because someone was of the *gora log* – the white people. Though display to whom, puzzled him. Georgiana, on the other hand, she'd received with delight.

Their own conversation was formal, but not stiff. She talked freely of the last time he was in Chintal, and spoke of her father as if her banishment were of no account. He wondered if there'd be occasion during his stay to ask of it, and what truly had lain behind it? He'd wish to understand for completeness, not just what bearing it might have on his mission.

'You are welcome in Chintalpore, you know, as long as you have care to stay. But how exactly are you come here?'

And now he must practise deceit, the soldier's art before battle is joined. But it was one thing to deceive an enemy in the field, and rather another to lie to his host. He could only dissemble.

'Very precisely, I come by way of Guntoor, in the suppression of dacoitee – of thuggee.'

He observed her closely as he spoke. Her expression remained the same.

The dewan said something, which Hervey's Hindoostanee could not quite catch.

Suneyla obliged. 'The dewan asks how is the great Lord Bentinck at Fort William.'

'I have not had the honour of his acquaintance, Your Highness, but I understand that he is well.'

Suneyla explained this to the dewan, though Hervey sensed he'd understood well enough. Yet just as he himself was sometimes reluctant to speak, fearing mistakes, he could hardly condemn the dewan for not wishing to practise his imperfect command of a foreign tongue before two expert speakers. It made, though, for tedious conversation.

The dewan asked if, in that case, he'd not lately been at Fort William.

Suneyla answered that he'd come from Guntoor, but the dewan appeared to want to be certain on the point.

Hervey smiled absently. 'I'm afraid that I have not been to Fort William in many years.' (Nine was a number that seemed to him reasonable to number as 'many'.)

In any case, it seemed to throw the dewan off his line, whatever that line was, and he returned to brooding silence. He was a tall, angular man, bearded, like most of his caste, and not without the appearance of physical strength; yet still the word 'reptilian' came to mind. A little later Suneyla turned to him, and there were rapid exchanges, which Hervey couldn't get even the gist of. She, however, looked uneasy rather than masterful. At length she turned away from the dewan and kept silent, her eyes distant. Hervey took the opportunity to look about the rest of the long table, content to wait for her to quit her contemplation.

Meat of all kinds – he thought it better not to know precisely – came on gold plate, and Cape wine in finely chased ewers. The ragas continued. There was plenty to distract from conversation, and to mask the absence of it. He began to wonder if his mention of thuggee had been ill-judged, putting Suneyla on her guard – the dewan too. But surely they'd known of it?

'It is very fortunate, is it not, Colonel, that you should have been in Guntoor?'

After so long a silence the question seemed strange, puzzling. Her manner was colder, too.

'Fortunate, ma'am? How so?'

She didn't answer.

'It was fortunate of course that I was in Guntoor when the news of the agent's death reached Fort William, and that I knew these parts. But such is life, is it not? There is pleasing happenstance, occasionally.'

Suneyla said nothing again for the moment, and then, 'Tell me of Georgiana's mother, Colonel.'

He thought it a strange locution, but knew it a mistake to imagine – for all her fluency – that he sat next to an Englishwoman. Though perhaps she knew more than he supposed.

He told her all that had happened.

'And so now you begin again, as it were?'

'My wife is with child, yes.'

She quickened. 'Ah, so you will not wish to be detained long from Fort St George?'

He smiled. 'I am quite used to the exigencies of the service, ma'am, as indeed is Mrs Hervey.'

'Indeed she must be, with a husband killed at Bhurtpore.'

It was said with hard edge. Hervey almost blenched.

Suneyla lapsed into silence once more. Dishes came and went. The ragas continued anon.

Then, suddenly, she spoke sharply to the dewan. He in turn gestured briskly to the sirdar.

The musicians fell silent and the khitmagars made themselves scarce. Hervey glanced to where Serjeant Acton stood, as the evening before, discreetly in a corner.

But soon he saw that he need have no worry. The little band began its music again, but this time much slower, and twelve sinewy, elaborately dressed 'ladies of the nautch' – young and of passing beauty – entered as if floating, bending this way and that like tall grass in a breeze. From neck to ankle they were aflash with mirrors, bracelets and rings, and in each bare navel an emerald shone.

Hervey smiled with the recollection of the first time he'd seen the nautch, here in this very place, and in the Ranee's company. He sat back in honest delight.

'From Maharashtra, as I recall, Highness.'

'Indeed they are.'

He wondered: had she brought them specially? The rajah had arranged the nautch for the delight of the Nizam, though little good it did him. Had she even remembered that first time? But he could hardly ask; and besides, he could hardly expect a truthful answer.

What did it matter, though? It would avail Chintal naught, even if Suneyla had brought them here for his amusement. The die was cast. Nor was it worth his regrets. He might as well enjoy what was laid before him.

The nautch girls swayed and swirled, silently – no singing – their eyes everywhere and nowhere, the movement continuous like an eddying stream: graceful, leisurely in gesture, mistresses of time. On and on it went, a full quarter of an hour; perhaps even more.

Captivating, enchanting, just as that first time. The years fell away . . .

Then suddenly the spell was broken – the frantic raga, the climax: spinning and shaking, extravagant motions; and then swift prostration.

And then loud applause. Even the dewan.

The nautch girls rose and stood quite still, hands together, and then, as one, bowed low – *namaskar*. That still they didn't smile, even at this ovation, only added to their allure. For they didn't dance for approval; they danced because it was their *karma*, the sum of their being in this and their previous life, and which would decide their fate in the next. Or so it was said.

Yet their fate was subject to temporal power too. They looked to the Ranee for their *congé*.

They got it – but an expressionless nod of the head, curt even.

Hervey wondered what displeased her (for so it seemed). What could compel her to crush a dozen Maharashtran beauties so? Was this, indeed, the root of her uneven rule, her *Lapse* – the pleasure in casual cruelty?

He remained silent – warily silent – as the nautch girls glided from the floor.

And then all refinement was gone in an instant. An outrageous chorus – shrieks, shrill voices, cymbals, bells, kanjiras and tambourines in hideous cacophony – gaudy sarees, extravagant bangles, beads and baubles. 'Girls' as thin as laths, tall, and some of riper years. Their singing – if such it could be called – was incomprehensible, their husky voices rhythmically repeating words that Hervey sensed had little meaning. This was sackcloth to the nautch's silk. They didn't dance; they cavorted. Cavorted for a full five minutes, gestures increasingly coarse – lewd, even – until the Ranee, smiling indulgently, clapped her hands to shoo them away, at which they besieged the audience with little begging bowls, and made hissing noises if they thought the contributions mean, before scuttling out with squeals as loud as when they'd entered.

Hijdas: 'neither one thing nor the other' – neither male nor female; 'he-she's', as they'd called them in Bengal. There were many bands of them in India, but none so far in Madras that he'd seen. They appeared from nowhere at birthdays, weddings, even funerals, and danced about and made a great deal of noise till given money to go away. To dismiss them without silver risked ill luck, especially near harvest. It could risk injury, too, for they were not without physical strength, nor the will to use it.

'They delighted us when first you came here, Colonel, if you recall.'

'I do, ma'am.' And her saying so told him everything about her recollection of those days.

What, in turn, that told him of his mission here, he'd have to ponder.

But they were gone as suddenly as they'd come, and the tamasha resumed its more stately progress.

At length, after a final procession of delicacies for the table, and excellent coffee, the whole assembly retired to take the evening air on the terrace. Except Fairbrother, who with one of the officers of the bodyguard went to smoke a cheroot with the hijdas. Fireworks and more music entertained the rest until at last the Ranee gathered up her ladies to take formal leave of her guests.

As she made to withdraw, however, she turned to the rissaldar of the bodyguard, who had detached himself elegantly from Georgiana and Annie to be by her side. 'You will bring me the principal of the dancers,' she said, in measured Hindoostanee and for all to hear. 'She has displeased me.'

Even the dewan looked uneasy.

Hervey, uncertain but believing he understood the import, mustered his own party to take leave of those who remained, saying little but what was strictly necessary. This was not a time to be witness to the Ranee's reproval.

In the corridor beyond, out of earshot, the Ranee dismissed the dewan imperiously: 'I will make example of those whores. I will do to their principal what the Begum Sumroo did to that conceited beauty of her household.'

The dewan, his look of unease now one of anxiety – for he'd no idea what had occasioned the anger of his 'sovereign', and must thereby cede a deal of control – touched his chest in submission. 'Highness.'

XIX

The Fatal Gift of Beauty

Next day

They began to quicken pace, amble to extension, and one or two to jog-trot. The horses had recovered well, even Acton's, who'd looked particularly sorry for himself the evening before. Minnie showed no sign at all of the exertion, as if the chase had been a mere canter on the heath at Hounslow.

Hervey had said little, just as last night when they retired. But he couldn't turn things over in his mind for ever. Nor could he reasonably expect to understand the intricacies of court etiquette against which the poor nautch girl had evidently offended. He could only trust that the Ranee's tongue did not leave her crushed for too long. He'd hoped to see their art again.

'The dancing – very graceful, was it not?' he said abruptly, glancing at Georgiana and Annie uncertainly out of the corner of his eye. There was just something about the nautch that was perhaps too . . . *advanced* for an Englishwoman's sensibilities, though as respectable a thing here as the ballet or quadrilles in London.

Georgiana smiled. 'Indeed, sir; there was much grace.'

'I fear the Ranee found fault that eluded us, though.'

Fairbrother chortled. 'But not with the he-she ladies, evidently! Deuced queer.'

Hervey sighed. He ought to have expected they'd come. (He'd glanced more than once at Georgiana during their cavorting to see if she comprehended.)

'But you found their company instructive.'

Fairbrother had joined the hijdas in the courtyard as they counted their coin. He'd hoped to find the nautch girls, but they'd been shepherded to a safe fold somewhere, the officer told him (and he'd been almost glad, for he'd found the hijdas prodigious tattlers).

'They knew exactly who we were.'

Hervey nodded. 'It was the same when first I was here. The rajah said they lived by such intelligence, always knowing when and where there'd be opportunity to intrude.'

'And I think they know why we're come. One of them asked "How much will you pay for Chintal?"'

'They're notoriously saucy,' said Hervey, with another sigh. In truth, he'd already concluded it was best to assume that everyone knew of why they were come.

He glanced again at Georgiana. He'd exposed her to a great deal these past months. India could overwhelm the senses if not taken in moderation, but she looked entirely composed. And Annie was such a level-headed girl – woman. Really, it was quite extraordinary how fortune could suddenly favour someone as she; though of course, without there being talent to take advantage, fortune wasted its time.

There was purpose, however, in their riding innocently *en famille* this morning. He wanted to speak without fear of the 'ears of Dionysius'. What intelligence was to be had of Chintalpore itself and its little army, Worsley was perfectly capable of gathering. The greater question was of will and intention. What was moving in the mind of the Ranee – and of her dewan?

It was a political's question, not so much a soldier's, but there was no political to ask it. Perhaps, though, ultimately the question didn't matter. Was it not his job merely to determine how best to execute the task given him? Yet that was as maybe; the execution ought to a degree to be determined by what it was the politicals actually wanted – and that in turn ought to depend on what they understood of the situation. So far, he'd not been assured that in respect of Chintal, Fort William's political intelligence was any better than their military.

'They made no pretence at liking the dewan,' added Fairbrother.

'And of the Ranee?'

'Nothing. But imitation being the sincerest of flattery, I conclude that they have a high regard for her.'

Hervey smiled. 'You hadn't opportunity to speak much with the Ranee herself.'

Fairbrother shook his head. 'I did, though, observe her a good deal. Unfathomable, I'd say.'

Hervey turned to Georgiana, though what he could expect of a child of an English parsonage he was uncertain to say the least. 'You found the Ranee agreeable, I think?'

'I liked her very much, yes, Papa.'

'It would be difficult not to, I suppose, for she paid you great attention.'

'Oh, but I knew she would, for I'd thought she must be intrigued to know how events had been with you since last you were here. You did, after all, help save her father.'

He smiled. She couldn't know all that had happened – and hoped fervently she never would; but there was truth in what she said. 'And so you were intent on seeing behind the mask, so to speak?'

'No, Papa, I wasn't intent, merely ready. The Ranee's eyes are large and I think they must therefore reveal more of her soul. And, in truth, I felt there was much warmth.'

It would have been difficult, of course, not to warm to one of Georgiana's age and ingenuous charm, but even so . . . 'I'm gratified to hear that. Did she ask anything of moment?'

Georgiana thought for a stride or two. 'She asked for how long we'd been travelling, which I suppose is not of much moment, but she did then ask how long we stayed at Guntoor and Sthambadree.'

'You spoke in English the while?'

'Yes.'

'No Hindoostanee?'

'No, nor when I spoke with the rissaldar. I thought it best.'

He smiled again. 'I think you were quite right.'

She smiled too.

'What did you observe of this, Annie?'

'Oh, Colonel, I'm not sure I could observe anything rightly.'

He knew that with Annie there was no false modesty, and also that her judgement was sound, unlikely therefore to be coloured by her dusty reception. 'What, then, did you observe, rightly *or* wrongly?'

She smiled, for so had he. 'Well, I observed a woman of the greatest beauty; and that, so I have read, can be a fatal gift. And I did observe her warm eyes as she spoke to Miss Hervey . . .'

'I sense that you're withholding a "but", Annie.'

'Only, Colonel, because evidently our observations are of some moment to you, and I don't wish to judge wrongly.'

'I'm excessively obliged, Annie; but I assure you that it's for me to judge. You should have no concern on that account. But I can't judge without information.'

Annie nodded. 'Well, Colonel, I couldn't but look at her frequently, as we dined and afterwards – and it was easy to do so unobserved, for her eyes were not on me, for I am a mere servant after all – and I believe

I observed someone who was . . . *apprehensive*. Not merely regarding her visitors; but that is very difficult to judge, is it not?'

'Indeed? That is a most telling observation.' And, were it so, one that he himself might – ought – to have made, except that, sitting next to Suneyla, he could scarcely have subjected her eyes to searching examination. 'Fairbrother, what think you?'

His friend smiled absently. 'I think that Miss Gildea has expressed it admirably. The fatal gift of beauty.'

Hervey sighed. Even if it were true – the beauty certainly was, but there was no knowing its lethality – it was hardly helpful. But then, that was Fairbrother's great worth: he didn't set out to be helpful, ever; only frank.

'And what did you make of that sourness at the end – summoning the nautch girl.'

'I wondered for whose benefit she spoke.'

'Did you indeed?'

Hervey lapsed into thought.

'Papa, where *is* Mr St Alban?'

It was a simple question, and a welcome one therefore. 'He's visiting with Colonel Bell, who was here when last I was. Or rather, he's trying to discover his situation, for I wish to visit with him too.'

Granite started to prance. Georgiana settled him with a check to the reins and more leg, wishing she could do so from astride rather than in this antiquated side-saddle. 'He does that when there's a snake.'

'How do you know?'

'Malik said, and he's the best of syces. And a krait just slid into the grass there.' She nodded to their right, perfectly calmly.

'Miss Hervey is excessively observant,' said Fairbrother, smiling broadly.

'How do you know it was a krait?'

'It's always a krait, says Malik.'

Hervey frowned. Was every Indian a fatalist?

*

At three o'clock Georgiana and Annie went to the zenana to take tea with the ladies of the court. It was a cool, quiet place about the size of a tennis court, set well apart, high-ceilinged and with trickling water to fill the silences, for it was not a place entirely of chatter. It was a place of domestic industry. The ladies were indeed skilled at embroidery. They showed their visitors their work and gave them samplers to demonstrate their own. Few words were necessary, and both Georgiana and Annie were sparing in what they revealed of their Hindoostanee. The ladies themselves spoke almost no English, except for Mira Bai, wife of Colonel Bell – tall, handsome, the image of a high-born Rajpoot, and about forty or forty-five years old. The others deferred to her, as if she had seniority beyond her years.

There were many easy smiles and gestures, and many expressions of pleasure that hardly needed translating. An hour and more passed agreeably for all, and then jasmine tea was brought, and sweetmeats – too sweet, indeed, for Georgiana's or Annie's taste, but which they accepted with many a '*mehrbanee*'. Mira Bai slipped out as the tea was poured, which put Georgiana on her guard, but after ten minutes she returned – with the Ranee.

They stood and made *namaskar*, Georgiana and Annie curtsying. The ladies of the court looked troubled, however, eyes lowered as if anxious not to meet the Ranee's. All except Mira Bai. She beckoned to Georgiana.

Georgiana approached the Ranee and curtsied again, Annie likewise, but the Ranee brushed her away roughly, which her ladies saw (and looked away even more nervously).

Georgiana held her countenance nevertheless. The Ranee's manner softened somewhat, and she asked her to sit with her by the trickling pool in the corner. Mira Bai withdrew with Annie to join the ladies of the court, who'd taken up their sewing again. 'All is well,' she said to her, softly.

The Ranee sat by the edge of the pool and bid Georgiana do the same. 'Why is Colonel Hervey's wife, your mother, not here with you?'

Georgiana was about to say she was with child, but checked. 'She is not entirely well, Your Highness. The heat: it became very tiring.'

Suneyla stared hard at her, the eyes Georgiana had found pleasingly large windows on the soul now hostile.

'Have you not seen Fort William then?'

'No, ma'am, not yet.'

'But you are to go there?'

'I know of no plans, ma'am. My father desires to return to Madras as soon as may be.'

'Are there a great many soldiers in Guntoor?'

'Highness?'

'I have heard there are many soldiers,' she said, but this time absently, as if trying to make nothing of it. 'It must be delightful for a daughter to see her father at the head of so great a number.'

Georgiana was unsure whether she ought to dissemble, for if the Ranee had heard there were many soldiers, she must believe it. And what would be the consequences of denying something that might already be proved? Was the Ranee testing her? And if so, why?

'Highness, there are a great many, yes. They have been hunting down the dacoits.' And then she thought to – as it were – flush out the game by frankness. 'But I understand that a great many more are soon to arrive.'

This appeared not to alarm Suneyla but somehow to encourage her. 'It is as I thought.'

But Georgiana did not know what she thought – other than that Chintal's spies did their work well. 'Ma'am?'

Suneyla fell silent for a moment, then made a gesture to the walls and her ear, and lowered her voice further. 'Miss Hervey, please give this message to your father: The hamadryads that he and I once observed in the forest are nothing to the court here. I am ready to consider any proposal.'

Georgiana stiffened.

Annie saw, and went to her at once.

Suneyla rose. Annie braced for the assault.

But Suneyla smiled warmly and took her hand. 'My dear, we have had such delightful talk, Miss Hervey and I.'

Mira Bai was now close. Suneyla turned to her and said, in English, 'It is accomplished.'

'How exactly did you learn of it? Common knowledge, do you suppose?'

Hervey had been tightening Minnie's girth strap. St Alban had found him just as he was about to leave.

'One of the bodyguard, just after I'd returned from Colonel Bell's. He said there was a great commotion in the palace, the dewan much agitated, and most others.'

Hervey shook his head. 'Bestial.'

'He said all the palace knew the story of Begum Sumroo, and if the Ranee could do to the nautch girl as the Begum did to one of her ladies, then she could do to any.'

'Quite.' Hervey wondered if he ought to go to the zenana. There was no reason to suppose that Georgiana was in any danger, but something as capriciously cruel as this . . .

'Do you know of this Begum, Colonel?'

'A very little. She was at Bhurtpore when we took it by siege. She'd brought her troops to assist Combermere – not that he needed any more. She was just after plunder. I saw her once – a hag, no less, though she was supposed to have been a beauty in her day. But that's by the bye. Mind, if the Ranee's imitating her methods . . .'

'What do you propose to do, Colonel?'

'What *can* I do? The Ranee entombs a nautch girl beneath her own bedchamber so she can hear her groans. You might imagine there'd be someone in the palace who'd take objection.'

'I gained the distinct impression that fear would overcome any objection.'

'Just so. Torture one; frighten a thousand.' He turned suddenly and took the reins from the syce. 'Edward, go see that Georgiana's safe. Have a corporal with her till I'm back. I shan't know how to proceed until I've spoken with Bell. Let's hope he's as forthcoming as you say.'

Colonel Bell's quarters were just as St Alban described: a fine old *ghar* in several acres of rhododendrons on the southern fringe of the city. There were hoopoes pecking on a very passable-looking lawn, a table and half a dozen cane chairs in the middle, and children playing – fairish-skinned children but dark-haired, the usual issue of British officers and their Rajpoot bibis.

The colonel greeted him warmly, rising from his chair with the help of a stick and calling for his bearer to bring lime water. St Alban had said he thought the old warrior might have 'gone Hindoo' – although he hadn't quite made *namaskar* – but although he wore a long white dhoti and mogul slippers, and shooed his children away in an accent that was more Dehli than Fort William (or, indeed, his native Scotland), it was not long before Hervey could fancy himself at the Horse Guards.

'Read of yer doings at Coorg, General. Admirable economy of effort. Sit ye down.'

Hervey told him the rank had been contingent on command of the field force, and that he'd thereby reverted, and that he'd simply not supposed his name would be known anywhere outside the military pales (a full despatch had been printed in the usual places) – and if it had been known, had soon been forgotten.

'Oh, it was read of here with great attention, I assure you. Indeed, as soon as I mentioned it to the Ranee she insisted on seeing it for herself.'

'The Ranee?'

Colonel Bell laughed. 'Of course! I imagine every ruler of every princely state's read it. They'd like to know how their little kingdom's to be annexed!'

Hervey suddenly realized there was two and two to be put together. If the Ranee had read accounts of Coorg she'd have seen his rank as brigadier-general. If he were now colonel but with general rank about to be granted again, it would suggest another field force was assembling. And if another field force was assembling . . .

He measured his words carefully. 'It makes for salutary reading, I suppose. *Sic semper tyrannus*?'

'Ah, so you suppose the Ranee to be a tyrant?'

Hervey shrugged.

'You don't suppose she might retain an interest in one who served her father so well?'

Hervey frowned. 'And in consequence saw her banished to the forest of the Gonds?'

'These things are taken as part and parcel of life in India, Colonel Hervey. But you'll concede, will ye no, that the appearance of *General* Hervey at any prince's seat will set the doocots aflutter?'

'I am a colonel of light dragoons. I am not a general.'

Colonel Bell smiled. 'I ought to congratulate you on your brevet, by the bye.'

'You are indeed well informed.' But otherwise Hervey was inclined to keep his peace, doubting the colonel could be persuaded even on such a demonstrably provable fact as his rank.

'And so?'

'The Ranee suggested I call on you.'

'I know. She told me.'

'Ah, forgive me. I hadn't known you were in her service still.'

'I was never in her service, Hervey, if you recall. I commanded the subsidiary force – temporary as it was – in the pay of Fort William.'

'That much I did know, yes, but when the force was withdrawn, I understood you to have transferred to her court.'

The colonel smiled again. 'More lime water?'

Hervey was beginning to wonder if there really had been any purpose in the Ranee's sending him here – beyond the natural decencies towards an old and infirm fellow-soldier and -countryman (except that the colonel was not so *very* old: his hair was streaked with grey; it wasn't white. And his stick, Hervey judged, was more ornamental than essential).

'You have a delightful establishment here.'

'Indeed I do, and a hundred-year lease. I regret that my wife is in attendance at the palace today, but I insist you meet her during your stay.'

'She's one of the Ranee's ladies? Was she at the banquet last evening?'

'She was, and said she observed you there but hadn't opportunity to be presented.'

Hervey thought it odd. If the Ranee was so keen he meet the colonel, why not arrange for his wife to be presented?

'Colonel, there is something I would speak of. I have just learned that the Ranee has perpetrated a murderous cruelty on one of last evening's nautch. I cannot pretend – I don't *wish* to pretend – that I know nothing of it.'

Colonel Bell inclined his head. 'How did you come by this?'

'It's common knowledge in the palace, evidently.'

The colonel smiled. '*Accha*.'

What a word was '*Accha*': Hervey had even found himself using it of late. It encompassed so much. 'And so?'

'And so her design is working.'

'What?'

'The Ranee has asserted herself.'

Hervey recoiled. Had Bell been so long in India as to be bereft of all Christian sentiment? 'You condone the interment of a young woman for such a purpose?'

'I assure you, Hervey, I don't condone it for any purpose. Nor does the Ranee.'

'Then the story is false?'

'Of course it is. Purposefully so. Bhikoba, the girl, is here, if you must know, and tonight she'll be away to join the rest of the nautchers back to Nagpore.'

Hervey shook his head. 'You'd better explain, if you will.'

'Just so. Last evening – you found it agreeable.'

'It was a fine evening altogether.'

'Shreemati Bell said the Ranee was much taken by Miss Hervey. She, the Ranee, hopes very much to become more acquainted.'

'I'm gratified. Georgiana liked her much too.'

'She also said the Ranee found you wholly unchanged – in both appearance and manner – and was delighted by it, and hoped that you and your party would stay for as long as you pleased.'

'Well, I'm gratified to hear that too, but the business of the agent won't require more than a few days.'

'The Ranee also wished to know of Mrs Hervey, but I had to confess I knew nothing.'

'She is well.' (He'd venture no more. He wanted no hostage information, and there was the business of the agent . . .) 'You knew him, the agent, I suppose – and the manner of his death.'

'The fellow was a sot. Choked in his own vomit.'

'Is that certain?'

'It was I who found him. And believe me, after years in India I have an eye for mischief.'

'Yes, I suppose you must have.'

'And not only was he a sot, Hervey, but a corrupt sot to boot.'

'Corrupt? How so?'

'Every one of his despatches was read first by the dewan in exchange for gold.'

'And you don't think he might have sent unseen the despatches that were unfavourable? It is not unknown.'

Bell shook his head. 'Nothing leaves Chintalpore without the knowledge and approval of the dewan. You've been chasing thugs these several months, have you not? They command the roads in Chintal on the dewan's behalf. That's why there're so many of 'em active in the Circars and Nagpore – and Haidarabad – with let of the dewan, because they intercept those whom he wishes and give 'im a share in their loot. They could be rounded up in weeks if he wished it – there're more than enough troops in the bodyguard alone – but they're too valuable to him.'

'How did you come by what we were doing in the Circars?'

The colonel smiled again. 'The dewan. Tyrants can't survive without spies. You must know that.'

'Elizabeth and Burghley?'

'Hah! You quite mistake the matter, Hervey. Elizabeth was the ruler, not Burghley. The Ranee rules merely at the pleasure of Ashok Acharya, on his behalf indeed. She daren't express so much as an opinion without his approval. As for doing anything, or even going anywhere . . .'

'You're saying that she's captive in her own state? Sounds deuced reachy.'

'How would you describe it then, General?'

Hervey simply raised an eyebrow.

'You had a hard ride for the boar yesterday, I understand.'

'Ye-es?'

'The rissaldar pressed you hard.'

'Tried to unseat me, I'd say.'

'Then let me tell you those were his riding orders.'

'From whom?'

'The Ranee, of course. She wanted to see if you were the same man.'

Hervey sighed heavily.

'You can hardly blame her, since she proposes to place her life in your hands.'

Hervey's face was all incredulity. 'She wants me to rescue her from her own devices?'

'I've already told you: she's no more her own mistress now than she ever was – from the outset, when she was brought back from the forest of the Gonds when her father died. It was bad enough with her first dewan, but Acharya is beyond evil. Doubtless you saw a few rubies at the palace last night; they're nothing to what he's been spending on the army – *his* army; they don't answer to other than him. What do you know of them? I'd hazard you don't know the half – that his artillery, for instance, now consists of over fifty pieces, and very well worked. How many of horse? I'd hazard too that you wouldn't put it at more than five hundred. Two thousand, I tell you. This is what Acharya's been doing these five years. His next move will be to contrive the removal of the Ranee, to take power completely.'

Hervey grunted. 'The fatal gift of rubies.'

'You might say that.'

'I can't deny it's a very contrary testimony to that which I've heard. Why now, though, am I hearing it?'

'Because your coming here has presented an opportunity that she – *we* – hadn't imagined would ever present itself, her very best chance of throwing off the chains. And that she now fears for her life.'

'Evidently with cause, and for some time. But what is all this of Mysore? How does making mischief there serve Acharya's purpose? It can only antagonize Fort William.'

'It serves to justify increase in the army. He has to have some pretence of legitimacy with her. In the end, though, her forfeit life's the stake, and this he's always subtly reminded her of, though of late he's become brazen. Doubtless you've heard of the snake pit at the palace?'

'Hah! There are always snake pits – and muggurs in the moats.'

'They're not unknown, surely so – if perhaps more in the imagination than in truth, though imagination will often serve powerfully enough – but let me assure you that there never was such a thing in Chintal until a year ago, when Acharya had it made to serve his terror. Few have actually been flung into it – its mere existence is enough to frighten money or information out of the stoutest heart – but two weeks ago a common felon was deposed thus, most unusually, for public hanging's the required entertainment, and under some pretext or other, Acharya forced the Ranee to watch, and had two of the bodyguard hold her by the arms at the edge of the pit, so that, he said, she herself didn't fall. But she understood perfectly that her life was his for the taking.'

Hervey began to think he might be hearing the truth – if there were such a thing in India. He took another glass of lime water.

'Am I to suppose, then, that the chastisement of the nautch girl is an elaborate ruse to out-dewan the man himself?'

'Just so. She buys time.'

'You've taken trouble to lay out the case at some length. Time for what?'

'I have, and for the very reason that I judged you to be of a careful disposition, and also – indeed, chiefly – because as well as the Ranee's, *my* forfeit life's the stake.'

Hervey looked grave. 'Evidently you have a proposition.'

'I do. The Ranee would make a treaty with Fort William, the same as Mysore's, and accept a subsidiary force here. The Company wouldn't annex Chintal, therefore, as it has Coorg, and therefore wouldn't profit materially much by it, but it might thereby save itself the charge of pillage.'

Hervey thought for a moment. Could he discuss the proposal without an admission that annexation was exactly what Fort William intended?

'How would you propose such a treaty be effected if the Ranee's a prisoner of the dewan? The business of the nautch girl's hardly likely to make much difference.'

'You would have to bring a force of such strength into Chintal as to overcome that of Acharya – something that must in any event be in contemplation as we speak, although the estimate will probably be greatly awry.'

There were now *two* assumptions to avoid confirming. 'What might such a strength be, in your judgement?'

'Twenty thousand.'

Hervey tried hard not to look perturbed. The plans for the field force were for twelve. He must continue to speak hypothetically, discursively. 'That's twice the number the Duke had at Assaye! Very nearly two thirds the size of the army of Bombay indeed!'

'Ashok Acharya's judged these things well, but not entirely. Every army in India is composed of mercenaries. They're therefore susceptible to defeat by financial inducement.'

They sat long together, Hervey gradually abandoning the pretence of the hypothetical, so that as it neared the time he judged he must leave, he turned to the one question that could not be considered in the abstract: how was the colonel's own life to be preserved? The dewan's spies would know of this meeting. What would he tell him when brought to question?

Colonel Bell had thought the matter through, however. 'You have come here to Chintalpore on account of the death of the agent. Fort William has invited me to become the agent in his place, and with the offer of much gold. I have declined, but you have said that you will visit with me again to try to persuade me to reconsider, although I have said that I am not open to reconsidering. That much the dewan will be inclined to believe. What further stratagems will be necessary we can only judge later.'

Hervey agreed. 'One last question, though, for the time being. Who is to be trusted in all this?'

'Hah! No one, save my wife, whose trust I try not to ill-use, and therefore tell her as little as may be, and Rissaldar Sikarwar, a fine Rajpoot officer. I've known him since he was a laddie.'

Hervey smiled ruefully, making to leave. 'He was nearly the death of me yesterday, but I'm inclined to take your word.'

Colonel Bell rose briskly, without the aid of his stick, and held out a hand. 'The Ranee will take a walk in the jasmine garden at dusk, as is her habit. She'll be alone save for an officer of the bodyguard – Sikarwar – and one of her ladies.'

Hervey nodded. 'I understand.'

'And to reassure you, on return Miss Hervey should have some words for you from the Ranee.'

At six-thirty he went to the jasmine gardens with Georgiana. They strolled among the sandalwood trees admiring the roses which climbed high and in profusion, and the peacocks beginning their nightly roost.

But they kept their voices low. 'Walls, ears,' he'd said.

The scent of jasmine was even stronger at this time of day – *Mysooru mallige*, the jasmine of Mysore. It was the same that filled the garden at Arcot House, and his thoughts turned momentarily to Kezia. And although campaigning had been his life – in truth still was – for an instant he would have traded all to be in that garden.

He was in no hurry to make the rendezvous. It was rare that he had opportunity to spend even a little time with Georgiana. She'd grown to age – well, almost to age – in his absence. Even their letters had been infrequent. Indeed, there were probably letters of several past years that were still on the high seas or at some distant post office trying vainly to deliver themselves – an ever-onward stern chase.

They strolled and chatted for a quarter of an hour – nothing of consequence: Granite, peacocks, the palace silks, but it didn't matter; they spoke easily. Strange that it should have to be in so distant and alien a place. He couldn't recall even five minutes of strolling in England – only occasionally some purposeful rush to see this or that, although there'd been those few days at Hounslow, when Kezia had been prostrated, and she and Elizabeth had come to stay (and when Annie had proved her true worth). How long might they have together, now, in India? 'The exigencies of the service' – there would be those well enough. And then the marriage market, though still just a distant prospect, surely – it had to be considered (and the market here unthinkable) . . .

They saw the Ranee come through the grove of fig trees to sit by the lotus pond that collected the water from the lower fountains when they were in play. At a respectful distance behind were the rissaldar and one of the ladies of the court.

There was good light still – half an hour at least.

'Do you recognize who it is that attends – the lady, I mean? One of your party today?'

'Yes, it's Mira Bai. She spoke to me at the sewing. The one I told you of, the wife of the colonel. Her English is at times a little uncertain, but she understands and can make herself understood.'

Hervey smiled to himself. It was a well-laid plan. Whether a plan to trap or to reassure was the question.

'Did you form any opinion of her?'

'No, not really, but she was kind to take such pains to speak to me.'

Or cunning? he wondered.

They strolled on – if observed, a stroll to a chance encounter.

'Why, Colonel Hervey, and Miss Hervey,' said the Ranee, smiling as she rose.

'Good evening, Your Highness,' said Hervey, bowing. Georgiana curtsied. Suneyla took her hand as she rose, then offered hers to Hervey.

'I like to come here at this time of day, when I am able. There is much peace. It is strange, but sometimes a snake will come to drink also, even a krait or a cobra, and I have no fear of them, for in their need of water they show their helplessness, just as you or I.'

Helpless: such an intriguing word – calculating, even? Colonel Bell had spoken of the snake pit, and Suneyla's message (the hamadryads in the forest being nothing to the court here) – what to make of it? Was a woman's life and liberty ever at the pleasure of men? Was that why women had their wiles? The apple, the serpent, the woman . . . the garden of Eden, here.

'I would hazard that their venom is diminished not one jot, though, ma'am.'

She smiled, and nodded.

She *was* extraordinarily beautiful, and the more so in her 'helplessness'. She must have excited many jealousies and desires, and still. The gift of beauty was indeed perilous.

'Did you find your day agreeable, Colonel Hervey?'

'Very, ma'am. I went to see Colonel Bell.'

'How did you find him? In good spirits, I trust?'

'I did.'

She beckoned to her lady. 'This is Colonel Bell's wife.'

Hervey bowed. 'Your servant, ma'am. It was pleasing to meet your husband again after so many years.'

'He, I am sure, was pleased to see you, Colonel Hervey.'

He nodded, turning again to the Ranee. 'I regret I was unable to persuade him to become the Company's agent, however, though I pressed him to consider it further, and he has at least agreed to do that.'

He followed, as it seemed, a script, but not knowing precisely what would be the lines of the other actors.

Suneyla spoke no lines though. She let her eyes speak instead.

Georgiana shivered. She'd no knowledge, only of Eve, but every instinct told her.

Hervey knew, by instinct and experience. The hamadryads – they'd coiled and coupled, but then female had killed male, her purpose accomplished. He'd seen as much often enough. He'd never let temptation overcome him again.

'Highness, you may always count on the protection of His Majesty's East India Company – *Honourable* East India Company.'

'I am no cipher of the dewan's, whatever he believes, but I am not free to leave this place.'

'I understand perfectly. And that it is necessary to gain leave of the dewan by force.'

'Even if I were able to leave, somehow, I could not as long as the dewan remained. I could not leave my people to such as he.'

Hervey caught his breath. This was the first intimation of nobility he'd had. Did he believe her?

'If, ma'am, you were to request the aid of the Company, how might the army answer?'

'The bodyguard would answer to me, once the commandant is detained.'

Hervey glanced at the rissaldar, who bowed to say that it was so.

'And the rest? There are a great many!'

'They are the dewan's creatures. I do not know.'

Hervey supposed that ultimately, like most mercenaries, they'd gauge the wind.

'And the dacoits, the thugs, ma'am?'

She stiffened. 'They do not answer to me. They never have!'

He wanted to believe her. He wanted very much to believe her.

That evening he kept to himself, thinking long on what he should do; and indeed what he could do. At length he went to consult with Fairbrother, finding him lying on his bed reading Southey's *Journal of a Tour in Scotland* by the light of a stearin candle that he'd brought from England.

'I commend your persistence,' he said ruefully, minded that he'd promised once that they'd make a Highland tour together, 'but I would have your opinion on a less agreeable prospect.'

'By all means. I was in fact reading more for the prospect here than Scotland – its observations on Mr Telford, wondering what capability he'd see in India.'

'He'd certainly have an even emptier canvas on which to display his art. One or two of his roads wouldn't come amiss.'

'For sure. And Mr Stephenson's railways. I thought I'd go and see the steam at the coal pits tomorrow, if you've no objection.'

'I've no objection in the least. But come take a turn with me now,' said Hervey, cupping his ear and pointing to the wall. 'I would see how Minnie's stood the day and all, give her a little mash perhaps, if they have such a thing.' (If the stable, too, had ears, then he supposed that nothing could avail him in his mission here.)

Fairbrother needed no explanation. He knew his friend well enough.

And, obligingly when they were come, Minnie and the others whickered just often enough to mask their talk, muted anyway as it was. Perilous, though, for Hervey had now firmly resolved to rescue Suneyla; or rather, not simply to spirit her away from the city, but to release both her and Chintal from the tyranny of Ashok Acharya. He had, he told his friend, taken leave of her in the jasmine gardens with an assurance not to be afraid, though he couldn't yet know how that might be.

'And how, meanwhile, is she to preserve herself?' asked Fairbrother.

'That is the material point. I said she must somehow allow Acharya to believe that he's secure. How, I can't suppose, but she's not without guile. It appears she can trust the bodyguard, and perhaps some of the Swiss officers that Acharya's brought to drill the others. His numbers are formidable though.'

'And this while you return to Sthambadree, collect your field force and come back here as knight-errant?'

Hervey scowled. Sometimes his friend tried him sorely. 'I can't pretend it will be easy. I don't doubt we can deliver Chintal from Acharya, given the men, but I can't be sure we can deliver the Ranee too.'

Fairbrother was silent for a moment, thoughtful.

'You'll need good intelligence in the meantime.'

'I'd thought of that well enough,' said Hervey wearily, for there was no obvious prospect of it.

'Then I shall stay here.'

'What?'

'I can't see another way. You can scarcely leave your dragoons. Tell the palace I'm to be Bell's assistant, till the new agent's appointed. And if the Ranee's courage fails her . . . Well, I'll have to contrive her escape somehow.'

Hervey shook his head. That he should have such men as Fairbrother follow him without bidding . . .

XX

The Chintal Field Force

Sthambadree, five days later

The troop serjeant-majors stood like petrified trees, fearing the slightest movement would bring down on the unfortunate individual the terrible wrath of the regiment's deity of discipline.

'I 'ave been in 'Is Majesty's Sixth Light Dragoons for more years than any of you've been able to tell left from right: an' never 'ave I seen aught *like it*!'

Armstrong stalked the line like a lion choosing whom to devour.

'Just because you've been in the field for two months, you think it's all right for boots to look like lead piping an' belts like old bandages – an' saddles as the day would quake to look on? Well let me tell you, one an' all of you, that even if it were just *us* – 'Is Majesty's Sixth Light Dragoons – on this grand scheme of 'Is Majesty's to bring light into this benighted land, *your* dragoons' boots an' belts an' saddles do not pass muster! *Understand?*'

'Sir!'

'An' if the belts an' boots an' saddles won't pass muster, what in the name of God is the state of them things as I *'aven't* seen? Swords rusted away are they? Carbines fouled so bad you couldn't squeeze a pea in, let alone a ball? *Eh?*'

'Sir!'

'But it isn't just us, 'Is Majesty's Sixth Light Dragoons, on this grand scheme to bring light into this benighted land; it's half the bloody soldiers in India! Half the white 'uns, anyway. An' you think it'll be good enough to parade with 'alf the King's men in India, looking like a regiment of half-washed *chimneysweeps?*'

'Sir!'

Armstrong halted abruptly, thrust his whip under his arm and braced himself.

'Listen very carefully, you troop serjeant-majors. Colonel Hervey, who is soon to be a general again, will be back at any minute. I would be shamed – *shamed*, I tell you! – for him to see his regiment in such bad order as this. An' if I am shamed, by God, so will you too be. Your stripes won't see the light of another day!'

The silence was profound. No bird sang, no dog barked, no horse whickered in the distant lines.

'Is . . . that . . . under . . . stood?'

'Sir!'

Armstrong glowered at each of them, his face as red as his tunic.

'Dismiss!'

The troop serjeant-majors turned to the right, paused to an unspoken count of 'two, three', marched sharply four paces, then without a word scuttled in different directions. In less than a minute they'd be in full throat too.

Armstrong's groom held out his forage cap and took his shako by return.

The serjeant-major nodded, said nothing, nodded again to him to fall out, then went to his tent and sank into the camp chair under the awning to contemplate the now empty maidan.

He was seething still. Bawling out serjeant-majors, all of 'em whipper-snappers – except Foxall . . . and Prickett (Prickett! God 'elp 'em all!) – an' all of 'em reckoning they could do 'is job, and wondering when they'd get the chance . . .

It was always the same: the boots, belts and saddles were never good enough; he could never *allow* them to be good enough – and then to hope like hell that what mattered even more would be good enough on the day. Not just on a parade – worthy test though that was – or even a field day, but when it was the true test: *With ball-cartridge, Load!*; *Draw swords!*; *Walk-March!*; *Trot!*; *Gallop – Cha-a-arge!*

Oh God, how often had he heard those words of command – and then set about some Frenchman or another of the King's enemies with his sabre? There were times – there'd always been times, first with Caithlin and now with Edie – when he'd just wanted a day or so without a trumpet call, without having to upbraid so much as a corporal, let alone a troop serjeant-major. Perhaps even more than a day – days without number . . .

The orderly serjeant appeared, breathless. 'Sir, the colonel's coming!'

The thoughts were gone like the wind. He sprang up and began re-buckling his swordbelt.

* * *

'Hervey, I've forwarded your despatch to Fort William, with the very strongest possible recommendation, but I am not of my own authority able to change the policy of the governor-general in council.'

Hervey had paced enough. He sat down with a deep sigh. The answer was not unexpected, but no less dismaying for that.

There were just the two of them, only the governor's khansamah and the sowars of the bodyguard within earshot. 'Somervile, I must ask to be relieved of command if the order stands.'

'*What?*'

'It's not solely the iniquity of deposing a sovereign – the unlawfulness I might say, though doubtless there'd be a jurist at Fort William who'd confound me with *jus ad bellum* and Lapse – but it's the practicability. I can conceive of no strategy to defeat so great a force as the dewan can dispose unless the Ranee is with us. I've assured her that at the very least the Company will give asylum, and it's my opinion that Fort William will be far better served by a subsidiary alliance with her than annexation. She is not without worth.'

'I have conveyed those thoughts exactly.'

'And the enormity of the task? *So* much artillery, *so* many horse; and his infantry – greatly more than that manifestly incompetent agent reported. You'll recall that when this began, it was with the promise of the unstinting support of the army of Bombay; yet now you tell me they're going north on some other errand instead. For what does Bentinck rightly wish? If he wishes the annexation of Chintal he must will the means.'

'I cannot but share your dismay. I've asked Fort William for two battalions, and sent word to Vellore for the rest of their brigade. At present I can do no more.'

He didn't add that, with but a few weeks before he took his leave of India, his lordship's attention might be difficult to detain.

Hervey nodded, still weary from thirty-six hours in the saddle and not yet opportunity even to plunge in the pool, let alone take an easeful bath.

'We'd lose five thousand, come what may.'

Somervile winced. 'Surely no?'

'I'm not a sorcerer.'

'You must not resign, whatever happens. There's no one who'd make so good a fist of it. There'd be many a man dead without need, and even more in despair.'

Hervey thought for a moment. 'As the orders come ultimately from Fort William, I must exercise the right to represent my opinion in person.'

Somervile nodded. 'Were I in your position, I should do likewise. And I'm perfectly willing to go along with it, but Fort William might overrule it, and then where'd you be? Let's at least proceed on the assumption that sound sense will prevail, and make plans accordingly.'

Hervey sighed heavily. What indeed was the alternative? There might be one or two who'd likewise refuse the command if he did, but ultimately there'd be one for whom promotion would be too great a temptation. And such a one who'd commit to so unpromising a venture would doubtless be the one least likely to bring it off.

'You are in the right.'

Somervile nodded again, but with a look of profound relief.

'*Qu'hai!*'

His khansamah appeared at once, like a djinn from the lamp.

'More coffee, please, Bulwunt.'

And thus the bargain was sealed. Hervey smiled. 'I want to send two or three good men to Fairbrother. I'd have left a cornet and dozen, but it might have invited suspicion, so just two corporals.'

'You did well to place him there. I still have no word who it is Fort William intends appointing. Indeed, I wonder that they'll be disposed to appoint anyone to be agent, in the circumstances. Nor that anyone will be inclined to accept, given the intention to depose the Ranee. A more perilous plum to pull I can scarce imagine!'

'We are greatly bounden to Fairbrother. Acharya accepted him readily enough, but as soon as he gets wind of our approach . . .'

'The thought had not escaped me,' said Somervile gravely. 'He must have some honour when the time comes.'

In the afternoon, Hervey went to see the 13th Light Dragoons, arrived from Bangalore the previous day. He found them well set up in tents and billets near the fort, but with fewer men than expected, and their commanding officer distinctly embarrassed by it.

'It's the deucedest thing, Hervey. I have every able man save the quarter guard here, and my sabre strength's barely three hundred. Fifteen years in India and its depredations.'

Hervey was sympathetic. He'd known their colonel since the Peninsula, Allan Maclean, scion of the Highland clan whose name he bore. He was but a couple of years his younger, yet had only lately come to command; but Hervey knew he wouldn't shrink from the present unhappy odds if it came to it.

They walked the lines without formality beyond the usual compliments. 'I would that you return the salutes, not I,' said Hervey, 'for I'm not dressed as a general, and it would only sow confusion if you failed to acknowledge them.'

All but the duty NCOs and picket officer were in watering order – white canvas overalls, looser cut than the parade dress worsted, and blue cotton-duck coatees. They too had been obliged to change to red when the new King had come to the throne (disliking, as he did, seeing soldiers in the colour he regarded as proper only for his sailors, among which, at heart, he remained).

After meeting the officers, who seemed to him a wholesome lot, Hervey took Maclean aside and told him confidentially what might be their predicament. They both wore the Waterloo Medal, and between men who'd been at Waterloo there could be extra trust.

Maclean listened in silence. He might only lately have been promoted, but long years' soldiering, much of it in India, had formed his opinion. When Hervey was finished, Maclean inclined his head and said, 'Well, for my own part, I am not dismayed. We were barely two hundred at Campo Maior and beat three times the number of French. These Pindaree horse, they won't stand the charge. For that's evidently what these Chintal devils are, fugitives of fugitives. If this Ashok intends using them to cover Chintalpore while he and his hoplites make a fortress of the city, then he'll go the way of Bhurtpore.'

Hervey was heartened by the Highland resolution, but cautious yet. 'We must hope he does, but if, as I say, his Swiss friends have trained his men to manoeuvre in the open, then we shall be sore pressed. That said, if they can be induced to attack . . .'

'That would be to break with practice.'

'But if they could be . . .'

'Then we'll drive them back.'

Maclean smiled, and Hervey knew why. The regiment still cherished Lord Hill's order at Waterloo when the Imperial Guard tried to force the line: 'Drive them back, Thirteenth!', for it was punctually obeyed.

'And so, we may take heart that whatever may be, you and I will do our duty.'

'Just so, General. Shall you dine with us this evening? I've sent word already for your officers.'

'I beg you would forgive me. I've despatches to attend to, which must go at dawn. Tomorrow, though, I'd be delighted.'

They parted with warm handshakes, Hervey much fortified. There was always comfort in Cromwell's 'A few honest men are better than numbers', and the assurance of Ecclesiastes that the race was not to the swift, nor the battle to the strong (even if in practice it usually *was*).

He'd intended returning at once to quarters, but, spirits high, he thought instead to ride over to the camp of the other, if much bracketed, 'Thirteenth': the 13th (1st Somersetshire) Regiment (Light Infantry).

It was not, in truth, a prospect that pleased him as much as Maclean's Thirteenth, for the Somersetshires had of late acquired a tempestuous reputation. He'd known them in Ava, where their colonel, Robert Sale, 'Fighting Bob', was grievously wounded. They'd been in garrison at Agra for the past three years. It wasn't in the Madras presidency (nor soon would it be in Bengal when the fourth presidency, of Agra itself, was created), but news of 'tempest' always travelled post in India.

The trouble appeared to have begun in their previous station, Dinapore, where in four years they'd lost some four hundred men, women and children through sickness and the like – not a shot fired – and too from the measures that 'Fighting Bob' had taken to improve discipline. Drink, evidently, and as ever, lay at the root of much of it, but inspecting officers had also made mention of the high number of courts martial and solitary confinements – if also of the attempts at reward for good conduct. The adjutant had even begun a temperance movement (with 'Fighting Bob' himself taking the pledge, so the stories went), getting himself made Baptist preacher, distributing bibles and even building a chapel. This, according to the hircarrahs of military gossip, had been all very well until the major succeeded to command, for Colonel Dennie made his priority not the flattering of soldiers into virtue, but bullying them out of vice. Not only had the courts martial increased, he'd authorized certain non-commissioned officers to administer corporal punishment – 'summary justice' as he called it – without informing the company commanders.

Hervey himself had been in two minds about the reports. There was many a vocal supporter in Madras of Colonel Sale's methods – he himself had instituted many an encouragement to sobriety in the Sixth – but command of a battalion of infantry in which the mortality rate had run at ten per cent was not for the faint-hearted. Certainly, an adjutant who married a missionary and got himself ordained was something he found curious to contemplate. He reserved his judgement of the – reportedly – far-from-teetotal Colonel Dennie.

It was as well that he did, for he soon found him at office in a bell-tent in the middle of the Somersets' camp. The picket had turned out and presented arms as fast as any he'd seen, and the picket officer and serjeant appeared before he was out of the saddle. Whatever was the regime of discipline, its first appearance was promising.

'Good afternoon to you, General,' said Dennie, rising. 'We're just come and you must take us as you find.'

It was not perhaps the most regular of beginnings, but there again, neither was his visit. A general arriving without ceremony could put a regiment in a spin.

Dennie was five or six years his senior in age and an inch or so shorter – wiry, bushy-browed, and with every appearance of a choleric disposition. Sleeman had told him he was fierce and fiery, irritably impatient of acts of injustice to which he himself would have been no party but which would scarcely have moved a less sensitive man. No doubt he perceived a slight where only courtesy was intended – and perhaps the reverse was true, that he intended only courtesy yet somehow managed to give offence. He, Hervey, reckoned he'd just have to see.

He shook his hand – uncommon custom that it was on meeting – and smiled unconcernedly. 'It is good to see your regiment again. The stockade at Rangoon was it not?'

There'd been 'trouble' there too, but no want of fight either.

'I do believe it was . . . And you're come now without a staff?'

'I'm come without a staff because I'm just returned from Chintalpore and thought to see how things stood with your quarters.'

'Well, there's too much canvas, but I'd rather have it that way, with the companies close to instead of boarded out, no matter how comfortable the billets.'

There was sense in that, for it was a good deal easier to keep out the hawkers of whatever it was the stills of Sthambadree brewed. 'How many are you?'

'Seven hundred and eighty-three all ranks.'

Hervey nodded. It wasn't a thousand, but it was more than some of the battalions in Madras could muster. He didn't suppose there was a single one in India save for the native regiments (nor anywhere else for that matter) that was up to strength.

'May I offer a libation, General?'

'A common drink will do.'

Dennie laughed and nodded to his orderly.

Hervey sat down. He'd let out the rope to see what he did with it. Dennie had been in regimentals seven years before he himself was made a cornet. Although that counted for nothing when it came to the Articles of War, it would count for much when it came to the *realities* of war. Dennie had been with Lake in the campaigns against the Marathas while he'd still been at Shrewsbury, and he'd come out of Ava with a brevet half-colonelcy and a CB. It couldn't have been easy for such a man to play second fiddle to Sale for so long. Hervey expected he'd need a tight rein.

Meanwhile he would take the glass and raise it to his host with a 'Your regiment, sir', and drink a full measure. (Whisky, too; good whisky – he'd expected arrack – and excellent soda water.)

He was not long back in his quarters, now at the fort, with Corporal Johnson still directing the bhistis drawing his bath, when his brigade major came. Hervey had chosen a young field officer of the Madras Native Infantry who'd bloodied his sword in Ava, been aide-de-camp to the commander-in-chief and then on the staff at Fort St George. Captain Parry had one of the neatest hands in the headquarters, and Hervey was of the same opinion as his father in the matter, that a neat hand betokened a calm mind; but one day, too, he'd seen him bang his fist on the table by return when a colonel of artillery had persisted in an unreasonable demand. A fair hand and the courage to speak his mind – the makings of a good executive officer (and deserving the pay of acting major).

'General, I intrude, but I've only just learned you're back. I was laying out lines for the Nizam's Horse.'

Hervey waved him to a chair. 'When did you come?'

'Three days ago. Major Sleeman's told me of the suppressing measures, and what's still to be done, and Sir Eyre of the change in the order of battle for Chintal.'

Hervey nodded. 'We're done with thug-hunting now, I trust. So Gordon's sowars are here, then?'

'Tomorrow. And a second of the Nizam's follows.'

'Well, that's all to the good, no doubt, but not directly in Chintal.'

Somervile had applied to the Nizam under the terms of the subsidiary alliance for a regiment of cavalry to police the dak roads. None from the contingent could be employed outside the presidency without permission of the Nizam, but he'd kept his intentions towards Chintal secret anyway.

'And their commandant is in the field.'

Hervey smiled. 'Better and better.' (The Nizam, evidently, wished to be helpful, since Gordon's were reckoned the most efficient.) 'I've not seen Sir John Gordon since France. You'll give me word as soon as he comes?'

'Of course, General.'

'And what others?'

'Three troops of horse artillery are at Guntoor, and the rest will follow within the fortnight, if there are no more mishaps on the Krishna. They lost two guns for a day embarking from Vellore. The Fifty-fifth will be here in three more days, and the Thirty-ninth a week, perhaps more, and their strength uncertain. Theirs was a short summons.'

'Indeed.' But he was pleased to hear of it; both they and the Fifty-fifth had been his comrades-in-arms in Coorg. 'And the native infantry?'

'The Third will be here tomorrow, the Fifth and Sixth in ten days. And the King's battalions and Madras Europeans from Vellore in three weeks, perhaps four.'

Hervey nodded again. 'It might be worse, I suppose. You'll not know the outcome of my sojourn in Chintal, though.'

'St Alban has told me all, General.'

Hervey looked glad of it, for where to begin? 'If St Alban's told you, then you may be assured there's no more to tell.' He got up again. 'See here, Parry, I'm deuced weary, but nothing that a bath and a razor won't amend. Join my family party in an hour, and we'll talk the more. Tomorrow I'll want to make plans – three plans, no less: in case we march in one week, in two or in three and more. You might in the meantime make up the march tables for each. Oh, and we'd better have the commissary come.'

'Very good, General; I'll begin at once. And thank you for the invitation to dine.'

'Speaking of which, you've not yet met Colonel Dennie?'

'Of the Somersetshires? No, I called on him this morning but was given my *congé* till tomorrow. He was at orderly room and not to be disturbed. I judged it best on that occasion to make nothing of it.'

Hervey sighed. 'No doubt it was for the best, but there can be no repetition.'

For a brigade major bore the brigadier's authority, and he, Hervey, would not put up with the door being closed to it. (He did, though, rather admire the assurance it signified.)

'No, indeed, General. By the bye, sir, I was given to understand Colonel Dennie is not enamoured of "Somersetshires" – that he insists instead on "Thirteenth Light Infantry".'

Hervey sighed. 'Yes, I too was given to understand it. Colonel Dennie said there weren't a dozen men from Somersetshire in the regiment, and that he was damned if he even knew where the place was.'

Parry smiled sympathetically.

Hervey smiled too. 'Oh, it served: I said I hoped that as light infantry I could count on their increase in celerity.'

XXI

Imperious Duty

Sthambadree, four days later

The Sixth, dismounted and in their red, were drawn up in hollow square on the maidan below the great fort, while the 55th (Westmoreland) and the 3rd Madras Native Infantry, likewise red-coated, provided the outer picket which would keep the spectators at precisely the distance Sleeman wanted – close enough to see the act, distant enough to threaten no part in it. They'd come from all quarters of the city and from the country miles about, for an execution was a pageant, and their lives anything but.

Sleeman had ordered the arrangements very exactly. The year before at Nagpore, the condemned men had turned the tables on their executioners, and to the watching crowd become the heroes. No sooner had they ascended the scaffold but they'd declaimed it was an everlasting disgrace to die by the hands of the common hangman, and each had taken hold of the rope, pushed his head into the noose, tightened the knot and then jumped off the beam into eternity.

But this time there'd be no opportunity for display, or for any declamation within earshot of the crowd. Nor would they, as at Nagpore, be able to receive gifts of money and clothes from the onlookers, useless as such gifts were – succour from the belief that a man about to meet his maker imparted a holiness to all he touched, thereby gaining reverence. No, Sleeman meant business. It was the Company that brought true peace to the people of this land, and he'd have the people know it.

The day was four hours old, the sun well up but with only moderate heat – a perfect morning for a parade. Sleeman was determined, too, that the despatch of the thugs would be business-like, and had brought three of the most experienced hangmen from Saugor District, wanting no ropes breaking and the hangman having to strangle the prisoners on the ground, as at Nagpore (nor any hamstringing afterwards to prevent the dead man's spirit returning to haunt the executioner). He also wanted the drop long enough so as not to have to place heavy fetters on their legs, which had also excited the sympathy of the crowd at Nagpore, Indian and European alike. No, these men from Saugor knew their business. And he certainly didn't want these thugs going defiantly to the gallows: they'd not be allowed to declare they were self-offerings to Kali. He intended making a solemn impression on those still fettered by error's chain: the spectacle was not simply the ultimate penalty of the law but moral example.

At ten o'clock precisely – or as precisely as the gun at the fort made it – the condemned men were brought out in two tumbrils pulled by oxen, hands bound behind their backs so that they could make no salute to the onlookers, and gags to prevent all but muffled protest. Men of the Fifty-fifth guarded them, with orders to use the butt of the musket if any became agitated, while others marched in close escort, with mounted dragoons of the Thirteenth to front and rear.

When after a quarter of an hour the procession reached the scaffold, Sleeman and his waiting hangmen ascended the ladders. The Sixth, in hollow square, were standing easy, resting on their sabres. Suddenly they were braced by Armstrong's '*Parade!*', three hundred blades coming back to the shoulder.

The crowd fell silent.

Sleeman began reading the proclamation, first detailing the condemned men's crimes – the last of which was the murder of Bunda Ali and his family – and the sentence of death passed by court martial. Carefully rehearsed repeaters with speaking trumpets translated for the crowd. Then came the exhortation:

> 'We must oppose to the progress of thuggee and dacoitee a greater dread of immediate punishment, and where our present establishments are not sufficient or suitable for the purpose, we shall employ others that are, till the evil be removed; for it is the imperious duty of the supreme government of this country to put an end in some way or other to this dreadful system of murder, by which thousands of human beings are now annually sacrificed upon every great road throughout India.'

The words were meant as much for the newspapers of Calcutta and Madras, and even London, as for the crowd and the troops on parade. They were not without effect, however.

'What a perfectly noble man is Major Sleeman,' said Georgiana, sitting astride, twenty yards or so behind the Sixth.

'He is,' said Annie, though knowing she'd have to close her eyes when the moment came.

At first, Hervey had forbidden Georgiana to come, but she said she couldn't be expected to know India if she weren't allowed to see its darkest side, by which she meant both the iniquity to which 'the heathen in his blindness' could sink, and the disagreeable obligations of those whose mission was the country's deliverance. But he'd conceded only on condition that she turn away from the moment itself. He'd seen enough men sent to their Maker thus to know what lasting impression it made. (And, indeed, Georgiana had been surprised that he'd thought she mightn't.)

''Ang ev'ry fookin' bastard one of 'em!' came a voice from the ranks.

Annie lowered her eyes. It was occasionally the language of the stable yard and kitchens of the Berkeley Arms, but not that of Georgiana's world. The dragoons always minded their language very well in her hearing, but they weren't to know that the commanding officer's daughter was posted within earshot.

Armstrong came unexpectedly to her support. '*Par-a-ade . . .*'

The voice silenced even the crowd again. And not the boldest, most impudent dragoon would risk a whisper now that the serjeant-major had 'spoken'.

'Atte-e-en-*shun!*'

The noble Major Sleeman may have talked of imperious duty, but for the Sixth it was more than imperious; it was regimental. Armstrong marched from the centre to the left flank of the open side of the hollow square, halted in front of the waiting major, saluted and pronounced the parade present and correct.

Major Garratt returned the salute and marched to the centre. 'Fall in, the officers!'

The captains and subalterns drew swords, marched along the open side, and halted.

'Officers, take post!'

They struck off left, right and centre to halt five paces to the front of their troop, turned inwards and remained at attention.

Hervey now rode onto parade.

'General salute, pres-e-e-ent, *arms*!'

The dragoons stood stock-still while the officers lowered swords. Hervey returned the salute with a hand to the peak of his shako, and then Garratt returned them to the 'shoulder'.

'Light Dragoons, stand a-a-at – *ease*! Stand easy.' It was the privilege of the commanding officer alone to use the cautionary 'Light

Dragoons', but no one on parade thought that Hervey had wholly relinquished command.

It was cruel to delay – the men about to be hanged could now see the actual instruments of their execution – but delay was cruel necessity.

'Light Dragoons, those about to die have been tried by lawful authority for the murder of many innocent men, women and children. They did so without remorse and most savagely, and for nothing but material gain – in some cases from people with little enough. They will shortly pay the price for that, and in so doing they will not be able to murder any more. They have been brought to justice by your actions these past months. You may be proud of what you have done for the good people of this country. But there is more. These men most cruelly murdered Moonshee Bunda Ali, and all of his family, including a child new born. The moonshee served the regiment loyally. His face was not white, and he did not wear the uniform of a dragoon, but he was one of *us*.'

Hervey paused and looked about the ranks, and would have forgiven a voice in agreement had any come; but a parade was a parade, especially with Armstrong posted. The only sound came from the distant repeaters, rendering his words – he trusted – into Hindoostanee.

'No one who murders one of the regiment can expect to escape apprehending – ever – and nor can he expect mercy.'

He paused again.

'For that is our *bond*.'

And with that he turned about and rode from the square.

Yet he cursed that it wasn't the whole truth. Until Ghufoor Khan was brought to the scaffold, justice was incomplete.

Major Garratt stood the parade easy and ordered 'eyes left and right' to witness punishment. Georgiana and Annie reined about, but did so at a walk, for otherwise it would have seemed unbecoming.

They were not out of earshot when the crowd gasped as one, and the thugs were – soon – no longer of that world.

*

An hour later, Hervey took up his pen to write to Kezia, as he had whenever there was opportunity and anything worthwhile – or seemly – to say. He'd written already of their time at Chintalpore, and there was not a great deal else to tell save some diverting – he hoped – story of the camp, or of Georgiana and Annie. And a little about the food, of course, and the weather, and the birds, and anything else he could think of that might reassure her. He ended, though, by saying that their first mission here, the suppression of thuggee, was complete, and not without success – but sparing any details of the measure of that success – and that their second charge would likely begin in two or three weeks' time, assuring her that it would be no very great thing once the force was assembled. And in the meantime – he always tried to make his campaigning sound more sport than war – he hoped to shoot snipe with Georgiana in the marshes of the Krishna.

He sealed it with the agate sealstone she'd given him before leaving England. It wasn't always easy to imprint the fine-limbed stallion cleanly in the wax, but this time the impression was as good as might be, and he handed the letter to Corporal Johnson with evident satisfaction.

'There *is* a hircarrah today is there not?'

'I'll go find out.'

He leaned back in his chair. 'Have you heard anything more of Mr Waterman's death?'

'No, Colonel, or else I'd 'ave told yer.'

It amused him that Johnson preferred 'Colonel'. It was, though, apt, for the general rank was local and they weren't on parade, and he'd be colonel again soon enough when the business of Chintal was done. Indeed, he was quite sure he'd be colonel indefinitely, whatever Kat had written.

'Frankly, it troubles me that I make such a matter of the moonshee and yet – if there has indeed been foul play – I'm not able to say as much about Mr Waterman.'

Johnson understood perfectly. 'Well, Colonel, you'd never've been able to say that about t'moonshee unless somebody'd ratted out them thugs.'

'That is true. And it vexes me that I've no one in Madras who can rat things out, as you put it. Or here, for that matter.'

'Well, nob'dy 'ere can 'ave done it, as they'd all left before 'e died.'

'They could have, indirectly. They could have paid someone – a thug like those we've just hanged.'

'Do thugs 'ave snakes, though, Colonel? I thought they just strangled people.'

Hervey conceded that Sleeman had not once mentioned it as even an infrequent practice.

'So why go to t'all that bother,' Johnson continued. 'Why not just strangle Mr Waterman, or smother 'im? Nob'dy'd be able to tell.'

Hervey said he didn't know if that were true – that a doctor of, say, Milne's erudition would surely detect the signs.

'Well, it were only accident that Mr St Alban caught them thugs and one of 'em ratted. All as can be 'oped for, I reckon, is that there'll be another accident, in Madras. Till then, there's nowt as can be done.'

Hervey conceded, and asked for more coffee.

There was a knock at the door, and Parry came with paper.

'General, this has come from Chintalpore, from Captain Fairbrother by corporal-galloper. He says the city's in confusion.'

Hervey took it, checked the seal – Fairbrother's stamp, unbroken – opened it and began to read.

His face soon disclosed the contents.

When he was finished, he handed it to Parry. 'Confusion's not the worst of it.'

Chintalpore
January 29th

My dear Hervey,

In the early hours, this day, without warning, the bodyguard, all except the rissalah, which does duty in the palace, was surrounded in their barracks by a force I estimate at 2,000 foot, & were disarmed. The artillery barracks were invested at first light & fighting occurred between, I understand, on the one hand the Swiss officers & some loyal natives, & on the other the rebel force. The rebels took possession of the barracks & all its ordnance in the late morning. The roads in & out of the city are closed by bodies of cavalry. As far as I can discover, the Ranee is fugitive – but unharmed – in the palace, which is now invested by a great force of infantry, & guns being brought thither from the artillery barracks. At the time of writing, the rissalah stands loyal under command of Rissaldar Sikarwar. For the moment I am not confined to my quarters & am able to communicate with him by irregular means. I am endeavouring to meet with Ashok Acharya. Colonel Bell is unmolested. He is of the opinion that this insurrection will succeed & with the gravest consequences unless immediate action is taken to relieve the palace. I have given no undertakings, but I have sent word to the Ranee that any appeal to the Company for assistance would be met with favourably and promptly.

Parry handed back the despatch. '*Will* it be met with favourably and promptly, General?'

Hervey smiled grimly, for he was without prospect of timely orders from civil authority. He had often said, though – indeed it had been his working principle – that it was easier to obtain forgiveness than permission. It pleased him greatly that he might claim the decision was justifiably his, though it disturbed him more than usual that there'd be no forgiveness for choosing ill.

'Depend upon it, Parry.'

'But when will Sir Eyre be returned?'

'I can't know. And it's for that very reason that I say you may depend on it that the Company will act favourably and promptly. I myself shall take the decision.'

Whatever the mind of Fort William, he would at least have the consolation of knowing that his old friend would not be held responsible.

'Shall I call for the brigadiers?'

'A moment if you please. Where is the galloper?'

'He waits outside, General.'

'I would see him.'

Johnson brought him.

His coat bore the dust of the road still.

Hervey nodded to the salute. 'Corporal Ledley.'

'Colonel.'

'Do you know what are the contents of the despatch?'

'I do, Colonel. Captain Fairbrother told me to commit them to memory in case of mishap.'

'You had no difficulty getting out of the city?'

'No, Colonel. The captain 'as some trusties. They know their way about and we was able to go by other ways. They get in and out of the palace too.'

'Capital. Bodyguard men?'

'No, Colonel. The he-shes. They seems to come and go any way they pleases.'

'The old game: Joshua had prostitutes, Fairbrother . . .'

'Colonel?'

'No matter.' He turned to the brigade major. 'Parry, sound for brigadiers and commanding officers.'

As the conference dispersed, Hervey spoke with Colonel Lindesay, who by seniority would in the event that he fell, take command. Lindesay had distinguished himself in Coorg, and was also, Hervey was certain, the right man to see through a siege if – God forbid – it came to that, but he impressed on him that his design was no more than *deployment*: what they found – when and wherever they found it – would determine what next. Bonaparte's plans were like a splendid leather harness, the Duke of Wellington always said: perfect when it worked, but if it broke it couldn't be mended; whereas he, the Duke, made his harness of ropes – never as good looking, but if it broke he could tie a knot and carry on.

'You'll be adept at tying knots, I fancy?'

Lindesay was older by at least ten years. He'd been a major two years before Hervey was a cornet, and had seen much service. A lesser man might resent the supersession.

'General, just give me a little rope.'

Hervey laughed, and clapped him on the shoulder.

He spoke also to Colonel Maclean of the Thirteenth, and to Worsley, for both their commands were independent, and impressed on them the paramount need for gaining as complete a picture as possible and as quickly as possible – in the first twenty-four hours – for it would be their *éclairage* that determined what to do next.

Then he asked Worsley to stay a moment, and spoke with him in an unusually confiding tone.

'Make touch with Fairbrother quick as you can, Christopher. He'll be in peril already, and greatly more once the insurgents learn we're coming. Most of all, he'll best know of what's happening. Ride clear of any fight unless it's unavoidable. You've seen the country. Take your risks early. And . . .' (he was conscious he spoke to a man who'd yet to see his son and heir) 'there's no reason we shouldn't bring this off without excessive blood.'

'That will certainly be my endeavour,' replied Worsley, with a wry smile. 'We'll be off by dawn.'

'Then I'll see you next in Chintalpore,' said Hervey, offering his hand. 'Go to it.'

Worsley drained his glass – Hervey had requisitioned a case of burgundy from Somervile's cellar, for a 'stirrup cup' after a council of war always got things off to a good start – then saluted and took his leave with an assuring 'Depend upon it, General.'

Orders given, questions answered (so far as answerable) and the words of private encouragement delivered, there was then for Hervey the strange 'hiatus' that came between a council of war and commencement of an enterprise. Brigadiers and others had their instructions and in turn must give theirs, while he who'd first given them their orders now had little or nothing to detain him, almost as if the clock stood still. He could sit apart in thought, or take refreshment, or rest – or else visit.

He ought perhaps to show his face – or, at least, the mask of command – to those least familiar with it, but instead chose those who knew it best. In truth, there was reassurance to be had from those with the shared experience of many years, and he was not above the need of it. (Besides, he'd only face another onslaught from Georgiana if he went back to his quarters at once, and he was determined in that matter: Chintal in its present state was no place for her or Annie. She'd be safe enough here with the rear party of Somervile's Bodyguard – and a sight more comfortable.)

There was no reason, either, why he shouldn't go to the Sixth's horse lines. The regiment remained his command no matter what the present arrangements (though he wouldn't want to make Garratt's job any harder by appearing to cling to it). Nor, with Worsley's troop detached and the other four disposed to screen the advance of the brigades – a squadron to each – was there much that Garratt could practicably do till they reached Chintalpore. After the conference Hervey had wished him well – suppressing as best he could all thoughts of the unresolved affair of venality – and shaken his hand.

Armstrong he found with the quartermaster in the storehouse counting out ball cartridge – his oldest 'Sixer' comrades (along with Johnson). Both of them braced up like dragoons on first parade as he came in, for Collins, though four years commissioned now, would not give up the discipline of half a lifetime, and the RSM knew no other.

Armstrong, his serjeant when Collins was still a corporal, spoke first – just a simple 'Colonel, General' to accompany the salute.

Hervey's face softened.

'For Captain Worsley's troop, Colonel,' said Collins, indicating the boxes separated from the rest. 'They're marching at three.'

Hervey nodded in satisfaction. Worsley must have sent word at once. But then, they'd been in the field a good many weeks now; no one wasted any time.

'How much corn are they taking?'

'Captain Worsley wants a day's worth on the saddle, and two on packs, Colonel.'

Hervey nodded again. Supply would be the deciding factor after a couple of days. The Sixth of late months had lost fewer horses than usual. Since returning from Coorg they'd cast forty-six and received by return sixty-five from the remount depot, all of them New South Walers.

'All but a dozen passed fit this morning by the vet'nary, Colonel,' said Armstrong.

There was plenty of grass where they were going, but even Walers, the best of doers, needed hard feed for real work. As for his soldiers and sepoys, he'd ordered the whole field force onto biscuit for the first three days, for he didn't want the advance tied to the pace of the commissary waggon. They'd have plenty of meat tonight, and bacon tomorrow morning, and they'd be at Chintalpore in two days if they marched fast and long and slept out, making no camp (and if they met no opposition) – and then the baggage trains could catch up. And there'd be plenty of good victuals in the city too.

If they met no opposition: it was a bold assumption. He knew he was trusting to a lot, not just his waggoners. But he'd supposed the insurgents' instinct would be to defend Chintalpore close rather than hazard a battle at arm's length as a seasoned soldier would. Besides, he still didn't know how strong Ashok Acharya's army really was. His 'Prussian mentor', as he called the manuscript – the thoughts on war of one of Prince Blücher's generals, which for the past three years he'd laboured in translating – held that men were always more inclined to pitch their estimate of the enemy's strength too high than too low. And yet he also knew it to be a sin to underestimate the enemy. Once, in the Peninsula when he'd been a galloper, his general concluded that the enemy had but two options, and had disposed his regiments accordingly; but the enemy had taken a third, and the brigade had been sorely pressed.

Here in India, though, there'd long been a saying that war was made with bullocks and gold. Before leaving Chintalpore, he'd told Bell and Fairbrother that if it came to a fight they could offer what inducement they thought best – gold, amnesty or both – to suborn any commander they thought fit. There was money enough in the mines in Chintal, as well as coin at Fort William, to buy off any mercenary army.

He chatted for a moment or two more with Collins about this and that – nothing of true consequence: the benefits of the supplementary dried pork, the additional rum ration, what and where they might spend the *batta*, the field allowance – and then took Armstrong aside.

'Is all well, Sar'nt-Major?'

He didn't need to elaborate. Their long association meant that the enquiry gave Armstrong licence to say whatever he wanted.

'There's not a thing to be troubling over, Colonel. I gave the SMs a rousting the other day, just in case.'

'I can imagine.' But Hervey narrowed his eyes. 'You'll allow the SMs their share of shot and shell, then, Sar'nt-Major – not try to take it from them?'

Armstrong smiled knowingly. 'I reckon I've had my fair share, Colonel.'

'Indeed you have.'

And that was that. He'd said what he needed to, and Armstrong had answered favourably. But when the time came . . . ?

It was useless to think on it. They'd (both) do their duty as they saw need. There was no other way.

*

Hervey and Major Parry worked long into the night, having sent immediately to Fort William a copy of Fairbrother's despatch. Hervey was determined to lay before the governor-general as complete a submission as possible before they set out, signing the covering letter in the small hours.

Sthambadree
February 1st, 1835

The Governor-General and Commander-in-chief
At Fort William

My Lord,

I am this day commencing operations in Chintal with the object of restoring good order to the country. I judge that I must do so without delay in order that the insurgents are given no time to consolidate their position, thus occasioning greater loss to my command, and also to take advantage of the favourable moon.

My method shall be to relieve the royal palace at Chintalpore presently invested by the insurgent force of the chief minister, and in which the Ranee of Chintal has taken refuge. Upon liberation of the Ranee, I shall take such steps to disband the present forces of Chintal as may be expedient, and to enter upon a provisional treaty with Her Highness for the establishment of a subsidiary force.

The troops available to me at the present time, and which comprise what Your Lordship was earlier pleased to designate the Chintal Field Force, are as follows:

Artillery

Four batteries of howitzers and cannon (32 pieces)
Three troops Horse Artillery (24 pieces)

Sappers
200

His Majesty's Cavalry
6th Light Dragoons (400 sabres)
13th Light Dragoons (300 sabres)

Native Horse (brigaded under Sir John Gordon)
Squadron 3rd Madras Light Cavalry (100 sabres)
4th Cavalry (Gordon's Horse), Haidarabad Contingent (400 sabres)
5th Cavalry, Haidarabad Contingent (300 sabres)

1st Brigade (Col Lindesay)
13th (Somersetshire) Light Infantry
39th (Dorsetshire) Foot

2nd Brigade (Col Craigie)
55th (Westmoreland) Foot
3rd Madras Native Infantry

My intention is as follows:

Exploring Force (13 Lt Drgns, & Sqdn 6 Lt Drgns) to discover strength and disposition of insurgent forces on roads west to Chintalpore, and situation in city.

1st Brigade to advance on northern road, 2nd Brigade on southern, covered each by sqn 6 Lt Drgns.

Reserve (Native Cavalry Brigade) on southern road. Sqdn Madras Light Cavalry to maintain communications with Sthambadree. It is my intention to keep the Nizam's contingent from the fighting to the greatest extent possible so as not to excite stronger resistance than may be.

Your Lordship will understand that such intelligence that I possess at this time is very little, and that I can only state broadly a plan of deployment. Your Lordship will further understand that the troops available to me are considerably fewer than those for which I had at first made plan, and that if it becomes necessary for prolonged siege operations I shall rely on the timely arrival of such other troops as have been promised from both Madras and Agra. I shall of course endeavour to inform Your Lordship of the progress of operations so far as is practicable.

I am Your Lordship's Obedient Servant, &c &c

M. P. Hervey, Brevet Col & Local Maj-Gen

Your Lordship will understand . . . Hervey had written more in hope than certainty, for Lord William Bentinck had assumed – appropriated, some held – the appointment of commander-in-chief when Sir Edward Barnes returned home unexpectedly a year ago. He'd no quarrel with Bentinck as governor-general, largely for the reason that Somervile hadn't, but he'd no great regard for his ability as a soldier. Indeed, as far as he could see, Bentinck could present no evidence of ever having *been* a soldier, in any sense that another soldier would recognize. 'Your Lordship will understand' was, indeed, forceful military judgement courteously expressed. His *plan de déploiement* was no more than he need explain, no more than military propriety and prudence required. If he were to fall in the course of the campaign, the design would bear witness enough to his military judgement.

XXII

A Few Honest Men

The Forest of Chintal, next day

Shots – not a volley or a fusillade, but more, for sure, than a brace of pistols. Difficult to be certain in the jungle.

For two hours they'd trodden the green road – wide enough for a waggon, and sometimes two – and for three hours before that they'd walked and occasionally trotted through open country with scarcely a soul to be seen save those too weak to run and hide. *Soldiers*: there was no knowing what they'd do. How might a poor ryot distinguish King's and Company's from less well-regulated corps? It had been the same when he'd taken the northern route three weeks before – sullenness. He was still uncertain whether it presaged good or ill.

'A mile, I think,' said Hervey. 'A hill makes no end of difference.'

'Hunters, perhaps?' said Parry.

Hervey looked doubtful. It was perfect country for advancing unseen, as he trusted that Worsley, and the Thirteenth, were, but damnable once discovered – the enemy concealed, movement difficult, order and control nigh impossible. Coorg had been much worse, of course: the hills there were *petites montagnes* – but in Coorg, time had been on his side. 'The commander's talents are given greatest scope in rough hilly country' said his Prussian mentor; and Hervey had smiled at it, for only a Prussian could treat with war as if it were a game. But as for jungle, it was true: it tested mettle like no other.

Colonel Maclean, at his side, spurred into a fast trot. No point waiting for the relays to report. But Hervey stood fast. They'd reach a fork, a track connecting with the northern road. If there was need to switch the effort from the southern, here was as good a place as any to begin. He'd not crowd Maclean and his squadrons.

Yet his every instinct was to ride forward. He got down from the saddle and spread the map on the ground – if 'map' it could be called. (What cartographical benefits would flow from a subsidiary alliance!) There was a road of some sort not far ahead that branched south towards the flood plain of the Nerbudda, but it wasn't clear whether it went as far as the plain or petered out in the forest. He wondered if he might get the Thirteenth to send a troop . . .

Half an hour passed, and still no word from Maclean. Nor any sound but avian and the odd monkey. That indeed was the jungle, which the Prussian couldn't know from experience: a commander knew nothing but what was told him, and if he tried to see for himself he only confounded things the more.

'The forest teems with life,' said Hervey suddenly to the baboo, 'yet it shuts up like a clam when anyone intrudes.'

'It is so, sahib, but it takes no side.'

Hervey nodded, and with a resigned smile. It was true – how could it not be? – but at times it felt entirely other.

He admired the baboo more with each day. He wanted him close during the march, for although he was confident enough that his Hindoostanee would get him by when it came to words of command, if it came to writing . . . (and there was bound to be writing when they made Chintalpore).

He began to chafe. Still nothing from the Thirteenth, and the covering squadron of the 2nd Brigade would be closing up behind them soon. He'd four gallopers and two orderlies. He supposed he could send one of them forward, but . . .

'Hurroo!'

A cornet at speed.

Parry spurred to halt him.

'Message for the general, sir!'

The covermen re-sheathed their sabres.

Hervey beckoned him forward.

'General,' he said eagerly as he saluted; 'Colonel Maclean's compliments, and the road is clear. There was a vidette a mile west. They fired in the air when our scouts approached and then tried to gallop back, but they – the scouts – ran them down. The colonel's questioning them now, two sowars, irregulars judging from their appearance.'

Hervey wondered. He'd expected something or nothing, not a brace of partisans. 'If there was a vidette there must be a fair body of troops beyond, within hearing, the shots to sound alarm; how far have you explored?'

'The forward detachment galloped three miles, General, but saw nothing at all.'

That was decidedly odd. Why post a vidette – or why its shots? Hervey thanked him nevertheless. There was only so much a galloper could suppose.

Time to see for himself – and for Minnie to have a gallop.

Ten minutes later they came on the Thirteenth's pennant, and with some surprise. Colonel Maclean was at his ease in an old nipa palm shelter chatting amiably in Hindoostanee with the captives, and his covering serjeant pouring them rum.

Hervey got down, returning the salute and the smile.

'Well, General, it appears I'll be able to take these fellows on strength. I've never known looser tongues – and I can't think they've any cause to be laying a false trail.'

'Tell.'

'They're Jats, silladars. Someone knew we were coming, evidently, for they were posted only last night.'

Hervey nodded. Silladars – yeomanry, but even more independent-minded than the English variety. Just the men for vidette duty, but perilous since they owed no allegiance.

'And the main force?'

'About ten miles, as far as I can calculate – you know how variable is the *kos* – where the road crosses a fair-sized stream they say. Might be this here.'

He pointed on his map with the leaflet of a palm frond.

'The forest's burned out there, they say. They reckon a thousand foot, and guns, but I doubt they know exactly.'

Hervey beckoned the baboo to come closer. He wanted to question them for himself, if only to gauge their manner. Both were clean-shaven but for a day's growth, tall, clear-eyed and active looking. A good stamp of soldier.

'What was your purpose in firing the shots?'

'Huzoor, they were my orders.'

'Who would hear the shots if the river is so far away?'

'Huzoor, the vidette behind me, one whole *kos*.'

Hervey frowned. *Kos* – a mile, two miles, three? But it scarcely mattered. It was obvious there was a relay of some sort. He told Maclean to have one of them taken aside, out of earshot, and then he'd question each in turn.

'How many cannon?'

This took a little more time, for Indians could be equally loose with terminology as distance, inclined to lump all shot together as 'artillery', whether *top* (cannon), *bundook* (musket), or anything else for that matter.

But in questioning them separately he managed to establish that there might be some twenty guns covering the crossing – 'wheel to wheel'. Even if there were half that number it was bad enough.

Did they know if there were troops on the other road, though, the northern?

It was a tall order. Why would two such Jats know the plan of battle?

But Hervey persisted: had they seen others marching in a different direction? Did they think the force at the river was the major part of the army? And so on.

Eventually he was satisfied there was no more to be had save the odd detail that might be useful as they closed up to the river – but that was for Maclean. The true import of the intelligence was that Ashok Acharya, or whoever was his field commander, intended confining them in the forest rather than defeating them in the open. If it were so, it were poor strategy, simply one of inflicting casualties, delay and discouragement. Did he not know His Majesty's troops better than that?

But, he'd concede, from a purely tactical point of view the river sounded like a well-calculated position. It was just about the furthest march from the frontier that could be had in a day, so that then the invader would be halted, there being no possibility of taking the position at night, and would spend half the following morning in preparation, and if checked in his first assault – as he surely would be by so many guns, whether twenty or half the number – and with no room to manoeuvre, night would come again with the defenders still in possession of the ground, and the invader exhausted. If they were then able to bring up new troops in the night – which ought to be possible – it would be the same the next day, and the next, and . . .

Yes, he could see that a man schooled in sieges and the like would think in such terms, but suppose the invader decided not to oblige him by continuing to batter his head against the wall?

The question Hervey now needed answer to was whether it was Acharya's 'strategy' on the northern road too, for so far he'd had no report from that line of advance.

Then it occurred to him: did not the strategy present him with an opportunity? If Ashok Acharya expected to compel the field force to make assaults, why not appear to oblige him? They could turn the tables, so to speak, pinning *him* in the forest – drawing in more and more of his men. It wasn't necessary to *take* the position, only to continue to threaten to. How he then took advantage of that depended on what he learned from Worsley, and from Maclean's squadron on the northern road. It would be well, too, and soon, to learn where Acharya actually was, and of course the Ranee.

But if he couldn't consider all of what his options might be, he could at least explore those that he recognized.

'Colonel,' he began, plucking a nipa frond to point with, 'you'll see by your map there's a road of sorts here that runs off to the south-west seemingly into nowhere. It may well continue to the banks of the Ner-budda, or it may be that the forest's passable on foot – you know how little's the undergrowth when there's been no fall of timber – and if that's so, I'm minded to try it. It can only be a mile ahead at most.'

'Yes, I see. I'll send a patrol.' He nodded to his adjutant. 'Mr Tysseu please.'

Then Hervey sat him down and explained his thinking about the 'demonstrations'. It was the very devil to risk men's lives trying to take a position of which there was no need, a feigned attack, a *ruse de guerre*, but the alternative could be even bloodier.

Maclean understood.

'Close up to them towards last light and make a great deal of noise, and again at first light – but spare your men; there's no need of actual attack. I'll have Lindesay's brigade come up and take on the action thereafter.'

'Very well.'

'Watch your flanks though.' He smiled wryly; 'It's conceivable they've read Tacitus.'

Maclean knew his Tacitus; they all did. Three legions had perished in the great ambush in the Teutoburgerwald, and Rome's finest at that. 'I'll keep a good watch. You'll let me have a little artillery?'

'I shall. I'll send a galloper as soon as I've settled with Lindesay. And . . .' (he held up his map again) 'this road may be nothing at all, an old animal track even, and if so, perhaps nothing at all to the Chintalees – quite forgotten indeed. And therein lies its promise.'

'If it'll admit so much as a hog-deer my dragoons'll prove the way.'

Hervey smiled to himself. He thought he heard his own voice.

A quarter of an hour later, back at the fork in the road, Vanneck's squadron came up at the trot, and with them Colonel Lindesay.

'Shots, General?' said Lindesay heartily, dismounting to salute and take a sip of coffee which Corporal Johnson had been brewing while Hervey was with Maclean.

'They carried to you? A vidette, yes. The Thirteenth drove them in. Some useful intelligence.'

Lindesay took out his map, though they could see but fifty yards.

Hervey told him his thoughts and what he'd asked of the Thirteenth, pointing to the indefinite – if promising – line to the south-west. 'And if Maclean says it's passable, I'll want you to send a battalion to the river. Yours to decide, but I'd reckon on Dennie's. Thereafter depends upon what Craigie finds on the northern road – and Worsley's troop.'

Lindesay nodded. He had no questions. It was all admirably clear. 'And Dennie'll do battle with the forest, right enough. I never met a man less content to march with his sword sheathed. He's cursed every step of the way.'

* * *

Fairbrother, his face darkened a shade or two with coffee, and *dupatta* (shawl) cast modestly over his head to defy too close an inspection, beat loudly on the kanjira, which he held firm under his left arm so that in an instant his right hand could be at the Derringer in the bodice of his saree. Others of the troupe agreed he made a passable-looking hijda.

He'd been generous in his promises of gold and rubies, but their loyalty was harder won than merely with jewels. Why they took to one and not another, who could tell; a sort of sixth sense, someone they could trust, someone who didn't deem them *Panchama*, not of the four *varda*, untouchable. Fairbrother had smoked cheroot with them after the Ranee's tamasha. That was enough.

They'd passed through the walls of the fortress-palace without difficulty – welcome even. The guards at the foot of the droog had cheered them, and those at the drawbridge had asked blessings. Chintal's ranee was confined along with her rissalah in the old palace – a fortress within a fortress – and there were soldiers everywhere, but in truth the city went about its business as before.

Were there muggurs in the moat? He'd seen none. But they stayed submerged by day, did they not? Had any seen them at night as they sought a place to lie up? One hijda told him a muggur was no great size anyway, that a man might fight with it, unlike the great beasts of the saltwater Sundarban. But a crocodile was a crocodile, and he wasn't inclined to try it. If it came to a siege, then they'd have to get across the water, and its narrowest part, the drawbridge, was of course the strongest. What occupied him most now, though, was how many guns the dewan could dispose, and in what strength were the defenders. That was intelligence he knew his friend would value most. The rest – where and in what strength were the troops outside the fortress – Hervey would discover for himself. As for the tunnel of which Colonel Bell had told him, that ran from the old rajah's quarters to a haveli on the north side, there would probably be no knowing. The dewan would surely have placed a guard on it somewhere, and they could hardly enquire of a secret passageway.

No, this morning he'd confine himself to simpler objectives. Yet one thing did give him hope: it was Mira Bai passing through the gates of the citadel without hindrance, exactly as she said she'd be able to – for a day or so at least, until the dewan would for sure take counsel of his fears and deprive the Ranee of all comforts. She'd glanced at him as she hurried by, with the look that one conspirator had on seeing another – uneasy but confiding. She'd take the Ranee his message, that help would come though he knew not when.

* * *

Hervey slept in his cloak on a bed of ferns. Campfires and torches blazed, for Johnson had taken charge to ward off – in the words of the chaplain – 'every creeping thing that creepeth upon the earth', words which had gained a peculiar following among the dragoons but with additional adjectives unfit for the chaplain's hearing.

Somewhat contrarily, however, as was his wont, Johnson (who'd not himself bedded down yet, instead playing dice with the orderlies) now reckoned he quite liked the forest, or the 'jungle' as he preferred, for that was what old India hands called it, which he considered himself to be. It was a bit like the place he'd rambled as a child when he slipped free of the Poor Law stewards of a Sunday. There he'd spend a whole day without seeing a soul and hearing nothing but a bird singing or the bark of a roebuck – 'that pleasant district of merry England which is watered by the river Don' and which, as he'd learned later, Ivanhoe loved. But in those pleasant green places there'd been no creeping things to give him more than a bit of a sting – an ant or a bee or a wasp; nothing in the remotest bit deadly, and which a dock leaf could ease. There were adders, people said; but he'd never seen one. And besides, an adder couldn't kill you, while here, they *all* did, one way or another. They'd strangle you or crush the life out of you, or poison you for no reason. And that wasn't the worst of it: there were good snakes and bad snakes, as poor Annie had almost found out for herself in the stillroom when she'd heard Allegra call out in fright and rushed to see what it was, and gathered her up in her arms to shield her from the cobra, and Serjeant Stray had killed it in the nick of time ever so deftly with his sabre.

Everybody thought the world of Annie after that. (Well, they had already, but . . .), especially the colonel, and Mrs Hervey, and when Allegra's governess had given her notice, they'd promoted Annie in her place to be 'Miss Gildea', and she'd become quite the lady now – but just as nice and friendly, and a real good companion to Miss 'Ervey. He wasn't sure it was right that Colonel 'Ervey had changed his mind and let them both come into the jungle, but if anybody was hurt and had to go to Dr Milne's, Miss 'Ervey and Annie'd look after 'em right enough, and the wives who'd come as well . . .

But now the peace of the hour was disturbed, and his game of dice. 'Colonel,' he said, with a hand to Hervey's shoulder to wake him. 'It's Colonel Maclean, come to report.'

Hervey sat up and looked at his watch. It was just after midnight. 'Very well. And some coffee, if you will. And have Major Parry come.'

He got up and shook his cloak. It was a soft bed, and no doubt he'd shared it with some minor fauna, but nothing too alarming that he could see in the lantern light.

The galloper on picket brought Maclean to the bivouac. He had a tin mug in his hand already – the Sixth's rule that visitors were offered hospitality appropriate to the time of day, and Johnson's pot of coffee simmering since dusk.

'My dear General, I'm sorry indeed to disturb you, but at least it's with good news.'

Johnson put a tin mug into Hervey's hand.

He took a sip, grimaced, took another and hoped it would soon have effect so he needn't drink more.

'No apology needed, Colonel.'

'I never would have thought it, but the Chintalees put up such a fire at the river as I've never seen for so modest a demonstration as we were able to make. Cannon and musketry as if their lives depended on it. And all of it wild beyond speaking; we didn't lose a single man. Evidently their purpose is indeed to draw us in. We'll oblige them, therefore, keep 'em awake all night and make another demonstration at dawn, and we'll then get ready for Lindesay's men to relieve us.'

'Capital. Any word about the mysterious road south?'

'Indeed there is, which is why I've come. I sent a subaltern's patrol – Tysseu – one of my best. The road does indeed run straight south-west, just as the map indicates – wide enough for four horses, and there are tracks made by more than one well-laden cart. It stops dead after three miles or so for no purpose whatsoever except that there's a shrine of some sort. Tysseu couldn't make out what. He made a sketch, but I myself am none the wiser, though it's evidently some snake deity – a naga, perhaps; or even Shiva – when he wears that cobra for a necklace. But that's by the bye. The material point is that the forest there's perfectly open. The canopy's so full, says Tysseu, that it felt like dusk even when it was still broad daylight.'

Hervey took a mouthful of coffee in satisfaction. Just as he'd hoped – a full canopy restricting the light, so that nothing worth speaking of grew but the trees themselves.

'So there'd be no hindrance to infantry?'

'Nothing, certainly, that infantry couldn't manage, says Tysseu, perhaps in places with the odd axe. He spoke of some disobliging thorn, but he pressed on till they debouched at the Nerbudda, four miles; five at most. Once out, as far as he could see was paddy-field.'

'And the distance between forest and river?'

'Half a mile or so.'

Better even than he'd expected. 'He must have moved at some speed.'

Maclean nodded. 'When he reckoned he'd be able to get to the river before dark he decided to post pairs of men with torches as he went so as to guide him back. He's also marked the way by notching the trees.'

'Admirable. Well, I will meet with Mr Tysseu in due course. In the meantime, my compliments.'

By now, Parry had joined them, and Hervey had modified his plan.

'Colonel Maclean says infantry should have no difficulty getting through the forest south, cavalry also. Perhaps even a few guns therefore, if they're able to break them down for the closer stretches. I think it has capability.'

'Is there nothing yet from the north, General? I'm afraid I'm only just come in myself.'

Hervey looked at Maclean. He'd told him not to waste relays passing 'nothing to report', but he was surprised nevertheless that the squadron on the northern road evidently hadn't had touch with the enemy.

'I sent Taylor, my major, about two hours before last light, but he's not returned yet. That squadron had the longer road, of course.'

'Indeed. Frankly, I'm more anxious to have word from Worsley's troop. Otherwise I risk merely taking the line of least resistance, as it were.'

He smiled to himself – the Prussian again: *Only the element of chance is needed to make war a gamble, and that element is never absent.*

'Still, in view of what you've just brought me, I want to make some preliminary arrangements. I'm excessively obliged.'

Colonel Maclean said he looked forward to wasting more of the Chintalees' powder at dawn, then finished his coffee and took his leave. Parry opened his order book.

Hervey slept till first light, when Johnson brought him tea and a piece of biscuit spread with honey.

'Can I 'ave a word, Colonel?'

Hervey sat up in his leafy bed, hoping the word wouldn't be too diverting. 'What troubles you?'

'I were listenin' to Colonel Maclean last night, when 'e said about that shrine. What if it's there because the place's crawling with 'em?'

'With what?'

'Snakes.'

Hervey sighed. Johnson had become rather too preoccupied with snakes: probably since their last time in India, when he'd bought a mongoose and found it afraid of them. Still, dawn in the forest was an agreeable time, and there were worse things on waking than a few harmless words with a man who'd served so staunchly for twenty years.

'I'd think not. I don't know what the Indian calls it, but to the Greeks a hamadryad was a tree spirit, so a shrine here doesn't strike me as unusual. And frankly, five hundred pairs of boots are going to send every living thing scuttling.'

'It were just a thought.'

'And I hold your thoughts in high regard, Corporal Johnson, make no mistake . . . This tea is uncommonly good.'

'Thank you. Are *we* going past t'shrine an' all?'

'Very probably.'

'Corporal Boyle's just come in, by the way.'

Hervey quickened. Boyle was one of Worsley's best NCOs.

''E's talking to Major Parry.'

Five minutes later, Parry came with him, and the news he'd been waiting for.

'Captain Worsley reached Chintalpore last night, General. His intention was to make touch with Captain Fairbrother at once and then report in person as soon as he has intelligence.'

Hervey nodded. He'd expected no more at this time, only confirmation that they'd made Chintalpore without mishap.

He turned to Worsley's galloper. 'What time did you leave Captain Worsley, Corp'l Boyle?'

'Two hours before dark, Colonel – sorry, General. The road was full of Chintalees though. I 'ad to lie up for a few hours, and then find the stream we'd come down to get back to the middle o' the forest. There was a good moon, when it could get through the trees. I didn't sleep or anything, General. I kept on.'

Hervey nodded again. 'I hadn't supposed you could have done, Corp'l Boyle. I commend you heartily.'

'Colonel. Private Prettyman was my second, also, Colonel, sorry, General. He's green still, but he didn't once hesitate.'

'*Prettyman* . . .'

'He came with the last draft, General. Been a postboy.'

'Ah, yes. Capital.'

Garratt had brought the rest of the recruits with him to Sthambadree, reckoning they'd learn as much in a month as they would in six drilling at Fort St George. They hadn't passed out of sabre and carbine yet, but that was no great matter compared with the advantage of having a couple of dozen extra horse-holders (at least, perhaps, not unless it came to really hot work).

'The Somersets will be mustering soon, General,' said Parry. 'Do you want them to proceed?'

Hervey smiled. 'So Lindesay did choose Dennie . . . Yes, better to take the risks early – and it *is* still early. We can't expect anything more from Worsley for a good few hours yet, and if his intelligence is contrary, Dennie can always be recalled.'

At that he kept the smile to himself, though, well imagining Dennie's indignation on being told to counter-march. His concern at that moment was leaving Lindesay and the Thirty-ninth to fight the battle at the river. (And the beginnings again of that battle were quite audible, now.) In truth Lindesay would need another battalion if they were to keep up the demonstration for long. Sending off Dennie's on a flank march was indeed a gamble: *If a segment of one's force is located where it is not sufficiently engaged with the enemy, or if the troops are on the march while the enemy is fighting, then these forces are being managed inefficiently.*

It was all nonsense, of course; typical Prussian purism, but it nagged at him nevertheless.

'Have we offered you refreshment, Corp'l Boyle? You and Prettyman.'

'Colonel? Sorry – General.'

'Corp'l Johnson, please see to it that Corp'l Boyle and Private Prettyman have their fill of tea, and an egg.'

'Tea and one egg, yes, Colonel.'

'One apiece, I mean.' He knew Johnson would have a bag of hard-boiled eggs strung on the bat horse.

'An egg apiece, Colonel . . . Come this way, if you please, Corporal Boyle,' he said, in his best imitation of a butler.

Parry was still looking quizzical as Hervey caught his eye. 'War's a grim business, Robert, but it needn't be solemn.'

It was nearing eleven when Worsley came. It had been daylight for almost four hours – time enough and more to cover the distance, but not when the insurgents held the road so completely as they appeared to do. For by now, Hervey had had a full report from the northern squadron via the Thirteenth's major. They'd got within three or four miles of Chintalpore – by their reckoning – and then found the road stockaded. Even trying to outflank it had brought casualties, as the palisading extended well to the north and south and was strongly garrisoned. The forest beyond wasn't easy either, with much undergrowth, the major had said, and Colonel Craigie, the brigadier, was bringing up the heavier guns, intending to probe a while with fire.

'Fairbrother's as safe as may be,' said Worsley, in answer to Hervey's immediate question. 'Or rather, he would be if he'd lie low. He's with the hijdas, but he insists on going about with them.'

Hervey was relieved nevertheless.

Johnson brought a coffee pot and two enamelled mugs. Parry shook his head when offered a third.

'Very well, Christopher,' said Hervey, his immediate concern allayed. 'Yours to report.'

'General, it was approaching dusk by the time I'd made safe with the squadron – we kept in the forest; there was no chancing otherwise – so there was little I could see for myself, but I found Fairbrother easily enough after dark. He believes the insurgents are in some disarray, since they've not been able to take the palace – not all of it, that is. They have the bailey and the outworks, but not the palace itself, which the Ranee and her bodyguard hold, and a few guns.'

'The old rajah fortified it for just such a contingency.'

'But they've brought in a great many cannon and mounted them on the walls, and they've flooded the moat.'

'That was only to be expected, the moat. How many pieces?'

'Fairbrother said he hoped to discover that once it was daylight. He reckons it may be the major part of their artillery – about fifty. He says the Swiss haven't been seen though, which didn't surprise him, as Colonel Bell had never supposed they'd throw in willingly with the dewan.'

'Carry on.'

'He expects to be able to get inside the citadel by way of a communicating tunnel.'

'Ah; I didn't know of a tunnel. There again, there's no reason I should have.' He thought for a moment. 'How strong do *you* reckon is the dewan – within the moat, I mean?'

'Fairbrother said he estimated two thousand, for there wouldn't be room for more, but they could be many fewer. He hopes to discover it this morning. For myself I can't judge.'

'And what of the troops that are *not* in the palace?'

'My own observation, though only of the east side, which is, I fancy, the direction which they would have greatest care for, is that there are none but a guard for the moat. I observed for the better part of an hour at daylight, and saw no other. I suspect the dewan's made the error of not being able to decide where most to place his effort and instead has placed it everywhere.'

'The cavalry?'

'The cavalry's another matter – the Pindarees as Fairbrother calls them – I've seen nothing of them but the odd patrol. Fairbrother neither. Their grass month has just ended, apparently, and he thinks they may be kept to their quarters for fear they'll desert. He has a few spies in their camp but hasn't been able to make touch with them yet.'

'Mm. And the road you came by?'

'Pickets and camp-followers the length of it.'

Hervey thought for a moment or two more, then told him what he planned with Colonel Dennie's. 'If things go well with him, I ought to have the regiment and the Madras Horse before Chintalpore in two days. Tell Fairbrother to have Colonel Bell use all means to detach the Swiss – and to find out what he can of this tunnel. And where those damned Pindarees are.'

'Colonel.'

'And, Christopher, take no undue risks.'

In truth, the whole enterprise was one of risk; judging what was due and what was not would tax a Napoleon. Hervey knew it, but the sentiment made him feel better. Worsley knew it too, but appreciated the sentiment nonetheless.

* * *

Colonel Dennie, eagle-eyed, his jaw set and sword in hand to do battle with the trailing vines that entangled anyone who tried to wrestle with them (the old Ava hands called it 'wait-a-while'), marched at the head of his battalion like stout Cortez. If his infantrymen – *light* infantrymen – were to be sent through country unfit for habitation by any but savages, human and otherwise, it would be with him at the fore. For if he himself, Colonel William Dennie, were at their head, then no man, no matter how low his rank or base his nature, could shirk or falter. Or, if he did, he could not complain at the lash.

Behind him was his adjutant with the compass by which they would keep direction in the dense green. Then came the regimental pioneers, their axe blades new sharpened that morning, and behind them two dozen sappers lest their progress require more than just brute strength with the blade. 'The crooked shall be made straight', he'd told them, enlisting Isaiah; 'and the rough places plain.'

Then came the light companies in double file: six *centuria* (on paper at least; their true bayonet strength nearer eighty), a quarter of a mile of red-coated soldiery seasoned by Burman jungle, hardened by strict discipline at Agra, and hoping for plunder as rich as at Rangoon. Behind them, the six-pounders of the 'flying artillery' and a cornet and two dragoons of the Sixth, and then a second column – the baggage and camp-followers, despite the express instructions to march light. But then, sutlers and wives didn't count themselves under command; and who otherwise would care for those who fell sick or to the bullet – or provide them with spirits? Hervey had his doubts about the guns, even broken down and ported, but if there were the remotest chance of getting them through it was worth taking. 'First reckon, then risk,' he'd insisted. Dennie himself was certain of the matter, however: his battalion would make the way practicable. *Any* regiment of His Majesty's Foot would be able to make it so, though none, he said, as fast and surely as his. Which was why he'd insisted an officer of the troop be forward with his pioneers.

He would send out no scouts or flankers to beware ambush, however, for how were they to maintain direction? They'd only slow the advance. Besides, what skill did an insurgent rabble possess that might disconcert the 13th Light Infantry, or, indeed, what art of war to march through forest to take them by surprise? No, Colonel Dennie believed, as Hervey, in reckoning and then risking.

But they struck, in great numbers and savagery. Pioneers, sappers and men in the leading company were assailed with shocking speed. Many fell to the ground, others staggered blindly, while some ran swearing blue, hands clenched to their wounds.

Hornets.

Faces swelled like pumpkins; hands like gourds. In minutes, two men were gasping their last, and the adjutant lay back against a tree, unrecognizable, his breathing too shallow for hope. Dennie himself, his face so bloated as to make him unrecognizable too but for the crown on his epaulettes, could only keep upright with hands to a tree, breathing deeply yet still cursing, angered beyond reason that his battalion be thus stopped in its tracks.

Brandy came to his aid, the colour ensigns rushing to his side. Then a horse to support him. He thrust his right arm angrily through the stirrup leather, refusing all entreaties to get into the saddle, cursing foully still, every thing and every one.

But recover they must. The jungle took no side. He'd allow them half an hour, no more, and then those that couldn't rise – two dozen and more – he'd leave for the surgeon and the camp-followers.

The Somersets thus forged on, Dennie's jaw set even squarer, his sword swinging even angrier. '*And I will send hornets before thee, which shall drive out the Hivite, the Canaanite, and the Hittite, from before thee.*' Those within hearing thought he raved, but Dennie was leading them into the Promised Land, like the people of Israel. He'd spare neither himself nor any other to drive out these latter-day Hivites, Canaanites and Hittites – these tribes who opposed the coming of his battalion to Chintal.

And so when at last, in the late afternoon, they broached the forest edge, he smiled with grim satisfaction and told his major to carry on – to make a marching camp in the way he said that morning – and sat down with his back against a peepal tree, and though utterly exhausted wrote a despatch for Colonel Lindesay – and thence for Hervey – and sent the gunner back for his troop. And then, dosing himself with more brandy, he pulled his cloak round him, told his orderly to wake him before dawn, and lay down to sleep off the poison. Colonel William

Dennie would wake ready for whatever the day or Hervey's gallopers might bring. That, or he'd not wake at all.

As for those left for the surgeon and the camp-followers, however, five would breathe their last before morning, and be buried with bayonets for grave markers and shakos tied to them to honour their regiment. It scarcely mattered that their names couldn't be inscribed, for who would read them in the forest? They were known unto God and, in due course, the regimental paymaster. That was all that counted.

XXIII

The General's Art

Next morning

Dennie's despatch had come just after midnight. And great relief it was. Hervey had made two plans for the morning: if Dennie's answer were 'nay', he'd recall them and bring the Madras Native Infantry from the northern road, together with most of the artillery, and begin the butcher-business of overcoming the defences at the river. 'Mere pounding', he'd said to himself disconsolately. If Dennie's answer were 'yea', however, he'd at once send the Nizam's contingent to reinforce him, then brigade the 13th and the 6th Light Dragoons under Colonel Maclean (but keeping Worsley's troop under his own command) and have them follow as soon as the infantry brigadiers were content to have them go. The dragoons would shock the Chintalees at the river and the stockade when they assailed them from the rear. Indeed, likely as not they'd scarce need to fire a shot.

His gallopers performed prodigiously in those early hours. He knew they would – picked men – but even so it was a relief to find Gordon's Nizams on the march so soon after sunrise. 'Into the hornets' nest', perhaps, real and figurative. The Prussian hornet was bad enough: seven stings to kill a horse, as they used to say, and *vier für ein Mann, und zwei für ein Kind* – but the Indian, real or figurative, was the very devil. Well, so be it. The jungle took no sides, though he meant to make it an ally.

As soon as it was light he wrote a despatch for Somervile, supposing his old friend would soon be back at Sthambadree, but promising no rapid success. Somervile's humour was not always that of the soldier, even though – like the old Prince Regent – he fancied himself the leader of men on occasions. Certainly, Hervey had no wish now to give him any pretext to join them. In a few days more – a week at most, he trusted – he'd be able to send word that the Governor of Madras was welcome in the capital of Her Highness the Ranee, but it wouldn't do to misjudge the matter now.

Judging anything, though, in this green fog of war would test a man. The art of the general, said the Prussian, consisted 'entirely and completely' in his *Überblick* – a tricky word, 'overview' literally, 'grasp of matters' – without which he was overpowered by events rather than dominating them. But here he fought blind, reliant wholly on what was brought to him by others. Indeed, he might as well sit in front of a chessboard as ride about the forest, for here there was no profit in the cavalryman's *coup d'oeil*. And yet he must judge what was brought him; and how might he do that without some sense at least of whence it came? He'd therefore spent the rest of the day before with the Dorsetshires at the river, and then gone to see the Westmorelands as they pressed the stockades. Both seemed to have mastered the game of 'demonstration', harassing the defenders without losing men (or rather, too many men), but he didn't suppose the Chintalees could be deceived for long, and he'd therefore warned the brigadiers to be ready to stand on the defensive in case of counter-attack. Afterwards he chided himself a little, but a general must be forgiven for occasionally making sure his subordinates knew their job, even if he himself were more acquainted with sabre and spur than boot and bayonet. He mustn't meddle, though: brigadiers fight the enemy; the general fights the battle.

It wasn't till the middle of the morning that the dragoons recovered themselves and Maclean got them into some semblance of a brigade. That scarcely troubled Hervey, for the Nizams would by his calculation take five or six hours to negotiate 'Dennie's Road', and he wanted also to see the Native Infantry come down from the north to join Lindesay's brigade (on which he'd decided late). It gave him opportunity, too, to speak with Major Garratt, who was all blitheness at the prospect of dismounted work if, as he put it, it came to 'winkling out'. The only question was if, when assailed both front and rear, the Chintalees would throw down their arms or scatter. By rights, taking them prisoner was the better course always, but who would be their gaolers? Hervey supposed that, being irregulars, scattered they'd take an age to rally, and therefore no trouble for a day or so, which might, contrary to the usual precepts of war, be the better. If they did yield, however, he said it would fall to the cavalry to take and keep them prisoner – though which cavalry he couldn't yet tell.

Armstrong was with the major, too, and in his element. They'd neither a lame horse nor a sick dragoon, 'and the farriers all idle'. Hervey walked aside with him while Garratt had a word with Parry about the gunners.

'What isn't clear to me is where the "Pindarees" are. Skulking in their lines perhaps, or nowhere at all, even, taken French leave, paid or unpaid. I've yet to have word from Captain Fairbrother.'

'Nor from Captain Worsley?'

'I didn't want them breaking cover too soon, showing we were close. In any event, this road the Somersets have opened – we'll have a thousand and more horse through by evening. It ought to serve.'

Armstrong agreed. He'd no great regard for the Pindaree relics he'd clashed with at Bhurtpore. 'Aye, Colonel; they're fleet enough, but they don't stand.'

Hervey nodded. He was certainly counting on it.

Garratt had finished his discourse with Parry.

Armstrong braced up. 'With your leave, then, Colonel – *General*?'

Hervey returned the salute. 'And you *will* remember to allow the sar'nt-majors their share of shot and shell, Mr Armstrong?'

'Sir!'

Half enquiry, half order – but, Hervey knew, without point.

It was towards five o'clock when they emerged from the cool and silence of the forest into the bright sun of the Nerbudda's flood plain. A picket of the Somersets directed him to Colonel Dennie's pennant atop a goat-house whose occupants had no further need of it, having the night before become mutton.

Everywhere was pleasing order, dragoons off-saddled and grooming, with running lines up and grass-cutters at work. The Nizams were no less exemplary, while the Somersets' marching camp would have done them justice on any inspection, with a picket line a good half a mile distant and the gunners' flying troop disposed to support. Whatever Dennie's prostration, his staff and company officers knew their business.

'General!'

Hervey was surprised to see him on his feet, and dismounted at once to return the salute. 'Colonel Dennie, my hand, sir; my compliments to you. And my condolences. I came on the graves an hour ago.'

'Thank you, General. Two were rogues and worse, but the others were good men.'

'And you yourself?'

Dennie shrugged. 'I can testify to their distress.'

Hervey nodded. Dennie's face was like a pug's who'd lost his wager. 'Is there anything more to report?'

'No, the night passed quietly. I had the horse troop make a clearing patrol after stand-to this morning – about three miles – and they saw nothing. There's a village of sorts a mile or so east, but they appear unworried, or unknowing. The dragoons'll make another clearing patrol later.'

'Capital. I'm minded not to wait, however. There's a good moon, and with no enemy abroad . . . Do your men have another march in them?'

'Certainly. They've full canteens and bellies, though biscuit mainly. To where?'

'To cork the bottles, so to speak. The sooner we belabour those Chintalees from the rear, the sooner we can invest the palace.'

Dennie nodded. Hervey had explained it before he'd marched. 'But I'm loth to divide the battalion.'

'No, I wouldn't have you do that. The corking'll be for the dragoons. I would have you make a demonstration before the palace. Cavalry alone won't fright them behind walls.'

Dennie agreed, but doubted the wisdom of marching at once. By his reckoning, Chintalpore was a dozen miles and more, and the going uncertain. It would take an hour to break camp, there were but a couple more of daylight left, and there was cloud looming. If they did march at once they'd hardly be fresh for a fight before midday; if they marched at dawn, however, they'd cover the ground quicker, and be better ready after a bit of sleep – and just a few hours later.

Hervey thought for a moment, then bid Dennie sit on the wall of the goat-house as they took coffee. For the advice of an officer of infantry on such a matter as a night march was not something to dismiss lightly. Yes, he'd known the odd old woman of a colonel who wasn't content unless he'd an hour for mustering and his fifes and drums every step of the way, but Dennie was no such colonel. Some officers needed encouraging, and some driving; but very few needed restraining. And Dennie, most decidedly, was in the latter category.

Then he understood. 'No, you mistake me. I'll not have your men make an assault. I'll hazard no more lives than strictly necessary. I mean to *manoeuvre* them out.'

Philanthropists, said the Prussian, with evident disdain, might easily imagine there to be a skilful method of overcoming an enemy without great bloodshed; and this was an error that must be extirpated. But Hervey was unconvinced. He'd no objection to the enemy spilling blood, but counted it a commander's first duty to spare as much of his own men's as possible. It was no great art to suppose that since men must die there was no point in troubling if they did so needlessly. There were some who counted men merely as ordnance, to be spent and then replaced at will – that was Bonaparte's way, as he'd seen for himself – but while well and good for Frenchmen, in the end it never did for 'gentlemen in red'. Besides, he'd been at Badajoz and Bhurtpore: the best-regulated troops could turn into fiends after storming a fortress. In the long run it was to no one's advantage, least of all to discipline.

XXIV

Fire and Manoeuvre

Next morning

The Ranee trembled as she spoke, though she struggled to master her dread. Show fear, and predators struck. Besides, if she were to be spirited away through that dark, dank tunnel – and who knew what perils lay therein? – few could accompany her. Death remained – certain death – for those left behind. The rissaldar and loyal sowars had their own lives to save as well as hers. Whose would they choose first? (It had ever been thus with Praetorians.)

'Tell your husband, Mira Bai, that it must be this day. As soon as the Company's soldiers appear before the walls, Ashok Acharya will force himself upon us, and the bodyguard will be overcome, and then my life shall be held forfeit. It must be this day. This mulatto captain, he is brave and true, you say. He must act, at once.'

Mira Bai could assure her that Fairbrother was brave and true, for though she would not say it, to come within the walls of the palace, even as a hijda, was perilous in the extreme. As for her husband, it surely went without saying – and yet he had her children to keep safe, and few enough to guard the house. 'I will go at once, Highness. Trust to Kali.'

The rissaldar beckoned one of his Sikhs, truest of his true, to escort the Ranee's lady to the citadel gate. He knew not precisely of what they'd spoken, but he saw that his Ranee was fearful – bravely though she tried to hide it (doubly bravely, for she was but a woman) – and for the moment it mattered not. As soon as she gave him leave he would order the entire rissalah – sixty sowars – to put saffron on their faces and a yellow cloak over their armour, just as a Rajpoot prince, riding out to fight, would vow that if he could not win he would die, and his bondsmen likewise would put on yellow, the clothes of the dead, vowing not to return from battle unless victorious – sworn to die. And this – this above all – would surely give heart to his Ranee?

Mira Bai slipped out of the gate of the citadel to respectful compliments from the guards – the dewan's guards keeping the pretence of ceremony rather than confinement. (Inside, men of the rissalah stood more serious sentry, a field piece loaded with grape ready to sweep the approaches.) She walked slowly but unhesitant, her eyes lowered modestly, her left hand at the skirt of her saree to lift it an inch or two clear of the earth, her right clutched to her breast. Her Rajpoot instinct was to walk with head held high, but women were few within the palace walls now – even the hijdas were fewer – and she would not tempt hindrance or insult.

As she reached the middle of the maidan a subedar of the dewan's auxiliaries, ill-dressed and rough in manner, barred her way.

'Your deceit is discovered, Mira Bai. Come with me. Begin your prayers.'

Ashok Acharya watched from the shadows of the great bastion. He himself recoiled from the actual exercise of force. The very sight of blood, even, troubled him. He'd contrived the business at the snake pit because there was no other way, but that was with the Ranee; there must be no doubt as to what he implied. But brute threats as now – he hadn't the stomach for it, and certainly no pleasure. Let the subedar do his work. He'd watched him with others. The subedar most certainly took pleasure in it. And with a woman doubly so, a highborn Rajpoot especially.

Mira Bai said her prayers. She prayed for the protection of Kali, and for mercy if she was not spared, but first for strength.

The subedar and his men took her to the far end of the bastion, to the snake pit she'd heard of but never seen. There was no light but for the torches – terror enough – but then the pit and waiting death in the spreading hood of the cobra.

'*Om Sri Maha Kalikayai Namah*,' she began – I bow my head to the Divine Mother Kali . . .

'You will tell what passes between the Ranee and the outside,' said the subedar, grasping her by her arms and pushing her to the edge of the pit.

'*Om Sri Maha Kalikayai Namah* . . .'

He shook her as if to let go. 'You will tell what passes between the Ranee and the outside, or you will not see her again or the sky, or your husband or your children.'

'*Om Sri Maha Kalikayai Namah* . . .'

'By the curse of Lord Shiva, you tell what it is that passes!'

But Mira Bai would not tell.

The subedar swore, and spat words to one of his men, who hurried away as if possessed.

He pulled Mira Bai from the edge of the pit. No one before had ever defied him, he cried.

And Mira Bai looked not defiant but terrified.

He half dragged her from the bastion, out into the sunlight of the maidan which she'd thought she'd never again see. She began to sob.

He pushed her to her knees and yelled to the man he'd sent running, who now drove his heel into the small of her back.

She gasped and fell on her hands.

Out of the shadows came a brute figure, not a soldier by any description. A bhuttote, a strangler.

The roomal swung round her neck in one movement. She had no time to gasp again. In half a minute she lay still.

The onlookers – there were many – kept silent. It took repeated words of command to turn them away to their duties. Kill one, frighten a thousand.

The hijdas were silent too.

* * *

A general who declines to attack the enemy in a defensive position, advancing instead by another line in pursuit of his object, will (if he is able to pass-by with impunity) immediately force the enemy to abandon the position. For the enemy always has a dread of his retreat being cut off.

This indeed was Hervey's intention, mindful too of what the Prussian said was the most powerful device in the art of war: surprise. And that consisted in 'opposing the enemy with a great many more troops than he expected at some particular point so that the actual superiority in numbers becomes suddenly of little – or certainly lesser – importance'. (Really, it was nothing that a common captain didn't know – one at least with five years in the field against the French – but ne'er so well expressed.) Colonel Dennie had therefore agreed that winning a couple of hours more by marching at once might save blood; and Colonel Maclean had agreed to dividing his dragoons – vexing though it was – to make a demonstration against the rear of *both* positions, the river and the stockade, and likewise to march before sunset. Major Garratt had needed little persuading to have his two squadrons re-saddle at once and clear and mark the route for them. So that only the reserve, the Nizam's contingent, would march after last light – a good two hours after – for there was nothing more trying for cavalry, even when horses were led, than to be slowed by infantry ahead of them; just as there was nothing more trying for infantry than to march over ground roiled by more horseshoes than was unavoidable.

The moon set just after three and Hervey's orders had been for commanding officers to judge the condition of their men at that point and to rest until dawn unless they thought there was advantage in pressing on in what would then be Stygian darkness.

At three o'clock, therefore, in the last guttering moonlight, the Somersets had lain down in column of route and slept. Dennie, at their head, had looked though his telescope with satisfaction at the distant watch fires of Chintalpore – a mile and a half, perhaps two. Thirteen miles they'd covered, in eight hours. It was hardly the pace Sir John Moore (of blessèd memory) had set at Hythe when he trained the first regiments of light infantry, but then he, Dennie, had at least kept his battalion in one piece and good order; and when the sun came up again they'd march off briskly in column of companies – and, as he told his captains, 'We shall shock them!'

The Thirteenth, with Colonel Maclean at their head, marching dismounted for all but the last hours of daylight, had made rapid progress too, reaching their objectives, the two debouches (to their surprise, not picketed), with the moon still up to light their bivouac. Maclean had sent word to Hervey by galloper – 'The corks are in the bottle.'

The Sixth, meanwhile, their marker work done with the passing of the Somersets, had also been able to rally by moonlight, under the direction of Armstrong's blue-glass lantern, off-saddling for three hours' rest till stand-to at first light. Theirs then would be to screen the Somersets as they alternately quick- and double-marched to Chintalpore. ('Same as herding cattle', the dragoons joked; or even sheep, said some, but slower.)

Hervey joined them just before moonset.

*

'Tea, Colonel.'

Johnson's hand to his shoulder again. It was enough somehow to wake him always from the deepest sleep, and the tea likewise to fortify his most doubtful spirits.

'Thank you,' he said, sitting up and letting the cloak fall from his shoulders.

'I meant "General", Colonel.'

'I know you did.'

Once it had been just 'sir' – *Mister* Hervey. They'd travelled a good many miles since then, and yet it was always the same (or so it seemed): a bed of turf, and soon the saddle, and then . . .

'Stay with the bat horses today, Corp'l Johnson. No need to muster.'

'Colonel?'

'There's no purpose.'

Johnson was puzzled. There was never 'purpose'; yet still he mustered. If Hervey – Cornet, Captain, Colonel – mustered, then so did he. He'd lead his second charger, or be additional coverman, or just be ready to take the reins if he dismounted. They had a bearer *and* a syce with them; why on earth did the bat horses need him suddenly?

'But . . .'

Then he thought better of it. There'd be opportunity enough to get him to change his mind. He'd always been able to about this and that, little things. (If there were going to be a fight, he'd be damned if he were going to miss it.)

Hervey rose, shook his cloak and said he'd shave – the business of a quarter-hour only (he wasn't dressing for a ball); and in that time Johnson could have Minnie fed, and then saddled as soon as the Somersets were ready to march. The razor was worth four hours' sleep. Besides, a general ought to look as if he were in possession of time, rather than pressed by it. It would, though, be another meagre breakfast for them, though at least with the visible prospect of fresh rations. The storehouses of Chintalpore would soon be theirs; and when the Thirteenth gave the Chintalees their shock, the commissary waggons would bring plenty of salt beef.

In these latitudes the sun rose without hesitating, and but for the shadow at the forest edge, the stage was now at last revealed. There, to the north and west, a league or so, was the city, with the fortress-palace prominent on the hill. Both looked at peace. The forest was its usual morning dissonance, all manner of birds, monkeys and heaven-knew-what-else waking to the new day and calling out in joy, or else in fear and warning. There'd been few shots during the night – none that Hervey had heard, certainly – and there were none now either. The brigadiers before the two Chintalee positions – Lindesay and Craigie – knew the plan: confuse and unnerve the defenders with silence at first light, and then as soon as the dragoons made their show, press the attack.

The Somersets, having stood-to-arms while it was still dark, now made short work of breakfast and breaking camp, and began mustering in column of company. Hervey knew he was asking much of them. Biscuit was no real good to fight on, or even just to march (Charles Stuart's men had learned that hard before Culloden, while the admirable Cumberland had fed his men on beef), and he thanked God he'd a man like Colonel Dennie in command. Dennie had led them every inch of the way; and Hervey was certain he'd *drive* them if necessary when the time came.

'Stand-to!'

It came suddenly, repeated left and right.

He was about to mount, but instead pulled out his telescope.

Horsemen; in the shadow of the forest; half a mile north.

'I do believe it's Worsley.'

Major Parry had his telescope too. 'Dragoons, certainly, General. They're in no hurry; no one in pursuit, evidently.'

Hervey put away his telescope. 'I'll let Dennie stand-down in his own time nevertheless.'

It was a full five minutes before Colonel Dennie was satisfied his battalion would not have to form square.

Two minutes later Worsley and half a dozen dragoons trotted briskly up to Hervey's pennant.

There were the customary exchanges, though perhaps with more relief than usual.

And then the report. 'As you instructed, I sent out patrols at first light. I've come at once, however, because we were able to scout during the night and I myself made touch again with Fairbrother. The communicating tunnel's flooded, by which he supposes that Ashok Acharya didn't know of it, as they'd never have flooded it otherwise.'

Hervey looked doubtful. 'It's a poor communicating tunnel that's flooded unintentionally.'

Worsley raised his eyebrows as if to say it was as much as he knew. 'But Fairbrother believes it's salvable.'

'How the deuce does he suppose that?'

'He wasn't awfully forthcoming, but Colonel Bell knows a great deal about it, it seems, and Fairbrother's hijdas come and go as they please.'

'No matter. But how's it salvable? I've but a few sappers.'

Worsley now looked sceptical. 'He's gone to the coal pits to bring a steam engine. He's found a place to pump the water unobserved.'

Hervey sighed. 'It can do no harm, I suppose.'

Frankly, though, he was beginning to wonder if Fairbrother's newfound fascination with steam was altogether sane.

'And the city itself?'

Worsley said he thought it possible the people had little idea that anything untoward was happening. Even the flooding of the moat hadn't seemed to excite much notice, and there were few if any in uniform on the streets. 'I got about with no difficulty whatsoever.'

Hervey nodded. It boded well for a long siege at least, a docile population at one's back.

'And what of the "Pindarees"?'

Worsley shook his head. 'Other than that their grand barracks are empty, nothing yet. I've tried to send word that riches beyond belief are theirs if they remain loyal, but have had no word by reply. I'm rather pinning my hopes on the patrols.'

Hervey nodded again. It wasn't easy, he knew. 'It's not unknown for a freebooter to take his troops some distance from the fight and wait to hear how it's going . . . All the more reason to make a demonstration before the palace as soon as may be.'

'The patrols have orders to send word as soon as they make touch.'

Hervey stiffened suddenly. Shots – a great many; muffled, indistinct, but the sound of battle, unquestionably.

Then he smiled with satisfaction. 'The Thirteenth beginning their work.'

'I saw their pickets.'

'The greatest folly the Chintalees didn't picket. Careless practice. No sign of communication with the palace. And I warrant the palace'll believe the noise to be frontal attacks.' He wouldn't tempt fate by saying so, or encourage any to drop his guard, but he was thankful nevertheless that he was evidently opposed by no great general.

'Quite,' said Worsley. 'An easy enough job, too.'

The sound was now of considerable cannonry, and growing.

'Well, Lindesay and Craigie know their business, and Maclean.'

Johnson brought coffee. Hervey took his knowing that in doing so he turned a blind eye to the disobedience. (Johnson always managed to interpret to advantage all but a direct order.)

A few minutes later, Parry pointed them to rear. 'The Nizams approach, General.'

Hervey turned. They were an imposing sight at the best of times: so many horsemen. His design for battle was now complete: he had his reserve at hand, and the way was clear. A risk, though, using them.

'They come most carefully upon their hour, too. I believe we're now as well set as may be.'

Parry beckoned the orderlies to take the word to Dennie and Maclean.

They cut about like lurchers on a hare.

In ten minutes the Somersets struck off to the bugle in column of company: *Advance!* – repeated semi-quavers, Gs and Cs.

The Sixth, with two guns of the flying troop – flank guards and screening – began their advance with a sabre signal.

Worsley finished his second cup of coffee. 'Orders, General?'

'Where and when will your squadron rally if they don't make touch with the Pindarees?'

'On the Somersets when they reach the palace.'

'Very well; till then, ride with me.'

Hervey wished he'd a decent artist with him: dragoons, flying guns, red-coated infantry, Nizam's horse – a field day, even, was nothing to the eye to compare with this; and all making their steady way across the green plain towards the castle on the hill, warmed but not oppressed by the steadily rising sun, with no noise but that of distant battle in the forest, the creaking of leather, jingling of bits and snorting of horses. This was the best of the soldier's art, before it became the work of the butcher. The eggs weren't yet in the pudding, but there was much to savour: *A general who declines to attack the enemy in a defensive position, advancing instead by another line in pursuit of his object, will (if he can pass-by with impunity) immediately force the enemy to abandon the position.*

Fortunes could turn in a moment, though. A plan rarely unfolded as desired. Yet a general must impart confidence to his command: 'I charm thy life / From the weapons of strife, / From stone and from wood, / From fire and from flood, / From the serpent's tooth, / And the beast of blood.'

'General?'

'Mr Southey, gentlemen: *The Curse of Kehama*. It's been my companion these past months.'

'An Indian story?' asked Parry.

'Indeed so, though whether it's a true representation of the Hindoo's religion I can't say, but it compels.'

'Our "beast of blood", I take it, is the dewan?'

Hervey nodded. 'Probably, yes. The other elements are plain enough.'

'Or else the "Tigress"?'

He certainly trusted not. He'd thrown in all with the Ranee. It wouldn't be the first time an Englishman had been tricked by a prince here in India, but for him it would be the end. 'An unhappy prospect.'

Worsley sensed his unease. 'I am with Blake and *his* tiger,' he said, intending to deflect the thought.

'How so?'

'I have these past days been in the forests of the night.'

They laughed. 'That indeed is droll.'

Then the scouts were active suddenly.

Horsemen . . .

Hervey halted and took out his telescope. 'Yours, I believe, Christopher.'

Worsley had his own 'scope to his eye. 'Cornet Kynaston, indeed.'

He came at a hand-gallop, two dragoons close on his heels.

A minute more, and . . . 'General!'

Hervey returned the salute. 'Report, Mr Kynaston.' (He supposed he'd be doing so too in due course to his uncle.)

'Mr Grace's compliments, General. Pindarees, one thousand perhaps, are proceeding south towards the palace and to its east. There are two thousand more encamped a league west of the palace, but at the time of observing, shortly after dawn, they showed no sign of leaving. Mr Grace maintains his observation of these, as does Mr Price the thousand.'

'No sign of artillery?'

'None, General.'

'Nor scouting patrols?'

'None.'

He turned to Worsley. 'Very well; you'll wish to return to your troop. A close eye, if you please, on the Pindaree camp, and action if they stir.' He'd no need to be any more explicit. Worsley would do what he had to.

'General.'

'Carry on . . . And, Mr Kynaston: good work.'

'General.'

They took their leave and kicked into a gallop for the forest edge, Worsley thinking only on how quickly he could gather up his scattered command. As for interference by the enemy, it was good to be mounted on corn-fed horses (even on short rations of late), for if there were need, they'd be able to out-gallop a grass-fed Pindaree's.

'Major Garratt, if you please,' said Hervey briskly.

A galloper sped off to fetch him.

Major Parry closed to his side again.

'Three thousand, General?'

'No matter. It's as we thought,' adding that with the Nizams, they'd not be so very greatly outnumbered – and they'd certainly have the advantage in discipline. 'But only a thousand on the move: d'ye suppose they reckon us an easy prize?'

'Or might the rest be, as you say, waiting to see the way of the wind?'

'Quite. But we'll see what we'll see.'

Parry could only admire his composure, and hope indeed that the wind was favourable.

Garratt galloped up. 'General?'

'We may soon see cavalry a mile or so distant. I can only surmise their purpose is to prevent our reaching the palace. We shall deal with them in customary fashion. I shall bring up one of the Nizam's – Gordon's – on your left, and the other as support, and the brigade will advance in two lines. You will command the first line and I the support. In the charge, your right troop will direct. Guns will remain with the Somersets until the rally. Judge your moment to charge, but give the enemy no time. They perhaps intend a good display for the palace, and if we catch them right it will go doubly to our advantage.'

'Very good, General.'

Parry looked troubled. 'General, with respect, leading the second line; you are commander of the field force. Oughtn't the brigade to be—'

'I'm obliged to you, Major Parry. There are two brigadiers in the event of mishap, and Lindesay the senior.'

'Sir.'

Serjeant Acton smiled. He could have told him that himself.

'Gallopers!'

Orders flew to the Nizams and the Somersets, and the guns, who cursed loudly at being made to unhook instead of going on with the Sixth.

Dennie's men began forming square, the first time Hervey had seen a battalion do so since Waterloo. Once dressed, the order came to load with ball, and then 'Fix bayonets!'

He touched his peak to them as he trotted by. 'Stand-fast, Light Infantry; your time will come!'

Colonel Dennie raised his sword to the salute, then turned and ordered 'Skirmishers out!'

In the far distance the host of 'Pindaree' horsemen at last made their appearance.

The Sixth were already forming two lines, with Gordon's coming up on their left. Hervey placed himself centre and fifty yards to the rear, the second regiment of the Nizam's trotting up in two ranks and halting a dozen lengths behind him. Armstrong saluted as he trotted past to take post at the rear of the Sixth's second rank. Hervey touched the peak of his cap by return – no point now wondering if he'd heed his words ('let others have their share of the shot') – then drew his sword. He'd have drawn it at the head of the first line if he'd not had regard for what Parry had been at pains to remind him. Garratt was anyway capable of leading a charge, and the captains knew their business. The real decision lay in when and where to commit the supports. If all they faced were a thousand, he was sure the first line would break them, even just a few hundred sabres – if, that is, they drove in pell-mell and the Pindarees didn't get their lance points down at too fast a pace. He'd just have to look out for trickery – a masked battery or some such (another thousand waiting in the wings, say). Then the supports would be decisive. It wasn't likely, but he couldn't entirely rule it out, no matter how sharp-eyed Worsley's troop had been.

'Draw swords!'

Garratt's words of command brought three hundred sabres from their scabbards, blades flashing in the sunlight.

The Nizams, flank and rear, drew theirs, making eight hundred in all.

Hervey could see now that the Pindarees were halted, with a frontage of several hundred yards. If they chose now to advance they'd almost certainly overlap his line on the right, and possibly the left if the Nizams didn't open out a little.

'Walk-march!'

Garratt's trumpeter sounded the order.

The line billowed forward.

Hervey's followed.

Fifty yards on, and no move from the Pindarees.

'Trot!'

The horses knew the trumpet call. Hooves began pounding the hard earth two-time.

With a nod to the commandant of the Nizams behind him, a brawny Deccani Mussulman, Hervey bid the supports follow.

Still the Pindarees remained motionless.

Hervey smiled grimly. It was a fault he'd observed before in India – waiting, in order to be sure. Fatal.

With a furlong to go Garratt put them into a gallop.

Down at last came the Pindaree lances – but only those on the flanks came forward to meet them.

Hervey quickened the pace but held short of a gallop. Both the right of the Sixth's line and left of the Nizams began extending so as not to be taken in flank.

'Good work!' (though no one heard).

Then the bugle sounding the charge, and the sabres pointing . . .

He quickened the pace again, but still a canter, a hundred yards behind the first line – perfect.

Now just twenty yards for Garratt to the Pindarees . . .

Then the crash of men and horses, blades and points.

And then the check; always the check – an age sometimes, in truth just seconds – before the effect revealed. Men – Pindarees – gave way, rallied, gave way again, turned once more to fight; or yielded, fled or fell bloodily from the saddle. The lance was supreme in the charge, useless in the melee. Those who threw them away and drew swords bore it longer. But the crush foiled many a one.

Garratt's line made progress, but it was time for more steel.

'Now, Commandant! Both flanks,' shouted Hervey, gesturing left and right with his sabre.

In joining the melee, the support line must not disorder the first line by too great a momentum.

Regulations. All well on paper but . . .

They drove in at a gallop.

In an instant the Pindaree flanks, inclined at too great an angle to see them bearing down, ceased to exist. Hervey made for the centre surrounded by his gallopers, Acton as ever a length and a half behind.

Regulations.

He drove with the point for a Pindaree battling with a stricken dragoon, pitching him from the saddle like a sack in a tiltyard, then cutting at a second trying to turn about, who took Acton's point a second later.

A pistol exploded so close as to deafen. Minnie stumbled over a falling horse but recovered – heaven knew how. Hervey grasped back the reins and dug in his spurs, lying along her neck and cutting left and right. She leapt at a gap, just missing a spear – which Acton dealt with, giving point as he followed through – and Hervey drove his own at another spearman who'd left it too late to draw sword instead.

Then he was clear; nothing before him but the backs of fleeing men.

But he was bloodied and breathless, the ringing in his ears as loud as the battle behind. He was exhilarated by the charge, as always – as every man – but this time strangely spent, though an affair of just minutes. Indeed, one of the quickest he'd known.

But now he turned to weigh the butcher's bill.

It was savage.

XXV

The Race to the Quick

That evening

'There's nothing more I can do for him, I fear, Colonel. His lungs are quite certainly full of blood. He can't last the night.'

Milne spoke softly. He was as fond of Garratt as he supposed Hervey was.

The major lay unconscious. The hospital was a fine haveli, which on Milne's orders the dragoons had cleared downstairs of all but a few chairs and instead brought in straw – better, he said, to 'muck out', like a stable, and as comfortable as a bed to men still in the remains of uniform. They'd stripped and washed those in the beds upstairs, the lesser wounded. Clean sheets for them were practicable as well as decent.

Milne had not been short of assistance. 'Annie and Miss Hervey haven't slept, I'd say. Nor the wives. I tell you, they've not spared themselves the filthiest chore.'

Hervey nodded. Whores and harridans the dragoons had called the camp-followers in Portugal and Spain – even some of the wives – but regular 'Magdalens' when it came to this.

'And the Indian women too,' Milne added. 'They've done fine service.'

'Capital,' said Hervey, trying hard to maintain the mask of the soldier steeled to the price of his profession. 'And Armstrong?'

Milne raised an eyebrow. 'I fancy a surgeon faced with a bigger bill would have amputated – so much blood – but the wound's clean enough. Not all agree, but I swear by permanganate. I've closed it with a great many stitches, I might add. But he kept insisting he'd return to duty, so I've trussed him like a lunatic to restrain the limb – and himself. A fortnight's light duties. I can't be held responsible if it's any less.'

'I shall see to it. And St Alban?'

'He too insisted on returning to duty, but I've strictly forbidden it. The wound's deeper than Armstrong's and he has crushed ribs. I believe he'll be well, but there's a risk of oedema of the lungs, which can be fatal. Indeed, it more usually is. I've dosed him with laudanum to reduce the respiratory distress. Miss Hervey's been tending him with especial care.'

Hervey nodded again. 'Twelve dead, and some I can scarcely afford.'

'I'm sorry. They were dead, or as good as, by the time I reached them.'

'The Nizams fared better, and they have a good surgeon.'

'Yes, a fine fellow. And what of your infantry, Colonel? I've not heard.'

'The Dorsets and the Westmorelands barely a dozen dead between them. They really were most skilfully handled. The Somersets none at all, except to the hornets. Extraordinary that a thing so small should be so deadly.'

'*Omnes feriunt, ultima necat . . .*'

Hervey sighed. 'Indeed. And one of the Thirteenth's succumbed to a krait, and another may do so yet.'

'Indeed? Were I not occupied here I'd see him for myself – to observe the symptoms; their surgeon's admirable.'

'Doubtless there'll be others when the grass-cutters begin work.'

Milne stooped to check Garratt's breathing, then rose again, satisfied there was no change. 'How, may I ask, do your operations proceed?'

Hervey took him aside. 'I'm excessively content. The only hostile troops are now within the palace – the fortress. Those in the forest threw down their arms soon enough, and the rest of the Pindarees yielded to Worsley without setting foot out of camp. Swore they'd been loyal throughout – doubtless a retrospective decision. The fugitives from the charge must've made a profound impression. That and the promissory notes of gold – not in my experience unusual in these lands.'

'*Condottieri* – was ever thus?'

'And we must be glad of it. Better to buy with gold than pay in lead.'

'Indeed.'

'Oh, and I have a battery of howitzers. Colonel Bell managed to buy one after all. And we have the guns from the forest.'

'You'll forgive me, Colonel: howitzers?'

'They shoot at a high angle – over the walls rather than battering at them. Explosive shell. They're in action as we speak.'

'"Now Jericho was straitly shut up because of the children of Israel: none went out, and none came in."'

Hervey nodded. Joshua had been his first hero. He'd had spies in Jericho, one of them a harlot. Then having gained his intelligence, he'd had the trumpets blow.

'I have my Rahab, too, doctor. Or rather, Fairbrother has – several of them.'

Milne allowed himself a smile. 'I had heard that. You count, then, on their asking for terms?'

'That would be a fine thing, except that the Ranee's life is all that Ashok Acharya has to bargain with, and that, by all accounts, is still not in his gift, and he daren't risk storming the citadel for fear of killing her. We could starve him out, but we might starve the Ranee too. There's a tunnel to the citadel, but he's stove it in, and flooded it under the moat.

I fear it'll only be to powder and the bayonet that he yields. But I'm damned if we'll do it like Badajoz.'

Milne had no idea what were the imperfections at Badajoz. He wondered instead, as he had since leaving Sthambadree, if it were the moment to speak of Kezia . . .

But Hervey had business to be about. 'Very well, doctor. You'll send me word if . . . when there's any change?'

'I will. But, with your leave, not before dawn, for I would that you had some sleep, and I wouldn't wish to disturb it. Be assured there'll be someone with him throughout. The chaplain at least.'

Hervey nodded again, looked once more at the unconscious Garratt and said a silent prayer.

'By the bye, he said more than once that he wished to speak with you. Something seemed to trouble him.'

Hervey fancied he knew. So did Milne.

'If he comes to, then I would that you send for me at once. The least I owe him is a peaceful end, his mind at ease.'

Milne nodded. In truth, though, he wasn't sure if he *would* send for him. It was the very devil of a thing to judge.

'No, Captain Hart, I must do it myself. I do appreciate that it is a sapper's business, but in the pitch dark without having seen it, you'll have the devil of a job.'

The captain of Madras Pioneers had done all that honour demanded. Even when he'd conceded that a boat of any sort was bound to be seen in the moonlight, Fairbrother was adamant that neither he nor any of his sappers enter the water with him. He would swim with just Abhina, the hijda with whom he'd 'fished' in the moat the day before (and who'd promised the sentries many good things to let them), and with Askew, whom he'd come to trust. Even if there'd been no moon, he'd have insisted on it. In truth, closing the sluice would be the easiest of things, especially for a sapper. It hardly needed exploration. But if the tunnel was to be the means by which the evil of Ashok Acharya – and all his fugitive thugs – was brought to an end, then he wanted it to be by his hand. For Abhina had told him of Mira Bai.

Nor indeed would the tunnel be retribution enough. He would seek out the strangler and do to him what he'd done to that brave, dutiful and noble-born woman, wife of that fine old gentleman-soldier and mother of his children – the man without whom they'd be hard-pressed now to know what was right to do, let alone how to do it.

'And I cannot persuade you to have a boat ready to assist in case of mishap?'

Fairbrother shook his head. 'The risk's too great. There are no muggurs, I assure you.'

Captain Hart was a man of scientific training. He accepted that Fairbrother had seen none, and that at night the muggur's habit was to come on land, but neither of these 'facts' was a basis for certainty. That the three were taking with them knives the size of hatchets seemed to argue his case for him. All he could do, however, was give him his hand and let them go into the night.

And then wait and trust he was right to do so.

A little while later at the champak bush, the marker for the crossing, the three of them stripped to just a loincloth, slid into the water and began silently to swim, Askew with a capped pistol wrapped in oilskin between his teeth.

The moat wasn't wide by the standards of the great fortresses of Hindoostan, or even deep, its purpose more to prevent the walls being taken by surprise than to withstand prolonged siege. Even swimming cautiously, reaching the sluice didn't take long, the moon giving them just enough light to see their line. Nor did closing it require any great effort, for gravity was on their side. There was just the faintest groan of the pulley as it lowered, nothing that the most bat-eared of sentries in the tower above could have heard. Yet Fairbrother wasn't content until he'd made sure the sluice gate was firmly seated. Three times he dived, coming up between for air with as little sound as a fish might make rising to the fly. Throughout they spoke not a word – as if anything much had been possible with Abhina – managing with hand signals alone.

In all, perhaps twenty minutes, twenty-five at most. And then the return, as carefully as they'd swum across, with Askew leading to make sure the bank was clear; and crawling out just as silently; and then, crouching, to the champak bush where they'd hid their clothes. And still not a word.

Only when they were back at the place where the tunnel emerged, a simple bustee fifty yards on and just below the moat, did Fairbrother break silence.

'*Shabash,* Abhina! *Shabash!*' he beamed, shaking hands heartily. '*Aap ka shukria.*'

And likewise with Askew.

'I conclude the tunnel's sealed,' said Hervey stepping from the shadows.

'*Caca faat!*' (Only rarely did Fairbrother allow himself his island patois.) 'General: I'd not thought you'd be here. It is sealed, well and truly!'

'And your hijda was with you.'

'Yes, indeed. And Askew.'

Hervey nodded.

'It was nothing but a pleasant bathe,' said Fairbrother, airily.

'If in the present danger of muggurs,' suggested Hervey.

Fairbrother shook his head, smiling.

Abhina gabbled something, which neither he nor Hervey could catch.

Hervey smiled benevolently.

Abhina's head shook side to side.

'With your leave, General,' said Captain Hart, holding up a hand to Abhina.

'By all means.'

'The hijda asks Captain Fairbrother if he didn't see the python.'

Fairbrother quickened. 'What python? Where?'

Captain Hart asked Abhina for details.

More strange words, much gesturing and waving of the knife.

'It was swimming towards you as you returned. He cut off its head.'

Silence.

Hervey sighed. What a place was this India, where a man mayn't put his hand in the grass without fear of a krait, or swim without fear of a multitude of deadly agents. And soon there'd be yet more storm and steel. Was there ever end of it?

XXVI

The Walls of Jericho

Evening the following day

'My God, Hervey, but that dragoon's been worth his weight in gold. I thought we were confounded.'

Fairbrother looked like a sodden chimney sweep, but his eyes were bright.

'How so? What dragoon?'

'Didn't you know? The enginemen bolted, damn their eyes. Your sappers were no help – said they'd never seen a steam engine – and I myself couldn't fathom it, though I tried every valve and pipe, and then Collins said there was a dragoon who'd been an engineman. Shaw. And he's damn-well done it. *Both* engines. There's only a foot of water left.'

'And you're certain it can't be flooded again?'

'Nothing's certain, Hervey, but I'd risk my life on it.'

'The remaining water – how long will it take?'

'An hour, I reckon. Two, perhaps. Not more, certainly, at the rate they've pumped so far.'

Hervey turned to Captain Hart. 'The sappers are ready?'

'They are, General. They've brought down sixty barrels from the arsenal. And if I might add, given more time to fathom its workings, I'm confident we ourselves could have got the engines working.'

Hervey had better things to do, but soothing Hart's wounded *amour propre* was probably in the circumstances worth his effort. Officers trained in scientific methods at Woolwich were invaluable in their way, but could be decidedly prickly. And dragging barrels of gunpowder the length of a submarine tunnel was a dismal prospect. 'I'm certain of it, Captain Hart. And I commend your sappers for the enterprise.' He turned to Fairbrother. 'And I'm obliged once again for your address. And Shaw's.'

His friend smiled quizzically. 'So it's to be the second, then?'

Hervey had conceived two plans. The first was to intrude a force via the tunnel, but that would mean digging out a part of it (or blowing out – perilous in the extreme). Surprise would soon be lost, and the defenders could counter in numbers. The second plan was to pack the tunnel with powder where it ran under the outer wall, and make a practicable breach. A storming party – he refused to call it a 'forlorn hope' as they did in the Peninsula – would then cross the moat in makeshift boats. There was perhaps a chance that they'd take the place without a shot, for by the old rule of siege, if the defenders held out when a practicable breach had been made, that meant no quarter would be given. But here, where the defenders were insurgents and oath-breakers, the gallows awaited them anyway. Who would choose to be spared death by the sword only to die by the rope? This did, however, simplify Hervey's position. For if the gallows awaited them by due process of law, there could hardly be qualms about summary justice by the sword. In the end, though, with great reluctance, he'd embrace the expediency he found so repugnant in Major Sleeman's system: amnesty for the dewan's 'foot soldiers'. But there'd be none for Ashok Acharya, for that would be a signal to every would-be usurper in India that his enterprise was one of limited liability; nor amnesty for any thug who'd taken refuge and could be recognized. Besides, would it not be the Ranee's prerogative that he himself would be usurping?

'Your Rahabs are ready?' asked Hervey cheerily of Fairbrother.

'They are.'

'And you trust them yet?'

'I've offered them so many rubies they'll look like Shakti on her wedding day.'

'Very well. Let them do their worst – and best.' He turned to Captain Hart. 'Your sappers to the tunnel, then, as soon as may be.' And then to Major Parry, 'Orders to the brigadiers.'

Parry looked content at last. 'Very good, General.'

And now Hervey knew he could do no more – nothing at least that would materially change the preparations; and when there was no more for a general to do, it was his duty to rest.

'Goodnight, then, gentlemen.'

* * *

And Joshua rose early in the morning . . .

'Tea, Colonel.'

Corporal Johnson's hand summoned him from his deepest sleep in weeks.

Hervey sat up and listened to the dawn. It was not given to a man to know when would be his last; to a soldier especially. *The Lord giveth and the Lord taketh away.* His thoughts were of Georgiana, though she was safe enough – and of Kezia.

As daylight came he shaved and put on clean linen, and took a leisurely breakfast of eggs, fruit and coffee.

Then he climbed into the saddle.

The morning was clear and fresh, the troops he passed were in good heart, well concealed, and the guns on the walls of the fortress-palace were silent but for the odd speculative shot, answered each time by howitzer and explosive shell – no doubt bringing curses from the dewan's poor foot soldiers for their own imprudent artillery. Here was the long game of siege as practised for centuries – since the days of the Ancients, indeed, when the catapult hurled Greek fire.

It was nearing nine o'clock, the time appointed for the exploding of the mine. Hervey rode out into full view of the walls with his staff and escort, and took post in the shade of a lone deodar – a tree as naturally alien to Chintal as was he in his red coat.

He took out his telescope to survey the walls, in particular that part under which the barrels would do their firework. Captain Hart had told him the powder would certainly bring down a good portion of masonry, but he could make no estimate of the length of wall or the extent of the collapse. (He thought it probable there would be a mound of rubble to climb, but that a deal of it would fall into the moat – a help thereby if it came to storming the breach.)

On the walls directly above the mine he could see a number of gunners and a huge cannon, its barrel long enough to send a ball half a mile, though to what purpose in a siege was unclear, and he felt a momentary pang of regret for what was about to be their fate. Until, that is, he smiled grimly at the thought of the Prussian's contempt of the *Menschenfreund*, the philanthropist. 'Cruel necessity', Cromwell had said of such things. And so he must play God again and send these distant figures to their own. He closed the cover of his watch, braced himself, and said, 'Well, gentlemen, we shall see what we shall see.'

The seconds ticked past – ten, eleven, twelve.

Then the deafening explosion.

It was greater than he'd heard in an age; greater even than Bhurtpore.

Minnie shied. Stones fell about them, disconcertingly if harmlessly. Larger ones made fountains in the moat.

The corner of the curtain wall was invisible in the smoke and dust. It was a full minute before he could see properly.

When he did see, it astonished him. The breach was fifty yards at least – as big as he'd ever seen – and a ramp of rubble almost filling the moat.

He snapped his telescope shut. 'Capital work, Hart; capital!'

Colonel Lindesay's brigade appeared from the cover of the havelis to the east, their orders to halt at the moat to make a show of what awaited the defenders if they chose to resist . . . *And it shall come to pass, that when they make a long blast with the ram's horn, and when ye hear the sound of the trumpet, all the people shall shout with a great shout; and the wall of the city shall fall down flat, and the people shall ascend up every man straight before him.*

Hervey sighed with more relief than he cared to show. Joshua himself could have wished for no more.

'Mr Hussey, your service now, if you please!' he called, once he'd settled Minnie.

The gallopers had drawn lots for the privilege of taking the terms to the palace. The cornet of the Thirteenth had won.

Hussey put his horse straight into a canter and made for the droog – with him a corporal carrying a flag of truce so large that it trailed in the earth, for it was Hervey's intention that everyone watching from the walls should know what it signified, and that they might therefore ponder on what he trusted the hijdas had been telling them all night.

Within the citadel, warned by the 'Rahabs' somehow that defied understanding, the Ranee stood with her bodyguard. She'd dressed in her finest silks – yellow, like her rissalah 'sworn to die' – with a jewelled sword at her waist and a pistol in each hand. She would not be taken alive by Ashok Acharya only to be put to death in ignominious fashion later. He would for sure storm her fastness once his own walls were breached, for what did he have to bargain with but her life? He had more than enough guns and men to do so. He'd pay dear, though. He'd made of her a 'tigress' – for his own purposes, and no doubt laughing at the deceit – and so now he would feel her claws.

Down came the drawbridge save for a last few feet, and Hussey rode up to place with great ceremony the ultimatum in the hand of the officer of the watch.

As he galloped back, the drawbridge rose laboriously. The walls – the cannon – remained silent.

'Were any words exchanged, Mr Hussey?'

'He said "*Namaste*", General,' replied the cornet, sounding perplexed.

'Promising.'

The ultimatum, in Hindoostanee, was stark:

> *Immediately upon the delivery of these presents, all troops and their followers within the walls of the palace are to surrender to the forces of His Britannic Majesty's Honourable East India Company upon guarantee of safe passage and amnesty, except the person of Ashok Acharya who must surrender unconditionally and quit the palace without arms. Flags of surrender are to be hoist at once. Or else the palace will be taken by the explosion of a second mine, and by storm, in which case No quarter for troops, nor followers of either sex, nor children, shall be given.*

But no one other than his closest staff, and soon Ashok Acharya (and, if the hijdas had done their work, Acharya's poor 'foot soldiers') knew what precisely was the threat contained in the ultimatum, for he wanted no Jericho . . . *And they utterly destroyed all that was in the city, both man and woman, young and old, and ox, and sheep, and ass, with the edge of the sword* – like Badajoz and its murderous blood-lust, rape and rapine.

The Prussian said that intruding a principle of moderation into the business of war was absurd, but that not merely offended his sensibility (which he might reasonably overcome) but went against his experience of battle so-won. The ultimatum was a ploy, a *ruse de guerre*. He'd no more intention of putting the dewan's men and their followers to the sword than he had the means of a second mine. But none within the walls could know that – or, at least, be sure of knowing.

Ten minutes passed, and no flags.

Then a gun from the south-east corner fired.

His heart sank.

Lindesay's orders were to begin the assault only when he himself sent word.

'Gentlemen, I have done my best to spare blood. But now no longer. Come.'

He would lead the storming of the breach himself.

'Wait! General – *look!*'

Not flags, but clothes of every colour being waved, and muskets and swords thrown from the walls like ballast from a foundering ship.

And then the drawbridge was coming down, and men not waiting for it but jumping into the water, rats from the same ship.

'By heavens, General, it's worked!' Parry was almost beside himself.

'Now God be thanked,' said Hervey quietly.

And Fairbrother; and his steam engines; and Shaw, from the black pits of Somerset. And Fairbrother's hijdas; he prayed most earnestly they were safe. *And the young men that were spies went in, and brought out Rahab, and her father, and her mother, and her brethren, and all that she had . . .*

But no, he himself would go in – and his young men – and bring out the Ranee 'and all that she had'.

Worsley brought the Sixth forward, their orders to enter the fortress at once to see what was what and do what they could. (No orders could have been more specific; for how even could Hervey have been sure the mine would explode, let alone the wall collapse and the garrison surrender?)

They lost no time, only the press of deserting men slowing them.

But Hervey could watch no longer. Down he galloped – Parry, Acton, half a dozen cornets and orderlies, the baboo and now Fairbrother all hurtling after him like a field in full cry.

The flat of the sword hastened their way up the droog and over the drawbridge.

Inside was the litter of siege – the bodies of the dead, the wounded, the cowering. The dragoons were making order of it, at least, and Worsley was already into the citadel. The hijdas, crowded in a corner of the bailey, began jabbering when Fairbrother appeared, rushing to him with their skirts held high.

'Huzoor! Huzoor!' – and a flood of words that only the baboo might understand.

'Sahib, they say man who kill wife of Colonel Bell is here, and also dewan is fast in tower.' The baboo pointed to the turret commanding the drawbridge.

Hervey jumped from the saddle. It was time to take his prisoner. It was a poor place to hide, but doubtless he hadn't had opportunity to choose.

Fairbrother was intent on the killer of Mira Bai, however. 'Where, Abhina?'

Abhina pointed to half a dozen men crouching by the wall of the bastion. Not soldiers, certainly.

'*Accha.*'

Hervey saw, and went with him. (Ashok Acharya could wait – in fear and trembling, he hoped.)

The men huddled the more, doubtless expecting the worst.

'Which one, Abhina?'

Abhina pointed.

Hervey told the baboo to make him show his face.

The man raised his head as far as he dare. Even so—

'Ghufoor Khan!' gasped Fairbrother.

'What—'

The Khan sprang like a hare and made for the bastion.

Fairbrother fell cursing at a leg thrust his way.

Hervey gave chase, pulling pistol from belt.

A ball from Acton's carbine glanced the Khan's shoulder but failed to slow him.

Hervey took aim, full stride.

Too late; Khan was into the bastion before he could draw bead.

Dragoons came running.

Hervey followed into the gloom, Acton close at heel.

Along the corridors, checking every room, every cell, every nook and cranny.

The length of the dank, dark bastion.

Until just the snake pit stood between the panting Khan and his escape.

Torches blazed on the walls. There was no more hiding.

Hervey stopped, took a breath and raised his pistol. 'Halt, Ghufoor Khan! There is no escape.'

But the Khan wouldn't yield. He snarled, cursed, and then leapt as he'd never leapt before – even to use the roomal.

He gained the other side, but with a foot only.

His fall was heavy.

Hervey lowered his pistol and edged towards the pit.

The spreading hood rose like a ship making sail as the Khan curled in a ball. Hervey brought his pistol up fast, but the hamadryad struck – once, twice, a third time and then a fourth.

A single bite would have been enough.

Hervey grimaced; looked away. It wasn't what he'd hoped for – deliberate, judicial, by the rope.

Nor was it instant.

But death would come in hours, at least, not days, for the hamadryad was a 'good' snake.

But a painful death.

Ghufoor Khan began pleading. 'Huzoor . . .'

Hervey recoiled. The man who'd murdered hundreds, even thousands, by his command or by his own hand; the man who in order to save his own skin had borne witness against those who'd followed him, and who had then, plainly, broken his parole to join this company of thieves and murderers; the man with the blood of Mira Bai still warm on his hands – Mira Bai, who'd been faithful to her Ranee even unto death; that such a man should plead to be spared a painful end . . .

Hervey turned to walk away.

Acton looked at him, puzzled. 'Shall I, Colonel?'

Hervey stopped, then turned back. 'No; the duty's mine.'

When they came out, it was to the hijdas' excited gesturing again. There at the foot of the tower in a bloody pool lay the body of Ashok Acharya.

'Mine,' said Fairbrother grimly.

It hardly mattered. A battle never ended tidily, the trumpet sounding ceasefire and all fire ceasing. There were always 'loose ends' to tie up – random shots. He'd not said 'no quarter'; but there was 'discretion'. The details, if needed, could wait. It was anyway convenient.

His, Hervey's, mission was done – as far, at least, as the Company was concerned. There were a great many thugs he'd sent to their maker, one way or another, and His Majesty's troops were in possession of the capital of the lapsed state of Chintal. There remained just the Ranee, the would-be 'tigress'; but instead a poor, caged thing; a 'paper tiger', as they said in China – *che lo foo*, a mere false device to frighten people.

And they'd certainly been anxious at Fort William.

In truth, he'd admit that Suneyla had become his principal mission, though it served the Company as well as his own conscience.

But did she live?

'Come,' he said simply to Fairbrother.

At the entrance to the citadel he found Worsley's second in command with Major Parry.

Both saluted, and keenly. 'The Ranee's safe, General,' said Parry.

Hervey nodded, not exactly with a smile but with evident satisfaction. He turned to Worsley's lieutenant. 'The details, if you please, Mr Edgeworth.'

'The insurgents tried but gained no foothold, General. The bodyguard, by all accounts – that is, by the evidence of what lies therein – fought stubbornly. The Ranee is secured in her state room. The troop, meanwhile, is searching the rest of the citadel.'

'And Rissaldar Sikarwar?'

'He is with the bodyguard.'

'Very well. Parry, have the dragoons here form a guard to pay compliments – when they've secured the walls and bailey properly – and call the brigadiers. I intend bringing the Ranee out. She ought to see the . . . *detritus* of this affair, and the men who've delivered her. And they her.'

'General.'

'Come, then, Edgeworth. And you, Fairbrother, for the honour's at least half yours.'

Hervey returned the pistol to his belt. Acton had already reloaded his carbine.

The bodyguard's stubbornness was in evidence as they made their way to the state room. The stench alone spoke of the fighting. But at the doors of the Ranee's refuge stood a sowar in good order, who brought his sword to the carry as they approached, and then to his lips.

Hervey returned the salute with particular care. Men who had stood their ground against the odds were always to be honoured.

The sowar opened the doors and announced 'the English general'.

Hervey and his party entered in step and halted.

'Your Highness.' He took off his cap and bowed.

Suneyla curtsied, the first time she'd done so. 'General Hervey.'

Her ladies did likewise.

'Is everything well with you, ma'am?'

'It is.' She spoke quietly, perfectly composed.

Hervey glanced at the pistols on the table before her, and the jewelled sword.

'There was no occasion for them, General. My rissalah were steadfast.'

He bowed to acknowledge.

'General, I would see your men, but first may we speak in private?'

'Of course, ma'am.'

Their attendants quit the room, though Acton, trusting no one, not even a princess, needed a confirmatory nod.

When they were gone, Suneyla said nothing for a moment, seeming to study him. Hervey himself, now standing at ease, was content to wait. Before him was indeed an arresting figure, one made yet more fascinating by what had just passed.

'So you are come then, General Hervey.'

It was a strange question, if question it was. 'As you see, ma'am.'

'I knew you would.'

'I'm gratified by Your Highness's confidence. I'm sorry, though, that it was not by means of the tunnel, which would have spared you the trial of the past few hours. You will know, I imagine, that it was not possible . . . and also that Mira Bai . . . has died.'

Suneyla lowered her eyes momentarily. 'I do know. And I shall make it my business that her children are not in want.'

Hervey supposed her reply was reasonable. He could scarcely expect a princess to show grief at the death of one who served her. Not before a virtual stranger.

'Ma'am.'

'I shall of course reward you also in fullest measure.'

'I am flattered, ma'am, but I should only be able to accept on behalf of my command.'

'I understand that that is the practice, but I intend some other token of gratitude. Though what will be left to me when there is a treaty with Fort William I cannot say.'

He'd no idea what her purpose was. She must know that his influence in the matter would amount to nothing.

She held out her hand, and he took it to kiss in the usual way. She spoke instead, though, holding his hand the while, and his eyes too. 'I believe I can count on our special trust always. We were once friends.'

That evening, when at last he'd shown himself and the Ranee to the troops, found her quarters in the old zenana, secured the palace, set in hand the urgent business of burial and cremation, disposed the field force in comfort and safety, and written a despatch for Somervile at Sthambadree, Hervey sat in an old cane chair at the window of the haveli over which his pennant flew, to contemplate the events of the past days. He supposed that Fort William would soon want to fete him as a great political, and his command, his regiments, salute him as a successful general – as some had tried to do that afternoon. For a while at least. But it was too soon to rejoice. There were too many men that the chaplains would have to read their words over – poor Garratt, for one, gone that very morning (and, God forbid, perhaps even St Alban). Too many of his dragoons and a good many others of the field force. The Duke had been right: *Nothing except a battle lost can be half so melancholy as a battle won.*

Fairbrother came later, and there was none he was more glad to see, for his friend needed no orders, nor his concern. A curious equality.

'Well, I never read, and certainly never saw, battle like it. What an extraordinary place is this India.'

He sat heavily and half-drained the glass of Malmsey. (The Ranee's cellars had yielded up uncommon quality.)

'Not a business for soldiers proper,' replied Hervey, still half absorbed in thought; 'but I suppose that only soldiers can do it.'

'And so what now?'

'We wait. That's what, now. I exceeded my authority in coming here. As a rule I've found it easier to gain forgiveness than permission, but I'm not inclined to try the principle too much.'

'Shall it be the ribbon or the rope, I wonder.'

'You may jest.'

'Only because Fort William couldn't be so blind as not to see the gain at such very little expense.'

'Then you don't know India.'

Fairbrother frowned. 'I am sorry to find you in such poor spirits.'

Hervey took another sip of his wine. They would need another bottle soon.

'Tell me: the dewan . . .'

'That doesn't trouble you, does it?'

'The Ranee asked. I said he was killed trying to flee.'

'He was. Would she have had him exiled instead?'

'No. She was excessively pleased to learn of it. I believe she had a fear he would haunt the place somehow, a martyr's death to his followers.'

'Well, he'd few followers when he died. One of your serjeants found him with just a bodyman, and he jumped to escape. He fell heavily but he was scrambling for the gate. I didn't know rightly it was him, but if he'd got into that horde outside we'd never have known.'

Hervey nodded.

'I'm only sorry I hadn't the satisfaction of knowing it when I fired. But at least I may tell Colonel Bell that I avenged his wife's murder.'

'Indeed so. I confess I quite dread to see him tomorrow.'

'But then you too can claim the same.'

'I suppose so – but in truth it was the snake.'

'Ah, so you haven't had tell?'

'Tell what?'

'They found the sampera afterwards and took him to fish it out so they could get the body to the pyre. Its mouth was sewn up. They only ever used the pit to fright.'

Hervey shook his head slowly. 'This . . . *country*.'

XXVII

The Fruits of Victory

St Mary's Church, Fort St George, two months later

TO THE MEMORY OF

LIEUT. COLONEL CHARLES MILL

HIS MAJESTY'S 55TH REGIMENT

KILLED ON THE 3RD OF APRIL 1834 WHILST GALLANTLY LEADING ON HIS REGIMENT TO THE ATTACK AGAINST THE STOCKADE OF SOMARPETT, IN THE TERRITORY OF HIS HIGHNESS THE RAJAH OF COORG. EMINENTLY DISTINGUISHED AS A SOLDIER THROUGH A PERIOD OF NEARLY FORTY YEARS, HE SERVED WITH THE BRITISH ARMY DURING ITS MOST EVENTFUL EPOCHS: AND HIS EXAMPLE OF COURAGE AND GALLANTRY INSPIRED HIS FOLLOWERS ON ALL OCCASIONS WITH THAT BRAVERY AND FORTITUDE SO CONSPICUOUS AT THE ASSAULT IN WHICH HE FELL. IN PRIVATE LIFE HE WAS UNIVERSALLY ESTEEMED. DEVOTED TO THE INTERESTS OF HIS REGIMENT AND THE HAPPINESS OF THOSE

WHO SERVED UNDER HIM, HIS MEMORY WILL LONG BE CHERISHED WITH SENTIMENT OF THE HIGHEST RESPECT, AND HIS PREMATURE DEATH CONTINUE A SOURCE OF THE DEEPEST REGRET TO ALL, MORE PARTICULARLY HIS BROTHER OFFICERS WHO HAVE IN HIM LOST A BRAVE LEADER, AND A KIND FRIEND, AND WHO HAVE ERECTED THIS TABLET IN TRIBUTE TO HIS WORTH.

ÆTAT. 54.

Fifty-four years of age – ten years and more his senior – and still commanding a battalion. Yet Mill was held in greater esteem than many a general. What therefore did he, Hervey, have to regret in being still at the head of so fine a corps as the Sixth?

Nothing.

The regiment was in as great a state of efficiency as it was possible – certainly as it was reasonable – to conceive. He would wager that he had the finest of officers of any in His Majesty's Land Forces. He had non-commissioned officers who'd be the envy of many a colonel, thanks to Armstrong and those who'd gone before. But these things could not abide: *To every thing there is a season, and a time to every purpose under the heaven*. Ecclesiastes, 'The words of the Preacher, the son of David, king in Jerusalem', words he returned to often, for they spoke truly. Now especially, perhaps, the Preacher's peroration was apt: *Wherefore I perceive that there is nothing better, than that a man should rejoice in his own works; for that is his portion: for who shall bring him to see what shall be after him?*

He was resolved that the Sixth would raise a tablet of equal elegance for Major Garratt, *In Memoriam*, 'In tribute to his worth', and to the others of the regiment who'd died in the territory of Her Highness the Ranee of Chintal. But for the time being, at least, the service that morning was their tribute, a church parade that for once few dragoons resented, for besides honouring their former comrades it was a promise that they in their turn would not be forgotten.

They'd sung heartily too, and the band had never sounded better – two dozen bandsmen, now, and the finest of instruments, the new bandmaster come from England with the best that money could buy: cornets by Köhler of Covent Garden, clarionets by Triébert of Paris; even an ophicleide – and all the bounty of Major Garratt's clever dealing in bills of exchange (and, indeed, his 'fines' on merchants who'd served the regiment ill). The band alone would be a fitting memorial, as well as a daily rebuke that he, Hervey, had doubted his second in command and then condoned (there was no other word for it) the 'crime' by arranging a convenient posting. 'Prudential judgement', he'd called it. But doubtless he'd reconcile himself to the condonation (and sooner than he ought).

'Thank you, Mr Coote. Admirable sermon.'

'Thank you, Colonel.'

In truth, he'd heard better. To begin with, the text (Samuel), excited too many passions: *Then Nahash the Ammonite came up, and encamped against Jabesh Gilead: and all the men of Jabesh said unto Nahash, Make a covenant with us, and we will serve thee* . . . For there could be no 'covenants' in a regiment. Officers must lead, and men must follow. That was an end to it.

Coote had made favourable comparison with the regiment's conduct at Chintalpore, though. They'd dealt benevolently with their captives; in the main, certainly. But it was done for no gain. Perhaps his mind had wandered. Doubtless the chaplain had thought it instructive and rousing; and he had, after all, detained them for really very little time. The lessons were well read, at least. Troop Serjeant-Major Wainwright had as good a voice for the chapel as for the parade. (If Armstrong had been laid low at Chintalpore for any longer than he had, he'd have made Wainwright his man.) And Cornet Kynaston's carried with the same clarity he must have sung with as a chorister at Westminster.

They were a fine sight too, his dragoons, as they fell in now for the march back to the lines. They had the look of men proud to be of their corps. It was true that on the whole the cavalry could count on a better class of recruit than the infantry, but even so, it was remarkable what riding school and skill-at-arms did for men of scarcely higher station or learning. There'd be English beer and best Madras pasties when they were back in the lines, but no speeches, just a toast: 'Absent Friends.' And all ranks would mingle, secure in the principle that in an association where one member was the subordinate of another, the superior would never think of it, and the subordinate would never forget it – assisted, of course, by the all-seeing eye of the serjeant-major.

The chaplain excused himself, never altogether at ease in Hervey's company. St Alban took his place.

'A fine church parade, Colonel.'

'I think it very properly done, Edward. It would perhaps have served better had we done it at once, at Chintalpore, but two months is hardly too long, and I would have had to wear a general's coat.'

St Alban was glad enough, too, if only that he himself might be present – might take charge, indeed – which he most certainly could not have done from his hospital bed. 'And it was right to include Waterman in the roll call. I shouldn't have doubted it.'

'If you don't speak your doubts, Edward, you're of no use to me as adjutant, as you very well know.'

'Indeed, Colonel. And we'll never know the truth now the provost marshal's concluded the scent is cold. That there *is* no scent, in point of fact.'

Especially now that Askew, given his free discharge, was on passage home. (The Duke had said that pardon ought to follow the performance of a duty of trust, but it was another thing to keep such a man in plain sight.)

'The truth will out,' said Hervey decidedly. 'If there *was* mischief. Though "when" is the question. In a regiment there can be no secret for ever.'

'No, I suppose not . . . With your leave, then, Colonel?'

'Go to it. March them off to a good swing. The band's in fine voice.'

Others then left him to his thoughts.

For this was the church in which Clive himself had worshipped – and married. That greatest of generals in India would surely have approved the parade, and in what cause – the extension of the King's Peace. Approved it probably a good deal more than Bentinck appeared to do, whose letter had seemed to Hervey a muted affair.

No, the other officers were giving their pensive colonel a wide berth. There'd be opportunity to speak at the tamasha, if need be.

Except for the surgeon. His age and calling always set him apart a little, and besides, there was a matter that wasn't for the festivities.

He raised his bicorn as he came up.

Hervey smiled warmly. 'Doctor, the dragoons did you honour. I've not heard the like before.'

When Milne had come into church, a little later than he ought, though all knew it would be on account of some invalid, the dragoons had shuffled their feet in acclamation.

'Aye, well . . .'

'You'll come to Arcot House later?'

'I shall, Colonel, don't you fear.'

'It will be as much comfort to Kezia as to me.'

'Aye, well . . . It doesn't do to trouble before it's time. It's like as not just a case of heat languor.'

Hervey nodded. Except that the heat was hardly oppressive. (He hadn't yet braced himself to ask if 'puerperal melancholy' could follow from still-birth.)

'But, Colonel, there's something I must tell you. Indeed, I ought to have done so many weeks ago. I think it only right you should know, for it touches on my judgement.'

'What troubles you?'

'When we were at Sthambadree, before Chintal, I had word of Mrs Hervey's miscarriage. I was minded to bring it to you at once, naturally, but was uncertain. I asked Garratt's opinion. He said he would not tell you, for although he believed it would not divert you from duty, such a thing was bound to intrude at some time on the judgements of any man of feeling, and he couldn't risk that intrusion being for the ill. The lives of too many men were at stake. He said that I must do what was proper as regards my profession, but also that as an officer I must have regard to the operation on which we were to embark. And so I chose not to inform you – until later, that is. I tell you this now, not to excuse myself by laying blame on Garratt, but so that you might judge for yourself.'

Hervey put a hand on the surgeon's shoulder. 'My dear Milne, your sensibility – nay, your integrity – does you proud. Your judgement likewise. Garratt spoke exactly as I'd have wished. And nor, I believe, would Kezia have wished it. Have not the slightest thought of the matter any more.'

Milne was quite visibly relieved. 'Colonel.'

'And you'll stay and have some supper?'

'Thank you, yes.'

In the circumstances it was hardly an invitation he could turn down. Besides, heat languor was a very speculative diagnosis – hopeful, perhaps even desperate. Observing Kezia at table (if she were able to rise from her bed) in the company of family would be of advantage.

Hervey cleared his throat. 'The gauskot – naught but a boy, says Sammy. Will he live?'

'Ah, the gauskot . . .' It was as good a way of changing the subject as any, if with no more certain a prognosis than he could give for Kezia. 'Kraits, Colonel: why does any man become a grass-cutter?'

But with his conscience now clear, Milne could take his leave, letting Hervey resume his thoughts – or rather, now, contemplation of the ladies. For it was a good turnout – even Dorothea Worsley, and so soon after giving birth, standing in admirably for Kezia and presenting the serjeants' wives to the Somerviles. (It was good of Eyre to come too, he thought, for he knew there was much to do in his last few days here.) Georgiana was speaking animatedly with a clutch of cornets, while Annie was doing so with rather greater reserve to Captain Malet. Poor Annie, he said to himself: she'd first met Malet when a chambermaid at the Berkeley Arms. What a trial it must be for her to comport herself as a governess, a lady, when all and sundry knew she'd served at table – not that it seemed a trial for Malet. But, he hardly need remind himself, Annie wasn't the chambermaid at the Berkeley Arms any more. She neither looked nor sounded the part. What a progress it had been. And if ever there could be doubt as to her goodness of heart, there were two dozen and more officers and dragoons who knew otherwise from the hospital at Chintalpore. And the bodyguard. Indeed, when Suneyla had bid him farewell, she'd made special mention of her, and given her a pigeon-blood ruby the size of a plumstone. If – God forbid – Kezia were to have any prolonged prostration, he'd have to rely on Annie more than ever. That is, if she'd want to stay in India now. Or if she did, that it wouldn't be to take up an offer from one of the Company ensigns. She must, of course, at some time; and she was sure to be well received here in India. Indeed, even on returning home she'd be received well, for like the matriarchs of Ancient Rome who made a point of never inquiring into the origins of a wife if her husband had been long on the frontiers, the hostesses of London did not bar their drawing rooms to those who could conduct themselves decorously . . .

'Hervey, a most fitting service. Capital, capital.'

Somervile had detached himself from the distaff side and advanced on him with a singularly hale expression.

'Rather a crush, I'm afraid,' said Hervey a little flatly. 'We ought perhaps to have taken the cathedral.'

'No, no; St Mary's was the place for it. No doubt. How is Kezia?'

'A little better today, thank you. Milne is sanguine, though, I believe. A heat languor, that's all. The past months, very tiring.'

'Quite.' Somervile cleared his throat. His old friend sounded not entirely convinced, but that was by the bye; there was business to be about. 'I had several communications from Fort William this morning. The Ranee has signed the subsidiary treaty and agreed to reparations. All very satisfactory. I think you can expect a vote of £10,000 from the Company, as before.'

Hervey nodded. It would make no difference to him personally. As was the custom – at least until Bhurtpore, when for some reason Lord Combermere chose to keep his portion of the prize money – he'd given his share of the Coorg vote to the relief fund, and as he'd said to Suneyla would do so again. But it was as well that Fort William was content, for had things gone ill with his decision to march without their leave, then it would have been cashiering, not prize money. (He'd yet no idea that Somervile had told Lord Bentinck that if they didn't treat with the Ranee as an ally, he himself would resign and take his case to London.)

'She gave Georgiana a very handsome necklace of rubies, and me a ring for Kezia.'

'And asked for you to command the subsidiary force.'

'I didn't judge it meet even to consider the offer – even had the governor-general approved.'

'I'm excessively pleased. It wouldn't have served, though very agreeable for a while, no doubt. "Can the Ethiopian change his skin, or the leopard his spots?" Or the tigress her stripes?'

Hervey smiled. 'At least my commander-in-chief would have been several hundred miles distant. I fear I'll have too much time for sport now that Sir Robert's returned.'

'Then what I'm about to propose may be agreeable to you.'

Hervey looked wary. Somervile was never happier than when plotting some scheme or other, and a little sport hadn't been an altogether unattractive prospect. 'How so?'

'Hervey, in five days' time I leave for Agra.'

'Yes, of course. I know it.'

'I shall be governor of what the Company has been pleased to call the Ceded and Conquered Provinces, but which are now raised to the status of a presidency.'

'Yes, yes; I know that perfectly well. I trust you'll have joy of it. I certainly wish you so. You asked me for an aide-de-camp, indeed, and I've given you one. '

Somervile was now smiling broadly. 'Hervey, I have just – by this day's hircarrah – had it given into my power to appoint a commander-in-chief. I choose you. It shall be in the rank of "major-general in India". I know that doesn't enter on the home gradation list, but it's a matter of time, only, before London adds your name. Meanwhile you would have all the pay and appurtenances of the rank, and the responsibility. And, indeed, you'd retain command of the Sixth, for I have it in my power to arrange too for their transfer to Agra. I didn't consult you in the matter for I wasn't in a position to. Now, what say you to it?'

Hervey could say nothing. He could think of no reason to decline, not least if the regiment was to move anyway. Except for Kezia.

Somervile sensed his concern. 'I know Agra to be the best of places, and the heat less unrelenting than here.'

Hervey knew likewise, but . . . 'I believe I must ask Milne's opinion first.'

'And what shall the surgeon say?'

Hervey sighed. He knew he ought to be overjoyed. 'What saith the Preacher indeed?'

Somervile was about to make reply when St Alban's words of command came clear across the maidan and the band struck up *Young May Moon*, the regiment's quick march.

Hervey's stomach tightened – the sight and the sound. And now the promise: major-general in India, brevet colonel, and yet for a little longer to remain lieutenant-colonel of the Sixth. What more could he reasonably desire? *For who can tell a man what shall be after him under the sun?*

He watched as they marched off, till the band changed to *Lillibulero*, another of the dragoons' favourites, and then turned to his old friend.

'Somervile, I'm excessively obliged to you. With your leave, then, I shall tell the regiment this day.'

HISTORICAL AFTERNOTE

The suppression of thuggee, along with that of suttee and female infanticide, stands as a monument to the humanity and capability of the Company's officials. 'Thuggee' Sleeman, as he became known, eventually took charge of the Department for the Suppression of Thuggee and Dacoity, in 1839, and with the help of various legal acts of the government of India expanded its operations, including efforts at rehabilitation. During these years, some four thousand 'thugs' were arrested, of whom half were convicted and hanged or transported for life. One of them, by the name of Bahram, confessed to having strangled over 900.

By the 1870s thuggee had been effectively eradicated, though the department remained in existence until 1904, when it was replaced by the Central Criminal Investigation Department. The suppression acts were replaced by the Criminal Tribes Act of 1871, by which ethnic or social groups defined as 'addicted to the systematic commission of non-bailable offences' were systematically registered by the government, with restrictions on their movements. The act was repealed in 1949 after Indian independence, de-stigmatizing some two and a half million people. However, there was such an upsurge in the criminal activity thitherto draconically suppressed that in 1953 the Habitual Offenders Act was passed, effectively re-stigmatizing the 'criminal tribes'. It is safe to say that the issue is still unresolved today.

For those who would read more on thuggee, there are Sleeman's own books, *Rambles and Recollections of an Indian Official*, the first volume in particular. Philip Meadows Taylor's 1839 novel *Confessions of a Thug*, based on actual confession, provides much grisly detail, some of which is no doubt true. Sir Francis Tuker's *The Yellow Scarf* (1961) is a lively, robust and imaginative account of thuggee and its suppression. John Masters's *The Deceivers* (1952), like all his India novels, is gripping. Mike Dash's *Thug* (2005) is the most up-to-date and scholarly account.

And yet there are claims that thuggee was merely a case of 'Orientalism' – the way of seeing something that exaggerates and ultimately distorts the difference of (in this case) India as compared with the West, the native culture implicitly uncivilized and at times dangerous. In other words, colonial imaginings. Further, there are claims that Sleeman himself exaggerated – indeed, invented – the phenomenon of thuggee simply to advance his own career.

I do not think this can stand. There were others engaged in the suppression of thuggee earlier and independently, notably Thomas Perry at Ettawah and William Borthwick at Indore. Besides, there was printed reference to 'thugs' as early as the fourteenth century. What is without doubt is that Sleeman got the bit between his teeth, and the governor-general – Bentinck – was pleased to give him his head, for reports from the Company's officials were becoming alarming.

In fact there has of late been a rather virulent bout of anti-colonialism among some historians, who paint a picture of rampant rapacity on the part of the Company – to the point of suggesting, if only implicitly, that India would have been better off if the British had never gone there. But better for whom? The transfer of wealth from a corrupt and sometimes cruel Indian to a corrupt and sometimes arrogant Englishman was no doubt a sin, but not one – it seems to me – that a poor ryot would have thought a very great one, especially when weighing it in the scales with the Company's *pax*; indeed, the Pax Britannica.

For the *pax* was a noble venture – of that I'm certain – if at times losing its way a little, and occasionally woefully. And the men who brought it, though not all of them worthy, were on the whole remarkably selfless and lacking in venality. They would of course have thought themselves superior to those in their charge – racially superior, not just by religion and education – but most would have given their lives for them, and frequently did. Philip Mason describes this magnificently in *The Men Who Ruled India* (written under the pseudonym 'Philip Woodruff'), especially the first volume, *The Founders* (1954), and in his study of the Indian Army, *A Matter of Honour* (1974). After Balliol, Mason served with the Indian Civil Service for twenty years until Independence. He is neither sentimental nor condescending, nor blind to corruption and misgovernment. He writes that 'in the end a man must be judged not by his worst so much as by his best, and in the end not even by his best but by what he aimed at. And so English rule in India is to be judged by the conscious will of England expressed in Parliament and by the aims of a good district officer, not by the nasty little atavistic impulses that came wriggling up from the subconscious when an official at the Treasury scored a departmental triumph over the India Office, or when a merchant fixed something over an opulent lunch.'

'Thuggee Sleeman' was later Resident at Gwalior, and then at Lucknow until just before the Mutiny. In 1856, aged sixty-eight, a major-general and knighted, he died at sea on passage home. He had served continuously in India for forty-seven years. The village of Sleemanabad in what is now Madhya Pradesh is named after him. Today, when many colonial-era place-names have been and are being changed – most notably, in the case of Hervey's story, Chennai for Madras – the fact that Sleemanabad remains must say something for the respect in which some at least of 'The Men Who Ruled India' are still held.

MATTHEW PAULINUS HERVEY

BORN: 1791, second son of the Reverend Thomas Hervey, Vicar of Horningsham in Wiltshire, and of Mrs Hervey; one sister, Elizabeth.

EDUCATED: Shrewsbury School (praepostor)

MARRIED: 1817 to Lady Henrietta Lindsay, ward of the Marquess of Bath (deceased 1818). 1828 to Lady Lankester, widow of Lieutenant-Colonel Sir Ivo Lankester, Bart, lately commanding 6th Light Dragoons.

CHILDREN: a daughter, Georgiana, born 1818; a son, Eyre, born 1833.

RECORD OF SERVICE

1808: commissioned cornet by purchase in His Majesty's 6th Light Dragoons (Princess Caroline's Own).

1809–14: served Portugal and Spain; evacuated with army at ⚔ Corunna, 1809 returned with regiment to Lisbon that year; present at numerous battles and actions including ⚔ Talavera, ⚔ Badajoz, ⚔ Salamanca, ⚔ Vitoria.

1814: present at ⚔ Toulouse; wounded; lieutenant.

1814–15: served Ireland, present at ⚔ Waterloo, and in Paris with army of occupation.

1815: Additional ADC to the Duke of Wellington (acting captain); despatched for special duty in Bengal.

1816: saw service against Pindarees and Nizam of Haiderabad's forces; returned to regimental duty. Brevet captain; brevet major.

1818: saw service in Canada; briefly seconded to US forces, Michigan Territory; resigned commission.

CONTINUED ☞

☜ *CONTINUED FROM PREVIOUS PAGE*

1819: reinstated, 6th Light Dragoons; captain.

1820–26: served Bengal; saw active service in ⚔ Ava (wounded severely); present at ⚔ Siege of Bhurtpore; brevet major.

1826–27: detached service in Portugal.

1827: in temporary command of 6th Light Dragoons, major; in command of detachment of 6th Light Dragoons at the Cape Colony; seconded to raise Corps of Cape Mounted Rifles; acting lieutenant-colonel; ⚔ Umtata River; wounded.

1828: home leave.

1828: service in Natal and Zululand.

1829: attached to Russian army in the Balkans for observation in the war with Turkey.

1830: assumes command 6th Light Dragoons (Princess Augusta's Own) in substantive rank of lieutenant-colonel, Hounslow.

1831: brevet colonel.

1832: posted to Madras with 6th Light Dragoons.

1834: commands Coorg Field Force, Coorg War, in local rank of brigadier-general; reverts to substantive rank.

∞ *MPH* ∞

The Matthew Hervey Novels

As the war against Bonaparte rages to its bloody end upon the field of Waterloo, a young officer goes about his duty in the ranks of Wellington's army. He is Cornet Matthew Hervey of the 6th Light Dragoons – a soldier, gentleman and man of honour who suddenly finds himself allotted a hero's role . . .

A CLOSE RUN THING
THE NIZAM'S DAUGHTERS
A REGIMENTAL AFFAIR
A CALL TO ARMS
THE SABRE'S EDGE
RUMOURS OF WAR
AN ACT OF COURAGE
COMPANY OF SPEARS
MAN OF WAR
WARRIOR
ON HIS MAJESTY'S SERVICE
WORDS OF COMMAND
THE PASSAGE TO INDIA
THE TIGRESS OF MYSORE

'Captain Matthew Hervey is as splendid a hero as ever sprang from an author's pen . . . What a hero! What an author! What a book! A joy for the lover of adventure and the military buff alike'
THE TIMES

'Mallinson writes with style, verve and the lucidity one would expect from a talented officer . . . His breadth of knowledge is deeply impressive even if it is modestly entwined in the fabric of this epic narrative. Kick on, Captain Hervey, we cannot wait for more'
COUNTRY LIFE

Military History

'Mallinson . . . combines the authority of a soldier-turned-military historian with the imaginative touch of the historical novelist'
Lawrence James, THE TIMES

THE MAKING OF THE BRITISH ARMY
From the English Civil War to the war on terror

From the Army's origins at Edgehill in 1642 to the recent conflict in Afghanistan, Allan Mallinson shows us the people and events that have shaped the army we know today. How Marlborough's critical victory at Blenheim is linked to Wellington's at Waterloo; how the desperate fight at Rorke's Drift in 1879 underpinned the heroism of the airborne forces at Arnhem in 1944; and why Montgomery's momentous victory at El Alamein mattered long after the Second World War was over. Here is history at its most relevant – and most dramatic.

1914: FIGHT THE GOOD FIGHT
Britain, the Army and the Coming of the First World War

It took just a month from the assassination in Sarajevo on 28 June 1914 for the huge armies of Continental Europe to be on the march. In his vivid, compelling and rigorously researched history, Allan Mallinson examines the century-long path that led to war, the vital first month of fighting, and speculates, tantalizingly, on what might have been had wiser political and military counsels prevailed . . .

TOO IMPORTANT FOR THE GENERALS
How Britain Nearly Lost the First World War

'War is too important to be left to the generals' snapped future French prime minister Georges Clemenceau on learning of yet another bloody and futile offensive on the Western Front. Why did the First World War take so long to win – and why did it exact so appalling a human cost? In his superbly researched, brilliantly argued and captivating history, Allan Mallinson provides controversial and disturbing answers to these questions that have divided military historians for nearly a century.

FIGHT TO THE FINISH
The First World War – Month by Month

The First World War lasted almost 52 months. It was fought on land, sea *and* in the air. It became industrial, and unrestricted. Four empires collapsed during its course, and casualties – military and civilian – probably exceeded 40 million. It was a conflict that can seem almost impossible to comprehend. Day-by-day narratives can be dizzying for those wanting to make sense of the whole, while freer-flowing accounts can lack that human dimension of time. Month-by-month seems a more digestible gauge and here one of the country's finest military historians gives us a unique single-volume portrait of 'The War to End War'.

Coming soon . . .

THE SHAPE OF BATTLE
Six Campaigns: Hastings to Helmand

Every battle is different. Each takes place in a different context. However, battles also have much in common. Fighting is, after all, an intensely human affair. And human nature doesn't change. So why were battles fought as they were? Why did they go as they did: victory for one side, defeat for the other? What gave them their shape?

The Shape of Battle tells the story of six defining battles, the war and campaign in which they each occurred, and the factors that determined their precise form and course. First is Hastings. We all know the date, but not, perhaps, the strategic background. Then, the Battle of Towton (1461), the bloodiest battle ever fought on English soil. Third is Waterloo (1815) – more written about in English than any other, but rarely in its true context as the culminating battle of the longest war in modern times. Fourth is D-Day – a battle in itself within a larger operation ('Overlord'), and the longest-planned and most complex offensive battle in history. Fifth is the little known battle of Imjin River (1951), the British Army's last large-scale defensive battle. And finally, a battle that has yet to receive the official distinction of being one: Operation Panther's Claw (2009). Fought in Afghanistan, it had all the trappings of 21st-century warfare yet its shape and face resembled, at times, something out of the Middle Ages.

The Shape of Battle is not a polemic, it doesn't try to argue a case. It lets the narratives – the battles – speak for themselves.